HATE TO LOVE YOU

CHARLY NICOLE

Charly Nicole
VILLAINS YOU HATE TO LOVE

AUTHOR NOTE

While this book is the first in a series, Abby and Roman's story can be read as a standalone.

This book contains dark themes and concepts, and it is recommended that you read the content warnings before you dive in.
Your mental health is, and will always be, more important to us than you reading this book.

The full comprehensive list of content warnings are available on our website.
AuthorCharlyNicole.Net.
Alternatively, you can scan the QR code below.

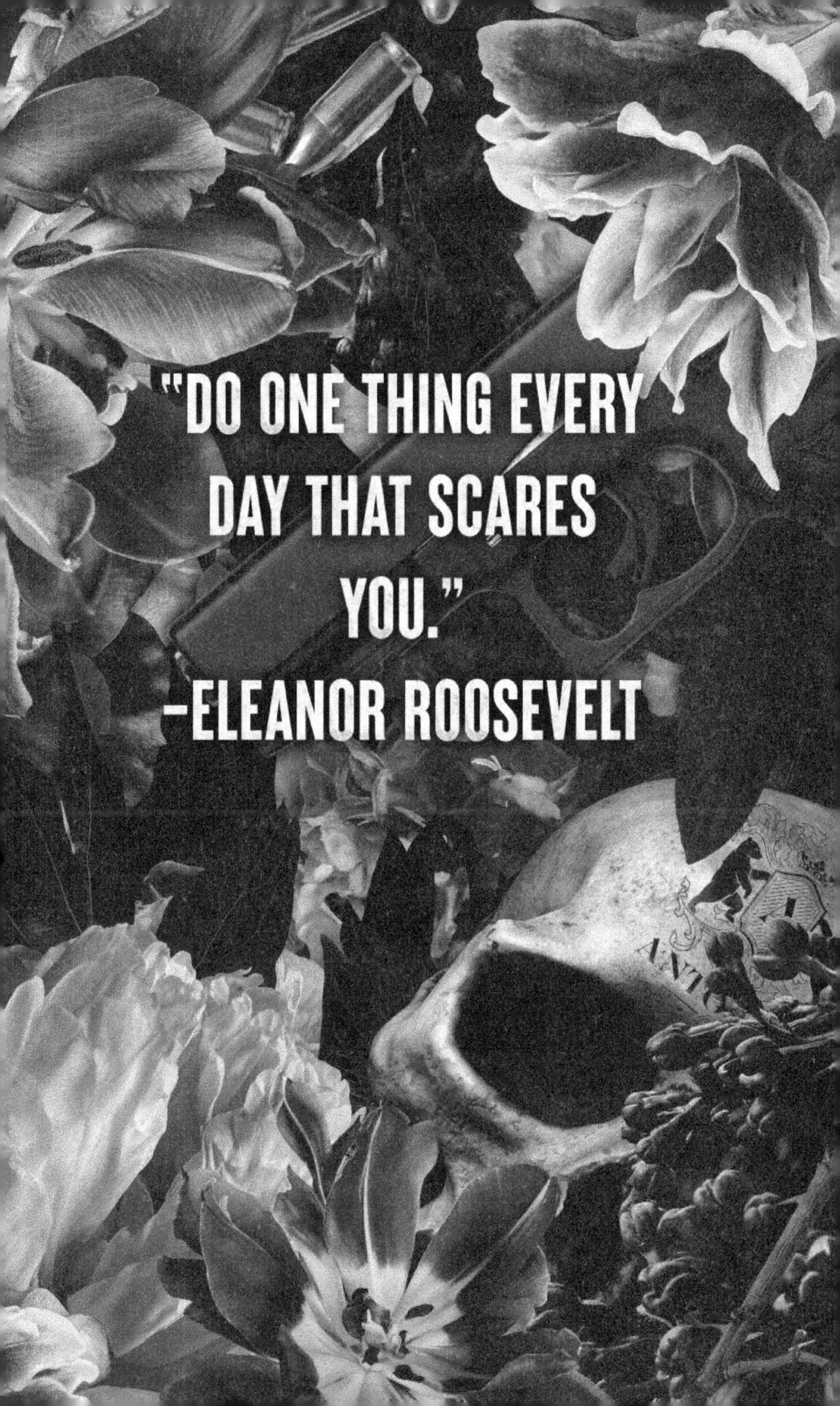
"DO ONE THING EVERY
DAY THAT SCARES
YOU."
-ELEANOR ROOSEVELT

To my younger self,
It wasn't your fault. I love you.
Look how far we've come.

PS: Don't worry, we all have someone we wish we could stab
in the neck with a dagger.

PLAYLIST

SWEET BUT PSYCHO - AVA MAX
ANGRY TOO - LOLA BLANC
AMERICAN HORROR SHOW - SNOW WIFE
WORST PART OF ME - I PREVAIL
DARKSIDE - NEONI
LABOUR - PARIS PALOMA
LITTLE GIRL GONE - CHINCHILLA
NAMELESS - STEVIE HOWIE
KISS FROM A ROSE - NO RESOLVE
INIKO JERICHO - TRAP MASTERY
MURDER IN MY HEAD - KORDHELL
WOLVES - SAM TINNESZ
SHATTER ME - LINDSEY STIRLING
THE DEATH OF PEACE OF MIND - BAD OMENS
DAYLIGHT - DAVID KUSHNER
I'M HER - NATALIE JANE
DESPERATE - NEFFEX
DANGEROUS HANDS - AUSTIN GIORGIO
SUPER VILLAIN - STILETO
RUNRUNRUN - DUTCH MELROSE
CHAMPION - NEONI
HOT GUM- SOFIA ISELLA
I MISS THE MISERY - HALESTORM
MY SONGS KNOW WHAT YOU DID IN THE DARK - FALL OUT BOY
ONCE IN A MILLION - BRYCE SAVAGE
DO OR DIE - NATALIE JANE
DIE 4 ME - HALSEY
HAUNT ME - KASKADE
I'LL WAIT LE YOUTH REMIX - LANE 8
WHITE FLAG - BISHOP BRIGGS

"THE ENEMY DOESN'T STAND A CHANCE WHEN THE VICTIM DECIDES TO SURVIVE."

-RAE SMITH

HELPFUL RESOURCES

As this book does contain scenes of domestic violence, we, as the authors, want you to know that there is help out there.

The National Domestic Violence Hotline is available 24/7 with advocates to help anyone experiencing domestic and intimate partner violence.

Call 211 for access to local community services
(for United States)
www.thehotline.org
www.nationaldahelpline.org.uk
www.988lifeline.org
www.samaritans.org
www.refuge.org.uk
https://www.domesticshelters.org

PROLOGUE

My hand burns.

The imprint is already visible on his defined face. I didn't think, I just reacted. His head turns to me slowly, his eyes dark, glistening, a dangerous rage held within them.

It's a look I've seen only once before…

He's pissed.

His body stiffens, and I know what's coming. The anger. The pain. My heart stops.

And then he pounces.

His hand wraps tightly around my throat, slamming my back into the door behind me. My lungs heave, trying to regain the air he slammed out of them, but I can't. His fingers twitching in time with my racing pulse.

Can he feel it too?

Instinctively, I raise my fists, preparing to use my claws if I have to, only for him to grasp them with his free hand, locking them almost painfully above my head.

I wanted this reaction. Fuck, I needed it.

But I *shouldn't* want this.

My pulse racing and my body is vibrating with a need I've never experienced. What is this electricity that's sparking between us?

No man has ever made me feel so…*alive*.

I kill men like him. I kill men who hurt people. I kill men who hurt me. But not *him*.

I can't hurt him…and I don't understand why.

"Why do you do this, Abby?" He growls, stepping into me. "Why do you constantly push and push?"

I can feel the hard lines of his body pressed tightly against me. As if I don't know where I end, and he begins.

"Because… I fucking can," I murmur, my eyes focusing on his lips. "And you know you *like* it."

His eye twitches.

"Don't ever do that again," he smirks, touching his nose to mine. "Or I'll have to punish you."

"*Punish me*?" I laugh. "Like hell that's happening."

He laughs, such a rich sound, one that vibrates through me and instantly puts me on edge.

He knows. I mean, he *has* to know? Right?

My eyes dart down to the spilt coffee soaking into the rug.

Along with the poison that was meant for *him*.

His knee slides between my legs, pressing against my heat, sending shockwaves through my body, rattling me to my very core.

"I can feel how wet you are for me, Foxy. Fuck, you're practically soaking my leg."

"No, I'm fucking not!" I snap, my cheeks heating.

"Yes, you are," He grins darkly. "I bet you regret wearing this skirt now, don't you? I told you what would happen if you kept disobeying me." His knee presses harder, causing my head to drop back against the door with a thump. His fingers clench around my neck as he pushes himself away from me.

"Now be a good little slut…and bend over my fucking desk."

My breath hitches in my throat.

Roman Nikolai Antonov was supposed to die today.

…So why do I find myself walking over to his desk?

ANTONOV

ANTONOV

CHAPTER ONE

ROMAN

"This is the place?" I ask, pulling on my gloves.

I stare up at a solid brick colonial townhome, on the upper East side of the city.

"Yes, Boss," my driver nods. "Number 912, the tan one in the middle."

"And we're sure the fucker's there?"

"Yes, Boss, O'Brien is inside. Has been all afternoon."

"Alone?"

"Harry reported four men stopped by around midnight. He hasn't seen any of them leave."

"Roommates?"

"Maybe. Could explain how he's affording the place. Especially in this zip code."

"And especially with what *you're* paying," Pasha, my brother, snorts from the front passenger seat. "Then again, I guess you're not the only one paying him, now are you?"

I glare at him.

Careful, Little Brother…

He pops his gum in his mouth and turns around to grin at me. But, when he sees exactly how unfunny I found his little crack, his eyes go wide and he quickly whips back around, adjusting his collar.

"So what now, Boss?" My enforcer Igor snarls. "Can I go kill them now, or are we plannin' to just sit around holding our dicks all night?"

Igor has snorted enough cocaine to take down an elephant and is clearly itching to bash in someone's head tonight.

I rub my chin.

"Send them in," I nod quietly.

"You got it," Igor chuckles to himself, licking his lips.

However, before he can step out of the car, I grab his arm, stopping him in his tracks.

"Don't fuck it up," I growl. "Keep it quiet. I don't need any nosy neighbors calling the cops, and I don't want a fucking mess, do you understand?"

Igor nods.

"And I don't care what you do with anyone else in that house, but O'Brien is mine."

"Of course, Boss."

He grabs his walkie and holds it to his sweaty lips.

"Simon, go open the door. Boss says keep it quiet."

As he climbs out of the car, I see Pasha reaching for the door handle on the passenger's side.

"Where the fuck do you think you're going?" I snap.

"But I thought—"

"You thought wrong," I hiss, "sit your ass down."

He takes his hands off the door handle defensively.

"My bad," Pasha shrugs, snapping the gum in his mouth and pulling his phone from his pocket. "Whateva you say, Big Ro."

I clench my jaw.

Everything's a joke to this kid.

And why shouldn't it be? He's soft. Just like Mother was.

Before she died, she used to call him "Солнце," because she said he was her "sunshine." Pasha got our father's blue eyes like the rest of us, but he's the only one of my six siblings who got Mother's blonde hair.

Armed with the Antonov good looks, and our powerful reputation, the world had always taken it easy on him. And it shows.

I love the little shit, maybe the most of all my siblings, and Pasha certainly has his strengths. But sometimes his cavalier attitude really grinds my patience. Especially when he forgets his place and gets too chummy with me in front of the other men.

That's when I have to step in and check his ass back in line.

"We never go in first. That's what the men are for."

"Gotcha," he says, waving me off. "While we're waiting, do you wanna see Isabel? She's the influencer I met on—"

"No," I snap irritably. "I want you to stop using the head between your legs more than the one between your ears."

I yank the door open and step out into the cool autumn air. At nearly quarter after three in the morning, the street is quiet, aside from the rustling leaves scraping across the pavement. Pulling my cigarettes from my pocket I light one, turning to the dark brick building and leaning back against the car.

I'm certain that Igor is inside, stalking room to room, subduing anyone he finds…searching for Murphy O'Brien.

The *rat*.

To be fair, I've suspected he's worked for the Irish since the very beginning. After all, his background was far too clean for any drug dealer I've ever known.

Which is exactly why I hired him.

It was also why I had my sister Anastasia do a profile for me. And since she's one of the best hackers in the world, she found all the dirt on him that he and his little Irish pals tried to hide when they sent him into my den.

For the last few months, we've been letting him think we're oblivious, while secretly monitoring Murphy's activities. His mission was clearly to try and gather intel on our shipping operations in order to report back to the Irish, with whom we've been embattled in a bloody territory war here in New York.

So, we let him do his "job."

After all, every good rat needs to think he's undetected.

But I know. I know everything. Because that's *my* job.

The war has been going on for nearly two decades, but after a messy confrontation last year, me and Cillian McCleary, head of the Irish Mafia, came to a shaky agreement on boundaries.

Which makes men like the little rat up in the townhouse, extremely valuable, as their movements and contacts help us navigate the murky waters of what was always a superficial truce at best.

But last week one of my men, and technically my cousin, Mikhail, was killed by two Irish guys in a bar over in the Bronx. And while I didn't particularly care for the crackhead Mikhail, who was a stupid drunk who likely just wandered into the wrong pub…*They* still killed him.

Which cannot stand.

And what's more, rumor has it that one of the men who killed him was none other than my little rat.

So now I must exterminate him.

The door opens behind me and Pasha steps out into the street with me.

"Can I have one of those?"

"No," I say firmly. "You don't need this shit."

"Fuck off, Ro," he sighs, annoyed.

I glance up at him before rolling my eyes. Handing him the pack, I turn back to the dark silent house before us.

"Are they alright in there?" Pasha asks. "I mean, they haven't made a peep."

"That's how we know they're alright. They know what's expected," I say, exhaling. "As do you."

I steal a glance at him, watching as he slowly lowers his eyes to the cigarette in his hand.

"I'm sorry," he says quietly. "I know you said you'd only bring me tonight if I didn't annoy you."

This fucking kid.

He's lucky he's my favorite, otherwise I might've strangled him a long time ago. But I also just can't seem to stay mad at the little shit.

I sigh, turning to face him.

"Look, you're a good kid. You're smart, and you're quick on the draw," I say, shaking my head. "But these men are dangerous. And you're not taking this seriously, and you fucking need to be."

He nods.

I grab the back of his head and pull him close enough to whisper in his ear.

"I need you to be sharp, and pull your head out of your ass. I cannot be worried about your mind being off in the clouds, or dwelling on fat-assed whores when I'm supposed to be handling business, alright?" I say, punching his shoulder gently. "Alright?"

"Yeah, don't worry, Ro," Pasha replies. "I've got you, brother."

"Good," I say, tapping his shoulder. "You can show me the bitch later."

Pasha grins, and I feel slightly better.

"Boss, we're ready for you," Igor's voice seeps through the walkie. "And you're not going to believe what I found…"

What?

I nod to Calvin, who is both my driver and my right hand. Cal signals Giorgi, the driver of the other car, and together the four of us walk up the old brick steps and head inside.

In the front parlor room, four men sit on the couch, bruised and bleeding.

Their hands are zip tied behind their backs, and their mouths duct-taped shut.

"The cunts didn't see us coming," Igor laughs, kicking one of the tied men in the shins.

"Where is he?" I growl.

Igor nods in the direction of another one of my enforcers, Oleg, standing in the kitchen.

"Bring them in here," he mutters in Russian.

Them?

But as Oleg pulls Murphy O'Brien into the room, I hear terrified cries coming from the kitchen.

A *woman's* cries.

"No! Please! Don't take him!" She wails as a bloodied Murphy is dragged into the living room. "He's innocent!"

"Someone shut her up!" Cal shouts beside me. "Why the fuck didn't you gag her too?!"

"Because," Igor grins, biting his lip. "Me and my men might want to use that pretty mouth of hers. Among *other* things…"

If I thought the woman was crying before, it's nothing to the frightened scream she immediately lets out, suddenly thrashing and clawing at Igor, trying to get away.

"Shut up, bitch!" he shouts, backhanding the crying woman across the face. Her head spins around violently and she falls immediately to the floor, unconscious.

"Jesus, Igor," Pasha scoffs, looking at him in disgust. "You're such a pig. You seem to have forgotten you have a fucking wife. You know, Polina? My *sister?*"

"And it seems you forget that your sister doesn't fuck me anymore, kid," Igor laughs as he grabs the unconscious woman's hair and starts taping her mouth closed.

He tosses her limp body into an armchair.

"…And that she's a royal bitch," Oleg jokes beside me.

That cannot stand either.

Without thinking I crack Oleg hard in the jaw sending three of his gold-plated teeth flying out of his mouth. He falls to his knees, and I kick him hard in the ribs before grabbing the back of his hair and yanking his head up.

"And *you* seem to have forgotten your place," I thunder at him. "You don't get an opinion. You don't even get a fucking thought! You are a servant, and you're here to respect and obey. So if you dare to mutter another word about my sister, I'll cut your tongue out and fuck your corpse with it!"

"Y…yes, Boss!" Oleg sputters, blood dripping down his nose. "I'm…I'm sorry!"

I shove him to the ground, my blood thumping in my veins and my adrenaline spiking.

"And you," I snarl, pointing at Igor. "You'll watch your fucking mouth too. I don't give a shit if you are my brother-in-law. I don't care about your marriage problems, or if she is a bitch. She's still an *Antonov*. Which is more than can be said for you. So if you don't watch your step, you'll end up like your toothless friend."

Igor nods, shifting uncomfortably. Pasha glares at him before locking eyes with me from across the room.

Neither of us like Polina.

No one in the family does. Because she *is* a royal bitch.

But that's not the point. The point is, you don't fuck with the family. And that's why we're here this evening—to deal with a rat who attacked my family.

I yank my gun from its holster and fire one bullet into each of the four men cowering wide-eyed on the couch.

The gunshots, although muted by my silencer, seem to startle the woman awake. She screams into her duct-tape, screwing her eyes shut, burying her face into the tattered old armchair.

That's when I turn back to a shaking Murphy O'Brien, who is now sweating profusely.

"And you, *rat*, are vermin." I growl, a wicked grin spreading across my face. "Would you like to know what we do with vermin?"

I nod at Calvin who steps forward carrying a bag of bright green pellets.

"We exterminate them."

Igor steps forward and holds Murphy's mouth open, allowing Calvin to pour the entire bag of poisoned rat pellets down his throat. He struggles for a minute, before foaming at the mouth and collapsing on the floor, seizing.

The crying woman on the chair wails, her entire face turning purple, aside from the streak of bright red blood dripping down her cheek from where Igor slapped her.

"What about her?" Igor asks. "What do we do with her?"

He runs his hands through the woman's bright red hair as she squirms, trying to get away from him.

"Nothing," Pasha snaps, stepping up into Igor's face. "You'll do absolutely nothing with her."

"And why the fuck not?" Igor laughs.

"Because, she's innocent." Pasha continues. "Murphy and his goons earned their fate. This woman has not."

"You're joking, right?" Igor laughs.

I sigh.

Oh Pasha. So fucking soft.

"No," I say, holstering my gun. "We're not savages."

"But Boss, she'll talk!"

"No, she won't," I say, narrowing my eyes at the woman. "Cal, take her phone, ID's and wallet, and drop her off…I don't know, somewhere in Queens I suppose. By the time she makes her way back to our side of town, I'm sure she'll have forgotten everything she saw here tonight."

I kneel down in front of her, gently reaching up and ripping the duct-tape off her mouth.

"Isn't that right, sweetheart?"

But the woman says nothing.

Instead, all she does is glare up at me with her bright green eyes, as a single tear slowly streaks down her cheek. Beautiful, proud, and strong, this woman watched her boyfriend murdered in front of her, and yet, there's no trace of fear in her eyes.

Only *hatred*.

But hatred is something I understand.

"Igor, cut her loose."

"Boss, wait a—"

However, before he can finish his sentence I snap, and decide I've had enough of Igor's mouth tonight. I immediately yank my gun from its holster and point it at him.

"I said," I growl, my voice low and lethal. "Cut. The. Bitch. Loose."

"S…sure, Boss," he says, swallowing hard.

Keeping my gun pointed at him, I watch as he walks over to her and takes out his knife. She trembles slightly as he grabs her hands and cuts the zip ties.

Good. Now that's settled.

"Cal, you can drop her off," I say, turning back around. "A few miles from the bridge and—"

"Fuck you all!"

The woman's pained cry suddenly rings out in the room.

"Roman, look out!" Pasha shouts.

I turn just in time to see she's grabbed Igor's gun from off his belt, and is pointing it at me. Before I can even raise my own, I hear the shot ring out.

But Pasha shoves me out of the way just in time.

The two of us tumble to the floor.

"What the fuck?!" I shout.

Another shot rings out as she fires again at Igor, and then at Oleg, and then at Calvin, all of them scrambling to find cover.

"Argh!" I hear Pasha cry, grabbing his shoulder. "Fuck!"

He rolls over on his back, bright red blood pouring out all over the floor and wall.

Pasha. She just shot Pasha.

I gave her mercy, and she shot my little brother.

Fuck this bitch!

And just like that, all my mercy evaporates.

I point my gun and fire a bullet straight into the bitch's forehead. Her head explodes all over the back of the blue armchair and her body slumps limply against the fabric.

The entire room goes silent for a moment, followed only by Pasha's heavy breathing.

"You're alright," I say, frantically grabbing his arm and checking the wound.

I can see the bullet's entrance, but not its exit, meaning it's likely still lodged in his shoulder.

"Motherfucker, that hurts," he winces.

"Cal start the car!" I shout, helping Pasha to his feet. "And someone get me some fucking rags!"

"Is it…bad?" he asks, gasping hard. "Oh shit. It feels bad."

"Bullets never feel *good*," I say, yanking off my jacket and wrapping it around his shoulders.

I doubt anyone heard any of this commotion, but just in case I don't want them to see a bleeding man exiting the townhouse. We make it to the car, where I help him inside before running around to the other side and getting in.

Calvin walks quickly out to the car with a few towels and tosses one to me.

"Doctor Avery lives six blocks away," I say to him.

"The *vet*?" Pasha asks sarcastically, wincing. "Wow, Ro, thanks."

"Shut up. I trust her with Caesar, I can trust her with you. Besides, she's close. Cal, if she doesn't answer on the second ring, text her 505. She'll know what it means."

"And if she doesn't answer your text, Boss?"

"Then I'll bust down her fucking front door."

"Ahh shit," Pasha winces. "That really fucking hurts, man. Am I going to die?"

I snort.

"I'm not that lucky," I tease. "But you're probably going to have a scar. So, I guess that just means you'll have to stop taking all those shirtless pictures for your lady friends."

He snorts.

"Nah, the ladies love the scars, Bro," he grunts as I press the towel down hard on his shoulder. "I keep telling you that. And with all those tats of yours, you should be going shirtless everywhere in your building."

"Okay…"

"The pool, the gym, even the mailboxes. You know, where you used to creep on that little brunette you liked, with the thick ass. I mean if you'd shown a little bit of skin once in a while maybe—"

"Alright, that's enough, Casanova," I say, pressing harder. "I'm not taking romantic advice from my kid brother."

"If not me then who?" Pasha chuckles, leaning his head back against the seat as we run through an intersection without stopping. "I'm the master."

I roll my eyes.

"Doctor Avery," Calvin says, interrupting my thoughts. "We have a bit of a situation. Yeah, Pasha's been hit. Yep. Shoulder. We're five minutes away. Got it."

Well, at least that's good.

"Am I going to make it?" Pasha asks, chuckling to himself.

"Yeah, just try to stay conscious and not bleed too much in my car, alright?"

"Whatever you say, Big Ro," he says, his words slurring a bit. "You're the Boss."

The sun is nearly coming up by the time me and Pasha make it back to my building. I thought it best he stay with me for the night, and miraculously he didn't even put up a fight.

Although, to be fair, that might be due to the immense amount of painkillers Doctor Avery pumped into him before fishing the bullet out of his shoulder and stitching him up.

I've just poured myself a drink when Calvin walks into the room.

"Boss, I just wanted to let you know that the guys have taken care of the situation at the O'Brien house. It's cleared."

"Good," I say, flicking through channels on my massive television.

But Calvin doesn't leave, lingering until I look up at him.

"What?" I sigh, my exhaustion from the night's activities starting to take a toll on me. "What else?"

"Boss, I think you should know that when the men pulled the woman's ID's from her wallet they found out what her name was."

"And?" I snap. "What is it, Cal? Are you expecting me to guess?"

He shakes his head.

"No, Boss, her name is Saoirse…*McCleary*."

"McCleary?" I ask, the blood freezing in my veins.

"Yes, Sir, Cillian McCleary is her cousin."

"*What?*"

The words escape my lips as I immediately try to remember the frazzled redhead, suddenly connecting the similar eye color and distinct cheekbone structure they both shared.

There's no denying it. The bullet I fired tonight had more meaning than I realized.

…And has ignited a war.

ANTONOV

CHAPTER TWO

Abby

I was twenty-three the first time I killed someone.

It wasn't like I suddenly snapped one day and went on a rampage. My thoughts had always been dark and somewhat twisted, and my rage had been bubbling beneath the surface for quite awhile.

Rage that stemmed from *him*.

Garrett Adams.

My husband. My world. My abuser.

Our story started off like most good old fashioned fairy tales.

Or at least the shit teen movies are made from anyway. Popular boy meets a neglected invisible girl and sweeps her off her feet.

I loved him immediately. My God, how I loved him.

He was the sun, and I was a little rock lost in the orbit of him. By some miracle, the sun noticed that small pathetic little rock, altering the course of its trajectory forever. He was the center of my world, my entire universe.

Perhaps that's why I ignored all of the red flags.

I suppose it's easy at first. When you're so wrapped up in your bubble, enamored with the attention and affection you're receiving, you tend to let the little things go.

But then they punch you in the face.

Which is exactly what happened. Well…*he* punched me in the face.

In the beginning I believed him when he said it was an accident, and that he didn't mean to fly off the handle and hurt me when he was angry. Of course I believed him.

After all, he was my *sun*. And he said he loved me.

I couldn't see it then, but his "love" was the most vicious of his lies.

He knew I was desperate for it, and he knew that by asking me to marry him, my love for him would keep me bound to him. No matter how awful he was, or whatever tortures he wanted to inflict.

My sun, my world…became a monster with a wedding ring.

It all came to a head the night of our fourth wedding anniversary.

That night he nearly killed me.

…And that night I decided to kill *him*.

The cab jerks to a stop, my body jolting forward in the seat, shaking me from my memories. So much has changed in the four years since I decided to leave my husband.

"Thank you!" I say, tossing the driver the required cash and jumping out, slamming the door behind me.

The street is full of busy people rushing around like the world is ending. Men and women dressed for work, weaving in and out of shoppers weighed down by bags. Or even the little group of elderly women dragging carts behind them, cooing at all the babies and dogs they pass.

Everyone in New York is always going so fast.

Walking down the sidewalk I take in the view before me appreciating the autumn colors in full effect, the golden leaves raining down in the cool breeze, making me glad I'd paired my fleece tights with my skirt.

I've come into the city for my monthly *book club* meeting.

I smile to myself.

Women all over the country come to little meetings like these. Hidden behind the ruse of a book club, it's actually a support group for battered and abused women. Trouble is, women often show up expecting someone to give them a magical fix-all solution, and are sorely disappointed when the answers are always the same:

"Just leave."

"Get help."

"Stay away from him when he's angry."

Blah. Blah. Blah.

Here's a fucking thought: why doesn't anyone just tell the *abusers* to not put their hands on their partners?

For many women, this group will help them, and set them free, but it didn't for me.

I found my own solution.

My *late* husband hated that I joined this club. He bitched about any time I spent away from our prison of a penthouse, our marital home that was a gift from his wealthy parents.

He had no idea this was the beginning of the end for him.

I owe this book club more than most people realize. My *life* really. Because if I'd never come to a meeting, then I wouldn't have checked out the book on plants… and Garrett Adams would still be alive.

Funny, because I like him better dead.

But as a widow, I have a different reason for coming here these days.

This is where I fish for my next *mark*.

Abusers. Stalkers. Rapists.

I never know who it's going to be, or what they do. And honestly, I don't care. They prey upon women. They are *monsters*.

Which makes them my target.

The police can only help so much, and usually only if a woman has *evidence*. But unfortunately, most victims don't have presence of mind to start recording when their attacker starts wailing on them. They are left to fend for themselves, because no one steps in to help.

No one…until me.

I do what I do because of what was done to me. And nothing will ever stop me.

The library is warm, the smell of books soothing my splintered soul.

Every time I come to these meetings, my fractured heart cracks a little bit more. I don't actually participate in the meetings anymore; I just linger in the library listening to the conversations taking place.

But I show up every month, in hopes that maybe, just maybe, I can save another woman from what I experienced.

Dr. Downing was the one who told me about my "accident."

My little trip down the stairs. He explained in detail how I must've lost my footing and tumbled down two flights of stairs, landing directly on my stomach.

My *pregnant* stomach.

He also told me all about how my panicked, flustered, "doting husband" brought me in, yelling for help as he cradled me to his chest.

Garrett never did win an Oscar for that performance.

The doctor told me I was so lucky to have a husband so willing to support my healing. But then he delivered the devastating news: that I had lost my unborn child as well as my ability to conceive in the future.

I head down the aisle that houses the self-help books, trailing my finger across the spines until I finally pull out *Your Time to Thrive*, from the shelf, hugging it to my chest.

As I get to the end, I stop, leaning against the wall. This is my favorite spot in the entire library, its central location allows me to hear everything around me, and I can see through the gaps in the shelves.

I twist my capsule necklace in my fingers, biting my bottom lip.

Who will it be tonight?

However my attention is pulled to a thin, petite lady, cowering nervously in the corner, dressed in high end clothing.

But even from where I'm sitting, I can see the light dusting of bruises, canvassing her neck and cheeks. Her hair falls limp, frizzy and clustered together, as if it hasn't been washed in a week. Yet it's only when I see her sunken brown eyes, staring lifelessly in my direction without seeing me at all, do I realize how serious her situation is.

I know that stare. I know it well.

My grandmother once said that the eyes are the doors to your soul. She said that if you really look, they will tell you everything you need to know about a person.

But all I can see right now, in the woman before me, is a broken soul drowning in despair so deeply that they've just given up.

Makeup might hide her bruises, but it doesn't hide her pain.

My chest tightens.

This is why women of affluence, or women associated with men of affluence, tend to be better at hiding the evidence of their pain. And when their pain is being caused by an influential man, you can almost guarantee he is the one funding the coverup.

People will look at the bumps and bruises of a top tier woman and shrug it off to her being clumsy. After all, she's deliberately crafted her image to be one of harmony and happiness, so the idea her injuries could be the result of abuse isn't even a consideration.

But as the meeting begins, and the women take turns listening to each other's horrendous accounts, I still can't take my eyes off the woman with the lifeless eyes.

From her body language, it's clear that even in this safe space, she doesn't *feel* safe.

She reminds me of a dying star, collapsing in on itself. As if she's hoping that the floor will swallow her whole, so she doesn't have to continue this miserable charade anymore.

But like so many women, she wouldn't be here if she could just pack up and leave her tormentor.

It's *never* as simple as that.

Abusers are smart. They don't start with breaking your body, they start by breaking your mind.

They brainwash you into believing you deserve the abuse. They tell you it's your fault, and that *you* pushed them to the point where they have to hurt you…in order to teach you a lesson. They make you believe that this hellish existence is the best that you could possibly have.

My husband was especially good at that.

He weaponized my unconditional love for him, so that I believed I deserved his torture.

And then there were days where there was no physical abuse. But mentally? He played me like a well-oiled violin. Conditioning me, molding me, until my sense of self completely evaporated.

I wasn't even human to him anymore. I was property.

Over time I was reduced to a shell of a human, alive but not living. Not for myself, but for him.

But what I learned by coming to these meetings is that my experience wasn't as isolated as I previously thought. I learned there were other women like me, suffering similar abuse from men like my husband.

As if they all shared a common core.

I listened to other women talk about their pain, or about trying to avoid their abuser's triggers, and realized I wasn't the only one impossibly trying to navigate a room full of landmines. And I wasn't the only one trying to convince myself that the man who tortured nearly every hour of my waking life, did so out of *love*.

It was then I realized it wasn't love.

It was hell.

And so I unlocked my *demons*.

"…He locked me in the cupboard under the stairs for four days with… a bucket," the woman with the lifeless eyes says, her voice carrying across the library.

Another lady gasps, her dark brown eyes widening as her pale hand covers her mouth. She's also dressed well, the red sole on her heels visible as she sits with her legs crossed, a designer handbag at her feet.

All eyes turn to the speaker, as empathetic murmurs go up from around the circle.

It just gets worse, sweetheart. Every single time. Trust me.

Even with the sympathy written on their well-meaning faces, and the fact that this poor woman just admitted to being locked in a cupboard for four days, I still doubt any of them will actually reach out and try to *help* her.

But I will.

"Leah, you have to be careful… they could be listening!"

Immediately 'Leah's' eyes dart around the room furiously, anxiously appraising the people surrounding her.

This is exactly why I like to hide in the shadows. Because if these women realized how closely I was listening to their conversation, they'd stop talking.

Leah turns back to her friend, her chest heaving.

"I just can't live like this anymore Brittany! I can't! He locked me in there because his *wife* came home early."

Ahh, she's a mistress then.

This was common enough, especially among the aristocracy in New York—everyone is fucking everybody, and commitment holds very little value.

Coincidentally my last kill had been another monster with a mistress.

John Bishop.

I remember the feeling I had seeing his name on the death certificate sat in front of me on my breakfast counter.

Years ago, I'd deliberately befriended a guy who worked for the county. One day, when he wasn't looking, I'd managed to "borrow" his logins, so I could have a way to obtain the death certificates of my marks.

My little *trophies.*

In the case of John Bishop, a piece of paper stating that the trust fund baby died of an "overdose."

Only *I* knew it wasn't an overdose at all.

I was so happy, imagining the relief the woman would feel to be finally free of the prick.

But he still won though. She killed herself four weeks later.

That's the cold truth: even when you're finally free, you're never fully free. The damage they do to your brain chemistry lasts a lifetime.

Even from the grave, Garrett still controls aspects of my life. He's been dead for years, and I've healed, but every now and then he reappears in my mind…stalking my nightmares.

Tonight, I lurk quietly in my little spot, closing my eyes and simply listening. Sometimes, being silent gives you an edge that others don't have. I hear everything, I see everything. Like a fucking god.

"Would you excuse us for a moment?"

My musings are interrupted as 'Brittany' grabs Leah's hands, pulling her out of the circle of trust, and unknowingly closer to me. They settle down in the soft cushioned chairs directly in front of my bookshelf hideout.

"Leah, they'll kill you, if they find out you're talking to people about this. Fuck, they'll kill you if they find out you're talking at *all*," Brittany murmurs in a harsh whisper.

How… intriguing.

"I know! Fuck, I know. But I can't do this anymore," Leah says, tears streaming down her face.

"We'll figure it out, together," Brittany says, taking Leah's trembling hand.

"Maybe we could run away while he's at The Studio? Take some money and just run!"

"Don't be ridiculous! *We* have no money. It's all theirs! You know this. Look at what happened to Brandy. They got tired of her, and she just disappeared into thin air," she gestures between them. "If *she* didn't get out… What chance do we have? It's a death sentence to run."

"It's a death sentence to stay!"

"Leah, be sensible. We knew who they were when we opened our legs to them," She murmurs, the hysteria rising in her voice with each word. "And we both know we won't be able to outrun Igor Ivanov."

I smirk to myself.

Igor Ivanov.

Why would you outrun him, Sweetheart?

When I'm finished, he won't even be able to *crawl*.

ANTONOV

CHAPTER THREE

ROMAN

"We shouldn't be here," she whispers against my lips as I shove her into a set of bookshelves. "If my husband found out he would—"

"*Disappear*," I smirk, slipping my hand in the slit of her black satin dress…and between her thighs.

Crushing my lips to hers and pushing her panties out of the way, I run my index finger along the length of her slit before pressing it deep inside of her. The moment I feel how tight she is, how *impossibly* tight, I nearly cum myself.

"Fuck!" She groans, throwing her head back and knocking several dusty old books to the floor as she tries to steady herself against the shelf.

"You'd best stay quiet," I growl, slipping another finger in and swirling it around. "It's a private event, but it's still a public library. If you keep being so loud, we might attract more than just your husband."

She opens her mouth to say something, but I ram my fingers into her again, harder this time, relishing the way my merciless probing makes her gasp.

Jesus Christ I've wanted this.

For longer than I care to recall, I've wanted to have this woman, right here, groaning like a whore for me.

Even though she's *not* a whore. And she's not *my* woman.

But tonight, I don't care. That floor length tight sequined evening gown she wore tempted me past the point of restraint, and I just had to have her.

The feisty little minx suddenly grabs my crotch, squeezing my throbbing erection through my slacks.

"Oh wow, you…you're…" she says, her brown eyes going wide.

I grin.

"I know," I say, biting my lip as my hands wrap around the backs of her thighs as I pull her up. "I'm bigger than your small-dicked prick of a husband."

"Oh God yeah," she snorts, as I press her ass into the shelf, using it to leverage her weight, allowing me to grab my cock and position myself at her entrance. "Like, you might *hurt* me."

"Well, you know what they say," I smile, running the head of my cock between her dripping pussy lips. "Small things, must give way."

And before she can say another word, I ram myself into her.

Her yelp is silenced only by my mouth on hers, and she breathes in sharply as I slowly pull myself out of her and shove back in again.

"Holy fuck," I grunt, burying my face in her neck, feeling her dripping cunt squeezing me hard with every thrust. "You feel so fucking good, Little Fox."

The scent of her floral perfume mixing with the delicious oils on her neck fills my nostrils, driving me crazy.

"Shit," she breathes heavily, wrapping her arms around my neck. "You're not using a condom."

"So what?" I whisper, thrusting harder.

"So," she gasps, trying to focus. "What if I get pregnant?"

"Then we have a baby," I smile, pressing my forehead to hers and squeezing her thick juicy ass in my hands.

"But…what about my husband?"

"If he knows what's good for him," I say, thrusting even harder, feeling my cock swelling at the thought of impregnating her right here, in the middle of the New York Public Library. "Your husband will take a long vacation, somewhere far far away."

"And," she breathes, biting her bottom lip. "If he doesn't?"

"Then he'll take a *short* vacation down a long flight of stairs." I chuckle, slamming my cock in and out of her, hearing the sound of her dripping pussy with every thrust. "No one will ever hear from him again. And you getting pregnant with my baby won't be a problem for anyone, will it?"

"Wait, Roman," she groans, but only superficially, as it's clear by now that she's lost in the ecstasy of the moment too.

Fuck, I should do it.

I should put my baby inside of her. Breed her. Mark her. Claim her as my own, right here, in the middle of the fucking Annual Children's Benefit. It would certainly be ironic.

And it would also certainly be everything I've wanted since I first laid eyes on her two years ago, when she moved into my building…with her twat of a husband.

But his existence meant that every glance I've had of her has been stolen. That ring around her finger acting as a barbed wire fence and the only deterrent I've had to snatching her up myself.

"Roman," she moans, gripping my shoulders tightly. "I…I…I think I'm going to cum!"

"Me too, Little Fox," I whisper.

However, just as I'm about to explode up inside of her, a loud noise echoes around us.

Beep! Beep! Beeeeep!

The trilling sound of the obnoxiously shrill ringing in my ears suddenly interrupts what's happening on my cock.

"What the—"

But I haven't even finished my sentence before I find myself no longer in the New York Public Library…and instead waking up in my bed. In my room. In my penthouse.

And that's where the unfortunate, and offensive truth hits me like a slap in the face: It was all just a *dream*.

A sinfully delicious dream that has already slipped from my fingertips and evaporated into thin air.

Beep! Beep! Beeeeep!

That's not a motherfucking dream though…that's a motherfucking fire alarm!

The siren echoes down the hall into my bedroom, blaring in my ears, making them pulse. However, somewhere between the monotonous beeping I also hear voices echoing from somewhere out in the hall.

"Shit! What the fuck did you do, Tate?" Pasha shouts, nervously.

"I don't know, man! I think I burned some milk on the glass top! Shit! What do I do?"

Beep! Beep! Beeeeep!

"How the fuck should I know?!" Pasha hisses back at him.

"Is Roman still sleeping?"

"Not anymore, dude!" Pasha snorts. "He's going to fucking kill you!"

I groan.

Not only did I just get yanked out of an illusionary romp with the woman I've affectionately deemed "The Brunette," I'm now being yanked out of my *bed*.

By a fucking idiot.

And given that Pasha just referred to "Tate," that also now means that I have to go deal with not one, but *two* fucking idiots in my penthouse.

Beep! Beep! Beeeeep!

God damn it, Pasha.

I quickly pull up the software app on my phone for the home fire alarm, and silence it, before throwing off the covers. I storm out of the bedroom and down the hallway as the last round of beeps sound before abruptly shutting off.

"What the fuck is going on in here?!" I thunder making idiots one and two jump to attention. "What the fuck have you shitheads done now?"

"S…sorry, Boss!" Tate, who is furiously scrubbing chemicals on my glass top stove and who is the blond haired, blue-eyed, non-Antonov version of my little brother, says nervously. "I brought your dog back from the groomer, and I was trying to steam the milk for Pasha's coffee, you know since he's injured and—"

"I don't give a rat's ass what you were trying to do, you fucking imbecile!" I hiss, nearly slipping in all the water he's dumped on the smoking stove. "Go to the fucking coffee shop!"

Suddenly, I hear Pasha chuckling, seated at the table beside me.

"Something funny, little brother?" I say, turning to glare at him.

"Good dream?" Pasha asks.

"Yes, actually," I seethe between gritted teeth.

"I can tell," he snorts.

"Excuse me?" I hiss.

But somehow this just makes him laugh harder.

"Bro," he finally says between his chuckling, holding up his hand and averting his eyes. "You're still half-mast, my man."

That's when I look down and see that I do in fact, still have a raging erection from the dream these two cumstains interrupted.

Shit.

"Yeah, well take a good look," I say, grabbing my crotch and kicking Pasha's kitchen chair hard, causing him to wince in pain. "Half-mast for me is more than you have on your best day, fucker."

Pasha submissively raises his hands in the air, but still can't hide the smirk on his face. If he were anyone else, I'd have beaten it off of him.

He's lucky he's my brother.

"Now," I growl, turning back to Tate and the counter, pointing between the two of them. "I don't care how long it takes, but you two are going to clean up this mess and get the fuck out of my sight."

I lock eyes with Pasha.

"And you have work to get to," I say, raising a brow. "You know, for that big boy role you wanted?"

"Well, yeah," he says defensively. "But, I thought since I'm here I'd just wait for you and—"

"You thought wrong," I say flatly. "I'm not going straight to the office."

"Oh," Pasha says, confused. "Where are—"

"My plans are not your concern," I snap, cutting him off. "I need a briefing about what happened yesterday and I'm not going to be waiting around for them to mosey into the office whenever they feel like it."

I slap Pasha on his good shoulder.

"That's your job, Bud. You get to round them up."

He sighs and nods in silence. Turning on my heel I head down the hall toward my bedroom.

"I don't want to see either of you assholes here when I get out of the shower," I shout, pressing open the door to my bedroom. "Or any *mess.*"

My bathroom is perfection.

And it should be for what I paid for the bitch.

It's dark, like *me.* Gray slate tiles line the floor, wired with heat to keep my feet warm, even in the cold New York winters. The twelve-foot walls of solid imported black Italian marble surround the entire room and there's a large copper freestanding tub along the floor to ceiling windows that face central park.

I snap at Alexa to start the shower before stripping off, taking a second to rub my hands over my chest in the mirror, noticing I still have that bruise along my ribs. Me and the boys got into a scuffle a few weeks ago at The Studio when a heated game of cards with the Italians turned into an all-out brawl. I smirk to myself and shake my head, stepping under the hot water.

Those drunken dickheads do too much coke.

Inhaling deeply, I press my hand against the wall and close my eyes.

However, the moment I do, images of *her* immediately come flooding back to me.

The Brunette.

As if she is standing right in front of me, I can see the curve of her face, the flecks of gold in her brown eyes, and the way her lip curls when she smirks. She was stunningly beautiful.

That's all I knew about her. Not because that information wasn't available to me, as I have the best information and intelligence team on the East Coast.

No, it was because I wouldn't *allow* myself to know anything about her… because she was married.

Not much is unattainable for men in my position, and realistically most of my circle would never let a little thing like a pesky husband get in the way of their pussy conquest.

But that was the problem.

Affairs might be common in mafia families, but unmanaged they can be dangerous. And deadly.

I know from experience.

My father had been a loyal husband to my mother for nearly half my life, until he wasn't. When he met his mistress, he changed. Hell, everything changed. That wicked bitch of his caused a lot of drama with my mother, which resulted in her declining health…and eventual death. And while my father did express remorse for his part, a part of me still resents *him* for it too.

When he finally came to his senses and cut his whore loose, he realized what a fool he'd been…when she ordered a hit on our family. We survived, and we handled it. Permanently. Just like we always do.

And we handled ol' dad too, when the time came.

I spit at the drain, the thought of my father making my blood boil within my veins.

Hope the worms are eating the fucking prick.

The only benefit to his bullshit, was I learned a valuable lesson: affairs are messy. And I don't have time for mess.

A jilted mistress can cause you a lot of embarrassment should they out you to the press. However, in our world, a jilted *wife* could literally destroy your life simply from how much access they have. And not just to assets or the children, but to information that could put you behind bars.

…Or the grave.

Which is why I don't fuck with any of it. Commitment. Marriage. Mistresses. I have enough chaos as it is as head of this insanely complicated family filled with over privileged narcissistic nepo-babies that are all borderline psychopaths.

I'm well past borderline though.

Regardless, my siblings keep me busy, as do their affairs.

Especially my sister Polina and her oafish husband Igor, who is always shoving his dick in the nearest soft pouch he can find. In Polina's case, however, she actually plays an active role in *choosing* her husband's mistresses. Knowing my conceited sister, her reasons are selfish, likely wanting to insure none of his "side chicks" steal her precious spotlight. But I could also imagine it's so that she doesn't have to subject herself to any of his…sexual preferences.

Actually no, I *can't* imagine that. I won't.

Immediately I put my entire face under the blast of hot water, hoping to wash away that entire train of thought.

No fucking thank you.

However, it's not as if Polina and Igor are the exception.

This is just how things are done in our…world.

The men do as they please, with whom they please, and unless you're of high rank like my sister, you don't get a vote. Hell, you don't even get an *opinion.* Our life, and our world, is still lost in an archaic time, and it's not as if anyone is interested in changing the status quo anytime soon.

That's not my problem though.

I have more pussy than a guy could ask for and I don't owe anyone anything. The sluts I fuck know they will never get loyalty from me. After all, I'd have to be insane to give up a fuck-list longer than the Dead Sea Scrolls.

But…then there was *The Brunette.*

The very thought of her causes an immediate reaction, and I have to reach down and stroke my swelling cock.

I *wanted* her. From the moment I laid eyes on her the first time we passed in the hallway at our building, I instantly wanted to see her naked, riding me.

Fuck I still do.

Under the warm soothing water, I stroke my erection, taking my time to squeeze the tip between my thumb and index finger, seeing the drops of precum forming.

She had the perfect cleavage, a deliciously thick ass, and was also adorably shorter than most of the girls I fucked.

From seeing her at multiple social events, The Brunette couldn't be taller than 5'6 even in heels, and as a 6'4 man myself, I was used to the tall stick-thin models who loved to hang on my arm at press events. And while perhaps that's what some men preferred, and the girls looked good on the cover of whatever tabloid was propping up my face, at the end of the day, not one has ever made my dick *this* hard.

I wanted a woman with an ass I could bury my face in. All. Night. Long.

I lean against the wall, running my hand up and down my pulsing cock, thinking about pulling her leggings down and stroking her smooth little slit. My heart beats faster as I picture her, laying on her stomach, legs together, with that ass up in the air as I slide into her from behind, burying myself within her, biting her neck, and pulling her hair in my fist.

This is what does it for me, and with a final pump, I cum, exploding all over the shower wall.

I stand there for a moment, catching my breath as the aftershocks shake through my body. And while the release feels amazing, it also suddenly makes me feel a bit unsettled.

How can a woman I've never actually spoken to have such an effect on me?

It feels a bit…insane.

Rinsing the rest of my body I turn off the shower and step out, grabbing a towel from off the rack, still thinking about her.

I'd seen her around our building for nearly two years; her and her pencil-dicked husband, that rumor has it, was some trust-fund fuckhead who worked for his daddy's brokerage firm. Likely because he couldn't make it in the real world, and his family couldn't stomach the embarrassment.

But there were no rumors about *her*. No whispers either. It was almost like she wasn't there. So, when the couple disappeared from the building, it was like she'd never existed.

How could a girl that pretty be that invisible?

She was stunningly beautiful, even in those frumpy sweaters she always wore. Which I never understood, as then I'd see her little twat of a husband parading her around some party in some form-fitting evening gown that left little to the imagination.

It didn't make any sense.

My phone pings on the counter, and I pick it up, realizing I have a text from Pasha.

8:24am:
Kitchen is clean. Got in touch with the clan, everyone will be there. But heads up, Polina's riled up about something. You've been warned.

Great. That's just what I fucking need.

Tossing the towel on the floor in the bathroom, I make my way into the bedroom, where Caesar, my purebred German Shepherd sits on his bed, staring at me eagerly. With one short whistle he immediately dashes across the room, and sits before me, nudging my hand with his long nose and awaiting my command.

"Good boy," I smile, kneeling down to give him pets. "Let me get dressed, and we'll go, okay?"

I snap my fingers and motion for him to return to his bed, and he obeys without complaint. As he always does.

If only my men were that fucking easy.

But even after I select an outfit, I find my mind drifting back to The Brunette's haunting brown eyes.

Last night's dream wasn't the exception.

In fact, it was a regular, if not weekly occurrence. She's the specter that occasionally stalks my subconscious, and if I had to wager a guess as to why, I'd say it's because she was going to *be* my exception.

I actually wanted her to *be* my one exception, to one of the few rules I govern myself by.

The night of the Children's Benefit I'd finally had enough of restraining and wanting and was ready to take her for myself. To be honest, I didn't care if she wanted me back, or if her husband objected. I had ways of dealing with both of those little hiccups, and that night I wasn't above using any and all means to claim her for myself.

And the look in those brown eyes told me that on some level, she wanted me too.

I decided I was going to break my own deep-seated rule about fucking with someone's marriage. I was going to have her if it was the last thing I did.

Because I just didn't care anymore.

I watched her all night, biding my time and inching my way closer to her with every minute that ticked by.

But then she just disappeared.

And not just from the gala, but from existence entirely. I stopped seeing her in the hallways, I stopped seeing her at the gym in our building. She was just gone.

Could I have looked harder for her? Sure. But it rattled me to my core, as if perhaps my willingness to discard my own morality had upset the universe… so the universe stepped in and took her from me.

Fuck the universe. And fuck this shit.

I've dwelt in fantasyland enough today. I have real problems to solve that require my full attention. I can't be distracted by the ghost of some mystery woman. No matter how sexy.

She's just a woman.

And as if confirming my acknowledgement, my phone pings in my pocket as I fasten my new favorite watch around my wrist. Another text has come in, and this time it's from a number I've apparently labeled "AccounTits."

AccounTits.
8:57am.: My pussy is still sore. Among other things. But I'm ready for round two anytime, Mr. A.

I smirk to myself, shoving the phone back into my pocket, but deliberately not replying.

AccounTits is actually an employee that works in my accounting department.

Some petite little blonde who found her way to The Studio a few nights ago, and after two bottles of vodka, took a good fucking on the poker table… with an audience. It was fun, especially since the big-chested girl was more than willing to do whatever I wanted, in every way imaginable.

But I'm Roman Antonov. I don't do "round twos."

I don't see the point.

After all, who wants to conquer the same pussy twice?

A
ANTONOV

CHAPTER FOUR

The scent of flowers fills my nose as I inhale deeply, the harsh thorns taking root within my chest, locking the cracks of my heart together. These four walls became my happy place, my safe haven.

My justice.

It took months for my pretties to grow, to flourish under my care, just as I flourished under theirs. My greenhouse is now full of Oleander, Deadly Nightshade, Henbane, Strychnine, Lily of the Valley, and my personal favorite, Foxglove.

Pretty and deadly.

My first time at the *book club*, I checked out *Plants That Kill* and then my collection was born. I chased down seeds online, went on walks, dug them up and brought them to the penthouse, where I made a makeshift greenhouse on the balcony. Garrett had no idea what I was doing, and he stopped asking when I told him they were herbs for dinner.

The first time I tried to kill him, with Morning Glory seeds, placed on top of a fresh loaf of bread, my heart was racing with adrenaline. I nearly chickened out, I sat on the chair in the living room, my knee bouncing as I chewed my nails…but all he experienced from that was hallucinations of me fucking the guy who lived above us. By the end of the night, I was beaten and bleeding, with him dripping down my thighs.

After that, all doubt had vanished.

He was a dead man.

The following morning, my sore body limped around grabbing the book again, while he drank himself silly on the couch. For hours I hunted through the pages, looking for my answer, my solution, my savior.

Foxglove.

It was the final piece of the puzzle that I needed, it tied it all together in a pretty little bow.

My concoction of death.

A widow maker.

A mix of Deadly Nightshade, for the nervous system, Strychnine for the respiratory system, and lastly Foxglove, for the heart.

The mix of these three becomes the perfect poison, each attacking a different part of the body, dancing simultaneously in beautiful harmony until they peak together, and the mark draws their last breath.

Beautifully poetic if you ask me.

It takes just two grams of my Widowmaker to kill a person. I heard a mark say it has a spicy, bitter taste, but they never seem to mind. It certainly hasn't stopped a single one of them from finishing my deadly cocktail of karmatic justice...forever sealing their own fate.

Yes, each plant could kill a person on their own with the correct dosage, yet each one had a fatal flaw, one that didn't benefit me: *Time.*

Time for the mark to get help. Time to be treated. Time to survive their fate.

That was unacceptable.

They do not get to survive the torment they have caused on another human being.

They do not get to survive *me.*

I've always thought Foxglove to be my favorite, it was after all the final piece I needed, it called to me in a way that no other plant did. It sang a song that only I could hear.

When researching it at the local library, I ended up down a rabbit hole, fascinated by Foxglove and its ability to kill, but also its ability to heal. It was often used in medication focusing on healing the heart.

It's a bit ironic that the correct dose can also stop it.

Finding information on grow-it-at-home poisonous plants is near impossible, it's clear that the powers that be have spent time burying it. I suppose it would be a nightmare for them if people started digging them up and killing their enemies with it.

The only real way to find out any information on these specific plants would be behind the scientific composition of them, and science was something I was good at. Something that I thrived in.

Yet, something I had to leave behind.

The moment I said yes to marriage, was the moment I gave up my dream of working in medicine. Not the sort that was dealing with humans or animals, but in medicinal chemistry. I'd always wanted to be someone working behind the microscope, cutting, slicing, and breaking down chemical compounds.

I traded in cutting, slicing, and compound composition for, cutting and slicing for dinner parties, and knowing what cleaning agents I can and can't mix.

Foxglove contains compounds called cardiac glycosides, they disable cell sodium-potassium ion pumps leading to increased cell sodium and calcium ion concentration, which results in the heart slowing down and eventually… stopping.

Kind of amazing that something so beautifully fragile can be so incredibly dangerous.

I walk out of the greenhouse, checking the lock three times, my mind drawing up images of my little Lily, the stray cat I saved as a kitten. She often roams the garden, basking in the sun just outside of the greenhouse. My pretty plants would kill her, and that's something I could never live with.

My eyes scan the cobblestone path heading toward the door of a red brick three story house, located just on the outskirts of lower Manhattan.

It was like the universe was rewarding me for killing my husband. The day after his funeral, a default notice was delivered. Apparently, my lovely husband's grandma Bettie died, and had left her Victorian style townhouse to him. And because he was dead, and his will left everything to me, it defaulted ownership…to *me*.

I never met the woman, but darling Bettie had kept this place in tip top condition and had upgraded it several times over the years, making it the perfect home for me to start over.

Stopping briefly at the hose, I quickly wash my hands and feet, removing any traces of the greenhouse, or my plants from them, the water circling down the drain. Once finished, I turn off the hose, and quickly ring my hands, now cold from the brisk fall air.

The clouds move with the wind, the colors blending together, creating a beautiful canvas of watercolors.

I take in the scenery for a moment, before I walk in through the back door, almost tripping over Lily as she bolts between my legs diving inside for warmth. Kicking the door closed behind me, I twist the lock, rattling the handle to make sure that it is secured. Lily brushes against my leg, silently scolding me for being out there so long, and demanding something to eat.

"Hey cutie, are you hungry?" I coo at her.

She meows and runs into the kitchen, the little bell around her neck ringing as she goes. I may have rinsed my hands before I came inside, but I still won't touch her till I've fully washed them with soap.

It is not a risk I'm willing to take. Not with her. Not ever.

Once they are clean, I'll snuggle her and give her all the love she could possibly want, until she runs away to sleep.

It didn't take long for her to come to understand my routine, but once she did, she now greets me with a chirp before darting off to wait for me by the sink.

My feet carry me through to the kitchen, my nose scrunching as I flinch at the cold seeping through the tiles on the floor. Turning the tap to hot, I wait for the water to heat up, smiling as I hear the familiar bang of the pipes upstairs. Steam floats from the sink before I dunk my hands under, a sigh escaping me. Zoning out, I practically rub my hands raw, only to be brought back by Lily headbutting my shoulder.

"Okay girl, okay, Salmon or Tuna today?"

It's strange, talking to an animal that can't talk back, but I'm positive that she understands me as she meows in response.

"Tuna it is."

Reaching up on my tip toes, I grab a foil packet from the cupboard, using my elbow to slam it shut behind me.

Dumping the foul-smelling contents into her bowl, I tug her tail gently before heading upstairs.

I open the door to my walk-in closet, full of clothes that I was never allowed to own, let alone wear.

My late husband never liked me showing any skin, he would've kept me wrapped in a sheet if he could, no shoulders visible and I always had to wear pants, because shoulders and knees were so…*distracting*.

Once a month, he and his mother would go clothes shopping while I remained at home. Being the girl with no family and not a dime to my name meant I wasn't trusted to dress myself. They picked everything, down to my underwear.

And if I was caught wearing something that wasn't on the approved *Abigail's List*, then I would pay the price.

When our marriage was finally dissolved after his death, I sold it all. The penthouse, the car, furniture, and then went to the mall and bought anything and everything that struck my fancy. Short skirts, tights, booty shorts, crop tops. The works.

With each swipe of the card, I felt my power coming back to me, each ding of the register stitching my soul together.

Retail therapy really is the answer to everything.

My husband would roll over in his grave if he knew the amount I'd spent, as well as every single piece of fabric that showed a centimeter of my skin.

Well, he would if he had a grave.

I cremated the bastard and then threw his ashes in the trash behind a fast-food joint just ten minutes from the crematorium.

Smiling to myself I grab my laptop.

It's time to find out who Igor Ivanov really is.

The computer hits the floor with a thump, my blood heating in my veins as my teeth grind together. Rubbing my hands over my eyes, I lean back in my chair as I take in a slow and deliberate breath, trying to calm the throbbing in my temple.

I couldn't find anything personal about Igor online.

Like…nothing.

Leah had said Igor had money and was well connected, but there's no social accounts, no business website, and no personal information in the public record about him.

It was intriguingly infuriating.

I've never had an issue finding someone online before, especially in this generation that practically lives on their phones. Nowadays, idiots document their entire life, even snapping pictures of food, something that I personally find to be absurd. We live in a day and age where we're more focused on capturing things on camera, than actually living it. We're simply watching life through a screen or documenting it for a like count.

But Igor Ivanov was practically an online ghost.

Minus the high-profile reports on his business practices at Nikotech Investments, which told me where he worked, I only found him tagged in a few social media posts. This told me what circles he ran with, but his lack of personal social media was strange for someone of his status. The only thing I'm able to confirm is that he's married, with a mistress that he keeps locked up when the wife is home.

That, and the fact that he, like every red-blooded male with a small dick complex, spends a lot of time at The Studio.

The Studio is the most popular club within New York City. It's expensive, exclusive, and requires men to have a membership to attend, stroking the egos of every man in there.

Women however don't need a membership, just a pretty face, and a lot of skin on show.

I haven't been to the club since putting down the trust fund baby a few weeks back.

John Bishop was a monster that forced himself on his victim. He never told her he was married, and when she found out she tried to do the right thing and leave… but he didn't let her.

She was his prisoner.

…But I was her savior.

I remember *his* death vividly. I studied him for weeks.

A preppy man child with mommy issues and a drug problem. He was the easiest kill for me, predictable, open, and down to party *hard,* after the weekly family dinner of course.

I'd placed a tracker on his car and followed him around. He never stayed in his own place and was always warming someone else's bed, while his wife was at home, feeding their baby.

I did wonder, however, if the wife knew what he was doing, and who he was. Did she turn a blind eye to it, or was she receiving the same treatment as his bed warmers?

The only routine stop John made was to his parents' mansion on the edge of the city, for his family dinner. On the outside, he looked like a good son attending a cozy get-together. But a cozy get together wouldn't include the best PR fixer in New York, likely hired to cover up his multiple transgressions.

I lurked in the shadows, using the groomed hedges to hide in plain sight. He was in the house for less than thirty minutes before he stormed out, throwing the door so hard into the wall that the old brick dusted around it. Then he sat in his car, blaring his music, and punching his steering wheel, making the horn blast. Repeatedly.

All while his mother looked through the window at the scene he was causing, before letting the curtain fall back into place.

Out of sight, out of mind I suppose.

Eventually he sped off, his tires tearing through the gravel of the drive and throwing pebbles everywhere.

I paid the driver of my cab to follow behind him making sure he kept a three-car gap between us. If we were any closer, I worried John would get suspicious. Of course, the driver was suspicious too, staring at me through the mirror. So I spun a lie, saying he was cheating on my best friend.

I followed him until he arrived at The Studio, throwing his keys at Teddy, the bouncer who usually mans the door. Before I even got inside, he was drugged out of his mind, with a young working girl sucking his cock down like a delicacy.

On Sundays, The Studio often had themed nights, where there were no limits. Anything could happen, and anything often did.

Even from across the club, I could see his neck straining as her head bobbed rhythmically. He fisted her hair and held her down, forcing her to choke so hard on his dick that after he finished, she crumpled to the floor, tears streaming down her face. Her knuckles white as she tightly gripped the wad of cash, he threw at her.

A normal man would've been done for the night.

But John? No.

That's when he went after Lizzie.

He stormed over to the bar, slamming his hand down repeatedly demanding she give him another drink. But Lizzie bravely declined, wisely cutting him off.

I wasn't planning on killing him that night, but the opportunity was right there. So, I took it.

I brought myself a drink, and ordered him a whiskey, neat. As I walked away from the bar, I dropped the Widowmaker in, swirling the glass in my hand. He gave me a dazzling smile as he patted the seat next to him, before he slurred something about me being a 'good girl'.

I will forever remember the way his lips formed the words.

Ugh. It still makes my skin crawl.

But that night had been successful.

And tonight will be too.

Forcing myself to move from the chair, I snatch my phone off the nightstand, and load up Igor's face, his balding head distracts me temporarily, but my eyes zero in on his eyes.

"The eyes are the doors to the soul; they show you all you need to know about a person."

My grandma was right. As always.

Because Igor's eyes in this headshot suck all the light out of the room, the shadows making them appear darker than the pits of hell.

A smile curves across my face.

It's time he met the devil.

ANTONOV

CHAPTER FIVE

ROMAN

"Caesar!" Pasha exclaims, dropping to his knees and calling my dog the moment I walk through the doors of my executive floor. "Heyy budddy! Get over here, good boy!"

Even though I know Caesar would love to go running to Pasha, I click my tongue, signaling for him to disregard the excited invitation, and like the intelligent dog he is, he stays directly at my side, looking up at me for affirmation.

"Damn, Ro," my brother snickers, slowly lifting himself up with the help of the nearest desk. "What the hell did you do to this poor dog to make him so obedient?"

"I *trained* him, Pasha," I say as I walk past him. "You know, that thing where you put time and effort into teaching an animal commands, expecting they will obey those commands? Something I apparently failed to do with you fuckers since none of you assholes listen."

"Yeah, well, maybe you should offer better *treats*," Pasha chuckles, snapping his gum in his mouth. "Perhaps you'd get a better return on your investment."

Rolling my eyes, and deliberately ignoring him, I head directly into my office.

The furniture is a black and white mix of contemporary Scandinavian furniture, and the walls are made of solid clear glass. However, in the event that I actually *do* want privacy, with the flick of a switch I can make them go opaque.

It was something I saw once at a BDSM club in Chicago several years ago and found to be extremely unique.

But given that everyone working on *this* floor of Nikotech Investments knows exactly what I do when I'm not fronting capital for upcoming projects around the city, I don't feel the need to use it very often.

Silently I point, and Caesar makes his way to his elevated dog bed in the corner and picks up his bone.

Cal, who has posted up temporarily today at the desk just outside my office, joins Pasha and the two of them follow me inside. He takes a position in the corner, standing respectfully off to the side, while my little brother on the other hand, pulls out his phone and crashes down in one of my chairs, resting his foot on my desk.

Cal clears his throat, and Pasha quickly removes it, but not before rolling his eyes.

I've just finished unbuttoning my jacket when there is a gentle knock against the glass door.

"Good morning, Sir," Kristinah, my decently attractive redheaded assistant, says with a smile. A very *loaded* smile, reminding me that Kristinah wants to fuck me.

But then again, who doesn't?

She sets my coffee down at my desk, careful not to spill a drop of the perfectly flayed cappuccino design.

I say nothing, and she wisely doesn't linger, having been the recipient of my pre-coffee wrath in the past. As I take a sip, I pick up the file on my desk, perusing it slowly. A daily report that's prepared by Cal, and despite rain, sleet, or shine, is *always* waiting for me before I arrive, giving me the updates on everything I need to know before the entourage arrives.

As head of this family, it's my job to always be in the know, even if the people in charge of keeping me in the know don't always do a good job of that...deliberately or otherwise. And while my dear siblings might think I insist on these early Monday morning meetings just to torture them, it's just to see who's going to be honest with me about the status of our various enterprises.

...Or rather, be *completely* honest with me.

Cal's reports are the ones I can *trust*, and how I gauge how much bullshit my family tries to feed me. That's because he's the one person I know I can rely on. He's also the one person that I would consider to be more than just my subordinate, or employee. When we were kids, Cal's father died in service to our family, and instead of dumping the orphan kid into the cracked foster care system, my father made a uniquely compassionate decision and took Cal in.

Perhaps it was because at that time, my closest siblings in age were Anastasia and Polina, my twin brothers Lev and Nikolai were just babies, and cheery ol' Pasha here wasn't even a twinkle in my father's wrinkly ball sack yet. So, it's likely it was a decision made less out of compassion, and more so because my father decided I could use a male playmate and friend…as well as a good sparring partner.

However, even if that friendship has always been intentionally one-sided, Cal has always had my back.

He's fearless, smart, reliable…and punctual.

Also unlike my fucking family.

"Pasha," I say, looking up at him. "You said they'd be here on time. It's quarter after. Where the hell are they?"

But just as I say the words out loud, I immediately hear the commotion coming down the hallway.

"Sounds to me they're right on time," Pasha says, holding his finger up in the air, but refusing to tear himself away from his scroll of the latest bikini-clad social media influencer he's trolling. "For *them* anyway."

"The entire car smelled of pussy Igor!" Polina snarls at him. "Cheap pussy!"

"What do you care, eh?" Igor snaps. "It was my night to be with Leah!"

"I know for a fact that Leah was at her stupid book club meeting!" Polina screeches. "So, want to try that again? The agreement was you could fuck around but only with the bitches I approve!"

"Christ, Pol," I hear Lev whine. "Can't you and your little *whoreband* here have these disgustingly illuminating marital discussions at home?"

"Shut up!" Polina snaps.

"Pretty sure that's exactly what Lev is suggesting," Nikolai chimes in, backing up his identical twin. "We don't care to know this much about your private life, or lack thereof, and it's getting a little weird at this point."

"Not to mention just…gross," Lev finishes.

"He's a fucking idiot!" Polina thunders, smacking Igor across the back of the head. "And a fucking pig!"

"Ow!" he bitches.

Suddenly she swipes a stapler off the nearest desk and flings it directly at her husband. It ricochets off his bald lumpy head and smashes into the glass wall of my office, which is thankfully bulletproof.

…And stapler-proof, evidently.

"Ow! What the hell?!" Igor snaps at her, rubbing her head. "What is wrong with you?"

"You! *You* are what's wrong with me, you asswipe!" Polina snaps, grabbing a decorative desk plant off Kristinah's desk. "Do you have any idea how long it took me to curate and train that whore for you?! You had no right to go *outsourcing*!"

She lobs the plant at Igor, sending Kristinah and the other office girl scurrying out of the way, and barely missing Igor's head a second time.

"Fuck you, you crazy Antonov bitch!" Igor shouts.

"*Igor!*" Anastasia suddenly hisses viciously, as every one of us suddenly glares at him. "Watch your fucking tongue!"

"Hah!" Polina smirks arrogantly, glaring at her husband as she grabs my office door handle.

"But really though, Pol," Ana says, narrowing her eyes at our sister. "Shut up, Bitch."

"Thatta girl, Ana," Pasha chuckles still without looking up from some fat-assed bikini model. "You tell her."

"Fuck off, little *Puppy*," Polina snaps, using her not-so-affectionate nickname she's had for Pasha since we were kids. "You should know, this bitch bites."

"Woof woof," Pasha chuckles antagonistically back at her, winking at her as he finally puts his phone away.

I clear my throat loudly.

"Good morning," I say sarcastically, lacing my hands together on my desk. "You're all late. As usual."

"You can thank these two for that," Lev says, pointing his head at Polina and Igor. "She set his car on fire this morning, so we had to turn around to go pick them up. After waiting for the fire department to clear off."

Pasha starts snickering, until Ana kicks his chair.

Jesus fucking Christ.

I sigh, looking up at Polina.

"Of course, you tell him *that* part, but you have neglected to tell him that the entire car smelled of pussy! Cheap, white trash pussy!" She scoffs, pointing angrily at Igor. "Wild dogs could have smelled it a mile away!"

"Wild dogs?" Igor laughs, infuriating Polina more. "There are no 'wild dogs' in the city! Unless you count your crazy bitch ass!"

Polina is yelling so loudly that Nikolai, who unfortunately is standing closest to her, rubs his ear. Swearing under his breath, he quickly moves across the room to stand by Ana and Lev.

"Roman," my sister demands. "You need to do something about this asshole! He's out of control!"

"*I'm* out of control?!" Igor snarls back at her. "You just set my fucking car on fire! You're insane!"

"Oh! And he came home plastered the other night, and crashed his car into my roses!" Polina continues still waving her arms wildly at her husband. "My *Juliet Roses,* Roman! The ones I've been growing for three years!"

"Oh God," Igor groans, throwing his hands in the air. "Here we go with the fucking flowers again, eh?"

"They were imported from Europe, you disgusting trash goblin!" She hisses. "Do you have any idea how hard they were to get? They came directly from the original greenhouse!"

I rub my eyes.

My headache has a name today: *Polina.*

She continues to ramble on, as if anyone in this room is actually listening.

"...And there was cum all over the back seats!"

"What the...?" Pasha asks, scrunching up his face. "Yuck."

"Exactly what I said," Nikolai snorts, looking at him with a grimace.

"That's what I've been saying this whole time!" She whines, desperate for sympathy. "I came out this morning to find some bitch's panties on the steering wheel and cum all over the back seats. I *had* to set the car on fire! I'm not getting diseases from your trashy sluts who don't know how to wash their pussies!"

"Again," Lev says, shaking his head, disgusted. "*Gross.*"

Polina begins exchanging curses at Igor in Russian, and makes a step toward him with her fist raised, but I bang my hand down hard on the desk.

"Alright, enough!"

The rattle of the sturdy oak desk is enough to make everyone jump, and make Caesar, who has been happily munching on his bone, look up at me.

"I don't give a flying fuck about roses, panties or mistresses," I glare at Igor and Polina. "But I swear to God, this fucking nonsense needs to stop."

"Tell him that, he's the one who—"

"*No!*" I growl, standing to my feet and storming over to her. "I'm saying it to *you.* You're not a teenager anymore Polina, so this shit isn't cute or funny! You can't just go screaming your tripe out first thing in the morning or setting cars on fire in a neighborhood like yours!"

I step up into her space, my face just inches from hers, my blood boiling in my veins.

"I keep trying to drill into your thick fucking head that your antics will draw attention to you, and us! And I'm not going to see all of us go down because of your marriage that you two shitheads can't seem to figure out for yourselves!" I thunder at her so forcefully I accidentally spit on her in the process. "Save this dramatic shit for the family dinner. This is a business meeting and therefore is not the place. I'm not going to tell you again, get your fucking shit together or I will cut you off, Polina. For good! Am I clear?"

Polina stubbornly opens her mouth to say something, but I cut her off.

"Am I fucking clear?!" I shout in her face, banging my fist on the glass wall behind her, making her flinch.

She slowly looks up at me, fury in her eyes before she pushes past me and storms out of the room, back toward the elevator.

"Do you want me to go retrieve her?" Ana, my favorite sister, and *my* twin, asks quietly.

"No," I sigh, rubbing my chin. "I think we can all agree this shit is easier without her. It's always easier."

"You got that right," Igor snorts, leaning against the wall by Cal, pushing his hands in his pockets.

"*You* can fuck off too," I snap at him. "I won't tell you how to conduct your relationship because frankly I don't give a damn about your shitty marriage. But I won't have it causing drama for me, this family, or the fucking business I am trying to run. So, if you can't keep your dirty laundry out of sight, I will remorselessly find some other juiced-up meathead to replace you. And God knows my sister won't weep for you should you disappear. Understood?"

"Yes, Boss," Igor swallows hard, bowing his head in submission. "Understood."

"Now," I say, walking back around to my chair and taking a seat. "We have more important things to discuss."

"Fifteen minutes," Pasha says, looking down at his watch. "That's a new record for us."

I shoot him a glare, silently informing him that if he says another fucking word, I might strangle him.

"Last night," I say, turning back to the rest of my family. "There was a bit of a situation."

"What kind of situation," Nikolai sighs.

"The kind that ended with this one getting shot in the shoulder," I say nodding to Pasha. "...And us executing one of the McCleary clan."

"*Which* member," Anastasia asks, her brow suddenly furrowed.

"Cillian's cousin," I say, pursing my lips as murmurs go up around the room.

"Which cousin?" Lev asks.

"Saoirse," I reply.

"Wait… you mean the *girl* cousin?" Nikolai asks, his eyes wide.

"Well," I say, clearing my throat. "She wasn't a *girl*, she was a full grown woman. And she shot Pasha."

"Technically she was shooting at *you*, Bro," Pasha shrugs. "I just jumped in the way. Like the badass hero brother I am."

"Jesus, Roman," Anastasia shoots me a disapproving look. "What the hell happened? I mean, I literally gave you guys everything you needed. It was just supposed to be a quick job. In and out."

"It was," I say, clicking my tongue. "It just went a bit sideways at the end."

"You're not kidding," Lev says, shaking his head. "That's not going to go over well with the Irish. You know how they are with their kin. Especially with their women."

"Yeah, Bro, they aren't going to take that well," Nikolai chirps.

Oh, for fucks sake…

"Yeah, well, regardless of what your opinions are on the matter," I snap irritably. "What's done is done. What I need you people to do is keep your heads out of your asses and pay attention. I don't know how or when, but they *will* retaliate. It's only a matter of time. So, you need to be on your game."

The room goes silent.

"Lev," I say, turning to him. "We need to ramp up the recruits. We need more men."

"How many?" he asks.

"As many as we can get. Any man for us, is a man we take from the Irish."

"…Or *woman*," Ana says flatly, crossing her arms raising her brows at me.

"Or woman," I concede, forcing myself not to roll my eyes. "Regardless, get on it. And get some foot soldiers out into the city. Reliable foot soldiers, ones who can observe and report without being noticed."

He nods.

"Niko, I need you to inventory our investments. I don't want anything to go wrong with the Walston Building deal. I've heard rumors that Cillian's been sniffing around, and I want to make sure that we are ten steps ahead of them."

"You got it, Roman," Nikolai replies.

"Pasha, you need to check in with Ethan White," I say pointing at him. "The shipment arrives this week, and he's supposed to be sending a guy to handle it and make the drop off. Wesley Lee, I think was his name."

"Wesley *Lee*?" Pasha snorts. "What a weird name choice."

"Hey! Don't be stupid," I snap, slapping my hand on the desk to grab his attention. "Get in touch with White and coordinate the drop off."

"Wait…I'm not going?"

"Anything with them I handle personally," I say firmly. "You know this."

"Boo," Pasha groans, pursing his lips.

"Ana—"

"Yeah, yeah, you don't need to tell me anything, Roman," Anastasia says. "I'll monitor all channels. As always."

I nod.

That's why she's my favorite sister.

"And you," I say, turning finally to Igor. "You will go collect your wife, take her home, and then go make our collections. After that, I don't care what you do. You can get back to screwing hookers, knocking off grannies or drowning kittens, or whatever it is you do."

Igor chuckles.

"Are we…still going to The Studio tonight?" He asks, eagerly. "I got a great girl for you. She will swallow your dick."

Is he for real right now?

But the truth is, I *am* looking forward to going to The Studio. And after that dream about The Brunette, I feel like I need it. But Igor and Polina's bullshit pissed me off today, and I want him nervous enough to button his lip.

"Fuck off," I say, catching his eyes.

"Yes, Boss," he says, nodding and quickly exiting my office.

He nearly trips on Kristinah, on the way out, who is standing at the door, with a priority mail envelope in hand.

"Um," she says sheepishly, sliding the cardboard envelope across the desk. "Sorry to interrupt, Sir. But this came for you. I signed for it, but it was marked as urgent."

"It's fine," I say, waving her off but looking back to my family. "They were just *leaving* anyway."

Anastasia looks at me, and then at Cal, but then turns and silently follows the boys, and Kristinah, out of my office.

No one lingers. They never do.

Except for Cal.

Hmm. That can't be good.

"What is it?" I ask.

"There is something I left out of your report this morning," Cal says, deliberately dropping the use of formalities once the members of my family have left. "But I couldn't risk anyone else seeing it."

I snort indignantly.

"Who else would see it?"

Cal doesn't respond, but instead, his eyes follow Kristinah as she walks across the vacant floor and sits on the edge of the other administrative assistant's desk.

I sigh heavily.

"What do you know," I say quietly, rubbing my eyes.

"I caught her reviewing the files on your desk one morning before you arrived," Cal says, still not taking his eyes off of Kristinah. "...And several times since."

Fuck. And I was just starting to not entirely hate Kristinah.

"Well," I say, motioning with my hands. "She's certainly been naughty, but curiosity isn't necessarily a crime, Cal. At least it isn't in my book."

"No," Cal says softly. "But I'm assuming that her passing along information about your Walston Street deal to the McCleary's would be."

My blood boils, and I find myself glaring at Kristinah, who takes a sip of her coffee, before throwing her head back in a mirthful laugh...unaware of the conversation taking place in this office.

"You're certain?" I ask, but I already know the answer.

"She's the only one who had access to that information," Cal says. "We've deliberately kept that very discreet. And there's no reason for it to even be on Cillian's radar. However, my sources tell me that she's connected by blood to one of his enforcers, and she's one of the only ones who could've seen all the financial paperwork and—"

"Alright," I snap irritably, raising my hand in the air. "Just handle it."

Cal nods once, and then heads out of my office.

I sit at my desk, watching as he walks up to Kristinah and with a well-practiced smile asks her to "come with him."

Shame. She had just learned how to get my coffee right.

"Oh my God! Please! Don't...don't do this!"

Screams echo through the old factory, scaring away a few pigeons squatting in the rickety old rafters.

"I've already told you everything I told them!" She wails as her hands and feet are bound with rope.

"You know what," I say, loudly chewing on a bite of filet mignon. "I actually believe you."

I had dinner reservations, but obviously with the way things developed today, I had to pivot my plans. So, Giorgi, one of my younger men, picked up takeout from my favorite steakhouse. My dinner table, placed atop an old barrel, consists of a porcelain plate, my gold silverware, a silk napkin, and a bottle of wine in a bucket of ice.

And perhaps out of amusement that we were inside an old candle factory, or perhaps just out of convenience, he's also set up a single lit candle in a discarded beer bottle.

"Y…you do?" Kristinah asks, her mascara-stained face looking up at me, her eyes wide. "You believe me?"

"Yes, I actually do," I nod, grabbing my glass of wine and taking a sip. "I've found people are always the most truthful…right before they die."

"Oh, God," she groans.

"Apparently, they think clearing their soul will bring them closer to the "Big Man Upstairs, or something," I say, pointing my fork at her, and smirking. "But I *am* the big man upstairs. At least for you little people anyway."

"Roman, Pl—"

But Igor cracks her hard across the face.

"Bitch, you will address Mr. Antonov by his proper name," he growls. "Or I will sew your mouth closed!"

"Jesus, Igor," I cringe.

Kristinah, albeit bewildered, looks up at me, a fleeting look of hope skating across her face.

"I mean, at least let me finish my dinner first before you start carving up the girl," I say, cutting a piece of steak. "This is delicious by the way. Alberto knows how to cook a steak."

"Mr. Antonov, please! Mercy, I beg you!" She pleads.

"You know, Giorgi," I snort, pointing to the candle in the beer bottle. "This is a nice touch."

"Thank you, Boss," Giorgi says, staring straight forward.

"Mr. Antonov!" Kristinah shouts in the background.

Screaming and flailing about as much as she can with her hands and feet tied, she is forcibly picked up by Oleg and Pavel, two of my oldest soldiers. They carry her up the rickety metal staircase leading to the main wax-melting drum in the center of the room, which is currently churning at nearly 300 degrees.

"See, you veterans could stand to learn a thing or two from the *kits* once in a while," I ignore her, instead motioning to Pavel and Oleg. "They have something you don't."

"Boss?" Igor asks me, confused.

"*Hunger*," I say, slicing the rest of the steak and popping it into my mouth. "You seasoned men think you're above growth, and you tend to get comfortable and lazy, because you've been gorging yourselves from the generosity of my table. Meanwhile these kids here, well, they are just willing to do more to try and make a good first impression. I like that."

"Yes, Boss," Igor says, who has been keeping his formalities up all afternoon and evening, ever since I scared him shitless in our little meeting today.

Maybe I should make that a weekly thing for him.

"Mr. Antonov, I swear, I had no choice!" Kristinah pleads again, reminding me of her unfortunate existence.

"You're new here, aren't you, kid?" I ask, ignoring her.

"Yes, Boss," Giorgi replies.

"Would you like two pieces of free advice?"

"Yes, Boss."

"The first is that the faster you adapt the more likely you are to survive," I say, going back to my dinner and looking up at the twenty-something year old kid in front of me. "You see life in the mafia is a delicate balance. On one hand, you kids need to be taught how to serve, and mentored. However, on the other hand, if you aren't also put in dangerous situations where you might die, we won't ever know how good you are, do you understand me?"

"Yes, Boss," Giorgi agrees.

"And the second thing is that none of these veterans really want to see you succeed at that. You know why?"

"No, Boss."

"Because *if* you succeed, it won't be long before you'll be taking a seat away from one of them at the table," I say, narrowing my eyes at him. "See, here, it's survival of the fittest. One man's fall is another man's gain. And in this city and in this family, if you stop being relevant and reliable, you stop being fed. So, at some point, you'll have to drop this whole good boy routine, and get your hands dirty. You'll have to fight and claw your way into a meal. Or you'll *become* the meal, you got me?"

"Yes, Boss," he nods.

I lean in, a wicked smirk on my face.

"But here's the crux of it all," I whisper softly. "While it's good for you to be starving and threatened enough to fight for that seat, you need to be *not* threatening enough that one of these older dogs starts thinking that your advancement equals his "retirement." Otherwise, your life won't just be tested, it will be threatened. Consistently. You understand me?"

"Yes, Boss," Giorgi nods, without breaking his stoic stare. "I understand."

Cal must've mentored this one.

Usually making eye contact with me is the first thing the young ones fuck up, mistakenly thinking that they have any sort of right to look their Don in the face.

I know this because I used to get a kick out of beating the ever-loving fuck out of them when they did.

"Are you willing to fight for that spot, kid?" I ask.

But he doesn't respond.

"I asked you a question!" I thunder suddenly.

But to my surprise, he doesn't flinch. Instead, his eyes slowly find mine.

"Yes, Boss," he says, his words polite but his tone firm. "I am."

Well, what do you know?

Maybe there is some bite in him after all. I stare him down, looking deep into his unmoving brown eyes. The fire held within crackles with an intensity that borders on dangerous and disrespectful, as if he was a kid staring down a train.

But then, just before I'm prepared to knock all of his teeth from his mouth for his bold declaration, he changes course, and lowers his eyes to the ground, returning to his stoic state.

He also knows when to concede. Smart kid.

"Good," I grin.

"Put me down you asshole!" Kristinah's voice suddenly echoes loudly through the factory once more.

"Oh, that's right, she's still here," I say, wiping my mouth with my napkin and tossing it on the table in front of me. "Hold!"

My singular command causes the men carrying her to freeze, setting her bound feet back on the ground and gripping her tightly by the shoulders.

"Oh, God," she pleads, closing her eyes as I slowly approach her, pulling out my phone. "Thank you, Mr. Antonov! I swear, I really didn't mean to—"

"Say cheese," I say, holding up the cellphone in my hand, I quickly snap a picture of her.

"W…what?" she asks, confused.

"Oh, that's for your family," I shrug. "We'll need something on file to show them for the negotiation of your release, of course."

"Mr. Antonov, oh God, please!" Kristinah wails, now standing at the top of the scaffolding that lines the perimeter of the wax drum, feeling the searing heat radiating from the bubbling and boiling liquid below her. "I'll do anything to make it up to you, I swear! Anything!"

"*Anything?*" I ask, pulling out my wireless headphones from my pocket.

"Yes! Anything! You name it, and I will do it! Whatever you need!"

"Well, if it's really *anything*," I say, scrolling through my music until I find the song I've had stuck in my head all night. "Then why don't you just go ahead and die."

I wave my hand before pressing play and I am immediately lost in Tchaikovsky's Symphony No. 6, drowning out her curses and screams as the two men toss her into the boiling hot wax.

They stand watching as she slowly drowns…and melts.

God, sometimes it's just fucking great to be me.

I swear my nipples could cut glass right now.

It's my own fault, as it's just past 11:30 p.m., and I stand waiting outside of The Studio for Igor Ivanov in a skintight black jumpsuit, with a plunging neckline down to my belly button and an open back design exposing my tattoo that my late husband would have hated.

Where are you Igor?

The Studio is busy tonight, with the entry line curving all the way around the side of the building. Occasionally, an entitled or simply impatient partygoer breaks the line to try their hand at gaining early entry.

But when I see who's posted on the door this chilly evening, a smile pulls at my lips, knowing *none* of them will be successful in that endeavor.

Teddy is on duty, and he's the strictest bouncer the Studio

d while he does seem to enjoy sending the scandalously clad bitches with Daddy's plastic back to the end of the line, he's also always double-checking ID's and occasionally saving girls from the touchy-feely regulars. His muscular frame dominates the archway, his arms crossed over his chest, the muscles in his forearm flexing, threatening to tear out of the standard black polo shirt he wears.

The neon lights above him highlight his red shaggy hair.

I asked him once why his hair was so poofy, he said it wouldn't be if he had time to cut it, but work keeps him busy, and the unpredictable weather makes his hair frizzy.

Almost as if he's aware of my eyes caressing his body, he glances my way, his baby face lighting up the moment we make eye contact. He nods at me, shooting me a dazzling smile.

I know that if he wasn't working, he'd already be across the street in a heartbeat.

Our stare off is momentarily interrupted when the club doors burst open, the strobe lights pulsing on to the street, illuminating the faces of the people waiting anxiously in line. I watch as a handful of tipsy partygoers stagger from the doorway, bumping into the bouncers and tripping over their own feet, laughing as they fall.

Drunk people are annoying as hell, but at least they are amusing.

I rub my hands up and down my arms, trying to expel the chill that threatens to seep into my bones as I stand here, waiting for my mark.

I don't bother scanning the constant flow of arrivals popping out of the cabs. Because even with the little I know about Igor Ivanov, I'm certain a man of his status would rather be caught dead before arriving anywhere in a cab.

Even despite deploying my best resting bitch face, occasionally, some stumbling, sleazy, and royally desperate *man* approaches me, mistaking me for a working girl.

"Come on, Sweetheart, I promise I'll make it worth your while. Just name your price."

Hah! I promise, you couldn't afford me, buddy.

Even if they weren't drunk enough to piss on themselves, these assholes give me "one-pump-chump" vibes. They'd probably just end up smashing their limp whiskey dick against me and giving my poor vagina a rug burn.

No thank you.

But as the club starts its first round of drunk "purging," at around 11:40pm, I find myself inundated with more and more men propositioning me for sex. And while brushing off drunk men with subtle insults is one of my favorite things, and wouldn't normally bother me, it *does* start distracting me from my end goal.

Slowly, I find myself moving away from the sidewalk, eventually edging so far back that I'm leaning my back against the nearest tree, the bark rubbing against my skin with each shake of my body.

11:45 p.m.

A black Range Rover crawls to a stop in front of the entrance, my eyes are drawn to a singular rose thrown haphazardly on the dash.

Leave it to me to notice the flower before the mark.

I pull my lip between my teeth, hoping that my mark, Igor, has finally arrived.

Only the rich think they are entitled enough to demand someone park their car.

Despite being informed multiple times that The Studio does not have a valet, there's always a few who still insist on parking in front, throwing the keys to the nearest bouncer.

Might be funny if they mistook an eager patron for staff and someone actually drove off with it one day. Though it's not like it would phase them, they'd probably just buy another one.

That's what my in-laws used to do anyway.

Pulling my phone from my clutch, I pretend to read a text, tapping the phone a few times for good measure.

After a few seconds the driver's side door flies open, a man with a crinkled suit emerges. From the back I can tell he's older, with slicked back salt and pepper hair barely hiding the fact he's balding in places.

He stands there, staring at the line of anxious women, some of whom are now pointing and whispering to themselves. It's obvious they know who he is, and that his money is drawing their attention…not his looks.

Standing here watching him ogling the girls in line, is making my skin crawl. It feels almost predatory, like a lion perusing the herd, or a man at a meat market picking out his ribeye. While it's clear that the man has money and power, it also feels as if he's dangerous, his threat lying just beneath the expensive custom suit, embedded in the surface of his skin.

His fingers click together as a man runs to his side.

"Igor?" the man asks, his eyes trained on my mark.

There he is, in all his glory.

A hell of a lot older than his mistress, Igor Ivanov looks to be in his forties.

His head jerks toward the line, "That one, big tits, red hair, gray dress toward the back."

The man next to him nods, twisting on his heel and immediately making his way over to the woman, his expression and demeanor softening.

The eyes of the lucky girl widen as she stares at Igor, her red curls bouncing in excitement as she nods, taking his minion's hand and stepping out of line with him.

"Let's go get our dicks wet boys!" Igor calls out to the remaining four men in the vehicle, who instantly pile out, forming around him like a shield. My head tilts as I inspect the young well-built men, dressed in their black suits, white shirts and black ties, the uniform of bodyguards.

Igor turns to the tallest guy, throwing his keys at him.

"Park it."

There it is.

With a nod to Teddy, the entourage walks through the double doors, ignoring the complaints from the line.

Time to shine.

I shake out my arms and stalk forward, popping my hip as I walk, weaponizing my voluptuous curves on the one person who can let me in.

"Teddy!" I exclaim, my voice higher than normal.

"Abby, baby! I thought you weren't going to come over tonight?!" He steps forward, putting his hands on my shoulders. "Why would you stand out there so long?"

"Got stood up," I shrug, turning away.

"Well, his loss," Teddy grins broadly, rubbing my shoulders. "Girl, you are freezing. Go inside and I'll catch up with you later."

"Thanks, Teddy, I'll see you in there."

Teddy is sweetest.

I bet he would certainly be amenable to more than the casual friendship we seem to have, especially given how his eyes canvas my body every single time he sees me. And the fact that he always lets me in without making me wait in line.

If I was ever looking to settle down with someone safe, I suppose it would be with someone like Teddy. Maybe even Teddy himself.

But I have no desire to settle down. Not worth the risk.

I forget how much brighter the strobe lights are inside the club. I don't understand how people could work here every night. The bass thumps so loudly that you can't even make out the lyrics in the song that is playing.

Unlike other clubs in the area, The Studio has a strict dress code. Women can wear whatever they want, but men must be dressed in suits, tying into their exclusivity.

However, this presents a bit of a problem for me, as Igor and his men, look nearly the same as every man in the dark. It'll make scouting him out from a distance a lot harder.

I stand off to the side, my eyes scanning the room. Everyone is packed together like sardines in a can, sweaty bodies rubbing up against each other.

Even though it is hard to see, a part of me does like how dark it is here. The walls are black, with wood trimmings that are painted a shiny silver, making the room feel bigger than it is. The perimeter of the room has booths full of people all huddled together doing shots and laughing.

The dance floor spans the center of the room, packed full of people, with no room for personal space.

The song changes, the bass hitting harder as the DJ yells unrecognizably into the mic.

The strobe lights bounce around the room, working the floor and exciting the crowd. My eyes are drawn to a group in the center of the floor, four guys surround a stunning blonde, each one grinding against her body as she tips her head back, her hand running through one of the guys hair, before she tugs and pulls his mouth down to hers.

The happiness radiates from them, infecting the room.

Ahh, to be in love, and to be free.

My temple throbs as the bass continues to pound, my heart rate racing to match it. I glance behind me at the exit, the red words shining like a beacon.

Fuck, I wish I didn't have to be here.

Just once, I'd like a mark that spent all his time in a dive bar or something.

The bar is along the back wall, which is covered in mirrors, with alcohol bottles stacked across. I spot a flash of pastel pink hair behind the bar and I smile to myself. Lizzie always makes a statement of some sort, her long hair always an obnoxious color. But honestly, each time she changes it, it suits her.

And I support whatever makes her happy.

Lizzie is the closest thing I have to a friend I suppose, perhaps that's why I *almost* feel guilty when I pump her for information.

Considering how much information she gives me, I probably *should* at least try and appear interested in having a normal friendship with her. Even if that concept is foreign to someone who never really had friends.

Maybe I should invite her shopping? Or to get coffee?

I watch her for a moment, flying behind the bar, tossing ice in the cocktail shaker before throwing a bottle of vodka above her head. Holding my breath, I watch her catch it in her hand, her eyes still firmly planted on the drink she's making with the other.

She is really good at doing that.

The strobe lights flash over the bar, highlighting the glitter she has splashed across her cheeks.

Few people know that Lizzie is also a resident doctor over at North General Hospital. She had this job through med school, and kept it, claiming that the one night a week that she works here helps cover her payments on her student loans.

No one would ever suspect that the hot bartender with the body of a supermodel, also has a medical degree.

Someone bumps into my shoulder, her hand landing on my arm. I glare down at her, seeing her mouth move in what I can only assume is an apology. But, there's no way in hell I can hear a word she's screaming with the bass as loud as it is.

Ugh. I hate clubs.

I shake my head, too tired to try and read her lips and take off toward the bar, knowing that if anyone would know where Igor is, it'll be Lizzie.

I weave through the mass of bodies, bumping shoulders and stepping on toes as I head over to the bar. I keep my head down to keep myself as inconspicuous as possible so that I'm not approached by anyone.

I don't need any attention on me tonight.

As I slide onto the barstool, I tap my freshly done nails against the marble bar top. I twist my body, angling it so that I'm facing the dance floor.

It's then that I notice to the left there's a man standing stiffly in front of a set of stairs leading up to a second story loft.

A loft that didn't exist the last time I was here.

Well... that's new.

My eyes run across the glass balcony trying to make out who is up there, but between the smoke and the strobe lights, I can't get a clear view.

I need to get closer.

Impulsively I move, only for Lizzie to grab hold of my arm. She leans across the bar, her breath warming my cheek as she yells in my ear.

"Hey bitch! Long time no fucking see. The usual?"

"Rose martini," I nod with a smile, glad that Lizzie interrupted me.

"Coming right up!"

Shit! I won't be able to just walk up those stairs.

That's when I see *him.*

A man approaches the rope separating the VIP area at the bottom of the stairs, with a woman to his right.

He's tall, dark-haired with a tight-fitting suit that hugs his body in all the right ways, his hand is spread against the small of her back, leading her forward. I run my tongue across my teeth as I watch the guard step aside and open the rope.

"Here you go! One rose martini!" Lizzie shouts, as she slides the drink across the bar.

I lean forward, waving her back before she walks away, "What's up there Liz?" I say, tilting my head towards the stairs.

"Oh, the VIP floor, it opened just this week! Been great for business," Lizzie replies, she's so close to me now that I can smell the undertones of her perfume instead of stale beer.

"VIP?"

"Oh yeah, the Antonov family paid for it."

"Antonov family?"

"Where have you been bitch? They're only the richest family in the city," she says with a laugh shaking her head. "They own the place."

"Never heard of them," I lie with a shrug, "How does one become a VIP?"

I had heard of them. Igor worked at Nikotech Investments, which was run by the Antonov Family. But I didn't look too deeply into that, but clearly, I should have.

"Money, baby girl! Money!" She gestures with her hands, as she walks away to serve another customer.

I feel my brow furrow as I try to make sense of what she said.

The Antonov family built an entire floor in this club, in a week, and made it a VIP lounge. How did I miss this family creeping up the social hierarchy? And not even creeping, but dominating it mercilessly?

I'll have to look into that.

Mentally, I add that to the to-do list for tomorrow, but my interest is piqued. Because a family with a lot of money always means a family with lots of secrets to hide.

I pull out my phone and see that it's just past midnight. However, the screensaver of Lily makes me question if I locked the greenhouse and I sigh.

I locked it. I know I did.

The side of my face heats up, and the hair on the back of my neck stands to attention as a familiar feeling overcomes me once again.

It's something I haven't felt in a few years: eyes.

Those *specific* eyes.

While fiddling with my necklace, and stirring my drink with my straw, I resist the urge to seek out the source that sets my skin ablaze.

Normally, a man staring at me wouldn't make me feel so uncomfortable, but there's something so powerful in this particular gaze, that feels as if it is searching for any sign of weakness, any clink in my armor, hunting its way to my soul. And it's almost as if a part of me senses that if I let my guard down, it will tear through the layers of my defense, straight through my skin and bury itself into my body, devouring me and my secrets.

But I'm getting distracted.

Lifting the glass to my lips I toss it back, the cold drink sliding down my parched throat.

There's no way I can get into the VIP section tonight, but I *can* place a tracker on his car. He drove it here, usually the rich have cars that are hired, but not this time. No, that car is his. He's the type of man that would own multiple cars, he screams money and if he's in VIP then he definitely has some according to Lizzie. However, I'm positive that the Range Rover is his favorite. It's too polished, too well-kept for him to only use it rarely.

I throw a twenty on the bar and jump down from the stool, adjusting the straps of my jumpsuit. I still feel like I'm being watched, but it's probably nothing.

Lizzie waves at me, as I finger salute her and walk away. However, I turn and walk straight into Teddy's chest. I stumble trying to regain my footing. These shoes aren't exactly conducive for walking, but they went so well with the jumpsuit that I had to wear them.

Teddy grabs my arm to steady me, "Abby baby, leaving so soon?"

"Yeah, Teddy, I'm just not feeling it tonight," I shrug, running my hand down his arm.

"One dance?"

"Maybe next time," I yell in his ear. "I have work tomorrow."

He nods, running his hand through his hair, "Maybe we could get dinner? I could—"

"Bye, Teddy!"

I'm not going to be able to use the loud club as an excuse to avoid *that* forever. I have been kind of leading him on so that I could get unlimited access to this club when he's working.

He's an asset.

Might need to throw the dog a bone at some point.

I throw a wave over my shoulder as I walk toward the exit, still feeling someone's eyes burning their way through my back as I slide between sweaty bodies. It's only as I exit the building, the door slamming closed behind me, does the sensation finally fade.

The night is clear, and I inhale deeply feeling the cool air in my lungs.

Glancing around, I can't believe how quiet it is now, all that can be heard is cars in the distance.

I just want to go home and cuddle up with Lily. It's strange how a little creature can become such a big part of your life, and feel like family. Technically, she's my only family, and found me when I needed her most. I can't imagine my life without her.

As I walk around the side of The Studio to the parking lot, I do my best to appear inconspicuous, pushing my shoulders back and holding my chin high.

Now where is this fucker's car?

My eyes scan the area, looking for Igor's black Range Rover, as well as for any passersby who might see me lingering around. I might appear as if I belong, but that can only keep me unnoticed for so long, the last thing I need is for someone to report me.

Bingo.

Striding over, I pull the small tracking device from my pocket and lean down to quickly put it in the wheel arch. My eyes are drawn to the awful custom rims he has on it; wide and shining brighter than *his* future. Drawing in a breath, I place a hand over my ear, before standing to my full height, pretending that I dropped my earring, just in case there's security cameras. Relief floods through me as I walk out of the exit, a satisfied smile on my face.

Throwing my hand out to hail a cab, a chuckle escapes me. Overall, it was a good night. I secured the tracker to Igor's car and got a new lead, Nikotech Investments.

The floor thumps upstairs as Lily jumps down from wherever she was perched as I toss my keys on the table.

While I wait for her, I kick off my heels, flexing my toes, the instant relief sinking into my sore skin. I love wearing them, but they are deadly. I walk past the thermostat throwing it on max as I pass. The fall air has gone straight to my bones after tonight.

Lily comes running down the stairs meowing loudly at me.

"I know sweet girl, let's warm the house up and snuggle down in bed, shall we?"

As I head toward the kitchen, I flick on the hallway lamp. That's one thing that I have always done since my parents died. Little Abby used to think that if she left the light on, they'd come home.

They didn't.

My parents loved me, but they weren't really around. Even before they died, I'd spent most of my childhood with my grandmother for a babysitter.

I was ten when the police showed up at the door.

Drive-by shooting, they said. Outside of the mall. Because there were no suspects, no evidence, not even a single bullet shell recovered, it became a cold case.

Grandma insisted before she died that it was organized crime. She said that my father never could stay out of trouble, a walking magnet for disaster she called him.

"Organized crime is all around us, Bambi."

But I've never found it. And I've looked. I always wondered though, what did my parents do to deserve an ending like that?

I swipe my laptop off the kitchen counter, and creep up the stairs, not that I need to, but my late husband left me with some *habits*.

Be seen not heard.

After throwing my laptop on the bed, I peel myself out of the jumpsuit, and throw it in the washing basket in the ensuite. The ensuite was the only place in the house that I redecorated.

I went with white marble tiles all over, a large corner walk-in shower that has black glass framed screens and a 72" clawfoot bath to match. The bath was a requirement, it took me weeks to hunt it down, but it was worth it. The stress literally melts out of my body as I feel my muscles relax.

Part of me wishes I had time to soak in the tub now, but it is already well past 1:00 a.m. and I still have shit to do.

Luckily my late husband was very well off, and I could live off his investments as the sole beneficiary. However, funds will be running low soon. The greenhouse alone costs me thousands a month to maintain.

Only the best for my babies.

At some point I should probably look for consistent work. The freelance drawings I do currently, while great, don't provide a steady income. Especially as I focus heavily on tattoo sketching. The market for them died out after it stopped trending.

"Alexa, turn on the shower to 100 degrees."

I jump in the shower and lean my head back under the spray, my body relaxing and finally warming up after my little outing.

Teddy is going to be a problem.

I can't keep leading him on and playing cat and mouse.

However, I also don't want to burn the bridge. He's my entry when they close the club for exclusive events.

Not that I'd off a man at one of those. It would be too obvious.

But I can't keep having Teddy pining after me, it's not fair to him. It's been years since I dated or had any form of sexual encounter.

My husband ruined that for me too.

I used to love sex. The thrill, the power, the release it gave. But he took that from me. He wouldn't care if I wanted it or not, it was his wife's duty to provide it, and it was his *right* to take it.

Sometimes I wonder how different my life would've been if I *hadn't* said yes to prom? What if I didn't fall in love with Garrett? Would I have become who I am today?

It's because of him that I've killed fifteen men in the last two years, all of whom abused their partners.

I grab the shower gel, rubbing it into my skin, washing away the grime from The Studio.

"Alexa, shower off," I say, stepping out and grabbing a towel off the heated rack to wrap around my body.

I rub my hands across the mirror, revealing my weary looking face and body. I used to hate my appearance, my curves and was told I looked frumpy. And maybe I did, in those god-awful clothes I was required to wear.

Once dried off and I grab an *I Prevail* shirt that comes down past my knees from the walk-in closet and jump into bed, the glowing numbers from the bedside clock burn into my eyes.

2:00 a.m.

I've done all I can do, now I just have to hope that the tracking software does its job.

ANTONOV

CHAPTER SEVEN

ROMAN

"Gone? What do you mean she's *gone*?"

My voice is quiet, far too quiet for the club, but the immediate panic reflected in Igor's eyes tells me he heard me even in the noisy crowded VIP.

"Boss, I…I…went to find that woman you pointed out to me, but I can't find her."

"Are you fucking blind?! She was right there!" I snap, frantically looking out over the dark and smoky dance floor to the stool at the bar where I saw her. But Igor is right.

The Brunette may *have* been here, but now she's just gone.

I can't believe this.

After obsessing about her, dreaming about her, and wondering where she's been for the past four years, she was right here, in my club and finally within my grasp.

…And somehow, I've let her slip through my fingers. *Again.*

Goddamnit!

I'm furious, because a part of me knew I should've just gone to talk to her myself.

But my pride thought it would look more impressive if one of my men went and invited her up to VIP to meet me.

However, somehow this drunken dickhead lost her in the crowd.

"Look again!" I shout at him, shoving him hard in the chest with my finger. "You go down there, and you comb the entire building until you find her!"

"Boss, I swear, I've searched the whole club, and she's not here," Igor says, as apologetically as a two-hundred-and-seventy-pound Russian man made of sheer muscle can possibly say. "I even had Lizzie check the bathrooms. I think she just must've left, brother."

I'm not sure if I've ever felt a stronger desire to throw someone off a balcony. In an instant my hands are around his neck, pushing him closer to the edge.

"Boss! Wait!" Igor squeaks, stumbling backwards.

Despite him being larger than me, my fury overpowers his brute strength and I slam him hard into the steel railing.

"Maybe you misunderstood me, *brother*," I snarl at him sarcastically, grabbing him by the shirt collar and twisting it in my fist, squeezing his neck fat so hard it bulges out the top. "I told your bitch ass to look again."

"Shit!" I hear Cal shout behind me, feeling the suspended floor beneath my feet shaking as my men come scrambling over to us. But I ignore them.

"You know, lately it seems you've been forgetting what your function is around here, so let me remind you," I growl, holding a struggling Igor in place. "You aren't here to *think*. You are here to obey. You are not my brother, you are nothing. Nothing but a fucking shit stain, and I'm growing awfully tired of making excuses for your incompetence and inability to follow simple fucking instructions."

Beads of sweat now form on Igor's brow, as I suddenly yank my switchblade from my pocket and hold it to his scruffy peppered five o'clock shadow.

"But if you can't follow simple, basic instructions to use your fucking eyes," I say, moving the blade to his cheek, just below his eye. "Then perhaps I should just take them."

Knowing that fighting against me can only result in a death sentence either from my men shooting him, or me letting go of his shirt, Igor throws his hands in the air.

"Y…yes…Boss!" He pleads, trying desperately to keep his footing from slipping, knowing the fall backwards would certainly kill him. "You're right! I fucked up! I will look for her! I promise! I'll look all night if you want me to!"

"Boss," Cal says, firmly. "Not to question your methods, but people are starting to stare."

Part of me wants to tell Cal to fuck off, but I know he's right. Especially when I look down and see a couple of astonished girls pointing while staring wide-eyed at me practically dangling Igor over the balcony.

However, as I glance down at my sniveling brother-in-law, who's begging and pleading with me for forgiveness, I'm reminded that it's because of *him* I'm not already at my penthouse with The Brunette. My lip curls, and it takes every ounce of self-restraint not to just let go and send him crashing down to the club floor below.

But the mess I'd have on my hands...

So instead, I yank his collar forward, bringing him back over the railing and causing him to crash instantly to his knees.

"Oh, God!" he wails, trying to kiss my feet, muttering in Russian. "Thank you, Roman! Thank you!"

But I don't want his weeping snot-filled apologies. I kick him hard in the chest, knocking the wind from his lungs before leaning down low and hissing in his ear.

"Why the fuck are you still here?"

"Yes! Of course, Boss!" He says, climbing to his feet and practically bolting down the VIP steps.

"Jesus Christ, Roman," my cousin Stetson, who is visiting New York for a couple of days as a stopover on his way home to Moscow, chuckles loudly. "You're a cold motherfucker, doing that to your own brother-in-law!"

"Fuck that asshole," I hiss through gritted teeth, still glaring after him.

"Look, tonight was supposed to be fun," Stetson says, placing his hand against my chest. "Let's not let that twat ruin it, eh? Let's do some shots and get back into it!"

He heads off to find some sort of alcohol, as I slowly head back to my chair at the poker table.

But what Stetson doesn't understand is that Igor isn't what is ruining my night.

The Brunette was *here*. I saw her.

Yes, the dream with her this morning felt nearly as real, and yes, she stalks my thoughts and sleep like some vengeful ghost...But this wasn't a hallucination. I know I saw her.

I'd know that face and body anywhere. After all, I spent nearly two years staring at it from a distance.

And after obsessing about her for years and kicking myself for every missed opportunity...I just missed another one.

"Hey Ro, I've got some good news," Stetson says excitedly as he reappears beside me. "There's a girl here to see you. And she's hot."

"A *girl?*" I ask, instantly, whirling around, thinking for a second that my gorgeous ghost might be standing there.

But it's not her.

It's Heather Jenson. Or "AccounTits" as I call her.

"Hey Ro," Heather says, walking around the staring men in a very low-cut black dress. "What a…coincidence."

Coincidence my ass. Try insistence.

The woman doesn't seem to take a hint.

"I came with a girlfriend, but she took off, but then I spotted you up here and thought I'd come say hi," she says walking forward and standing next to me. "I hope that's okay."

Before I can tell her to fuck off, however, Stetson apparently sensing my mood, interrupts before I can.

"And we are soooo glad you did," he says with a big grin, staring at her huge tits as he wraps his arm around her. "We were just looking for a fun little distraction."

"Here we go," Stetson says loudly above the club music, licking his lips. "Two tits, two lines."

He sprinkles the fine white powder from a tiny glass vial onto the perfectly crafted tits of Heather who has lingered around me like a virus and is now, somehow, seated on my lap.

I blame the vodka.

Heather giggles, sipping her third martini while staring me down.

"Oiy, sweetheart, you can't move, or you'll spill the goods," Stetson says to her before tapping my shoulder. "One of these is yours, Roman."

I'm pulled back to reality as Stetson hands me the hundred-dollar bill rolled tightly into a straw. I think about refusing, but given the shitty direction my night took, and the fact that it's sitting right in front of me, I quickly change my mind.

Fuck it. Why not?

I snort the line, feeling it tingle a little. While I don't do it as regularly as Stetson, I do allow myself a little indulgence from time to time.

After all, I have to know the product I sell to my customers.

I throw my head back and pinch my nose, but the second I shut my eyes to avoid the blinding strobe lights of the club, I see *her* face again.

She was here.

"Feeling better, baby?"

I'm immediately reminded there is a woman in my lap when she spins around to straddle me.

"So I was thinking," she whispers in my ear, grinding her pantiless pussy against my crotch. "What do you say we slip off somewhere private?"

"No," I say, my mind still clouded by The Brunette. "Get off."

"Hmmm that's exactly what I wanna help you do, baby," she says, biting her lip and grinding harder, kissing my neck.

"I said get off."

"Aw, come on, don't be like—"

"Are you fucking deaf, bitch?" I snap, quickly grabbing the back of her fake blonde highlights in my hand and leaning in close to growl in her ear. "I said get. The. Fuck. Off. Me."

I release her, dumping her onto the floor before standing and adjusting my suit coat.

"Fuck her if you want, she seems desperate for it," I say to my friends as she glares up at me. "I'm leaving."

Irrationally I have lost all desire to be here, in this club, or with any of these people any longer. My men look at me in confusion, but quickly follow me out of the VIP section, and down the staircase. We make our way across the club dance floor, getting pawed at by beautiful women the entire time.

But this is normal for me.

After all, I'm Roman Nikolai Antonov, and as Heather upstairs just proved, there's no shortage of beautiful women desperate to choke on my cock. If I wanted to, I could fuck any one of them in the middle of this crowded room, and no one would even bat an eye.

And yet…all I can think about is *her*. The Brunette.

She was here tonight. In this club. Right where I'm standing.

Even with all the sexy bitches I see on a day-to-day basis, I've never seen a face prettier than hers, or a body more deliciously tempting. Tits, ass, and thick thighs in exactly the right proportions.

Christ, she was literal perfection.

I want her. And since I'm used to getting exactly what I want, exactly when I want it, the fact that I don't *already* know what her pussy tastes like is pissing me the fuck off.

There's something about her that has me mesmerized…and she's not even in the building anymore.

What the hell is wrong with me?

I walk out of the club, a part of me foolishly hoping to find her out here in the atrium, waiting for me. But I don't. Which just pisses me off more.

"David is bringing the car around, Boss," Cal says, standing next to me.

If it was anyone else speaking to me right now, I would probably deck them in the face, but since it's Cal, I give him a short nod.

My mind is spinning with more questions than I'm comfortable not having answers to.

Who is she? Where has she been? Why did she come back?

I need to know.

My Cadillac SUV comes around the corner, forcing some unhappy customers to step back closer to the wall. It stops in front of me, and Cal steps forward to open the door for me, before climbing into the front seat with David.

"Where to, Boss?" he asks.

"The office," I reply. "I have work to do."

I sit at my desk on my empty executive floor tapping a pen against the oak, and replaying the last hour. I may have also pulled up my club's surveillance footage to try and find her again, but even that was spotty.

It was almost as if she knew where the camera's blind spots were and was exclusively standing in them.

But that couldn't be true.

It had to be a coincidence, but it was a disappointing coincidence. All I had were tiny little fractions of frames that contained her still image, the last one sitting frozen on my computer screen.

Lost in my thoughts my eyes accidentally drift to the envelope that Kristinah dropped off earlier today that I never opened.

Which reminds me that I no longer have a fucking assistant.

I look at my watch, realizing it's just after two in the morning, and I sent my text to Anastasia about forty minutes ago.

Just relax. She'll be here soon enough.

In the middle of my internal pep talk, I pick up the envelope and grab my father's antique letter opener from the drawer of my desk.

I smile as I do.

This letter opener isn't a letter opener at all, it's a *dagger*.

…A dagger I was never supposed to *have*.

The pale ivory whalebone handle had been meticulously engraved with the Antonov Family Crest, and the blade, made of pure Russian obsidian, is sharper than any blade I have ever handled. And if you weren't careful, it could slice half-way through your hand before you even realized what you'd done.

Which was exactly what happened when I was eight.

I'd found it on my father's desk, while snooping around his office, and thought it was interesting. But when I went to pick it up, I bumped my elbow on the desk, which jolted the knife in my hand. It was only when my blood started pouring all over my desk and floor that I realized I'd accidentally scraped the sharp blade across the edge of my hand.

Thankfully, my father walked in at that exact moment, and saw me frantically bleeding all over the place. He promptly got me medical attention, but then of course, promptly whipped my ass for playing with *his* shit.

That night, however, he came to my room and told me about the dagger. How it was a gift from a Yupik Shaman to my great-grandfather, a grateful gesture after my great-grandfather had saved his wife from drowning after falling through a patch of thin ice. He told me that my great-grandfather had passed it down to my grandfather, with the hope that it would continue as a family heirloom passed down to each new heir.

But, my grandfather, for whatever reason, had no intention of passing it on to my father, going as far as to explicitly state in his will that the dagger was to be *buried* with him in the Antonov Family Crypt.

However, in our family we have a unique tradition when it comes to our dead. We call it "Обряд *Маркировки*," or the "Rite of Marking." Before an Antonov corpse is interred, their skull is engraved with our family crest. There is always someone in our family who knows the process. In ours, it's my father's cousin Artyom, and although he's nearing eighty, he still has the steadiest of hands.

But because defacing a corpse's forehead before the burial could seem gruesome and appalling for those non-family members attending the funeral, the marking was usually done afterwards, just before the body was sealed in the crypt.

This tiny window of time was exactly what my father needed. He waited until the guests had left, and old Arty's back was turned before swiping the dagger and replacing it with a plastic replica. His final "fuck you," to his own father.

The ironic part was that when my father kicked the bucket, we learned that *his* last will and testament had been conveniently amended to express that he too desired the blade buried with *him.*

Yet my father's death had been a bit chaotic to say the least. And given that the traitorous fuck was bedridden and senile, I'd already swiped the blade from his safe, and put it in my own. But no one in my family cared about some stupid dagger, and the attorneys in charge of the estate had more important business to settle and no desire to grapple with their new don over it.

Now it sits on my desk. Opening my fucking mail.

Hope you're smiling up from hell, Dad.

Turning the fine blade over in my hands, I'm not entirely sure of its origin story has any significance, or if that's just the way of our fucked-up family. My father never explained his reason for stealing it, and I can only assume it's because he didn't have one.

Dead men don't need daggers. And honestly, neither did I.

…But I *did* need a letter opener.

I reach for the envelope, but just as I do, my sister's voice echoes throughout the darkened office floor.

"Seriously, Ro?" Anastasia groans walking past the rows of unoccupied desks. "You think you can just summon me twice in a day? What, you think I don't have a life?"

"No, I just think I *am* your life," I snort arrogantly, winking at her. "So yes, I think I can summon you whenever I want. Just consider me doing your eyes a favor, tearing you away from a computer screen."

"What do you want, Roman?" she snaps irritably.

"A job posting," I say flatly.

"*What?*" She scoffs. "You're kidding, right? Please tell me you did not just drag me all the way down here, at three in the fucking morning, just to tell me you want me to post a job for you, when you have a perfectly capable HR department that—"

"Kristinah is dead," I say, sitting back in my chair. "And yes, before you ask, I killed her."

Ana's jaw drops.

"W…what?" she whispers. "Why?"

"Apparently, Cal discovered that she'd been slipping information to the Irish," I shrug. "He thinks there's a chance she's told them about our plans with the Walston Street deal and now they might be trying to compete for our prize."

"I mean, wow, that sucks about your assistant," Ana says, shaking her head. "But I still don't get why that deal was such a big deal."

"Because, Little Sister," I say, leaning forward. "The investor list for that build site has some of the fattest cats in all of New York on it. Well-connected powerhouses of industry, and if I can get them all grouped together on one dossier, *with* me, I'd ensure that none of them would ever use their power and influence to try and fuck me. I'd have leverage over them. Leverage equals pressure. And I wanted to apply that pressure to expand our territories, while simultaneously covering our asses."

Ana stares at me before rolling her eyes.

"*Wow*, Roman," she says sarcastically. "That all sounds really fucking interesting-oh wait, no, actually it doesn't."

"I mean, it's kind of interesting," I shrug.

"Not at three in morning, it isn't. I can assure you, it sounds boring as fuck. And your long-winded explanation still doesn't explain why the fuck you dragged *me* down here?"

I snort.

This is why I love Ana. She's no nonsense.

"I need a new assistant," I say, smiling at her. "And since my "fully capable" HR department fucked up with the last one, I'm not thrilled about trusting the process this time."

"So, you really do want me to post a job for you," she says, glaring at me.

"No, HR will do the posting, I just thought you could do some preliminary research on whomever applies. You know, the thorough kind."

"This could've been a text message, Roman!" she says, throwing her hands in the air. "Fine, I'll do it! Can I go now?"

"Sure," I nod. "I'll drive you back home."

"How kind of you," Ana says, folding her arms and sinking into the chair across from me.

"Just let me wrap up a few things first," I say, picking up the envelope.

But suddenly Ana's hand grabs mine.

"What are you doing?" she asks, her eyes wide with concern. "Isn't that the envelope Kristinah dropped off?"

"Umm, yes?" I say, raising a brow at her. "I just never got around to it."

Once again, I go to slice the thin cardboard but, once again, Ana stops me. And this time, she grabs it by the corner, and slowly walks it over to Caesar's bed, where he sits staring at us both.

Among the many things that my dog is trained to do, one of them is identifying explosives. And he's never been wrong. It's a useful skill, considering the Irish have an affinity for explosives, and we've been at war with them for over a decade.

After a few good long sniffs of the package, he shows no reaction whatsoever, indicating it's safe to open.

Carefully I slice the envelope open, but instead of a letter, the envelope appears to be empty.

"What the fuck?" I snort. "Who the hell pays to send a letter urgently, but then forgets to add the actual message?"

However, just as I throw it into the trash can, a pebble falls out, bouncing onto the floor. Except, as I pick it up, I realize that it's not a pebble, but rather what appears to be a seed.

Ana walks over to the desk and takes it from me, staring at it before pulling the envelope out of the trash. She rips the edge open, revealing the entire inside and the fact that there are several more seeds inside.

"Why the fuck would someone send me seeds?" I ask incredulously. "Unless they belong to Polina and are just more of those stupid Shakespeare flowers or whatever she was screaming about earlier."

"I don't think so, Ro," Ana says. "These actually look like citrus pips."

Suddenly, the word *pip* instantly causes a light bulb in the far distant crevices of my mind to illuminate…and it also causes my blood to go cold.

"I don't get it though," she says, picking up the envelope and looking inside. "There's no note? No message?"

"The pips *are* the message," I whisper, taking them from her. "They are a warning…of *death*."

"What?"

"Did you ever read *The Five Orange Pips?* by Sir Arthur Conan Doyle?"

"You mean that British guy who wrote Sherlock Holmes?" Ana says cautiously.

"*He* was British, but Doyle's father was an immigrant," I smirk. "An *Irish* Catholic immigrant."

As I stare down at one of the seeds in my hand, I notice that there is writing on it. Very faintly, I can see that carved into this small little seed, is the letter "V."

"Look at this," I say, handing it to Ana before picking up another. "And this one, it has a letter "A" on it."

"So, it's from the Irish, and there is a message," Ana says cautiously. "But, what is it, Roman? Do they want to meet?"

I flip over the rest of the scattered little seeds, and it doesn't take me more than three seconds to realize that there are exactly seven pips on my desk.

…And seven letters in "*Antonov*."

With seven little pips, the Irish have made their intentions known. "No, they want us *dead*, Ana," I say softly. "They want us *all* dead."

A
ANTONOV

CHAPTER EIGHT

Abby

THREE DAYS LATER.

There's always risks to the justice that I serve.

After the tracker pinged Igor's location, I discovered that he lives in the same part of town that I used to live in with my dead ex-husband. And not just in the same part of town, but in the *exact* building I used to live in.

Igor Ivanov had been a hard man to track down, elusive even. But a man with an ego as big as his wasn't hard to find in the end. It took me four days, but I learned a lot about him.

He prefers to travel at night, but when he moves about the city during the day, it's always with a small army of men. Additionally, he only routinely goes to three places within the city: his home, The Studio, and Nikotech Investments.

There's not a chance in hell I'm going to be able to get to him at his home, especially with a wife lingering around, so it's either his favorite club, or his place of employment.

Curiosity burns through me, as my fingers glide across the keyboard slowly, typing in Nikotech Investments. But the search returns barely anything at all, just some news articles about the company's birthday, its stock exchange IPO reports, and the company's CEO…Roman Nikolai Antonov.

Russian.

I wonder how he is connected to Igor?

However, as I search online for him, it's clear that like Igor, he doesn't have social media accounts. In fact, it's almost as if he's intentionally done a good job of burying any reference of his name on social media. And even after a few more extensive searches, all I'm able to locate is his estimated net worth, and a few names of his older, much smaller businesses. But that's it.

Jesus, the man is a ghost.

And then randomly, a job posting for Nikotech Investments pops up on page five.

You know it's bad when you're on page five of the search results. The listing gives more information on the company, and a few names of its board members, and descriptions of their backgrounds and roles at Nikotech.

It's here that I learn that Roman Antonov, became one of the youngest millionaires in the United States when he inherited his father's holdings at the age of twenty-three. However, seven years later, at the age of thirty, he's now a billionaire, having built Nikotech from the ground up.

My eyes roll.

Of course, he would name the company after himself.

Pretentious prick.

But…it appears Mr. Antonov is looking for a secretary to help with his calendar, emails, and various personal office tasks.

The ad says pay would be negotiated based on previous experience, and while I don't have any previous secretary or assistant experience, I managed my husband's busy calendar and social life, all while taking his horrific abuse.

How hard could this be?

Shrugging, I decide just to fill out an application, because I really have nothing to lose.

And, if I actually get the job, it might provide me with more than just a steady source of income…it would provide me access to more monsters.

Something I learned in high-school with my bitch-faced bullies, is that they tend to congregate. Bullies prefer to associate with other bullies, their insecurities feeding each other's monsters. They are like rats, colonizing and becoming an infestation.

…And I'm the exterminator.

Money *and* new marks? Fuck yes. Two birds with one stone.

Once I hit submit on my application, my next search is for the Nikotech

Investments blueprints.

While security blueprints for corporations are usually confidentially protected, the standard site blueprints for the building are normally a matter of public record. But with the logins I stole from my friend down at the city zoning commission, I shouldn't have an issue finding something on a big company like Nikotech.

"0 Results Found/No Records Exist."

That can't be right.

I try again, but receive the same message.

"0 Results Found/No Records Exist."

"Fuck me, who is this family?" I scoff out loud, my hand running through my hair. Lily chirps behind me, appearing in the door, her white fur shining in the morning sun that bleeds through the curtains. She jumps on the bed, her sparkling blue eyes staring up at me as she purrs and bumps her forehead into my leg.

I sigh, stroking her gently.

"Well, girl, I guess I'll have to resort to actually going over to Nikotech today."

As I walk down the bustling city sidewalk, I take in the crisp fall air, allowing it to fill my lungs. I stop at a small convenience store, rumored to have the best caramel hot chocolate and decide to test the theory. Additionally, I grab a sandwich and a newspaper, smiling at the cashier before continuing down the block.

Subconsciously, I'm glad I had the foresight to dress *business* casual, as my typical "casual" wear would've made me stick out like a sore thumb here in the financial district.

However, in my knee-length black skirt and candy-apple red blouse underneath a black blazer, today I pass for one of them.

I look as if I belong here, seamlessly blending in among the men and women scurrying from cabs to various buildings in their suits, carrying their briefcases and gourmet coffees.

Eventually Nikotech comes into view.

My eyes follow the building upwards, noting how it stands taller than the other buildings in this district. The reflection of the sun off the gleaming glass windows is nearly blinding, but the structure of the design is a work of art.

But even its beauty can't diminish the dominating essence the building gives, looking like a monstrous glass obelisk, towering over *its* city.

Finding an empty, clean bench just outside, I set my lunch down, before running my hands over the back of my skirt and crossing my legs as I sit. Tucking my bag against my side, I reach for my sandwich and newspaper, basking in the sun that warms my bones.

While I eat my sandwich, I survey the building in front of me from behind the safety of my large dark sunglasses. The revolving door never seems to stop, a relentless onslaught of people constantly milling in and out of it.

As one dark-haired woman leaves, I just so happen to catch the crest sitting proudly above the entrance.

The crest is formed of a shield in the center with a N and the I crossing through it. Adorning the top was a crown and, on either side, there's a bear. Below, the words Nikotech Investments were written in large shining silver letters. It was by all accounts a very bold company logo, but unlike its competitors, doesn't strike me as one that necessarily fits in the financial district.

Somehow it feels older, and more…archaic.

"Move!" A man yells, with a faint accent as he draws my eyes from the crest. His suit crinkled, his hair unbrushed as it blows in the breeze. Distracted, he crashes directly into a young lady in front of me, dropping his folder on the floor, a folder that just so happens to have the same Nikotech Crest embossed on the outside. He scoops it up quickly, muttering under his breath as he storms past reception, running to grab the elevator. His hand slams on the door as it closes before he reaches it. After a moment of hesitation, he pulls something from his pocket, slamming it against the panel.

Interesting.

It's no secret that most buildings in the financial district have heavy security. Access to the secure information of investors and banks, they have to be. But *this* building is locked down like Fort Knox, the main floor is open so that people can get in and out freely, but to access the higher floors, you need an ID badge… for an elevator.

How very *secure.*

As I chew the remainder of the sandwich, I take a final assessing gaze at the building.

I won't get Igor here, it would be impossible, it's too secure for me to even try.

That's Nikotech out of the running, guess that only leaves one place, which doesn't surprise me, The Studio is where so many of my marks seem to find their end. But luckily for me that's where the dark atmosphere, smoke machines and the flashing strobe lights come in handy, providing me with the cover I need.

My phone buzzes in my pocket, before my watch screen illuminates, as an incoming call comes in.

Number Unknown.

My brows pull down as I slide my thumb over the screen bringing it to my ear.

"Hello, is that Abigail Wayne?" A polite female voice says through the speaker.

"Speaking," I state, my brain racing to recognize the voice.

"It's Lucy Roberts, calling from Nikotech investments. We have just reviewed your application and would love to invite you to an interview with Mr. Antonov on Monday at nine, *sharp*. Would that work for you?" she says.

A smile pulls across my face, "Yes absolutely, is there anything you wish for me to bring?" I ask.

"No, we have everything we need. Be at reception at eight forty-five, someone will come down to retrieve you. Dress business casual, and don't be late."

"Thank you, Lucy, I look forward to it."

I shake the cat treats to tempt Lily back into the house, I have work to do, and I can't have her free roaming in the garden near the greenhouse. Glancing at the clock, I see that it's five-thirty in the morning. I've always thought that it's best to work in the greenhouse before the sun rises, less people awake to bother me then.

Lily chirps as she runs down the cobbled path toward the door, my breath clouds out in front of me drawing my attention to the temperature.

Fuck its cold.

"Come here sweet thing, let's get you warm," I whisper, bending down to scoop her up in my arms. Her little frame is cold to the touch, and her little paws are damp from the morning dew.

I walk toward her bowls, placing her down in front of them. As I sprinkle her treats on top of her kibble, I run my fingers through her soft fur, giving her tail a little wiggle as I reach it.

"I'll be back in a bit, Lilibug." I say, before quickly walking out of the kitchen, straight into the garden.

My greenhouse stands proudly at the end of the garden, the warm mist inside clinging to the walls and ceiling. The frame might be steel, but the rest of the structure is made of solid glass. It was the most expensive option, as it all needed to be custom fitted, but after doing an extensive amount of research, I felt it was the only material strong enough to provide protection for my *collection*.

At least it will be warm in there.

The lights flicker on as I open the greenhouse door, the warmth of the moist air hitting my skin. My shoulders relax as the floral scent wraps around me in a comforting embrace, and I gently pull the door closed.

The greenhouse is organized meticulously, there are four rows of plant beds. On the two outer rows I have fruits, vegetables and normal herbs, as well as many species of flowers in a wide array of colors. The two inner rows are where my Oleander, Deadly Nightshade, Strychnine, Henbane, Lily of the Valley and Foxglove are planted.

I decided that it was best to bed them in the middle to provide a level of protection to them.

While my neighbors don't tend to bother me much, if any of them decided to get nosey, my arrangement means that they wouldn't see the deadly plants first. If they peaked through the windows, they would only see the tomatoes and berries.

And, as an added protection, I deliberately planted comfrey around my Foxglove, knowing I could always say I enjoy brewing it into my tea.

As I walk through the greenhouse, I run my finger over the plant bed, feeling the dirt rub against my fingertip. My eyes scan the rows of marigolds and pansies, admiring how they reach for the sun that is yet to break the clouds.

I head toward the center where the workstation is located, which has a storage cupboard below, filled with all the supplies I could possibly need. I grasp the handle, pulling the door open to reach inside for a pair of latex gloves, the disposable pill capsules and my mortar and pestle.

Gently, placing them down onto the work bench, and using my foot to kick the door closed. I grab a pair of gloves before walking over to the back of the greenhouse to the small freezer.

Yesterday, I prepared my leaves to freeze dry them, delicately plucking them off the stems and placing them on a cooking tray before slotting them into the freezer. I flick my wrist to check the time. I have just over an hour before my sprinkler system kicks in.

Time to get to work.

I put on my gloves, hearing the satisfying snap against the skin of my wrist. I pull the tray out and head back to the work bench, placing the tray down with a resolute clang. I toss the leaves into the marble mortar, using the pestle to grind them down into a fine powder.

I've got this process down to a routine, but in the beginning it was hard. When I first started my arms ached, and my shoulders were full of knots. But now, I just zone out using my heartbeat as the rhythm to work in sync with. Once the leaves become powder, I use a small set of scales to weigh out the correct dosages, and then fill in the dissolvable capsules.

Originally, I thought I could just drop the capsules into a mark's drink, but I didn't do my research properly. While the powder dissolves quickly, the capsules themselves can take up to twenty minutes.

And twenty minutes is too long for a capsule to float in a drink undetected.

So, I use them now mostly just to *store* the powder in the correct doses and hide them in an old herb vitamin container.

When I go out to The Studio, I use my ring to drop the Widowmaker into their drink.

Oddly enough, pillbox rings used to be very popular in the sixteenth century, often used for exactly what I use it for. To slip poison into someone's food or drink. They made a comeback in the 80's when cocaine usage was at its peak, but then fell out of the spotlight when the government started cracking down.

Once I'm finished, I clean up my station, and scrub my hands down in the sink making sure I take nothing inside to Lily. Quickly walking out the door, I lock it behind me before pressing down on the handle twice.

Smirking to myself as I glance up toward the sky, seeing the clouds clearing to reveal the radiant blue hiding behind them.

I just know that today is going to be an excellent day.

Tonight, my cab takes me straight to the entrance of The Studio, as I step out onto the cool evening sidewalk, I notice Teddy already making his way over to me.

"Abby, baby!" he exclaims.

"Hey, Teddy," I say with a nod.

"Friday nights are always the busiest! It is packed in there tonight!" He sighs, his head dropping slightly. "I doubt I'll be able to get off the door to see you at all!"

Schooling my face to hide the relief, knowing that I don't have to worry about Teddy interfering with my plans.

"Oh no," I spin around, showing off my bright red dress. "And I got all dressed up too!"

"Babe, you look stunning!" He says, his eyes trailing down my body. "Did you do all this for *me*?"

I wink playfully, shrugging off the tiny bit of cringey shiver I feel from his intense gaze. I toss my thumb toward the door with a tilt of my head.

"It's chilly, I'm going to head inside, okay? I'll try and find you later!" He walks me to the door, swinging it open for me.

"For sure, babe. I'll try and get at least one dance with you tonight."

Oh God. No thank you.

But I gently place my hand on his arm, smiling at him as I walk inside.

Tonight, I don't waste my time orbiting the orgy of people grinding on the sticky dance floor and simply make my way over to the bar. My eyes bounce around the room, scanning to see if Igor is here but given that I'm here early, there's a huge chance he isn't even here yet.

Lizzie drops my usual in front of me with a smile, but the bar is so packed with demanding customers that she doesn't have a moment to stop for a chat. I raise my glass to her, with a nod of my head as I take a sip.

This part is always the most stressful, knowing that after all my careful planning, scouting, and hard work, one wrong move and I'd be caught.

…But that's always what makes it the most thrilling.

A deep voice suddenly rumbles next to me, startling me from my thoughts. "Move!"

The guy next to me jolts, spinning round.

"Hey man, I was here first, so why don't you… oh shit! Okay, I'm going, I'm going."

I take a sip, feeling the cool drink sliding down my throat as a large frame sits down next to me, the scent of cigarettes, sweat and far too much cologne overpowering my nose almost immediately.

"What's a lady like you doing alone in a place like this?" A heavy Russian accent breathes next to me, making my body tense and causing the hair on my arms to stand up.

I turn my head slowly, deliberately using my eyes to trail up his body, which isn't that impressive. Sure, the beast of a man has some muscle, but the majority of his bulk is fat around his midsection.

"Who? Little old me?" I put my hand on my chest, bashfully.

"Yes, you," he growls with a sleazy grin.

"Well, I'd say that the right guy just hasn't come along yet," I say with a wink.

He nods his head, his dark eyes flashing as a devilish smile splits his face, "Well it's your lucky day *Malishka*, what's your poison?"

"Rose Martini," I smirk.

If only he knew.

He taps his hand on the bar, drawing Lizzies attention as she walks past, her wide eyes darting to my face.

"A drink for the lady, and a whiskey. Neat. Now." He demands, causing Lizzie to smile in return, which doesn't quite reach her eyes as she gets to making the drinks.

He turns back to me, his beady eyes locked on mine, "What's your name *Malishka*?"

I twist my body toward him, and lean forward, my lips skimming the top of his cheek, to say in his ear, "Jasmine, like the flower. And you?"

The hand that he had resting on the bar falls forward, his fingertips brushing the top of my knee. "Igor."

Mark secure.

Lizzie slams the drinks down on the bar, causing the Rose Martini to spill. "I'm so sorry! I'll clea—" Igor jolts backwards, his face turning red as he points his finger at her.

"You bar whores are all the fucking same, you'll fuc—"

"Oh no, that was my fault, I set my clutch on the counter in the worst spot," I say pretending that I might've contributed to the spill. "I can be so careless at times."

I place my hand on his arm, feeling the rage that seems to be radiating off him in waves, causing his body to vibrate under my hand.

His eyes snap to mine, sharp and dangerous. For a moment I almost crack under their intense stare, but I've come too far to fold now. So instead, I run my hand up and down his arm, trying to draw his attention fully to me.

"It's no big deal," I shrug, biting my lip, and watching as his eyes follow.

"Yeah, well she should be paying better attention. She could have ruined your dress! I don't understand how she's still working here, she's a fucking mess!" he complains, his voice getting darker. "Always fucking tired!"

Out of the corner of my eye, I see Lizzie wringing the towel in her hands, her eyes misting with tears. She jerks forward, quickly wiping down the bar top before shooting me a small grateful smile as she retreats to the back of the bar.

"It's just a dress that I'll never wear again after tonight anyway!"

"Oh really…and why won't you wear it again?" He says huskily.

"Something tells me there won't be much left of it after we leave," I smirk with a wink, trying to hide the fact that my stomach lurches at the idea.

"Let's get out of—"

"Sir!" A short man interrupts.

Thank God.

"What, Oleg?!" Igor snaps, his hand running over his bald patch.

"The Boss wants a word."

Even in the loud club I can hear Igor groan.

"Of course, he fucking does," he slams his hand down on the bar, "Oleg, Jasmine here is mine for the night." He says, jerking his head toward me. Oleg tips his head toward me, his lips closed tight into a smile.

Igor leans in toward me, "Don't go anywhere. I've just got a quick phone call and then we can leave and go back to my place for a bit of…fun."

I have no intention of going anywhere… *yet.*

I nod, smiling up at him as he turns and walks away.

Briefly glancing around before I lean across and grab his drink, pretending to take a sip, as the powder slips out of my ring and into his drink.

I grimace, because I really don't like the smell of whiskey, but also so that if anyone is looking at me, they'll just assume the taste really isn't for me.

A couple to my left screams, making me jump as they laugh loudly and dance, taking a video on the phone in their hands, the flash momentarily blinding me from the other side of the bar as it penetrates the darkness.

I put his drink back, grabbing mine and sipping it continuously to drain it, so when he returns my excuse is ready to go. I pull out my phone, my eyes taking in the screensaver of Lily, who I know is going to be waiting for me to return for dinner.

When Igor returns his hands grasp my shoulders from behind as he leans into mumble "Sorry." He slides back into his seat that surprisingly stayed empty while he was gone and downs his whiskey in one.

Typical. Job done.

"Ready to head out?" He says, holding his hand out for me to take.

"Sure! Just let me go to the ladies' room first," I say, holding up my empty glass with a shrug of my shoulders. He laughs, his hand slapping down on the bar top. As I try to slide off my stool he doesn't step back, forcing me to slide down his body, where I can feel his length poking against me, causing a quiver in the stomach.

Keep it together Abby. Just keep up the facade.

I fight the urge to cringe away from him, slipping past him into the crowd. My heart is in my throat as I fight my way to the ladies' room, only to change direction when I see Oleg walking out of the men's.

Shit. Shit. Shit.

Turning I head straight to the door, fumbling as I pass people excitedly walking in.

Immediately I realize that I need a new plan. And *fast*.

"Teddy!" I yell, he spins on the spot, his face lighting up at the sight of me.

"Abby, baby! What's wrong?" He asks, concerned.

"Please tell me there's a cab here?! My neighbor just called saying there's police at the house and that I need to come home immediately!" I ramble out, my adrenaline from what I just did actually making my voice sound breathless and panicked as I bounce on the balls of my feet.

He runs out of the doorway, his head jumping from side to side, as he waves his hand out.

"Abby! There's one here!"

However, just as I reach the cab, a scuffle breaks out between two drunk people in line, and he turns to look.

But I can't wait.

"Thank you, Teddy! You're a lifesaver!" I shout, running past him and jumping into the cab that just pulled up.

"Wait…Abby!" he yells, forcing my eyes to his as the door closes behind me. It's then that I realize he's stood holding the door of a different cab.

Oops!

I throw him a quick wave, as we dart off from the curb.

"Where to?"

"Forest Hills," I mutter.

In the next six hours, Igor Ivanov will be dead.

ANTONOV

CHAPTER NINE

ROMAN

Ending the call with Igor, I shove my phone into my pocket. He was given strict instructions on what to do should The Brunette show up to The Studio tonight, and that asshole better not fuck things up a second time.

…Or he will be in a casket before the morning.

But just as I'm reaching to light a cigarette, I hear my phone chime.

Unknown Number
11:03pm: 501 Chelsea Pier. 12am. Come alone.

Seriously?

Me
11:04pm: First of all, I never come alone. That's what whores are for, dumbass. Second, this is a *parley*, not a bad 90's gangster movie. Third, you don't give me instructions. If we aren't negotiating, then I'll just get back to the whores.

I think I'll let these bastards suck on that for a minute.

It's about this time that I notice I also have another text.

And about fifteen missed calls.

Pasha
11:01pm: What the fuck, Ro?! You said we were all going at 11pm, but I just got out of the shower, and everyone was gone. Called all of you, and Niko just texted back and said you guys left 25 minutes ago!

Me
11:05pm: You just got out of the shower at 11:01pm. I think that answers your question, doesn't it?

Pasha
11:05pm: I'm always fast Roman.
11:05pm: …except in bed.

Me
11:06pm: Why don't you send some of those wounded shirtless pics to the booty girl from Instagram and get laid?

Pasha
11:06pm: She's going to be here in ten. Btw, we're finishing your scotch. The GOOD scotch.

I chuckle to myself as I sit in the car…at the Chelsea Pier.

It was a reasonable guess, as all my research into any sort of meeting with the McCleary's always led me here.

And Cillian isn't the only one who trains *rats*. I have a few little "pets" myself, hiding in the shadows amongst his ranks.

It wasn't easy mind you, getting someone inside. But I didn't try to send him someone new. I had my brother Lev, who's in of all our recruitment, find me someone old.

Lev, who sits in the front seat of my Cadillac, has several different ways that he sources men for our ranks, but his personal favorite is the underground boxing circuit. Most nights he is just an observer, sipping drinks and dropping hundreds on the fighters he thinks will win.

Occasionally he finds a diamond in the turd that is this city. Some scrappy kid, from a large poor family that is desperate to prove his worth. And his grit. Once Lev has a target he fosters that relationship, gets to know everything he needs to know, before finally picking a fight…*himself.*

Lev's always been a good fighter. The best of all of us in hand-to-hand combat.

Perhaps it's the fact that he grew up as the most middle child a middle child could possibly be. After all, Lev's a twin, and the third boy of four, and so naturally he grew up fighting for attention, and position.

He's never lost a fight. Honestly, I don't think he can because he simply won't *let* himself. Lev could be broken, bleeding, and completely delirious, and the kid still wouldn't back down. He's absolutely fearless, and I've seen him defeat fighters nearly twice his size by sheer grit and stubbornness.

So, when Lev steps into the ring, there's really only two possible outcomes: His opponents either concede the fight, or they get knocked the fuck out.

If they concede, that's the end. They walk. His interest evaporates, as he knows as well as I do that we have no use for quitters.

However, if they get knocked out, and are lucky enough to wake up, Lev offers them something money can't buy: a position within *our* ranks.

Looking down at my watch, I check the time.

11:15pm.

Fuck this.

I dial Ana.

"What?" She answers, her tone a bit flustered.

"I need you to do one of those lookup things you do for an unknown number."

"Why?" She asks. "Where are you?"

"That doesn't matter."

"Oh my God…you didn't," she sighs. "Roman, tell me you didn't arrange the parley. Please tell me you didn't. I specifically told you not to."

"Ana, I'm fine," I sigh, rolling my eyes. "I've got Cal and the boys and—"

"You involved the boys too?!" She screeches. "You took them on this stupid suicide mission?!"

"Hiya, Sis!" Lev chuckles from the front seat.

I don't even have to hold the phone to my ear, because Ana launches into a colossal scolding so loud that the entire car can hear her, even without being on speakerphone. I let her rant for a minute or two before deciding I can't waste any more valuable time.

"Ana…Ana!" I shout, breaking through her ass-kicking.

"I do need the reverse lookup information. It's important."

"No! I'm not doing it!" She says defiantly.

"It's not really a request."

"Well, that's good, because I'm not really going to do it for you. You're calling me outside of business hours. Again!"

"We don't *have* business hours, Ana."

"I do," she snaps at me. "And I don't have the time because I'm about to have company."

"No, you aren't," I smirk to myself. "You're sitting at your computer, stalking some internet executive or something, learning all of their dirty secrets."

"Fuck off!" She hisses. "For your information, I actually do have a friend coming over tonight. She'll be here any minute!"

"Then if she's clearly *not* there already, then you can just do as I ask."

"Oh, you pompous—"

"Careful, sister," I growl, a bemused smile spreading across my face.

"Why should I, Roman? You clearly never listen to a damn thing I say, because I explicitly remember telling you *not* to answer their parley invitation," she shouts into the phone, stunning my eardrum. "So why the hell should I help you?"

"Alright fine, if you do it, I'll give you a raise," I hiss. "And what was the name of that band you love? The screaming rock band with the goth clothing and all the black shit around their eyes? *Ink & Stain,* was it?"

The phone goes quiet for a minute.

"Are you talking about *Shrink & Pain?*" Ana asks, her tone suddenly lighter and more curious.

"Maybe?"

"My favorite band since high school that—"

"Yeah, that's the one," I say, cutting her off. "Let's just say if you *don't* agree to help me with this, you have my word that good ol' *Ink Stain* won't make it to their next tour destination. I'm thinking a pipe bomb explodes on their tour bus, but I might consult the boys to see what they think."

"Y…you wouldn't!"

"Wouldn't I, Ana?" I ask wickedly.

The phone goes completely silent.

"You know, I really fucking hate you sometimes."

"That's fine, you can hate to love me," I say. "But I'm sending you a screenshot for the number I need identified and just remember the fate of *Ink Stain* is up to you."

"It's *Shrink & Pain* you prick!" She screams into the phone before hanging up.

Lev laughs from the front seat. "Dude, you're such a dick."

"Yeah, I know," I shrug.

Within five minutes Ana sends me back the identified digits of the unidentified number that text me, a quick synopsis of the owner…and a bunch of middle-finger emojis.

I'll let those slide.

Immediately I dial it.

"Who the fuck is this?"

The voice on the other end of the phone sounds young,

"Roman fucking Antonov," I snarl.

"Oh shit!" I hear the kid say, panic in his voice as he tries to cover the receiver. "Psst! Cillian it's *him*! Fuck, how the hell did he get this number?!"

"Because I'm *God*, you cunt," I snap. "You should also know I've also got your home address, and the name of the assisted living facility where your grandma lives. So why don't you stop pretending you have hair on your balls and put me on the phone with someone who does."

There is a moment of silence, and shuffling before a man answers the phone.

"Evening, Roman," Cillian McCleary's voice sounds through the line. "I apologize for my associate. He's...*new.*"

"Clearly," I snort. "Tell me, Cillian, do you normally have pubescent teens do your dirty work? Last I heard there are rules about child labor, even in New York."

"You preaching about rules is a bit rich, don't you think?" Cillian says sarcastically. "You can't even keep to a truce. Perhaps they didn't cover that in your fancy mafia school."

"No, I just shot the teacher," I smile.

"I see you're already here. Why don't you pull into warehouse number one, we will see you in five."

"Looking forward to it, *darling*," I say, rolling my eyes.

Naturally, there's a part of me that worries that me and my men could be rolling into a trap, and for a second I think about Ana practically begging me not to go through with this meeting tonight, insisting that we would all get ourselves killed.

I'd really hate for her to be right.

Although, I bet she would get a little satisfaction saying it over my casket.

"We don't get to choose when we die, Roman, we're just guaranteed it will happen."

That was what my father said to me at my mother's funeral.

At the time I was furious with him because I felt that it was specifically his over-publicized antics with his stupid whore that had pushed my mother into an early grave. And perhaps it was.

But now, I realize he was right. In a way.

Unlike most of the bullshit my father fed me over the years, this little nugget of advice has stuck with me. Every time we're deliberately heading into a dangerous situation, and I feel my nerves start to strangle the air from my lungs, I'm reminded that we aren't owed shit from life.

…Which is why we must take it.

Silently, Lev hands me a fresh loaded clip, and we pull up outside of the warehouse. The first thing that strikes me as odd, is the fact that there are no other cars here.

"Is this the right one?" I ask, looking around before touching my ear. "Niko, do you have eyes on us?"

"Roger that, Ro," Niko says, the wind from his rooftop position breaking up his transmission. "But there really doesn't appear to be anyone else here."

"You've got the thermal imaging that Pace sent?"

"Yeah, and it's amazing!" Niko calls back. "I've got it on the drone, but the only heat signatures are coming from *your* car."

As he says this to me, I get a text from the same phone number as before:

Hairless Twat
11:25pm: Come on in. We're waiting.

The hair on the back of my neck stands up.

"Cal, are our little aqua-troops ready to go?"

"Yes, Boss," he replies with a short nod. "They're in the boats, on standby."

"…And I've got you, Ro," Niko says in my ear. "I'll let you know if any red pops onto the screen."

"Well then, what are we waiting for, ladies?"

As the three of us climb out of the vehicle, the potent smell of fish mixed with gasoline and dirt hits my nostrils. But confirming what Niko said, there doesn't appear to be anyone here. It doesn't even *feel* like there's anyone here.

Ever since I was a kid, I've always been able to feel when there was danger nearby. Almost like a sixth sense. When we were younger, Cal used to call it my superpower, because I could just feel when something in the energy was…off.

It feels off now, but not in the way it usually does when there's an armed gunman approaching me from the shadows.

"Keep your eyes open," I say softly.

I listen carefully, trying to catch a single sound out of place. But all I can hear is the faint hum of the drone above the waves splashing in the harbor or the groan of empty old fishing vessels bumping into the dock.

As a birthday gift, Jaxon Pace, a mafia don from Chicago, and longtime friend of mine, sent me the state-of-the-art imaging software that one of his tech men had designed. My brother Niko was fascinated and spent hours with

Ana figuring out how to upload it to his drone.

"Do you have anything now, Niko? Since we're out in the open?" I ask as the three of us on the ground approach the old warehouse door.

"Not a blip, Ro," Nikolai replies in my ear. "No sigs."

"Are you sure this is the right place, Cal?" Lev asks.

"All our recognizance says it is," Cal says quietly, scanning the windows of the buildings around us. "We've had people watching this place for weeks. This is their stomping ground."

When we reach the door, he scans it for boobytraps before knocking twice, but the door simply swings open into the darkened warehouse.

"Well, either they're wrong or we're wrong, because it appears that no one is home," Lev whispers. "There's no stomping happening here. Not tonight anyway."

Something *is* off, but I can't quite place it.

We step into the warehouse with our weapons drawn before pulling out the flashlights, splashing light around the room, terrifying some bats lingering in the rafters.

But as my beam pans over the wall furthest to us, that's when I see it. On the pale blank wall, covered in hundreds of peeling paint shards, there appears to be a small photo with red writing on it.

Silently, and cautiously the three of us make our way across the old factory floor, scanning the room and listening for any sound other than the cooing of pigeons cooing above us.

I yank the photo off the wall, and shine my light on it.

It's a picture of Saoirse McCleary, the woman I shot on in the head the other night, and the cousin of Irish clan leader Cillian McCleary. It's obviously a photo taken of her while she was in the morgue, as she's naked and lying on a cold metal table, her skin pale and untouched, and the giant bullet hole in her head hauntingly obvious.

I read the writing on the note.

Fuck your Parley.
An eye for an eye.

"Roman," Lev says, shining his light on the wall where the note was pinned, illuminating a large red arrow scribbled on the wall. "What does this mean?"

"I think I have an idea," Cal says, a few yards away from us.

Looking up, I can see he's shining his flashlight on something on the floor behind a giant piece of discarded sheet metal. Cal's stance is rigid, and his face is pale.

And when I reach him, I immediately understand why.

Because there, tied to a chair, is my cousin Stetson with a bullet hole in his head…and his eyes carved out.

Despite all the theatrics, there was no gunfight waiting for us at the warehouse. There wasn't even a fight. There simply was nothing. Not a person, not a bomb…only Stetson.

And Cillian had that number disconnected before we had even stepped back outside.

He'd left his message though, one that told me that he knew *our* movements as well as I thought I knew his.

Stetson wasn't part of my organization; he was just a casualty. And from what limited information I could gather, he'd left the club last night with a woman, but never made it home.

I did find it a bit surprising that Stetson would've left alone as he, like me, always had a small protection detail with him.

And although there's no way for him to know, Stetson was probably the *last* person that I needed to die on my watch.

Although he was technically my cousin, our extended family in Moscow is not one for affection…or forgiveness. And now I'm going to have to call my estranged uncle and explain to him why his careless manwhore of a son, who was only ever supposed to be here for a week, is coming back to him in an urn. And I already know it won't go well.

However, that's a problem for tomorrow. And if I'm going to sit and wallow in my worries, I might as well do it at The Studio, where I can wait.

…For her.

However, when the last call goes out, and the crowds start dissipating, it's clear that the only familiar female face I'm going to see around here is that of Heather, who has decided yet again to try her shot with me.

Tonight, I take it though, along with four vodka tonics, and allow her to suck me off right there in the VIP. And as I shoot my full load straight down the back of her throat, I admittedly feel a twinge of relief from the disappointment and stresses this night has placed on me.

But it doesn't last for long.

Heather has barely wiped my cum from her lips when a blood curdling scream echoes through the dimly lit club.

My hand is immediately on my gun, my eyes scanning instinctively for the source.

"Somebody help him! Please!"

A woman by the bar is pointing at the floor, her face painted with horror. However, with so many people on the dance floor, it's impossible to see what she's looking at.

…But then I get my answer.

"Boss! It's Igor!" Oleg shouts over the music, grabbing my arm. "He went down!"

"What the fuck do you mean he went down? Did the idiot fall off a bar stool or something?"

"I don't know, Boss, I only see him on the floor!"

We do our best to shove our way past through the crowd, but between the oblivious dancers, and the panicked patrons at the bar trying to back away we aren't getting anywhere quickly.

Fuck this.

I immediately just start shoving people out of my way, knocking a few of them over in the process but successfully clearing my way to the bar where I find Igor on the ground with his eyes rolled back into his head.

"Fucking hell, is he drunk?" I ask, rolling my eyes, wondering how the fuck my sister copes with such a shitshow for a husband.

"No, Boss," Boris says, pulling his finger from Igor's neck. "He's *dead.*"

It's nearly three in the morning when I collapse on to the couch at my condo, a glass of vodka in my hand.

Igor Ivanov, one of my most reliable enforcers, and reluctant brother-in-law, is dead.

Neither the imbecile paramedics or the limp-dick doctor at the hospital could give me a straight answer as to the cause, only saying that it appeared as if the asshole just straight up had a heart attack.

The entire family arrived, and Polina was a nightmare. Strangely inconsolable, she kept screaming that this was a hit, and between her hysterical weeping, she demanded I press the coroner for his report, and look into this further.

I have to admit her response is a bit surprising, considering Igor had quite a temper, and she knew as well as anyone else that he was constantly dipping his wick in anything with tits.

But she's not wrong, and something about that doesn't sit right. Igor might have drank like a fish, and snorted coke like a washed-up rockstar, but he was also oddly paranoid about his health and regular gym rat. He was too young to have just keeled over like that.

I don't know how or why, or even who did it.

All I know is that this wasn't an accident.

"I'm telling you, Roman," Ana says as the two of us take the elevator upstairs. "Something about this is…odd."

"Well yeah, Ana," I snort sarcastically. "Igor and Stetson are dead."

"No, I'm talking about Polina," Ana says, stopping and running her hand through her hair. "But we can talk about it later, after your interview."

"Her husband just died," I say, scrunching up my face as I continue down the hall. "What, do you expect her to be giddy about it?"

Suddenly I stop, turning to face her as her words sink in.

"What do you mean after my *interview*?"

"Roman," she snorts, crossing her arms across her body. "I told you about this last night."

"I was drunk last night!" I snort. "Ana, I don't have time for an interview today."

"You told me to find you a new assistant, remember? You told me to post the job."

"That was five days ago!"

"Yeah, and we already got a shitton of applicants," Ana says, throwing her hands in the air. "But she's one of the few that actually checks out. I already verified her."

I rub my eyes.

"Ana, this really isn't the best time for this," I groan.

"I'm aware of that," she hisses back.

Silence falls over the hallway before Ana throws her hands up in defeat.

"Look, I know you've got a lot going on. So, if you really want me to reschedule her, I can. But realistically, you *do* need the help, because as fun as it is doing all of this administrative shit for you, big brother, it's really not."

Taking a deep breath, my eyes meet hers.

I know I've been asking a lot of her lately. And, I know that she's been the one fielding most of the calls from Polina.

Fuck it.

"You have her resume?"

Ana smiles and hands me one of the files in her arms.

"She's waiting for you in your office," she says, taking a step down the hallway before turning around. "Oh, and Roman?"

"Yes?"

"Don't fuck her."

"What?"

"You heard me. At least not right away," Ana says, rolling her eyes. "Sourcing and verifying these girls takes actual work, so maybe let this one do some actual *work* first?"

"I'm certain I don't know what you're talking about," I shrug, smirking to myself as I turn down the hall, hearing Ana groan behind me as I walk away.

As I step onto my executive floor, I find Heather, sitting on the desk of the floor assistant, Alison, whispering animatedly. The moment she sees me, however, she jumps to her feet, adjusting her top and smoothing her pencil skirt.

"Good morning, Roman," she says far too confidently, the sultry tone in her voice overpowering her enthusiasm.

Immediately I understand: Heather thinks that because I let her blow me last night at the club that it means something.

"*Excuse me?*" I snap, glaring at her icily.

Her face goes as white as her thin nearly see-through blouse.

"Um…I…I mean, *Mr. Antonov,*" she squeaks, her cheeks turning a bright shade of red.

I say nothing, walking past her towards my office, convinced that the bitches in this city are getting bolder by the day.

And now I have to go fuck around with an interview.

"So, let's cut the shit," I say storming into my office, without bothering to look up. "I hate interviews, and I hate wasting my time. So why don't you just tell me what's wrong with you so that we aren't fucking around."

"What?" I hear the woman say quietly as I walk over to my coat rack.

"The fact is, this job was posted at the back of the classifieds," I say, hanging up my jacket. "It was deliberately buried. So, statistically speaking, *you* are either deliberately unhirable or deliberately desperate and—"

But as I turn back around my words freeze in my throat.

Because sitting there, in my office…is *The Brunette*.

My mouth has gone numb, and I feel as though my heart has stopped beating, and time itself is standing still, the room around us buzzing with electricity. If I couldn't smell her floral perfume, I'd be certain that I'm having some sort of hallucinatory episode.

Holy shit. It's her. It's actually really really, her. Here.

"Excuse me?" she asks, offended by my comment.

A comment that I've already forgotten, because in an instant I've forgotten my words all together. All of them. And even though I realize I'm staring at her, I can't tear my eyes away.

How? How is any of this possible? And why?

I'm not sure if my brain is working too quickly, or it's completely short-circuited, but no words have come out of my mouth, a fact that is making her slightly uncomfortable.

Come on Roman, say something.

"Who are…I mean…what are…" I say before clearing my throat. "What?"

The Brunette stares at me, appraising me with her eyebrow raised, confusion and annoyance written on her face.

"Well, that's what I was asking you?" She bites back. "It sounded as if you were saying something about me being unhirable."

Then she shoots me a semi-reproachful look, crossing her arms across her body.

"…And desperate?"

Fuck.

"No, that's not what I said," I say, trying to buy myself a few seconds without eye contact to think of something else to say instead. "Perhaps you misheard me."

"Oh, so now I'm just unhirable, desperate, *and* delusional?" She says, glaring at me.

Well, this is going great…

First words I've ever said to the woman I've secretly pined after for years, and I've insulted her. I need to pull it together, and fast, or I might fuck this up again.

"Look, Miss—" I say, grabbing the file in my hands and opening it. "Abigail Wayne, we seem to have gotten off on the wrong foot here."

"Perhaps that's because you're the one who stepped in here being an ass so…”

I snort, semi-impressed by her catty remark snapping back so quickly.

Remember who the fuck you are and get it together.

“Well, that’s just who I am, unfortunately,” I shrug, trying to hide my grin, and also trying to stop my eyes from drifting down the front of her blouse. “I’m an asshole. It’s part of the job description, so I hope that’s not going to be a problem.”

“Depends on how much you’re paying,” she says, a sly smile spreads across her face, as she gently bats her lashes at me, nearly making me cave on the spot. “I don’t do ‘ass’ for minimum wage.”

But that’s the moment her confident little facade falters, and her eyes immediately go wide, realizing what she just said.

“Is that so?” I say, raising my brow at her.

“Wait…no…I didn’t mean I *do* ass or anything,” she blushes. “I don’t do ass!”

“No?” I ask, locking my face to stop myself from smirking, staring her down, finding her flustered expression adorable.

“Not that I have anything against it,” she says, flustered.

“That’s a relief,” I say, clicking my tongue inside my mouth, and looking down at her resume in my hands to keep from chuckling. “It’s good to have an open mind.”

“It is?” She asks, her jaw dropping slightly before she shakes her head, putting her hand up. “I’m sorry, do you *normally* ask your interview candidates their sexual preferences, Mr. Antonov?”

It’s clear that her response is just her attempt to take the attention off herself, and the fact that I’m making her squirm is incredibly hot to me.

“Well, to be fair I didn’t *ask* you for that information,” I smirk at her, folding my hands across the desk. “You volunteered it.”

“Oh shit…I did,” she whispers under her breath, biting her bottom lip.

Oh God…those lips. Fuck. I want them on mine. Now.

No. I can’t lose focus. I was just gaining the upper hand.

By some strange providence, The Brunette, apparently also known as *“Abigail Wayne”* is sitting in my office, applying for a position with my company. And I’ve just been handed an amazing opportunity.

Abigail needs a job. I need a secretary.

It’s the perfect situation to covertly get to know the woman I’ve secretly desired for the better part of the decade…with an ideal role to play as cover: Her *boss*.

“Don’t worry,” I say, with a wink. “I’ll make a note that if we do make you an offer, ‘ass’ if off the table. And at the very least, I think we certainly can do better than minimum wage.”

“Great,” she says, tucking her hair behind her ear. “Well, at least that’s something.”

“Look, why don’t we just start over.”

“Perfect!” She says, enthusiastically, before clearing her throat. “I mean, yes, I think that would be good.”

“Miss…Wayne, was it?” I say, catching her dark brown eyes again. “Why don’t you start from the beginning, and just tell me about yourself?”

“What would you like to know?”

I grin.

“Everything.”

As she begins to tell me about her limited employment history, it’s clear she isn’t qualified to be my secretary. She has the education, but no real experience in the “secretary” or executive assistant department.

But I don’t give a shit.

There won’t be a second interview, and I won’t be seeing any other applicants.

This ‘job’ was Abigail’s the moment she sat her fine ass down in my office. I’ve wanted her from afar for longer than I can remember, and now that I have her, there’s no fucking way I’m letting her go.

ANTONOV

CHAPTER TEN

Abby

The cool air hits me straight in the face as I fly from the revolving doors, my entire body burning for a man I just met.

I have never, *ever*, had a reaction to someone like that.

It was so strong…and *primal*. It was like there was a voice inside me demanding I mount that man and consume him like he was oxygen.

I've never felt a need like that before.

His voice was like velvet, the rumble of it vibrating inside me, unlocking every single buried desire I've ever had. My entire being felt off balance, spiraling out of my control.

Roman Nikolai Antonov was a prick really, a rude, snobby, awful man. And he had no right to be that attractive.

He glided into that room, like he owned the place.

Well, I guess to be fair, he *does* own it.

But it wasn't just that. Nor was it the fact that he was so boldly attractive and confident. It was deeper than that. Everything about the man screamed power, as if he'd been born into it, and it permeated his entire being.

And Roman's "being" was very pretty.

He clearly cared a lot about his appearance. His dark brown hair was pristine and styled, bleeding immaculately down into his short well maintained facial hair that only further defined his chiseled jawline. His suit was crisp, without a single crease, and his shoes looked either brand new, or delicately polished and maintained to *appear* that way.

Then there were his *eyes*. They were the deepest blue I've ever seen, with flecks of gold and gray. The problem was, they pulled me under like waves on the ocean, and that was where I started fumbling around the interview like an idiot.

However, it was neither his appearance, nor his beautiful eyes that rattled me the most. No. It was the inescapable feeling, that buried somewhere beneath Roman Antonov's collected, polished, and immaculate exterior, the man had an edge. A dangerous edge, an untamable wildness that he was barely keeping contained inside his expensive designer suit.

…And it *called* to me.

I didn't understand it, but my God, did it call to me.

Against all logic, and even though I've only just met him, there's a pull to him that feels familiar, and safe.

Jesus Christ. What the hell am I saying?

What the fuck was in my coffee this morning?

Turning to head down the sidewalk, I shake my head, briefly wondering if perhaps I accidentally brushed against one of my Deadly Nightshade plants this morning in the greenhouse, as all of this feels like a hallucination.

But when I find myself stepping off the curb too soon, and getting honked at by an angry yellow cabbie, I know it wasn't.

It was real. He was real.

Well done, Abby. You clearly aren't getting that job.

Even though I'm a bit embarrassed that I bombed that interview so badly I do my best to shrug it off.

I don't necessarily need the money right this minute, but a steady source of income would keep me from dipping into my savings. Plus keeping myself busy during the day would have prevented me from doing something careless.

But Mr. Antonov has set me on edge.

It almost feels as if my fragile grip on reality and restraint is slipping, and I suddenly find myself questioning the face of every person that passes me on the street.

Are they good people? Do they hurt their partners?

What terrifies me though, is that somewhere deep inside my bones I feel as if I'm almost itching to punish someone.

…To *kill* someone.

This isn't like me. I'm not an emotional killer.

I'm meticulous and organized. I select and stalk my targets, savoring every bit of research, and basking in the thrill of every hunt, knowing I've just rid the world of yet another monster.

But…I just killed Igor Ivanov.

I have no *reason* to kill someone else, nor have I even spent the time identifying and trailing a suitable mark, following my carefully curated process.

A gust of wind blows my hair into my face and after I tuck it behind my ear, my hand absentmindedly falls to my capsule necklace. It burns into my chest, whispering to me.

Technically I have all I need to make a kill. Right here.

I always carry a dose of Widowmaker inside it, telling myself it's better to have it in case I ever need it in a hurry.

But that's not the only reason.

No, the truth is that I always carry it as my backup. My trump card. My contingency plan.

While I have no qualms about the work I do, and harbor no guilt about the justice I serve to the wicked men of New York City, I know the rest of the world wouldn't see it that way.

Particularly the *police*.

For me, having my control taken from me, and being locked in a cell, would be a fate worse than death.

I swore after Garrett died, that the only way I'd allow my power to be taken from me, would be over my dead body. And I intend on keeping that promise.

So, should I ever be discovered, I would simply accept my fate, open the capsule and swallow it down, ending things on my own terms, rather than be hauled away and locked up in a cage. *Again.*

Besides, orange isn't really my color.

Sometimes people ask me about the necklace, which hangs around my neck on a delicate gold chain. When they do, I put on the best sad eyes I can manage and tell them I always carry a part of my husband around with me.

Obviously, this is a blatant lie. But it has its benefits.

One, the sad widow routine seems to garner a lot of sympathy. And two, it's really good at killing a conversation.

But today, in my frazzled state, I'm reminded of the power I hold, right there between my fingertips.

The power of life and death.

I mean technically I could just waltz into the nearest coffee shop and drop this lethal dose into someone's coffee… anyone's really, it doesn't matter.

No. I don't just kill people without reason.

And being frustrated and angry at a man for being beautiful and dangerous, is no reason to kill someone else.

The unfamiliar morality battle suddenly warring in my heart, has it pounding inside my chest as I storm down the street, now has me ignoring anyone who passes me.

Which is probably safer, as these innocent pedestrians have no idea how dangerous I am right now.

I feel like Roman Antonov has pulled the pin of my grenade, and I'm about to explode and take out anyone in the immediate vicinity.

I need to get home. The sooner the better.

With every step, I try to calm my racing heart, focusing on breathing deeply, and ignoring my chaotic intrusive thoughts.

I'll go home and cuddle Lily, and everything will be fine.

But I know it's not true.

Something changed during that interview with Roman Antonov. Something massive.

The only problem is…I have no idea what it was.

As I start down the next block, I briefly make eye contact with the owner of the newspaper stand and shoot him a smile.

"Hiya, Carl," I say politely.

"Morning, Abigail," he calls as I stroll past.

But as I do, I just so happen to catch the headline of a newspaper that an elderly man is reading nearby on a bench.

"Business Mogul Dead at 42."

Oh shit! How did I miss that?!

Turning on my heel, I run back over to Carl, yanking a paper from the top of the stack. I drop my change in his cup and mutter my thanks before walking away, tucking it under my arm.

I'd been so distracted by the interview that I'd forgotten about the *best* part of what I do: *The Obituary.*

Learning my mark's fate was always the best part for me, especially after all the effort I'd put into curating, trailing, and drugging the bastard.

Because I never see my marks actually die, I always have to stalk the internet or the news for the obituary to get confirmation. Until I know for sure, the suspense keeps me on the edge of my seat, and I treat it like a surprise.

Igor Ivanov's obituary came up sooner than I thought it would, but then again, I didn't really know much about him personally. However, from the article, and the fact that he's made the front page, it appears he was a bit of a big deal in the business sector.

Finding a quiet spot in the sun, I stop and lean against the wall of the nearest building, my eyes trailing over the paper, digesting the words, *'impressive career'*, *'massive loss to the charity scene'*, and *'leaves behind his young wife'*.

I still wonder if the wife knew he was cheating on her whenever he could. Or that he was so cruel and sadistic to his mistresses.

My blood instantly heats just thinking about it, only further validating that he deserved the fate he got.

Frankly, I did his wife a service.

I fold the paper in my hands, tucking it back under my arm as I continue on my way.

When I get home, I'll add Igor's obituary to my collection. I like to keep a little box of souvenirs for each kill, either a printout of the obituary or the death certificate, but for *"Front Page Igor"* I'll be keeping the entire newspaper.

Before I know it, I've somehow found myself walking in Central Park. I always did find this park peaceful. No matter the season, it's always bustling, but this time of year and especially on a beautiful sunny day like today, it's practically *alive*.

Young children play amongst the trees, their parents watching dutifully as their youngsters giggle and laugh, the fallen red and orange leaves crunching beneath their boots.

On the soft dry lawn, a law student sits reading, while a couple on a blanket sit closely together, cradling their hot drinks and listening to music softly playing on a portable speaker.

Intentionally, I head toward the Turtle Pond in the middle, which I always thought was funny, as I've never seen a turtle there.

Truthfully, I usually avoid it, but with how out of control I feel right now, perhaps it's finally time to reclaim it, and take that control back.

The only time I've been to Turtle Pond was with Garrett, the day that he proposed.

It had caught me by surprise, as just the day before we had another one of our vicious fights. He'd thrown plates, smashed holes in walls, and stormed out of the penthouse.

I cried myself to sleep that night, my mind spiraling as to where he might be, or who he might be with, and what horrific fate awaited me whenever he'd return.

But the moment he walked through the door, he wasn't angry, or violent. In fact, he was nothing that I expected.

He apologized for his behavior the night before and told me he wanted to make it up to me.

He took my hand, and led me all the way down here to Turtle Pond, where a wicker basket was waiting on a soft red blanket, and a few candles lit around us.

He was so romantic that day, I was completely blindsided.

Of course, at that time I wasn't attuned to the fact that Garrett was clearly just playing another round of his "manipulation chess," and I fell for it like the pawn I was.

Once he'd slipped those rose-tinted glasses back on, he dropped down on one knee, and asked me to marry him, promising to love me forever.

What a fucking joke.

I smirk, reminding myself that his ashes are now spread all over the city dump. Because that's where *trash* belongs.

Pulling the paper from under my arm, I once again find myself staring at the headline.

Something about Igor's death is sitting off with me, like a violin playing a chord just slightly off key. Perhaps it's the thought that even after all my research, I still apparently had no idea that he was someone of affluence. And that someone connected enough to warrant the front page of the newspaper could very well warrant an inquest into his death…right?

I'm pulled from my thoughts when a soccer ball suddenly smashes into my leg, almost knocking me over. Bending down I pick it up, rolling it in my hands.

"Sorry!" A young boy calls over to me.

"See, Bobby! This is why you can't be on *my* team," a young girl yells, standing with her hands on her hips.

A smile pulls at my lips at the bossy little attitude she has. But when I look down at the ball in my hands, my stomach drops, the sad familiar longing creeping in between my bones.

What would life have been like if my child had survived?

How different would *I* be?

I'd never known the gender, but something in my gut always told me it was a girl. She'd be nearly five now.

My eyes burn as I consider the possibilities, all those "what-ifs" have plagued me for years. Wondering what my daughter might have looked like. Or if she'd have my eyes and his big nose. Would she have liked to play soccer? Or would she have taken after me, and found her joy amongst nature, or under a microscope?

"Hey lady!" The girl yells at me, pulling me from my spiral.

Clearing my throat, I look up at her.

"Can I have my ball back?" she asks, a small grubby hand pinning her windswept hair back. "Please?"

"Oh… yes! Sorry." I say with a smile, dropping the ball to the floor before kicking it over to her.

"Nice footwork!" she yells, pumping her fist into the air.

"Have fun!" I yell back before looking back at the pond.

Yeah, I think that's enough reminiscing for today.

I set off for the exit, inhaling deeply, and allowing the autumn air to fill my lungs, filtering out this emotional hurricane.

Flicking my wrist I see the time, sighing as I realize I've been walking around aimlessly for hours.

However, just as my watch face fades, it lights up again.

Number Unknown.

I let it ring, waiting for it to go to voicemail. But the moment it stops, it starts up again. Pulling out my phone, I swipe the screen bringing it to my ear.

"Hello?"

"Hello, is this Abigail Wayne?" Chimes a female voice.

"Speaking."

"Hello Abigail, this is Lucy Roberts. I'm calling in regard to your interview for the Secretary position with Mr. Antonov?" She says brightly.

Wait…the same interview that I just blew?!

I wait for her to continue, but the line stays awkwardly silent.

"Okay?" I say softly.

"Yes, sorry. Mr. Antonov would like—"

"Look, it's okay, I understand—"

I interrupt, cutting her off with a heavy sigh.

"To offer you the position as his secretary," she finishes.

"*What?*" I splutter. "I thought the interview didn't go too well…" I trail off, running my hand through my hair.

"Oh no! He loved you! In fact, I probably shouldn't tell you this," she whispers enthusiastically. "But Mr. Antonov *insisted* they cancel all other interviews, and I've never phoned someone back the same day to offer them the position!"

Her excitement is palatable, and almost infectious. She continues talking to me, but my brain mutes her.

If I take this position, it opens doors for me, allowing me to hunt down more monsters.

Yet after having met the man, I have all the more reason *not* to take this position, as my body's response to him is nearly debilitating. I genuinely fear that he would become my biggest distraction- something I cannot afford to have.

However, thanks to Lucy, I now know there's no one else competing for this role, and that Mr. Antonov himself insisted they make me an offer. *Today.*

That's what I'd like to call bargaining power.

"So? Would you like to accept his offer, Miss Wayne?" she asks.

"Well, that depends," I ask, standing a little straighter while glancing back at Central Park. "You technically haven't made me one yet."

"Oh, oops! My bad!" She laughs excitedly.

"What's the salary?"

"Starting salary for this position is fifty thousand," she replies without hesitation. "With benefits of course!"

"Seventy-five," I state. "I want seventy-five thousand."

"Erm, Miss Wayne," she laughs nervously. "Our salaries at Nikotech start at fifty thousand, and are above industry standard."

"Well, I'm not standard," I say, smirking, enjoying how uncomfortable I've suddenly made her.

"Of course, Miss Wayne," she says politely, her nails clacking furiously on a keyboard. "It's just with your lack of secretary experience..."

Her voice trails off, along with her bubbly enthusiasm.

"Well, seventy-five thousand is the lowest I'll accept." I say, my tone measured and firm.

"I...I...I'll take that to Mr. Antonov," she gulps, her voice trembling. "And see what I can do."

"I'd appreciate that."

ANTONOV

A
ANTONOV

CHAPTER ELEVEN

ROMAN

"Is everyone ready?" I ask, hitting the blinker on the Cadillac.

"Yep," Pasha says beside me in the passenger seat.

"Are they really?" I say, giving him a side-eye look. "Because you said that last time and they were late."

"Then why bother asking me again?" he asks jokingly, scrolling through his phone.

"Because, Pasha," I growl, stopping myself from ripping his beloved device out of his hands. "Remember that big speech you gave me a month ago, about how you wanted to start focusing on the family business? Well, this is part of it."

"What, wrangling our chaotic family?" He scoffs.

"Yes! I want to be able to trust you with big stuff, but I have to be able to trust you with the small stuff first. And this is just part of—"

"Relax, Ro," Pasha chuckles. "I'm just fucking with you. I promise, the whole gang is there. And Ana is there, and she says everyone is seated, waiting for us. The kitchen just brought out some appetizers to hold everyone over."

"Good," I nod. "That's better."

"...And Polina has already made the cook cry and threw a vase at Mrs. Devan."

Well, that's not 'better.'

I roll my eyes.

"Of course, she fucking did," I groan. "Because God forbid, we just have a normal family dinner at that house."

"*That house*," Pasha snorts, shaking his head. "You say it like it belongs to someone else."

"It does. That's father's house."

"No, Ro," he pulls off his sunglasses and folds them, tucking them into the collar of his unbuttoned shirt. "It's your house. It belongs to the leader of our family, and last I checked, that's you, ever since our selfish fuck of a father died."

This time I can't help but smirk.

Pasha is my real "Ride or Die."

And just like I watch out for him, he's always had my back, in ways that he might not even realize.

Pasha doesn't have a lot of memories of our father, but the ones he does have are brutal.

For the most part, my father ignored Pasha, which was honestly better than the alternative. Because when my asshole father did turn his gaze to Pasha, it never ended well. I can't recall the number of times I had to come to my brother's defense when he became the recipient of my father's misplaced rage.

I too have plenty of horror stories about good old dad, and plenty of justifiable reasons to hate him.

However, this is just the way of our life. From the moment I could walk, I'd been groomed and trained for the role I would eventually have one day. Heirs were taught to be smart, strong, and fearless, and in order to accomplish those desired attributes, my father had to be constantly pushing my boundaries, desensitizing me to the world around me, and to the gruesome realities of our world. Naturally, I had all the regular educational lessons, but the minute my school day ended, my mafia education began.

I saw a man die at seven.

I was able to fire a gun by eight.

I could hold my own in a fight by nine.

And the list went on and on from there.

Our father had a complicated polarity to him, but by Russian mob boss standards, he was mild. He was a gangster and businessman in every regard, including with his family. He was callous, hard, and cold, and in his mind, the best thing he could do was to make me into a man who didn't flinch when it came to danger.

He also made it repeatedly clear that if I ever disrespected or blatantly disobeyed him, he'd snuff me out and give the responsibility of his legacy to Lev, the firstborn of the twins. And after seeing firsthand the harsh realities of leadership, I made up my mind to try and protect my siblings from as much pain as I could.

"Show up. Do the job. Keep your mouth shut."

Another one of my father's favorite pearls of wisdom, which was also often followed by:

"Betray me and they'll never find you."

And he made sure to show me what he meant by that. Any time someone dared to cross him, or even question him, they were executed…and I was required to watch. So, no matter what it was, what I thought, or what else was going on in my life, if my father told me to do something, I did it, without complaint, and without fail. I did everything.

My twin brothers being next in line were also put through the ringer when it came to training, but not to the same degree. But Pasha, being my mother's favorite, and the least likely of the boys to take over the family, was spared the same grueling training. I doubt my father ever saw much leadership potential in Pasha, but what was worse was that he saw softness, which to a Russian gangster meant weakness.

He refused to tolerate weakness. So, for the most part, he refused to tolerate Pasha.

And then there were my sisters. While they couldn't be more different, they were both my father's princesses. And they were untouchable. Or at least Anastasia was. She was also the only one to ever make my father break tradition.

Typically, in our mafia families, boys are born for legacy, and girls are born for alliances. They are married off for whatever cause, or to whatever family provides their father the most benefit.

But Anastasia never fit that mold. My father referred to her as his "ugly duckling" but in his own, strange way, it was a term of endearment. And he didn't have many of those.

Perhaps it's because she defied the mold and never expressed any interest in the things typical girls did. Instead, she could often be found running with us, wreaking havoc with her crazy brothers, and was just as wild and untamed as we were. As she grew older, she developed a fast affinity for software and technology, and as the millennia dawned on America, she knew more about it than anyone in our family.

Or perhaps my father just saw an opportunity...or a liability.

He knew that if he forced Ana into an arranged marriage, even one that he carefully selected and curated, it wouldn't be what she *wanted*. And on the other side, he also knew that at eighteen she was already a proficient hacker and if she really wanted to, she could disable all of our enterprises overnight, leaving us fucked without recourse. So, my father broke tradition, and allowed her to choose her own path, as long as that path was loyal to our family.

Polina, on the other hand, got no such concessions. However, that was entirely her own fault.

Polina was your typical superficial, spoiled, and entitled mafia princess, who had an affinity for sleeping with our men. *Any* men really. My father had a hell of a time controlling her, and after her antics with the Pace's in Chicago, where she nearly ruined our biggest business proposal, my father had enough. When he heard about her shameless attempts to seduce the heir to the Pace Family, while also sleeping with my low-level security grunt, he arranged her marriage before our plane had even landed in New York, and she was married to Igor Ivanov within the week.

Their marriage was never one for love, but it was strategic. The Ivanov's had bought my sister by providing my father with money and men. And because Igor was older, my father thought that he would do a better job of handling Polina's chaos and attitude. And for the first year, it seemed like he did, and the two of them seemed to adequately tolerate each other's company.

But like many of our family's arranged marriages, it didn't last. Apparently, the novelty of my pretty sister wore off, but her attitude didn't. And that's when Igor started to wander. The two of these narcissistic psychopaths have been locked in this toxic cycle ever since, and after Polina nearly stabbed her husband to death at one of our weekly family dinners, I finally had to intervene.

I wasn't about to tell Igor, one of my best enforcers, that he couldn't have mistresses, so instead I told her that she would be allowed to choose his mistresses. Strangely enough, this seemed to pacify her, as this meant that she could delegate the less desirable sex acts to someone else, a prospect she sadistically enjoyed.

There are few things Polina enjoys anymore.

Which is further confirmed when Pasha and I pull up in front of the old Antonov mansion, and find her holding one of my maids at gunpoint while Lev and Nikolai desperately try to diffuse the situation.

Jesus fucking Christ! This bitch has no chill!

"Polina!" I snap, slamming on the brakes and jumping out of the car, storming toward her. "What the fuck are you doing?"

"This whore used to sleep with my husband!" She yells at me, while pressing her pistol into the neck of the terrified young girl, who is on her knees with her hands in the air, weeping.

"Yeah, and so did half the damn city," I throw back at her, grabbing her arm, and yanking the gun from her hand. "You'll have your work cut out for you if you intend on assaulting everyone who has seen your dead husband's dick."

Polina glares after the maid, who bolts into the house, before she turns her icy stare to me.

"My husband is dead, Roman! Which you don't seem to understand!" She snarls angrily. "I want answers. I want someone to pay for what they've done to me and my family!"

"*Family*? What family?" Pasha snorts, shaking his head. "Unless you're referring to those ugly little poodles or your fancy rose bushes?"

I see her reaction before it happens, and thankfully I'm close enough to knock her on her ass just as she lunges at Pasha.

"Pol! Stop it!" I shout at her. "No one in this house killed your fucking husband."

"You don't know that! It could be one of them! It wasn't an accident, Roman! It had to be someone who knew his movements and his schedule!"

"Which as you well know, doesn't apply to any of the house staff. They are never privy to that information," I snap back. "So why don't you stop acting irrationally and use your fucking head? Because if you can't act like a civilized adult, you can sit right there on your ass, like a child in time out. I don't give a shit. But I'm not having a lunatic in my fucking house!"

Disgusted at the dirt all over her hands, Polina wipes white gravel from her palm on the edge of her dress, before looking up at me. She says nothing, her hair a mess, her chest heaving, and her mascara streaking down her cheeks.

Even though she's crazy, and even though she's a bitch, she's still my sister. My recently *widowed* sister.

After she takes a few deep breaths, I extend my hand to her, offering to help her up. But Polina doesn't take it, slapping it away, and standing to her feet, brushing herself off.

"I look forward to hearing your plan, brother," she hisses, narrowing her eyes at me before turning up her nose and storming toward the door.

"Polina," I bellow forcefully, making her turn around.

"What?" She hisses.

"Give me the gun," I say calmly, extending my hand. "You know the rules. No firearms at family dinner."

My sister glares at me, pursing her lips and setting her jaw. But even though she looks as though she wants to tell me to go fuck myself, I know that ultimately, she wouldn't dare. And apparently Polina knows it too, as she stomps back over to me and slaps the gun into my hand. She then turns on her heel and heads back inside.

"Not your house, huh?" Pasha winks at me, an amused grin skating across his face.

I say nothing, simply shaking my head.

"Well," he says, clapping his hands together. "Now that the entertainment portion of the evening has concluded with Sister Succubus, I don't know about you, but I'm starving. So can we please go see what *your* cooks have prepared for *your* dinner…in *your* house?"

I roll my eyes, walking back to shut off the Cadillac since I had to stop an assault the moment we arrived.

"You're always starving. You're like a bottomless pit when it comes to food."

"Don't forget tits and ass," Pasha says, tipping what appears to be an imaginary top hat at me. "When it comes to indulgences, I try to keep a well-diversified portfolio."

His comment about *tits* and *ass* suddenly reminds me of my conversation with a certain brunette this morning.

Abigail Wayne.

My mood instantly shifts.

"Well, unfortunately, I doubt the chef was made aware of your peculiar dietary preferences," I grin, slapping my brother's shoulder as my Butler, Olfred, opens the door for us. "But I'm sure we can find something in the pantry to hold you over."

"What do you mean the coroner doesn't have an answer yet?" Polina shouts at Nikolai. "It's been over twenty-four hours!"

"...As I was saying," Nikolai continues, glaring at our sister. "They *did* have an answer, but they concluded it was a heart attack. So, they are re—"

"It wasn't a damn heart attack!" Polina screams, smashing her hand down hard on the table.

"He's not saying it is, Polina!" Lev shouts back at her, rushing to the defense of his twin. "If you let him finish, he's trying to tell you that they are doing it again to see if they missed something."

"They have missed something!" She says, throwing her hands to her head. "This is ridiculous! Igor worked out all the time! He was healthy!"

Pasha chuckles, nearly choking on his food.

"What?" She hisses at him. "What is so funny, *Puppy*?"

"The fact that you thought your lard-ass of a husband was healthy," Pasha says, taking a sip of his wine. "He thought cheeseburgers were a food group, Pol. Be serious."

"He had an iron deficiency!" She scoffs defensively.

This makes Pasha laugh, now coughing into his wine.

"Suck my dick, Pasha!" Polina snaps at him.

Unfortunately, this causes the twins to erupt in laughter along with Pasha.

"Enough," I say firmly, raising my hand as Ana elbows Lev hard in the ribs, shooting both him and Nikolai a glare. "Regardless of what you thought of Igor, he was part of this family, and now he's dead. As is our cousin Stetson. And while perhaps Igor's death could be explained away with poor diet, Stetson was *executed* by the Irish two nights ago."

The table falls silent, with the exception of Polina's angrily tapping foot, and the clinking of glasses and silverware.

"But," Lev says, tilting his head slightly. "I mean, when you look at all the facts, the circumstances of Stetson and Igor's deaths are so vastly different."

"Right," Nikolai says, nodding. "Couldn't it just be a weird coincidence?"

"I don't believe in coincidences," I say darkly. "Especially not where the Irish are concerned."

"So, you're saying that you're pretty convinced that the Irish killed them both?" Ana asks, her eyes finding mine over the top of her wine glass. "That just doesn't seem like them. They're always so proud of their kills, and they always want us to know. So why would they make such a point of us finding Stetson the way we did, but then having Igor die of a heart attack?"

"He didn't die of a fucking heart attack!" Polina says, pushing her chair back from the table. "How many times do I have to tell you people!"

"Polina," I say firmly. "Sit down."

"No! I'm not going to sit here and listen to you all—"

"You are going to do exactly what I fucking tell you to do, or I will tie you to that fucking chair and stuff that napkin in your mouth to shut you the hell up!" I roar, smashing my hand on the table.

Polina jumps. Hell, everyone jumps.

"We are trying to get answers for you, but I also need you all alert, and on edge," I say, pointing to each of them. "Until I hear, definitively, that it was just a heart attack or some other medical condition, I'm going to assume it was a hit. A hit well organized and planned by the Irish, because that will keep me alive, and I suggest you fuckheads do the same!"

The room falls quiet once again.

"Polina, we need to wait until we get the coroner's second report before we burn everything down, or shoot the hired help," I say, giving her a reproachful look. "Our staff is carefully curated and trained to keep their mouths shut. But if you go flying off the handle, threatening them with guns and acts of violence then you risk one of them going to the police."

I run my hand over my chin.

"Right now, we need to keep all of our alliances open."

"Alliances?" Polina whispers, glaring at me. "Oh, you mean like the alliance that father made with my absentee in-laws? The parents of my late husband, and the same people that haven't said or done jack shit to help me since their son dropped dead in the middle of the club floor?"

"Pol——"

"Tell me, Roman, what good is your precious alliance now?" Polina snaps angrily. "Because that's all I've ever been to this family, right? An asset. A *possession*. Just a piece of ass to marry off so that you and father can line your pockets?"

"Polina, be reasonable," Ana says sympathetically, placing her hand on Polina's arm. "No one here is saying that, and we're going to help you through this."

"Fuck you!" She screams, pulling her arm away. "I'll be damned if I let any of you assholes feel good about yourselves for one minute at my expense!"

"That's not why we want to help," Ana tries to say, as calmly as she is able to manage. "We're trying to tell you that this is going to be a lengthy process and you're going to have to learn to adjust."

"Yeah, and also how to not spend as much money," Pasha says, deliberately taunting her. "You know since you're going to have a smaller income now."

"Pasha!" I hiss between gritted teeth, shooting him a very direct look. "Shut the fuck up. Now!"

But instead of biting Pasha's head off, like she normally would, Polina laughs quietly to herself, shaking her head.

"You know, I don't need any of your help," she says, her voice low and venomous. "And I certainly don't need your fucking charity. I can provide for myself just fine."

She then slides her chair backwards and grabs her purse.

"You know," she says sarcastically. "I think I'm not actually hungry anymore."

And without another word, she turns and storms out of the family meeting.

"Well, I think that went well," Ana says sarcastically as we watch the twins and Pasha drive off together. "At least no one got maimed or murdered this time."

"Yeah, I was fearing for Pasha for a second there," I rub my chin, shaking my head. "I swear the kid doesn't know when to keep his mouth shut sometimes."

"That's kinda rich coming from you, ya know," Ana snorts. "And it's not entirely Pasha's fault. Polina can be a lot."

"That's an understatement," I say, turning toward the ballroom.

"She was worse before you got here. She'd insulted all of us, as well as every living breathing human in this house. I was sure that Mrs. Devan was going to quit if you hadn't shown up when you did."

"The maid *did* quit," I say, walking over to my chair. "But then changed her mind, when Mrs. Devan delicately explained that it doesn't really work like that."

Ana chuckles.

"If that's how you're handling staff turnover then no wonder you've got rats for assistants. They're all just looking for a way out."

"They don't get out. They know too much, Ana," I shrug, reaching under the table.

"What are you doing?" My sister asks, confused.

But when I rip my gun, securely stuck to the underside of the table by a Velcro strip, she murmurs to herself.

"Oh, I see so your little rule about no guns at dinner only ever applies to *us*?"

"Exactly," I reply with an unapologetic smirk. "Someone has to maintain order around here and I'm the only one I can trust to not lose my shit when things inevitably get heated, as they so often seem to do."

"The only one?" She asks, raising her brow, pointing to herself.

"Well, the only one who carries a gun," I smile at her. "You know, since you seem to think you can just use your *words* to diffuse a deadly situation."

Anastasia rolls her eyes.

"I never said that, Roman. I said that statistically speaking if you *carry* a deadly weapon, you're more likely to be *assaulted* with a deadly weapon."

"Well, if you don't carry a deadly weapon, and are attacked with a deadly weapon, then you're going to be dead."

"That's why I have Kane," she smiles at me. "Kane carries a deadly weapon and is practically one himself."

"Which reminds me, where *is* the dedicated bodyguard I assigned to you, sister?"

She opens her mouth to say something before shifting and clearing her throat, looking uncomfortable.

"He's…at my building."

"Oh, I know," I say, pulling out my phone, scrolling through my texts. "Good to know that he's clearly doing his job."

"Don't go biting his head off or anything," she snaps at me. "I'm the one who told him to stay behind. I'm not in danger with all of you," she scoffs defensively. "At least I shouldn't be, considering it's family."

"Well, statistically speaking," I say, patting my gun belt. "With *our* family, that's when you're in the most danger."

"I'm not even going to try and unpack the ridiculousness of that statement," she says, throwing her hands in the air.

"Good, we never agree on this debate anyway."

"My personal opinions are not a debate, Roman!"

"No," I smile at her arrogantly. "They're just wrong,"

"Annnnyway," she groans, clearly annoyed. "I do have something else to discuss with you. Two actually."

She reaches into her large tan purse and pulls out a file.

"Tell me in the car," I say as we step out into the foyer. "I'll give you a ride home."

"You're not staying here tonight?"

"Definitely not," I snort. "I never do."

"What, are you afraid that father's ghost might haunt you in your sleep?" She says, wiggling her fingers at me mockingly.

"Oh no, dad is welcome to come haunt me," I wink at her, clicking my tongue. "But if he's making the trip from hell, it's going to be to the penthouse I paid ten million to have remodeled this year. God, I'd love to know I was making the bastard jealous from beyond the veil."

Ana snorts quietly.

The two of us nod silently to Mrs. Devan, the widowed housekeeper who maintains the Antonov Estate, before walking out to the car. We've barely made it down the driveway before she shifts in her seat, opening one of the files.

"It's Polina," she says softly. "We all know how toxic her relationship was with Igor, and how much they hated each other. So, her reaction at the hospital felt so…odd."

"Well, not that I want to make excuses for her, of all people," I say. "But it's easier to hate someone that's still breathing. Much harder once they're gone."

"Right, I get that," Ana says, folding her arms across her chest. "But I couldn't help but feel like all of this was just a little over the top. Especially given the fight the two of them had the day before."

As I turn onto the highway, visions from the hospital come back to me.

Igor's body. Polina in hysterics. The entire family on edge.

"His phone," I say quietly. "I did find it odd how much she wanted his phone. But I just reasoned that perhaps she just wanted access to things."

"…Or didn't want *us* having access to things," Ana says quietly, thumbing the pages on the file.

"What are you saying?"

"I'm not sure," she says, sighing and leaning back against the seat. "But she didn't want us going through his phone, even when I told her that it could potentially give us some clue about what happened to him."

"You think she's hiding something," I say.

"Maybe? I mean, maybe I'm just being crazy, or paranoid," Ana shrugs. "But I just feel like we aren't getting the whole story."

"Well, we never really get that with Pol," I say, tilting my head. "She's never been very forthcoming with anything."

"Which is why I requested her text records," Ana says softly.

"What?"

"You heard me just fine," she practically whispers.

This makes me chuckle.

"You know, for someone who claims to trust her mafia family with her life, it's a bit amusing to hear you be this suspicious of your only sister."

"Hey! I'm just looking out for you, Roman," Ana says defensively, pressing her hand to her chest. "And yeah, maybe I'm paranoid, but let's not forget that because I'm her sister, I know better than most how conniving and evil Polina can be."

"Fair enough," I say, raising my hand, sensing her mounting frustration. "I'm not putting you on trial here."

"Feels like it," she says, sulking back against the seat. "I'm just trying to have your back. Which is exactly what you pay me for, and why you wake me up in the middle of the night or interrupt my plans. So, how about you just say, "thank you Ana, I appreciate you."

"You know I do."

"Yeah, well saying it once in a while wouldn't kill you, you know," Ana says a bit bitterly. "And neither would listening to me instead of just running off to play mafia don with Lev and Nikolai."

"Are you still upset about that?" I snort, as the traffic around us begins to thicken, having passed back into the city. "No one got hurt that night."

"Um, Stetson did," Ana says, waving her palm at me. "And that was just a technicality. You went to their turf and—"

"The Chelsea Pier isn't their turf, Ana, that's specifically why I chose it," I say. "It's shipping space, which means it's neutral ground."

"Maybe it *was*, but not anymore!" She scolds. "Forgive me, but I really don't think that Cillian is going to be honoring any part of the truce you had. Not after all of this. Which means that you can't rely on *any* safe spaces. Which brings me to my second point, and that is that you should be doubling our patrols at our secure warehouses at Chelsea Pier. Because If I was Cillian I would—"

"Careful, sister," I caution, raising my finger in the air as we stop in front of her building. "You know I value your opinion, maybe the most out of everyone, which is why I allow you to speak freely with me. But I won't have you disrespecting me, or telling *me* how to do *my* job."

"Oh get off it, Roman," she says, rolling her eyes. "We both know I'm not disrespecting you. I'm warning you. About Cillian, and about Polina. You need to treat them both like they are powder kegs that could blow at any moment. And…"

She goes to continue but then stops when she sees Kane, her six-foot five bodyguard walking out of the building and toward the car.

"You texted him?" she says, looking back at me.

"Of course, I did," I smile at her, leaning across the seat and giving her a peck on the cheek. "Because I'm always looking out for you too."

"More like babysitting me," she groans, rolling her eyes.

"Then Kane here is the most expensive sitter in the world."

"Evening, Ma'am," Kane says, his deep voice louder than the bustling city traffic behind us as he extends his hand, and helps her out of the car.

"Evening, Boss," he nods to me.

My sister rolls her eyes as she steps onto the sidewalk. But instead of just walking back into the building she turns and sets the second manilla folder down on the passenger seat.

"What's that?" I ask.

"That's the additional information I pulled on your interview today," she says, pursing her lips. "You know, the only interview you conducted before ignoring the advice from your sister and head of your Human Resources department, and impulsively having them make her an offer? An offer she enthusiastically declined by the way."

"She did?"

"Yeah, she did," Ana says, pointing at me. "She wants seventy-five."

I grin.

Of course she does.

"I'll reach out to her," I say, licking my bottom lip.

"Oh God," Ana groans, rolling her eyes. "Roman."

"What?"

"You know exactly what," she sighs, judgmentally. "I can see that look on your face. But if this backfires, you best believe I'm never going to let it go. Oh, and you should also know that I have a concert to attend next week, so I won't be around to post jobs at three in the morning. Or conduct background checks. So, do me a favor and don't murder this one."

She turns on her heel and starts to walk away.

"Wait," I call after her, watching her stop. "You never told me, what did Polina's text messages with Igor show?"

"Nothing," she says, her face blank. "There were no text messages."

"What?"

She nods.

"That's not possible," I say softly.

"Hence why I'm concerned," she says, folding her arms and raising her brow. "Perhaps you need to actually read the files and the briefs I give you occasionally. Or, ya know, just listen to me once in a while."

And before I can say another word, my sister turns and storms up toward the building, with the massive Kane hot on her heels.

All in all, Abigail Wayne's file was relatively…boring.

There was nothing in there that would suggest she was part of our world, which is why I could rule out the possibility of her working for the Irish or any of our adversaries.

So, despite Ana's reservations about my "enthusiasm" to hire her, I now find myself standing at my kitchen island, in just my gray sweatpants, sending an email to the personal email Abigail has listed on her resume.

FROM: RomanAntonov@Nikotechinvestments.com
TO: AWayneLovesPlants@myemail.org
SUBJECT: Offer
Miss Wayne,

It was a pleasure meeting you this afternoon for your interview. I thoroughly enjoyed our conversation, and I think you would be a great fit for Nikotech.

However, I heard that you have refused our standard salary offer of $50,000 for the Secretary position and have requested $75,000.

May I ask why?
Roman Antonov.
CEO of Nikotech Investments.

After pressing send I walk over to the fridge and pull out Caesar's nightly snack. He's happily licking his bowl when I hear my email chime.

A reply already?

FROM: AWayneLovesPlants@myemail.org
TO: RomanAntonov@Nikotechinvestments.com
SUBJECT: Offer
Dear Mr. Antonov,

It was nice to meet you as well. And I do think I would be fit for Nikotech as well.

But I am not standard, and neither is my work performance. And my grandma always said that when you're good at something, you should never accept less than your worth.

Which is why I cannot accept your standard offer.

However, I would accept your offer, if the amount was increased to $75,000, and the title changed from "Secretary" to "Executive Assistant."

Sincerely,
Abigail Wayne

I chuckle to myself.
Alright, Miss Wayne, I gotta hand it to you. That's ballsy.

FROM: RomanAntonov@Nikotechinvestments.com
TO: AWayneLovesPlants@myemail.org

SUBJECT: New Offer

Miss Wayne,

After consideration, I have attached a new offer letter, reflecting a salary of $75,000.

I look forward to seeing the "above standard" work performance of my new Executive Assistant at 8:00am on Monday.

Roman Antonov.

CEO of Nikotech Investments.

A reply comes almost immediately.

FROM: AWayneLovesPlants@myemail.org

TO: RomanAntonov@Nikotechinvestments.com

SUBJECT: New Offer

I accept.

See you on Monday.

Sincerely,

Abigail Wayne.

"I accept."

I read those two words over and over, probably a hundred times before I finally crawled into bed.

The Brunette, also known as Abigail Wayne, has accepted my offer.

And is now my new Executive Assistant.

CHAPTER TWELVE

My first two weeks at Nikotech Investments flew by.

To be honest, I didn't actually see much of Mr. Antonov, let alone spend any time actually assisting him in those two weeks. I spent those first few days training.

And then training some more.

The majority of it was standard office protocol, like how to use the elevators, or how to answer the phones. But given that Mr. Antonov was the CEO, they even taught me how to tie a tie.

At least Lucy was nice. In fact, all of the girls in the Human Resources department were. They were all managed by Ana Antonov, who was apparently Mr. Antonov's favorite sister, and while she wasn't in her office very often, she made certain that everyone in her department was incredibly helpful and friendly to me.

I learned early on that the two girls who worked on my floor were cold and uninviting, so the time I spent training with Lucy and the HR girls became my favorite part of the day. I learned so much about Nikotech, but also about the man behind the wheel, Mr. Antonov himself.

All of the HR girls seemed to have an affection for Roman, and I did notice that when he did come down to speak with Ana, he was always extremely polite and warm with them, more so than anyone else in the office.

Off the record, Lucy also confided in me the electric brain-rattling sensation I felt in my interview was the "Antonov Effect," and claimed that he seemed to have that mysterious power to make your brain go fuzzy.

At least it wasn't just me.

Yet while being relatively easy work, it was also incredibly boring and completely uneventful.

I came here to hunt monsters, yet, the only monsters I've met are men with more money than they know what to do with.

But today is my first day with Mr. Antonov.

His office is on one of the top floors of the building, and I'm told that the only floor above us is his penthouse.

I find his executive floor to be lonelier than I anticipated. I assumed that I'd have someone to talk to at least, but as the floor is exclusive only to his executives, and the two frigid floor assistants that assist them, I find I'm disappointed.

It's almost as if everyone avoids even looking at me.

Thankfully, I'm kept busy with the emails that keep pinging my inbox every few minutes, regarding reports, meetings, events and dinner plans.

All of it completely normal, and to be expected for a corporate company, but also completely overwhelming.

It's clear to me now that this role is something that I'm not at all qualified for, I know it, HR knows it, and so did Mr. Antonov. Which makes me wonder why he hired me at all.

The phone rings, jolting me from my thoughts, "Nikotech Investments, Abby speaking how may I assist you?" I ramble off, reading from the script that was placed on my desk when I arrived.

"I need to speak to Roman," a male voice says confidently.

"Can I take a name?" I say sweetly, my pen bouncing off the notepad. I hear the man sigh before he responds.

"Pace."

"Do you have an appointment, Mr. Pace?" I ask, pulling Roman's planner toward me.

"No."

"Erm, may I ask what it's concerning, Mr. Pace?"

"Put him on the phone. It's personal." He snaps.

Mr. Antonov explicitly said no personal calls at the office, and that if people wanted him, then they'd either get him via the appropriate channels, or they'd fuck off.

"I can't do that. Mr. Antonov is out of office." I reply, glancing quickly at Mr. Antonov's door.

As if reading my mind, he continues.

"You're new. I know he's in his office. Go and tell him I'm waiting."

I roll my eyes, "Of course Mr. Pace, please hold." I say as I press the hold button, and jump up to knock on my boss's door.

"Enter," he yells through the door.

Gently, I push the door open, coming face to face with Mr. Antonov, sitting behind his desk, paperwork piled around him.

"What do you want Abigail?" He spits.

Clearly, he still doesn't like me very much.

"There's a gentleman on the line, wishing to discuss something privately with you, regarding a *personal* matter, Mr. Antonov."

"For fucks sake, I do not take personal calls at work, Abigail. You were told this when you started!" He sighs irritably, rubbing his temples. "I also told you not to call me Mr. Antonov. *You*, call me Roman."

My eyes narrow.

"And," he continues. "That skirt is too fucking short. Make sure that you don't wear it again. Burn it if you have to. It's not professional."

"Well, you are in a great mood today, *Roman*," I sneer at him, my jaw tight. Twirling slowly on the spot, I continue, "Is my skirt distracting for you, Sir?"

I watch as his eyes flash before narrowing at me, making me shiver.

"Yes." He snaps darkly, still staring at me like he wants to eat me alive.

I hum in response, smirking at him as I turn away. Shrugging, I start to close the door, before peaking my head in at the last minute, causing his eyes to snap up from his desk once more.

"Okay, well I'll tell Mr. Pace, that you're unable to take his call."

"Fuck! Put him through on line one!"

"Yes, Sir!" I finger salute, shooting him my best dazzling smile as I slam the door shut with a bang, hearing him mutter "fuck me" as I walk away.

As I sit back down in my desk chair, I grab the phone, placing it back to my ear, "Mr. Pace?"

"Hello Abby," he greets in return.

"Thank you so much for holding, Mr. Antonov will speak to you now. You'll hear a dial tone as it connects, okay?"

"Thank you, Abby."

"My pleasure, have a great day!"

I quickly transfer him through to Roman, as I lean back into my chair, straining my ears trying to hear their conversation.

I could pick up the phone here, and listen in as he is on the open connection to my desk…My fingers twitch to reach out to the receiver, my decision made as I reach for it—

Suddenly Roman's door flies open, "Abigail! Come here!"

Flying from my desk, I stride quickly toward his office, finding him slouched back down on his chair, the phone still to his ear.

"Hello, my friend, what can I do for you?" He asks, his hand tugging through his hair. "He said what? No. That's not correct, hold on for one second." He suddenly looks up from his desk at me.

"Abigail, get hold of Oleg for me. Tell him to get his ass up to my office. Now!"

The blood in my veins freezes instantly.

Oleg? As in Igor Ivanov's Oleg? God damn it.

"Yes Sir, anything else?"

"No, get out, Abigail. And while you're at it, go find a new skirt." As I stand there, just staring at him, he shakes his head and returns to his phone call. "Nah man, she only started this week. Doesn't know how to dress appropriately…Oh shut it Pace…"

Despite his cold demeanor I can't help but admire him, sitting here, his jaw tensing. He swipes a black stress ball from off the top of his desk and squeezes, the muscles in his arm flexing, further accentuating the veins in his wrist.

"Abigail?"

Roman's voice suddenly snaps me out of my trance and my heart lurches.

"What the fuck are you doing? Get out."

"Yes!" I squeak in response, darting out of his office.

Such a prick.

I've been staring at the number for Oleg Mikhailov for fifteen minutes, but lacking the courage to actually dial it.

Get over it Abby, he won't recognize you.

I push my shoulders back, straightening in my chair and pick up the phone, dialing through to his office.

He answers on the third ring.

"Hello," he says, his voice sounds exactly as I remember from the club, confirming that it's him.

"Mr. Antonov wants you in his office."

"Can it wait? I'm just about to head into a meeting," he sighs, "Did he say what it was about?"

My head tilts back against the chair headrest, as I quickly consider what to say.

"He can wait right? This meeting is with the shareholders for the charity fundraiser, this was the only time I could schedule this meeting! Especially with him asking me to babysit his sister after Igor died," he rambles on, my eyes fall closed as I continue to listen to him, the pitch of his voice increasing with each word he says. "She's crazy, you know? Still thinks it was a murder, and she's determined to find out who did it."

My eyes fly open as I'm immediately pulled back into this conversation.

Oleg is a very chatty individual, considering he has no idea who I am.

I resist asking him for more information.

Surely a personal assistant could be a bit nosey?

After all, I've seen all the women downstairs, walking around in packs, gossiping among themselves about everything. In fact, I haven't seen a single woman alone in this building since I arrived.

Well, besides me.

My heart pounds while I consider my words, but just as I open my mouth, something thuds against Roman's door.

Great, he's throwing things now.

"Mr. Antonov requires you immediately."

I hang up before Oleg has the chance to respond, smashing the phone down into the receiver as my head leans against the desk.

Roman's door opens, and I feel his eyes burn into the side of my face as my forehead remains resting on the desk.

"Is the workload that hard for you already?" he sneers, "Sleeping on the job and it's only your first week."

"Mr—I mean Roman, it's not exactly like I received much training or guidance on how to work for you. I've been winging it mostly, just thrown into this chair trying to decipher the sticky notes your old assistant left behind, in handwriting I can't even read." I sigh, "I'm trying."

"Where the fuck is Oleg?" he spits, completely disregarding what I just said.

"I just got off the phone with him, which is why he's not here yet. I didn't know what office he was in, or what floor. Or even his last name. I had to find his contact information in the system, and for the record you have a lot of employees," I state, rolling my eyes.

I'm not going to keep apologizing for not knowing how to do my job. After all, he just threw me in at the deep end.

However, with the mood he's in, I'm momentarily concerned that Oleg is about to take the brunt of his anger.

He storms over, crowding me in my desk as he leans over, and standing so close that I could lick his neck.

What the fuck Abby.

As he fumbles through the folders slotted to my right, my body reacts and I inhale deeply, filling my lungs with the scent of him. Roman freezes, his body tensing above me.

I sniffed him…and he heard me.

Fuck. Me.

I feel his eyes searing into my forehead, but I refuse to look up at him. My cheeks heat, and I know how flushed I must look. My thighs clench together as I try to ignore my body's impulsive reaction to him.

Of all people to reignite my long-dead sexual desires, of course it's this fucking man.

I bite my lip as images flash in my head.

Images of him bending me over the desk, biting, slapping, kissing me on every inch of my skin. I swallow, my breath hitching in my throat as I squirm in my chair, crossing my legs, and bumping my knee into his.

Jesus Christ, Abby, get it together.

Desperately I try to think of something else, anything else, to distract me from my own devious thoughts and delicious desires. My legs clench together, and given how long it's been, I almost have to fight the urge to moan at the tiniest bit of friction that provides.

With how close he is to me right now, I feel as if I can barely breathe, teetering on the edge of restraint. A part of me fears that if I look at him now, I might spiral into a loss of control, and jump on him.

Given how much I need and crave my control, a reaction like this should intimidate me. Yet, with Roman I want to surrender it.

"Here," he snaps, suddenly slamming a notebook down in front of me, his finger tapping against the page, "This is the contact information for the Department Heads I will ask for the most."

As my eyes meet his, I gulp, seeing his drop to my exposed neck.

"And when I say I need them immediately, I need them immediately." He murmurs huskily.

Clearing my throat, I glance down at the notebook, my eyes widening at the scribbles on the page his finger is pressed to.

The writing is a hybrid between cursive, and lines, multiple numbers are circled in a different colored pen. Some of them are underlined multiple times.

It reminds me of when your doctor writes you a prescription, but you can't read it because it's nearly a different language, made up of symbols and swirls.

How does anyone read this?

I glance back up at the beast of a man still towering over me, having not moved an inch.

Usually, I would move away from anyone standing this close to me.

But the fact that I'm completely at his mercy, and yet still have no desire to move, confuses me.

"Erm, Roman?" I say softly, clearing my throat.

"Hmm…"

"I can't read this. How does anyone read this?" I huff.

"Well, my previous assistant managed." He states sarcastically.

"And, um, where are they now?" I smirk, batting my lashes and raising my brows at him. "Because if they were so good, where did they go?"

A wicked grin skates across his face, one that I notice does *not* meet his eyes.

"Betray me and find out." He snaps, pushing off the desk and walking backwards away from me. The air around us cackles with electricity.

Roman turns, gliding into his office and closing the door behind him quietly.

Okay buddy…way to be cryptic and ominous.

Betray me and find out? What the hell does that even mean?

I stare at my screen, before glancing over my shoulder at Roman's closed office door.

Who is Jaxon Pace? And why would Roman take his call, especially after saying no personal calls?

Quickly, I open a tab on the browser, and type in his name, hundreds, if not thousands, of results stare back at me.

Jaxon Pace in Times Magazine being one of them.

"Setting the *Pace*—Billionaire Jaxon Pace, 34, leads the way on new Eco-Friendly hotels by 2030."

"Hearts Break in Chicago! Most Mysterious Bachelor Marries in intimate ceremony!"

"From Playboy to Philanthropist-Mr. & Mrs. Pace restore and expand St. Stephen's Outreach Program with Addition of Ismena-Eliza

Minute Clinic!"

Suddenly, I hear the elevator ding, quickly I close out of the search results, fumbling to get the system back up as Oleg rounds the corner, wringing his hands together, almost… nervously?

"Hey, you're the new assistant, right?" he asks, without looking at me, staring at Roman's office door like he's waiting for it to reveal why he's here.

"Yep, that's me."

Finally, he looks at me, his eyes scanning my face.

"Hang on, I know you right?" He says, clicking his fingers together.

"No, I don't think so."

"I swear I do," he pauses, as his eyes squint, "a face like yours isn't easily forgotten."

Realization floods his features.

"That's it! Jasmine, right?"

Fuck.

I tilt my head, widening my eyes as I lean forward, forcing my breasts together as I point to my new desk sign.

"Jasmine? No, I'm Abby." I smile sweetly at him, watching his hungry eyes practically gawking at my tits.

But that's exactly the distraction I'm hoping for, something that's enough to draw his mind elsewhere.

He stares at me, the confusion clouding his eyes, "Ah, right. Sorry. Long week."

I tilt my head toward the door, "He's waiting."

Oleg pulls at his shirt collar, the sheen of sweat visible under the fluorescent lighting as he swallows hard, the sound echoing in the empty space.

He runs his hand over his hair, before walking forward toward Roman's office.

There's no way for him to know, but Oleg Mikhailov has just signed his own death certificate.

How inconvenient.

I've worked here for two weeks, and I already have to kill someone.

ANTONOV

CHAPTER THIRTEEN

ROMAN

"Sorry, that took so long," I grumble, glaring at Oleg. "My man here just confirmed that the warehouse *will* be ready for your shipment. He was just… misinformed."

"That's good to hear," Jaxon says. "So…when did you get a new assistant?"

"Recently," I wave my hand, silently telling Oleg to get the fuck out of my office. "Let's just say the last one had to go."

"Ahh, I see. Well, my condolences. Staff turnover is always unfortunate," he says, clicking his tongue. "But you know, I don't remember the last one ever getting you so…worked up."

"Fuck off, Pace," I growl.

"What? She sounds very *nice*," the cocky smirk on his face is evident even through the phone. "Don't tell me the famous "Russian Rooster" is finally considering settling down with just one little hen?"

Somehow, the pencil in my hand mysteriously snaps in half, the splinters shattering all over my desk.

"No, he's still just a *cock* who likes to leave the marriage and monogamy shit to old men." I hiss through gritted teeth. "Like *you*, asshole."

Jaxon laughs, a deep hearty chuckle that's so unusual for him, and one that irritates me even more.

"Oh, man, I had no idea it was *that* bad," he continues chuckling. "If that's true, then you're properly fucked, brother."

I want nothing more than to be able to reach through this phone and strangle my old friend…but only because he's *right*.

"Yeah, well that's the beauty of not having just one woman who owns my balls," I reply, my voice quiet. "I can always make sure I'm properly *fucked*."

However, as I say this, Abigail bends over her desk, playing with her desk phone cord. As she does, her tight black mini-skirt strains to cover her round perky ass, and if she wasn't wearing black tights, I might be looking directly at her pussy. In fact, I think I am.

Jesus Christ, is she doing this shit deliberately?

"What?" Jaxon asks. "Doing what deliberately?"

Fuck! I must've said that out loud!

"Nothing," I say, clearing my throat and shifting my swelling erection in my pants. "I was just talking to myself. About some…shit."

Jaxon laughs again.

"As I said, my friend," he says, with an annoyingly elated sigh. "Fucked."

"Anyways," I snap, finding his amusement increasingly irritating. "So, when can we expect your associate? What was his name again? Weston?"

"Wesley," Jaxon says, his voice shifting seamlessly back into business mode. "He'll be there when the shipment is scheduled to arrive, so next Friday at ten. He's one of my munitions experts, and he's intimately familiar with the products."

"And will that complete the, uh…*full order*?" I ask, knowing that I don't have to imply too hard for Jaxon to know that I'm wondering about the larger artillery pieces I ordered from his South African warehouse months ago.

"No, but I'm assured all pieces have been completed and are just waiting on a departure," Jaxon says. "They're already packed with a bow, coming directly from manufacturing. Once it passes through customs, it'll be all yours."

"And you're assured it will?"

"Without fail," Jaxon says confidently. "I make a point to foster a good relationship with customs."

"That's good to hear," I smile, repeating Jaxon's words back to him. "As always, my friend, it's a pleasure doing business with you."

"Likewise."

I end the call, licking my bottom lip as Abigail saunters her fine ass down the hallway toward the bathrooms. It takes everything in my power not to follow her in there, shove her in a stall, and rip her tiny little excuse of a skirt to pieces…just so I can finally feel my dick inside her.

If my cock was pulsing before, it's throbbing now.

I can't explain it, but there's something about her that draws my attention whenever she's near. And not just because she's beautiful, and deliciously shaped, but because she's not as simple as she appears.

At first glance my new assistant might give the appearance of someone as quiet and as meek as a church mouse. She doesn't talk to the other girls in the office, she isn't pushy or bossy like the sluts from accounting.

She just keeps to herself.

Unless my men decide to pester her.

And yet, I've watched from this desk as her big brown doe eyes have disarmed every one of my men unlucky enough to come up to this floor today. I say *"unlucky"* because the moment I'd inevitably catch them gawking at her, I'd want to push them off my twentieth story balcony directly into New York City traffic.

However, since trained mafia gangsters are time-consuming to source, and even harder to retain, I've changed my mind, and instead found some horrific or tedious task for them to do.

Abigail opens the bathroom door and I make a point to look down at my desk, refusing to make eye contact with her as she makes her way back down the row.

When it comes to me, well, I've been a deliberately difficult CEO today, determined to see how the girl responds under pressure. Yet despite being surrounded, and ogled, by 200lb meatheads that break bones and crush skulls for a living, and running every stupid errand I can think to send her barely clothed ass on, the little church mouse hasn't flinched.

I smile, looking up just as she sits down at her desk.

No, she's not really a mouse at all.

More like a fox. Beautiful, sleek and quiet…with a bite.

Foxy little Abigail Wayne. What do I make of you?

I'm staring out over the top of my glasses when suddenly I see the one person who can literally suck all of the joy out of any room: *Polina*. With her ugly little gray poodle in tow, she comes storming onto the executive floor, making a beeline for my office.

But just as I'm bracing for the hurricane that is my sister, my assistant steps into her path.

"Excuse me," Abigail says firmly. "Who are you?"

I don't know whose jaw hits the floor faster, mine, or Polina's.

"*Excuse me?*" Polina repeats, her offended gasp echoing through the glass panels of my office.

"Oh, I'm sorry, did you not hear me?" Abigail repeats. "I said *who* are *you*? Do you have an appointment with Mr. Antonov?"

My sister's vicious gaze sizes Miss Wayne up and down before she removes her Bulgari Sunglasses, and blinks at her.

"I don't need a fucking appointment," she hisses. "I'm here on personal business."

"I'm sorry, but Mr. Antonov doesn't take personal business here at his office," Abigail says politely.

Oh fuck.

And yet still, in the face of my absolute bitch of a sister, my clever little fox doesn't flinch.

"Now listen here you little cunt," my sister growls, stepping past her. "I don't know who the hell you think you are, but if I were you, I'd be very careful speaking to me this way."

"Certainly," Abigail smiles, as my sister stops and turns back to face her once more. "But to do that, I still need to know who you are first."

I'm on my feet and around my desk just as my sister takes a step toward Abigail.

"Why I ought to smack that—"

"Polina!" I thunder, yanking my office door open and making her jump. "Why the hell are you interrupting my afternoon?"

My sister scoffs, glaring at me, and then back at Abby, her eyes lingering on her once again.

"Hello?" I snap my fingers, shaking my head at her. "Is there a point to this intrusion, or do you just like to hear the sound of your heels clacking across my floor?"

"I need to talk to you, Roman," she hisses, narrowing her eyes at me before glaring once more at Abigail. "I just wasn't aware of this new rule that *I* apparently need to make an appointment first."

"It's not new," I say, clicking my tongue. "You've just never followed it."

Despite my desire to send her away, I know that if I do, she will just return to my office tomorrow or blow up my phone.

So instead, I wave her inside, rolling my eyes.

"You can come in, but hold your little lap-rat," I say, bitterly. "I'm not going to be responsible if Caesar decides to eat him."

Shooting one more side-eye glance at my assistant, my sister throws her nose in the air and with a huff, stomps her red-bottomed heels into my office.

Perhaps it's because I'm impressed with Abigail's fearlessness in the face of my snobbish sister, but as I close the door, I can't help but wink at her. And before I can even regret letting down my grumpy facade, I catch the blush that skates across her face.

I also happen to catch the *smirk* on her lips, coincidentally putting one on mine at the same time.

Given my situation, I walk straight over to the bar, which sits next to Caesar's bed, who is staring pointedly at Polina and her yappy little dog.

"Easy," I say firmly, hearing his low growl, meant probably more for Polina than the poodle. "Easy boy."

He looks up at me and his ears, which were previously back in warning, go up in expectation.

"I don't think he likes me," Polina says, matter-of-factly. "He's always looking at me like he wants to eat me."

"Good dog," I say, patting his head, before turning to my bar and pouring myself a drink, knowing alcohol is my only hope of surviving this conversation.

With my bourbon in hand, I head back to the desk. However, the moment I set it down my sister swipes it, pulling it over to her side.

"Just so you know, I actually prefer vodka," she says arrogantly.

"Then next time, I suggest you actually bring your own," I smile back at her.

But as I stand up to make myself another drink, I suddenly have an idea, and pull my phone from my pocket, quickly typing out a text.

Pasha
11:49am: SOS-Polina. My office. Now.

"So, when did you get another dog?" Polina asks, looking at me over the rim of her glass.

"What?"

"Well, I thought you got that beast over there for protection," she says, motioning to Caesar and pushing her lips together in a bitchy little smile. "Which is why I'm confused as to why you needed that stocky little Pitbull *bitch* out there too."

I've never liked my sister, and even she knows that. But the moment she insults Abigail, I immediately want to grab her by the hair and smash her face into my desk so hard her nose is crammed into her skull. But I can't.

…And at least not here, where there's witnesses.

"I know this might seem trivial to you, little sister," I smile at her, folding my hands across my desk. "But some of us adults have these things called jobs that we do during the week. So how about instead of wasting time on small talk that neither of us really want to have, we skip the pleasantries and go straight to you telling me what you want. That way I can get back to my job, and you can get back to popping Xanax and deepthroating your pool boy?"

Her fake smile instantly fades.

"I don't know what you think you've heard," she says, scoffing to herself as her face pales. "But you really shouldn't listen to gossip."

"What do you want, Pol?" I snap, my own smile fading. "I really am a busy man."

She rubs her lips together before sighing heavily.

"Well, I heard from a friend of a friend that Igor's second autopsy was stalled. So, naturally I went straight down to the morgue this morning, and talked to some pinch-faced bitch who tells me it wasn't stalled. No, no, it was canceled! Can you believe that shit?"

"You know for once your gossip actually has paid off," I say, leaning back in my chair. "Because it was."

"What?!" She scoffs, her jaw dropping. "By who?"

"Me."

The joy I get from watching the utter shock on my sister's face is unparalleled. I'm convinced I'd happily give her my entire bottle of bourbon just to enjoy this moment once more.

"Why, Roman?!" She demands when I don't answer.

"Polina, we aren't the only ones who have people downtown," I say slowly, as if I am explaining a difficult concept to a child. "And I've gotten wind, from my own reliable sources, that *Cillian's* sources were making inquiries as to the status of your husband's autopsy. And someone even went as far as to request a death certificate."

"B...but..." she breathes, still clearly stunned. "I...don't understand. If they issued the hit, then why would they need to check how he died?"

"Look at you," I gasp condescendingly. "Way to go! Using your head for once and finally asking the right questions! You know, I bet if you think *real* hard about it, you'll be able to answer that question."

"Fuck you, Roman!" Polina snaps at me. "You know as well as I do it was a hit!"

"According to the coroner, it was a heart attack," I shrug.

"Oh, come off it! You know it was a hit! And I want to see someone punished and I don't think that you're doing anything to—"

But before Polina finishes her sentence, Pasha bursts into my office.

"Roman," he gasps, clearly winded. "I need you...it's...it's...an... emergency."

"What?" I ask, confused. "What is it?"

"It's Raquel," he says, walking over to the other chair in my office and plopping down.

"Who?" Polina and I both say at the same time.

"Raquel?" Pasha says, looking at us both like we are the ones not making any sense. "The Miss Hawaiian Tropics Winner?"

I stare at him, blinking and trying to make sense of what he just said, wondering if it's code. But Pasha just rolls his eyes.

"The Instagram model who wants to meet me? You know, the one I showed you with the fine ass and those fucking cantaloupes?" He grins, squeezing a pair of imaginary tits.

"Oh my God," Polina groans, rolling her eyes. "Are you serious right now?"

"Like a *heart attack*," Pasha says dismissively before placing a sarcastic hand on Polina's shoulder. "Oh, my bad, Sis. Is that still too raw for you?"

"Fuck you!" She snaps angrily, jumping to her feet. "In case you didn't notice, we are actually in the middle of something, so why don't you run along, Puppy."

"This is more important," Pasha says, ignoring and turning to me. "Roman, I'm nervous. I've got this big date with her, and I…well, I don't want to fuck it up."

"What?" Polina scoffs.

"You?" I snort. "Nervous? About a *girl*? I don't beli—"

But then it hits me.

He's lying to get me out of this meeting with Polina.

"Yeah, she's like, oof, sooooo hot, you know?" Pasha says, using his hand motion to demonstrate his brain exploding. "And like, I just don't want to fuck it up, so I need your advice. Especially, you know, for that first night?"

"Ugh, gross," Polina says, throwing up her hands.

"Well, it is important to make a good impression," I say, nodding along with him. "Do you have a plan?"

"Yeah, check it," he says, biting his lower lip in a grin. "I got a table at Albertos, and then I was thinking that she's gonna be expecting me to take her to a club, or something like that, so instead, I'm going to do the carriage ride through Central Park! Totally stun her!"

"Smart move, honestly," I say, rubbing my chin, deliberately furrowing my brow.

"Roman!" Polina whines, throwing her hands in the air.

"Quiet, Polina!" I snap at her. "Can't you see the boy is in the middle of explaining his first date plans with a very elusive bikini model."

"With cantaloupes!" Pasha adds excitedly. "Oh my god!"

"*What*?!" She gasps incredulously.

"Please, continue, Pasha."

"Okay so then I'm going to take her back to the apartment and like slowly take off her clothes and go down on her for I dunno, probably an hour or so? Give or take?" Pasha shrugs. "I'll act like I *want* to keep going, and pretend like I don't want her to go down on me, but obviously I ain't gonna stop her or anything if she wants to return the favor. Cuz like, you know sometimes when I get nervous, I get that erectile dysfunction thing, so my dick just doesn't—"

"Ew! Ew! Ew!" Polina says, waving her hands in the air and storming out of the office. "You're both fucking disgusting!"

Without so much as a look back she stomps all the way to the elevators and hits the button.

Pasha and I step out of the office, and after doing a quick little verification that the Wicked Witch of Central Park West is indeed gone, we immediately break into laughter.

"Fuck, that was amazing," Pasha laughs, clapping his hands together so loud that it makes Abigail jump. "Did you see the look on her face?"

"I did," I chuckle, slapping his shoulder. "I have to admit, that was actually pretty impressive, little brother."

"Well, you know me, Heh," he says, popping his collar. "Impressive is my middle name."

All I can do is just roll my eyes.

Suddenly Pasha turns to Abigail.

"By the way, um, hi," he says with a grin, extending his hand. "I'm Pasha Antonov. I know I said that, before I ran into Roman's office and all, but I feel like that was kinda rude, and I should formally introduce myself. I'm Roman's kid brother. The youngest. But like, also the best looking. *Obviously*."

"Pasha," I say firmly, feeling a slight tension rising in my stomach at the way my brother is smiling at her and the way she giggles at his shameless flirting.

"I don't know how much you heard or anything," he continues, ignoring me. "But like, just so you know, I don't actually *have* any erectile dysfunction. I was just trying to—"

"Alright you," I say, grabbing him by the back of his shirt and walking him toward the elevators. "I think your Romeo hero duties are done for today."

Abigail giggles behind me.

"Well, I don't have any plans for lunch if you—"

"I have work to do," I grumble, hitting the elevator button. "Besides, I'm sure you have imaginary bikini models to woo and seduce."

"Oh, she *wasn't* imaginary, Big Ro," Pasha grins as he steps on to the elevator, clicking his tongue. "I have a date with her tomorrow night. And I'm definitely gonna smash."

Pasha. Pasha. Pasha.

As the doors close behind him, all I can do is shake my head and walk back to my office.

"Well, *he* seems very nice," Abigail says to me as I pass by without looking up from whatever she's typing. "Not sure about your sister though."

"Polina is just—"

"Or *you.*"

Slowly her brown eyes find mine.

"Oh, I'm sure you'll learn quite quickly, Miss Wayne," I say, a wicked grin spreading across my face. "I'm definitely not nice."

CHAPTER FOURTEEN

Oleg "Ollie" Mikhailov was easier to find than the others.

The beautiful man had every single social media account you could think of, as well as a handful of backup accounts.

He had the jawline of a model, and the body of a fuckboy, so naturally his face was splashed in dozens of tabloids and internet blogs, as well as making a regular appearance at the most up-and-coming clubs in New York City.

In one blog I found, the author, presumably a disgruntled ex-lover, referred to him as a "twenty-nine-year-old playboy, with a blonde fetish." She went on to detail that the only women who made their way onto Oleg's radar were girls who are under five-feet, platinum blonde and no bigger than a size zero.

Otherwise, good ol' Ollie didn't even notice them.

But, if Oleg wasn't with a long-legged bottle blonde, he was with Igor. They were practically attached at the hip, they spent most of their time attending events, mingling with other well-dressed men, shaking hands, and smiling for cameras.

However, for a man he had publicly referred to as his "brother from another mother," in a news article that I read online, he didn't seem too distraught when talking about Igor's sudden death to me.

The best thing about Oleg? He likes to location tag himself everywhere he goes. Maybe the man thinks of himself as an undiscovered celebrity, but he 'checks-in' to every restaurant, club, or gym he steps into. And often his food, his date or his well-toned abs end up on the social media page for that particular establishment.

It means that at least I won't have to waste money on a tracker, as the man was practically tracking himself for me.

It wouldn't be hard to kill him, it might *actually* be the easiest one yet.

I could always use Roman as an excuse and make up a reason to go downstairs to Oleg's floor.

Lucy informed me that my ID badge would get me into any door, on any floor, in any building that Roman owns in the city. I've also learned that people are so scared of my boss, that all I have to do is drop his name, and they will do whatever I ask, afraid that resisting could result in Roman's wrath.

So, in some ways, it feels as if the power and fear they have for Roman… has now transferred to me.

However, despite my concerns, my stomach churns at the thought of killing him. Because unlike Igor, there was absolutely nothing to indicate he'd done anything dark and wicked. Despite a few jilted exes, there were still no reports of him being anything other than a gentleman with whatever woman he's currently fucking.

The pen I'm chewing on cracks in my mouth, the ink leaking out onto my tongue, the taste making me grimace.

Damnit.

I close my monitor and head over to the bathroom. As I walk through the corridor, his men step out of my way, their eyes downcast to the ground.

I'm not going to lie; I really enjoy the confidence that being around Roman gives me. It makes sense to me now how rich, powerful men can become drunk on this feeling. This high is electrifying, awaking parts of my soul I had forgotten existed.

Shaking my head, I fight against the desire to let that power consume me too. Normally, it wouldn't be an issue, but this feels different, almost addictive.

The first time I actually felt it was when Polina arrived, I knew I should have stayed out of her way, yet there I was, pushing back. And enjoying my little power trip.

Usually, I never see the wife, or victim of someone I put down. I deliberately try to stay as far away as possible to avoid any suspicion.

But the moment Polina walked onto our floor, I couldn't stop myself.

I stare at myself in the mirror, my emotions swirling.

I keep to a strict code, I don't kill unnecessarily, and while the argument could be made that this *is* necessary, in my heart, I know that it's not. The only reason I have to kill Oleg would be for self-preservation.

With each second that passes, I gradually watch my eyes darken, as I continue to play God with Oleg's life, as judge, jury and executioner. It's usually a clean-cut case, the man's a monster, he's guilty, and I'm justified in putting him down.

He might be guilty of something, as everyone always is. But as it stands right now, he isn't guilty of the crime I usually punish.

But…he did recognize me. And even if I successfully managed to deflect it once, it doesn't mean he couldn't reiterate those concerns to Roman…or worse, Polina.

He's a liability.

It's too much of a risk to stay here, knowing that any day, any one of them could discover me.

Then again, I could always eliminate myself from the equation, and hand in my notice, even if that means sacrificing my proximity to Roman…and power.

Bending down, I swirl my mouth out under the tap, rinsing the ink from my tongue.

"Fuck," I mutter, my decision made.

Folding the letter into an envelope, I place it in the top drawer of my desk. For some reason, I just can't find it in myself to walk this straight into Roman's office and hand it to him.

Although, it's not like I could right now, as he stormed out of here so fast that it nearly gave me whiplash.

So, I've decided to just wait until the end of the day and leave it on my desk for him to find in the morning.

A shiver runs down my spine.

Since I started on this floor, I've noticed that each day I come in, it's almost colder than the previous day. And yeah, the weather is changing outside, due to the season. But it's not even this cold *outside*.

Almost as if someone has deliberately lowered the temperature.

The ding of the elevator echoes loudly through the quiet floor, and I can feel Roman's presence before I see him. Since he stormed out of here, the floor has been eerily quiet, the only sounds coming from the AC as it clicks on and off.

Raw energy vibrates through the floor, an energy that is off balance, and chaotic. The hair on my arms stands, as a wave of goosebumps coats my skin.

Roman rounds the corner, a man basically running behind him to keep up with his strides.

Swallowing, I cast my eyes from him, as I fight against that unknown force that keeps pulling me toward him.

Without hesitating I grab a notebook, and flip it open, pretending to be busy before his furious attention is aimed my way.

Suddenly, the executive floor is now flooded with gigantic grumbling and thundering men, who materialize from the elevator, the stairwell, and practically out of thin air.

"…I told Ana last night that I wanted an asset management report from Heather first thing," Roman snaps, as he thunders down the aisle leading from the elevator to his office.

His obedient and loyal pup Caesar trots along beside him.

"Why the fuck don't I have that already?"

"Um, I…I don't know, Boss," a stocky young man says.

He's a man that I've never seen before, and I notice that he has several, intricately detailed neck tattoos. The two of them pause just before reaching my desk. Closing the notebook, I go to stand, but before I even get up, Roman shoves his long coat into the man's arms unceremoniously.

Well, I guess he doesn't need me to take his coat…

"Have we heard from the contact at Stein and Company?" Roman asks, looking down at his phone.

"I'm not sure," he replies.

"Where's your brother?" Roman continues, storming down the aisle without looking up.

"Um…well, I don't—"

"I swear to fucking God, Noah," Roman suddenly snaps, screeching to a halt and poking his finger into "Noah's" chest. "If you say, *I don't know,* one more fucking time, I might just toss you over the goddamn balcony."

"Yes, Boss," Noah gulps, stepping forward and tossing Roman's coat onto my desk before raising his hands in the air. "Sorry, Boss, I can find out where Jacques is right away."

Reaching forward, I grab the coat from my desk, folding it delicately as my fingers run over the fabric. It's still warm and smells distinctly like Roman.

"No need, I'm right here, Boss," another man chimes in, also materializing out of thin air.

Jacques might not have the same distinctive neck artwork as Noah, but their build and facial similarities are undeniable.

"You're late," Roman growls, whirling back around toward his office. "Do you have my report? Or am I just supposed to imagine the fucker?"

"Noah, run down to accounting and get the report from Heather," the man named Jacques says firmly, turning to his brother.

"Noah," Roman snaps, turning back round, "I gave *you,* my coat. Put it away."

"Yes, Boss," Noah says sheepishly, holding his hands out toward me, without a word I pass him the coat.

With a nod, he promptly jogs away, tossing the coat on a hanger before heading to the elevators. Not that I blame him. With the mood that Roman appears to be in this morning, I'd want to get away from him too.

"I want Boris, Oleg, Jacques and you in a conference in ten minutes, or I swear I'll use your balls for bookends."

"Good morning, Mr. Antonov," I hear Alison say in a nauseating sing-song voice.

I fight the urge to roll my eyes.

Of course, *she's* magically appeared on the floor now as well, she tends to hover whenever Roman, and his men are around.

"Do you need anything? Or would you like me to take notes for—"

"Coffee, black," he quips without looking up at her as he steps into his office. "From Roast."

A dejected Alison turns a bright shade of red, and based on the way she angrily snatches her purse and jacket off the back of her chair, it's clear that *this* was not the answer she was hoping for.

However, as she stands waiting next to the silent and equally dejected Noah, the elevator dings again, and suddenly Cal appears carrying a stack of papers.

Alison steps on to the elevator, but Noah is redirected by Cal who grabs him by the arm, and evidently tells him to disregard his task.

With the young man in tow, Cal walks down the aisle and directly into Roman's office.

"Your reports," he says, laying the stack of papers on the desk. "I took the liberty of stopping by Heather's desk on the way up."

"Thank God, at least someone around here has their head screwed on straight," Roman sneers, glaring up at Noah. "Well? What are you waiting for? Make yourself useful! Go round up the rest of the asshole brigade and make sure they're in the conference room by nine."

Noah says nothing, before high-tailing it out of Roman's office and heading toward the group of men gathering near the conference area.

Standing, I walk over to Roman's office, intending to close the door so that they can discuss whatever he's fuming about without disrupting my peace.

With the mood he's in, I don't want to be anywhere near it.

And after all, today's my last day anyway. I don't need to talk business or even be involved.

But just as my hand touches the cool metal handle, Roman's eyes snap to mine.

"Abigail," he suddenly barks at me. "What are you doing?"

"Um..." I shrug, feeling my face heat. "Giving you privacy... and *secretary-ing*? I'm answering your phones, mail, and emails. Besides that, I really don't know how to answer that question, Roman."

"Get in here."

Taking a deep breath, I hesitate at the threshold, I should have given him my notice earlier and just left. I really don't have time or the patience for whatever fucking corporate bullshit this is.

However, my hesitation is clearly visible, as he stands, prowling toward me with an icy scowl. And even though I stopped giving a fuck what anyone thought of me years ago, I can't help but feel my body begin to tremble under the weight of his silent, intense stare.

Stopping directly in front of me, his eyes widen slightly, before narrowing again.

"What the fuck are you wearing?" he whispers, his voice low as his eyes canvas my body slowly.

"Do you not like it?" I ask, hating how breathless I sound. "You all seem to wear a lot of black, so I went with black."

"Your skirt," he swallows, before clearing his throat. "Is too fucking short. *Again.*"

"Well," I say, crossing one arm behind my back. "It's longer than the one I wore yesterday. At least I think so."

Shaking his head, he walks back to his desk silently, sitting back down in his chair. He closes his eyes, and takes a deep breath before resting his elbows on the desk, grabbing his stress ball and squeezing it, clenching his hand into a fist.

God, I really shouldn't enjoy teasing him this much, but I'm going to miss this.

"Regardless," he finally breathes. "I need to have a briefing with my team, and I need you to notate this meeting."

"No problem, let me just grab my—"

But before I can walk out the door, Roman is around the desk and slams it closed in front of me, making me jump.

His masculine scent fills my nostrils as he leans in close.

"...And I'm sure I don't have to remind you that anything and everything you might hear in that meeting, is strictly *confidential*," he says, the gravel in his voice making me listen harder. "And that your NDA prohibits you from discussing anything you may hear or see in that meeting...with *anyone*."

I want to say something, but unfortunately, I can't think of anything to retort, so I just nod once in response, looking up into the beautifully terrifying blue eyes of Roman Antonov.

"And also, on a personal level," he growls lethally. "Should I find out that you have broken that silence, I promise I will *bury* you."

"Ex...excuse me?" I snort sarcastically. "You're going to bury me? Where?"

Roman says nothing, only glaring at me icily.

"Get your ass to the conference room, Abigail," he hisses. "*Now*."

...And just like that I'm engulfed in the chaos that is Roman Antonov yet again.

Less than ten minutes later I find that I am one of seven people seated around the Nikotech executive conference table.

"I don't know how, but somehow Cillian McCleary managed to pull the resource funding together and is about to out-maneuver us on the Walston Street deal," Roman growls. "Which *cannot* happen."

The table full of giant burly men, who were all so animated seconds before setting foot in this room, are now all as silent as the grave.

"It cannot fucking happen!" Roman suddenly shouts, slamming his hand down hard on the table.

Tensing, I stare at him, admiring the clear fury that this man is, his rage palatable. Even from my seat, a few feet away, I can see the vein in his neck throbbing.

"So, what are we going to do about it?" He asks.

However, it is at that exact moment that I slowly feel six other pairs of eyes fall to me, the weight of them nearly suffocating me.

"Don't worry about Miss Wayne," Roman says, without looking up at them. "She's been reminded of her duties, her limitations, and also to forget anything and everything you say here."

Cocking my head, my eyes pass over each and every one of the men in this room, each one of them well built, tattooed and terrifying.

Only a handful of them look like they actually belong in a suit, the rest of them look out of place and uncomfortable in the crisp suits they wear. Almost as if they are rarely worn.

Or perhaps they're all just rich enough that they can afford to wear a new one each day.

One by one their eyes drop from mine, returning back to Roman as I fill my lungs with air, finally able to breathe clearly again.

"From what I understand, his funding is with the bank," Cal offers cautiously. "If we could figure out which bank, and who helped him do it, perhaps we could…intervene."

Without missing a beat, Roman walks over to me, snapping his fingers before leaving his palm outstretched. Caesar to my left immediately sits up, staring expectedly up at Roman.

"Oh, sorry!" I say, clearing my throat as I quickly rummage through the stacks of papers he gave me for safekeeping, before handing a file over to him. He slides it over to Cal.

Without thinking, I reach over and scratch Caeser behind his ear, and his tail starts thumping against the floor, drawing Roman's attention.

He blinks, looking between me and the dog with confusion before shaking his head and turning back to his men.

"I had Ana track that down," Roman nods to the file. "I believe there's a name. But then what?"

"Well, we could always try it *my* way," Jacques smiles wickedly. "As you know, I'm very good at getting people to do things they don't want to do."

"Yeah, you sick fuck," Noah snorts. "That's because you just love to hear the screaming."

"Jesus," Oleg mutters.

Hold up… *screaming*?

I thought this was a business meeting?

I know that my lack of experience in a corporate position is likely showing, but… I don't think business takedowns usually involve screaming, well, at least not the way he's implying.

"Does he have any…*leverage*?" The big guy named Boris growls in a thick Russian accent. "And if so, what are we talking? Wife and kids? Sick grandma?"

"Well, as my father used to say," Roman says with a shrug. "You can't avoid that which is meant to happen."

Holy fucking shit.

My fingers freeze over the laptop that Roman basically threw at me, all rational thought exiting my brain.

Thankfully my mental implosion is momentarily halted, when there is a gentle knock at the conference room door.

"What?!" Roman bellows.

It creaks open slowly, and Alison appears in the doorway, holding a dark blue cardboard coffee cup.

"Um...I have what you asked for," she gulps, stepping into the room gingerly.

"Set it down and get the fuck out," Roman hisses, obviously annoyed by her interruption.

As she places it on the table, however, she looks up, her eyes widening as she sees me, here, and petting Roman's dog.

I smirk, knowing it has to burn her, seeing me here, assimilated with Roman's most trusted entourage.

Suck it bitch.

"Out!" Roman snaps, yanking the door open for Alison, who scurries out of the room.

As the door clicks closed, he turns back to the room and pinches his eyebrows together before leaning both hands on the back of the chair next to me.

"I want a plan here, people," he sighs. "I need this buttoned up, and fast. This isn't our only agenda item here."

"For now, we need to get our hands on this guy," Cal says quietly.

"Agreed," Jacques says with a nod, "Once we have him, Noah and I can work out magic and see what kind of information we can...*extract.*"

"Just make sure you don't make a mess, like you did last time," Roman snaps at Jacques, who immediately drops his smile. "It took forever to get the smell out."

My stomach churns, as a chorus of low chortles and dark laughter go up around me. I scan the room, analyzing their faces and reactions.

They're enjoying this. Every single one of them.

"And where are we with the Pace International Transport shipment?" Roman asks. "Have they been paid? Is it still arriving on schedule?"

Luckily, after researching Jaxon Pace, I know all about his shipment company, and how highly rated they were. They delivered nothing less than excellence.

"Yes, Boss," Boris nods. "Debts are settled, and according to our contact, if the ship has favorable weather, they should set sail by the end of the week. And Mr. Pace confirmed that he's sending his weapons expert out here on Friday to personally supervise the deal. Smart guy or some shit like that."

My heart drops to my stomach.

Holy. Fucking. Shit.

This is it. This is exactly what I was looking for.

I've actually found them. I've found the monsters. And for some reason, these monsters feel very different than the rest.

Biting my lip, I have to fight the smile that tugs at the corners of my mouth. *Jackpot.*

The monster meeting concludes just shy of six in the evening.

Roman's men disperse disappearing back into the aether from whence they came.

Yanking open the top drawer of my desk, I snatch out my resignation notice.

After what I just witnessed, there's not a chance in fucking hell I'm quitting this place.

Carefully, I make my way over to the copy room, making sure no one sees me enter, and promptly drop the envelope into the shredder, watching until it's been torn to pieces and all traces of my doubt have been destroyed.

Grabbing my purse and coat, I decide to stop off at the restroom before heading downstairs.

I knew that accepting the position here at Nikotech Investments was a gamble, but it was a risk I was willing to take because my gut told me that monsters like Igor tend to congregate.

But having this many of them under the same roof?

It's a fucking goldmine.

And it's all mine.

I'm standing in front of the mirror, smiling to myself, when my thoughts are interrupted by the door opening.

Jenny and Alison walk in, their heads held high, both wearing black knee-length skirts, and white blouses. Alison's face darkens as she looks at me, her heels clicking to a stop. She sneers at me, before turning back to Jenny, and whispering in her ear.

"I thought Mr. Antonov had standards," Alison laughs, turning to herself in the mirror as she touches up her makeup. "I can't believe he took *you*... to that meeting."

Jenny rolls her eyes, looking away from me.

"Well, I guess he has been slumming it lately. After all, you did hear about Roman the other night? In The Studio?" Jenny says.

"No! What happened?"

I feel awkward just listening to their conversation, so I turn to one of the cubicles, locking myself inside.

However, as they continue talking, it's obvious they want me to hear what they are saying.

"He went with Heather from accounting, right?"

"Yes! I hate to say it, but they look good together."

"Yeah, actually, don't say that." Jenny snorts.

"Don't get me wrong, I hate her and all, but they make a good-looking couple," Alison laughs viciously.

"Lucky bitch," Jenny snorts, and they both giggle, the sound bouncing off the tiled walls.

I don't know why, but I feel myself tense as I continue to listen, however, the idea of Roman touching someone else… makes my blood boil.

"Like, I was watching from the dance floor, watching her throwing herself all over him while he and Stetson snorted lines off her fake as fuck tits." Alison hisses.

"What a skank!" Jenny squeaks out in uproar.

Oh God…

I roll my eyes, amused with how fake the entire interaction is between these two vapid bitches.

"Right!? Honestly what a fucking slut, anyway! He legit threw her… like threw her…on the floor…"

"No!"

"Yes! I thought they were going to fuck right in the open with the way she was grinding herself against his dick. I mean, the bitch wasn't even wearing underwear."

"No way…"

"Yes way!"

A giggle escapes me, my hands darting up to my mouth with an audible slap.

Fuck.

The idea of Roman throwing a girl off him is hilarious, as it's clear the man has women literally falling all over themselves just to get his attention.

But he wants nothing to do with any of them.

My thoughts are interrupted with a bang as one of them hits against the cubicle door. I guess they figured out I wasn't using the facilities.

"Get out here, you little bitch," Alison snaps.

With a sigh I stand, opening the door with a smile.

"I'm sorry, do you find our conversation amusing, Abigail?"

"Yeah," I scoff. "I actually do. Imagine being that consumed with someone else's personal life."

"I don't know why you're laughing," Jenny quips venomously. "He fucked his last assistant, and then, from what I've heard, no one has seen her since."

Her words hit me like a punch to the gut.

What?

"Oh pssh," Alison says, rolling her eyes and waving Jenny off. "I'm sure that's just a rumor Jen."

"Is it though? Tell me then, why has no one seen her since?"

"Just a thought," I shrug, deciding not to let these bitches have the satisfaction. "Maybe she just moved on. People do that, you know."

Alison throws her head back and laughs. She narrows her eyes at me before crossing her arms across her chest.

"Yeah, not *here* you don't," she snarls, batting her lashes at me. "But you should know, they went to her house, and found it empty. No luggage missing, and her clothes still hanging neatly in the closet."

She glares at me one last time before clicking her tongue inside her mouth and smiling.

"So, I guess, best of luck, *bestie*."

And without another word, she turns on her red-bottom pumps and her and Jenny saunter out the door.

Standing here, I can feel my body shaking and my lungs heaving as I process what they just said.

I wouldn't usually believe bathroom gossip like this, especially from the office mean girls, but I've always trusted my gut. It has never steered me wrong.

And right now, it's telling me there is at least some truth to what Jenny and Alison just said.

But…I'm not afraid. Not at all actually.

I turn to myself in the mirror, leaning forward against the sink.

Well, well, well. What do you know? Roman Antonov is dangerous too. Just like me.

I knew there was something about him that rang the bell of familiarity, a likeness my subconscious must have recognized.

Oleg, Boris, Jacques, Noah…Roman.

He's a bad man. They all are. Maybe even killers.

But at the end of the day, there's only one thing that causes a wicked smirk to skate across my face: A *challenge*.

Lurking behind his eyes are demons as dark as mine. Determined to fight their way out, and once they were free, they would be all that remained.

Roman Nikolai Antonov has demons, but so do I.

Let the darkest demon's win.

ANTONOV

CHAPTER FIFTEEN

ROMAN

I stand next to Abigail's desk watching as she types something into the search bar on her computer and a bunch of flowers come up on the screen. Flowers that appear to have complicated names that I could never hope to pronounce.

What is it with women and flowers?

"Let's go," I snap deliberately, enjoying how she nearly jumps out of her skin and almost knocks over her cup of coffee. "We're leaving."

"Roman!" She gasps, her eyes wide and her cheeks turning that bright shade of crimson.

God, I love it when that happens.

"I…I…swear I was just finishing my break," she stutters nervously, spinning back around to quickly close her browsing window. "I promise, I wasn't—"

"Abigail, I don't care if you browse the internet in your downtime," I say, watching as she smooths her long brown hair. "However, I *do* care that you're still sitting here when I just said that we're leaving."

"Oh…okay!" She says, turning back to her desk and trying to pull up her timecard to log out.

But she's obviously flustered, typing the wrong passcode twice before finally getting it right and then trying to close down the barrage of programs. She reaches for her purse but then sets it down, reaching instead for her mug.

"I should probably wash this out, yes?" She says, looking up at me, her eyes widening. "Wait, I…I guess I don't even know where we're going?"

"Does it matter?" I ask, raising my brow. "I said we're leaving. So, we're leaving."

"But…are we…you know, coming *back*?" She asks, twisting her necklace between her fingers.

"Abigail."

"Yes, yes," she gulps, jumping up. "I'm ready I just have to grab my—"

That's when her eyes drift to what I have in my arms. Somehow, I'm able to stifle my smirk and hold her coat open for her as she sheepishly slips one arm in at a time.

However, my stoic facade nearly fades, because having her in my arms I can smell her perfume and the bright intoxicating floral scent of her hair.

Thankfully, I'm distracted by Jenny and Alison gawking at us from the large bulk printer in the corner. As soon as we make eye contact, they both immediately pretend to be adding paper to a tray.

Those bitches do more standing around than actual work.

And since I already know exactly how mediocre they *both* are in bed, part of me wants to spin Abigail around, cup her face, and shove my tongue down her throat right here…just to make them jealous.

But I don't want our first kiss to be like that.

What the fuck? Where did that come from?

"You finally ready?" I ask quietly, as she clumsily grabs her purse, her sudden anxiety apparent.

"Yes, sorry," she says, trying to pull her long brown hair out from under her coat. "I'm ready."

I reach forward, instantly hearing her sharp intake of breath as my fingers gently caress the skin on her neck, helping to brush the last disobedient strand out of the top of her coat collar. In the brief moment our skin collides I feel an almost static electricity, crackling between us and it makes me pause.

Is that even possible? I've never felt this before.

"Good," is all I manage to whisper.

"Mmmhmm," she gulps, breathing shakily.

Her eyes drop to my lips as she bites her own. It nearly derails me, as I would give anything to do that myself.

No! Stop it! This is ridiculous!

If she looked down right now, she'd immediately see my growing erection, and I'd look like some pathetic teenager who's never had his dick touched before.

"After you," I say, gently placing my hand on her back and motioning her toward the elevator.

We walk in silence past the stunned office hoes, who aren't even trying to stifle their astonishment anymore as I press the button for the garage on the elevator pad. Perhaps that's why I deliberately let my hand brush her lower back as we step into the lift.

"Am I, um," Abigail asks softly, the moment the doors close. "Allowed to ask where we're going?"

"You can," I say, leaning against the wall and trying to avoid looking at her big brown doe eyes for fear that I'd want to ravish her right here. "But it doesn't mean I'll tell you."

Abby goes quiet, pressing her lips together and anxiously bouncing up and down on her heels. When the door opens, we're in my private parking garage where Cal is waiting with the cars.

"Boss," he nods. "Everything is prepared."

"Good," I nod, heading to the nearest one and opening the door for Abigail. "We'll go alone. You can follow."

"Yes, Sir."

If I thought she looked nervous before, it's nothing compared to how it looks as I wave her into the open door. Every step she takes is slow and calculated. Eventually she makes it inside the car, and I close the door behind her. I walk around to my side and hop inside.

The car is silent until we pull out onto fifth avenue.

"Am I…being *fired*?" She finally asks.

Her voice is shaky and quiet, and it catches me off guard.

"*What?*" I ask, looking up at her, seeing her fidgeting with her hands. "No. Why on earth would you—"

"Well, I just thought that maybe I did something wrong," she says, shrugging. "Or that you're unhappy with me?"

"Abigail, no…I…" I say, frustrated, that this is immediately where her mind went. "Of course not."

"Because if I was too aggressive with your sister, I'm sorry," she says. "Again, I honestly didn't know who she was and—"

"I'm taking you to *lunch*," I say, interrupting her.

"You're what?"

"I had a busy afternoon, and I noticed you hadn't taken yours yet either. So, I decided to take you to lunch. That's all."

"Oh," she says, chuckling to herself and looking almost relieved as she stares down at her lap. "Yeah, I actually didn't *bring* lunch today."

I know she didn't. But obviously I can't say that.

Because that's creepy as fuck, Roman.

"I, uh…have a standing table at Albertos," I say, clearing my throat. "It's one of the best restaurants in the city."

"Yes, I've heard it's very hard to get a table there," she nods. "But I guess I'm confused about why you'd want to bring *me*?"

Shit.

I didn't anticipate her asking this question, and for a moment, it throws me off my game.

"Why not?" I say, trying my hardest to sound as indifferent as possible. "You eat. I eat. And I don't like eating alone."

"Fair, I guess it's that I'm just, well, me," she shrugs. "I'm not very important."

"I think I'll be the judge of that," I say as we turn the corner. "Last I checked, I'm the only one who gets to decide who I spend my time with, Abigail."

"Abby."

"What?"

"You keep calling me Abigail," she says, tucking a strand of her brown hair behind her ear. "Which is fine, because that's my name, but I prefer to go by Abby."

I grin.

"Alright," I say slowly. "Well, Abby, just consider it a business lunch," I say, sadistically enjoying watching her squirm. "I'll be sure to give you the receipt so you can file the expense report when we get back to the office. Since two grown adults enjoying a meal at the best restaurant in the city is going to be an issue, apparently."

"It's not an issue!" She snaps at me, frustrated. "I just was confused because you didn't give me any heads-up."

"As you already know, my schedule doesn't allow for much of a heads-up these days," I say matter-of-factly. "I have to work with what I have."

"Okay, well that still doesn't explain why you'd invite *me*?" She shrugs. "There's always men coming and going from your office, or you know, you could've sent me to pick up takeout for you."

"Is that what you'd prefer?" I ask, my heart beating a little faster. "Does the idea of lunch with me make you that uncomfortable?"

"No!" she sighs, exasperated. "I guess I just don't understand why you'd even bother with…me."

Oh, little fox, I very much enjoy bothering you.

But I suddenly realize that perhaps after my cold and callous demeanor with her all week, kidnapping her for lunch, might actually *be* a bit confusing. And, even though I really am enjoying watching her seesaw between being sassy and confident, to nervous and fidgety, it might not win me any points in her book.

I need to try a different approach.

"Look," I say, swallowing hard. "Truth is, I wanted to bring you to lunch because I owe you an apology."

"What?" She gasps. "An apology? For what?"

"My ridiculous family, especially my cunt of a sister," I say, feeling Abby's gaze on me. "It's my way of saying thank you."

Abby stares at me, before snorting quietly to herself. And as silence settles over the car, I feel the static electricity return.

"What are you thinking?" I say, trying my best to make it sound more like a question and less like a demand.

"I'm shocked," she quips, her nervousness seeming to dissipate. "Wow. And here I was starting to think they didn't teach you things like gratitude in fancy CEO School."

There's my feisty little fox.

"I'm just out of practice," I say, throwing on my black aviators. "Usually in my line of work I'm used to people saying it to me."

"Is that a fact?"

"Well, they alternate."

"Alternate?" Abigail asks.

"Between saying thank you," I grin, turning to her as I bring the car to a full stop at the light. "Or begging for mercy…On their fucking *knees*."

I glance over at her, watching her arrogant little grin disappear.

"Oh, and by the way, *Abby*," I say, lowering my glasses to look her up and down. "Your skirt is *still* too fucking short."

"Right this way, Mr. Antonov," Cassandra, the attractive hostess, says politely.

"Holy shit," I hear Abby say under her breath as we walk through the crowded restaurant.

"What is it?" I ask, seizing the opportunity to once again put my hand on her lower back.

"There's just a lot of people here," she whispers.

"Well, yes," I chuckle sarcastically. "It has great reviews. And, of course, three Michelin stars."

"Here you are," Cassandra smiles, batting her lashes at me. "I'll have someone alert Mr. Caruso that you're here, Mr. Antonov."

"Thank you," I say, swallowing hard, and hoping that Abby didn't catch the girl's lingering stare, or the suggestive way she said my name.

"You know," Abby says, as I pull out her chair. "When you said you got a table here, I guess I thought that you were going to do that celebrity thing."

"That celebrity thing?"

"You know, where they have a private room, or they shut down the restaurant for an hour for you to eat in private without all these people staring at you?"

I grin. And not just from her comment, but from the fact that as I push in her chair, I catch my rebellious assistant pulling at her tight black skirt.

"Considering that this place already has a five-month waiting list, that would be incredibly selfish of me."

Abby rolls her eyes.

"Somehow I doubt that would stop you."

"That's true," I wink at her as I take my seat. "But forgive me, I thought you *liked* people staring at you, Abby? I mean, why else would you wear skirts that short?"

She glares at me, but then slowly a devious little grin spreads across her pretty face.

"Maybe because I know it bothers you."

Holy fuck.

The room suddenly feels warmer, and I instinctively have to adjust my shirt collar.

"I just can't help myself," she continues. "I guess I just enjoy torturing you, *Mr. Antonov.*"

However, the tone in which she says my name matches the exact way that Cassandra had said it, which tells me that she *did* pick up on the fact that there was at least a carnal history between us.

…And it bothered her.

"Oh, no, Miss Wayne, not in the slightest," I smile darkly, locking eyes with her. "I do love some good torture. I'll just have to be sure to return the favor."

And once again, I watch in real time as the power dynamic shifts, and her momentary arrogance shatters on the table before me. Her eyes find mine and once again I'm reminded of the real reason, I decided to bring her to lunch: To understand her. And her motivations.

Typically, when it comes to my employees, especially my female employees, it's not hard to figure out what they're after, because it's usually just *me*. Or at least the part of me that is partially bulging between my legs as I stare back at Abby's deep brown eyes, now sheepishly peaking at me over the top of her menu.

At first I tried to tell myself that I'm only struggling to read her like the others because I've harbored a buried physical attraction to this woman for longer than I can remember. But every day that I spend with her, picking up the tiny fragments of her cues and personality, I'm learning that's not the case.

It feels as if Abby and I are locked in a chess match. On the surface we're both deflecting and downplaying our true intentions. We're both playing a strategic long game to discover our opponent's weakness…while burying our own.

I'm having difficulty reading Abby because she's deliberately difficult to read. And I find that incredibly intriguing.

After all, what dark secrets could an assistant *really* have?

I wasn't sure, but I was determined to find out.

As we wait for Alberto, I cleverly begin to grill Abby about her life. I ask about her childhood, education, and even her past relationships, trying to get her to tell me as much about it in as much detail as possible.

"Hello there!" A young male waiter says, stepping up to the table with a smile. "What can I do for you today?"

"Excuse me," I hold up my hand. "What is this? What are you doing?"

The man's face pales, and he looks back at me, stunned.

"Um, I think he's here to take our order, Roman," Abby says sarcastically. "You know, for food?"

"Yeah, except *I'm* not waited on by the help," I snap, appraising the man up and down. "I'm waited on by Alberto."

"Oh, um, yes," the man says nervously, smacking his forehead with his hand. "I knew that and should've started with that."

What the…

"Alberto…shit…I mean, *Mr. Caruso* wasn't feeling good, and he went home for the day," he says, stumbling over his words before swallowing hard. "My name is Trevor, and I'm the head waiter here so I'll be waiting on you today."

Something isn't right.

"No, you won't," I snap, irritably. "We're leaving."

"What?" Abby scoffs, waving at the young man. "Roman, that's rude as hell. I'm sure Trevor here is an excellent waiter and will—"

"I said we're leaving!" I snap at her, smacking my hand on the table and kicking my chair back at the same time. "Let's go. Now."

"Oh, my fucking God," Abby gasps, snatching her purse from the chair. "I cannot believe this!"

Brushing past "Trevor," I follow after Abby as she starts storming for the door and I immediately dial Cal.

"We have a problem," I growl into the phone. "It's Al."

But as soon as we step out onto the street corner, Abby is immediately in my chest.

"That was so fucking rude, Roman!" She snaps at me angrily. "I know that you're a big powerful CEO and you think you can do whatever you want, but it does not give you the right to shit on the little people who are just trying to make ends meet!"

"Abby, I—"

"That man was just trying to do his job, and you acted like a total asshole to him!" She continues, shoving her finger into my chest. "God, I'm so embarrassed to even be seen with someone who could be that—"

"Observant," I snap back at her, making her jump. "I wasn't being a dick, I was being cautious, Abby."

"What?"

I glance around quickly, the hair on the back of my neck standing on end. My heart is beating loudly in my chest, and yet I'm not entirely sure why. It's as if there is an energetic crescendo happening around us and I want us to be out of here as quickly as possible.

"What the fuck are you talking about, Roman?" She demands, confused.

Cal arrives on the scene with the car, and I immediately open the door.

"Get in," I bark at her, my eyes still scanning the street around us.

"What? No!" She says, crossing her arms. "You still haven't answered my question and—"

"I said get in the fucking car!" I snap, grabbing her arm and shoving her ass through the open door of the car and onto the seat. "I'll explain inside."

Stunned, but shocked enough by my forcefulness to at least be obedient, she pulls her legs inside and yanks the door closed.

Quickly I walk around the back of the car and hop into the opposite side.

"Cal, we need to take Abby home," I say quickly as he pulls away from the curb.

"What?"

"Yes, Boss," Cal nods from the driver's seat.

"Roman, what the fuck is going on, I don't understand what the hell just—"

BOOM!

The car is suddenly rocked by a massive explosion behind us. Turning to look, the front room of the small building that used to be Albertos is now a blazing ball of fire.

"Holy shit!" Abby gasps, throwing her hand to her mouth. "That was—"

"Yes," I say, still staring at the flames shooting out of frames of what used to be windows.

"Shouldn't we go back and help?" Abby asks, staring out the back window before shaking her head.

"No," I growl, staring out the windows of the backseat. "It's too dangerous."

"But how did…" she says, looking at me in disbelief. "You…you knew that was going to happen. How did you know?"

"No, I didn't," I say, shaking my head.

"Yes, you did, because you knew we needed to get out of there," she snaps, pulling back against the wall of the car.

I sigh. It's clear to me now that I'm going to have to explain something to Abby. But I have to be cautious in how I do that.

"I didn't know that was going to happen," I say quietly. "But I knew something was off."

"What does that even mean?" She scoffs throwing her hands in the air.

"Because of my…status," I say slowly. "I'm very cautious in who I allow to serve me. In any industry. I've been going to Albertos for years now, and the only person I've ever allowed to wait on me, was Alberto himself. Because I trust that man."

"Okay, but I still don't understand how you knew that bomb was about to go off," Abby demands, eyeing me suspiciously.

"I didn't know anything about…*this*," I say firmly, my eyes finding hers. "I only knew that I deliberately confirmed with Alberto that I was coming today, and there is no sickness under the sun that would have made that man miss waiting on me. I knew something was wrong, and I'm just grateful we got out of there in time."

Abby stares at me before looking back at the smoking street behind us, the sounds of sirens wailing in the street.

"Some lunch date," she says quietly.

But the look in her eyes tells me that for the first time Abigail Wayne isn't just afraid of me…she's suspicious.

After we dropped Abby off, there was only one place I wanted to go: Alberto's home.

The problem was that the media had the same idea.

It was expected, considering an award-winning chef's flagship restaurant had just been hit with a bomb, and according to the reports we were getting, nearly a dozen people had died with dozens more taken to the hospital with serious injuries.

And so, everyone was waiting on Alberto Caruso, expecting him to make some sort of a statement as to the cause of this tragedy.

But they would be disappointed.

Because when the police knocked on the door of Alberto's residence, they got no response. And when they entered, they found no one there.

I know this because my team and I were monitoring every police band in the area, listening in on their conversations. When we discovered that Alberto was not found at his residence, I knew immediately where we'd find him.

As a long-time married man with an estranged wife who preferred to spend the cold New York winters overseas in Malta, he'd found himself a mistress.

Stefania Rodero was known to our circle, as was their not-so-secret affair. She was the widow heiress of a packaging company, and she lived in a penthouse in Soho.

While the clumsy and confused police were rummaging around his empty apartment, speculating that Alberto had left town, Cal and I headed back to my penthouse and changed into more casual clothes, then we drove to Soho, to visit my old friend.

Given that the police were looking for Alberto, and likely surmising that he himself had something to do with the tragic fate of his restaurant, it wasn't going to take them long to find out about his affair and track down the couple.

So, we needed to get there first, in hopes of finding him, and getting him to explain what had happened.

We do a casual screen of the apartment, from a neighboring block, and using Lev's drone we found it dark, and seemingly vacant.

"Let's go see if they're home," I say anxiously, pulling up the hood around my head.

We park on a neighboring street and make our way into the building from the back exit to avoid the cameras. However, when we eventually make our way upstairs, Cal makes me aware of the fact that the security cameras in the hall have all been sprayed with spray paint.

"Someone came here for them," he says, as the two of us simultaneously pull out our guns and cautiously make our way down the hallway. "And they were professionals."

His assessment is confirmed as we reach the door to Stefania's apartment and find it ajar.

"Don't touch anything," I whisper using my elbow to open it.

My stomach twists. But nothing could've prepared us for what we find the moment we push the door to her penthouse open.

It's a bloodbath. Or at least it *was*.

Right there in the center of the expensively decorated living room, the stiff bodies of Alberto's security staff, and Stefania's maid, lay slumped on a giant Persian rug. Their mouths are gagged, their hands are tied behind their backs…and they each have a hole in the back of their head.

"Well, you were definitely right," I whisper carefully, unsure if Stefania had her own security cameras, or Bluetooth speakers set to record. "They were professionals. Because this wasn't a home invasion."

"No, Boss," Cal mumbles gruffly, staring off into the room to my left. "This was an execution."

As I turn the corner, I am met with a horrific sight. There, seated across from each other at Stefania's giant maple dining room table, are the happy couple.

They were each tied to one of her taupe cashmere dining room chairs, and their throats had been slit. The white walls are splattered with spray patterns that could only come from their severed jugular arteries, and their lifeless bodies now sit in a puddle of their own blood.

The oddest part, however, is that in stark contrast to the gruesomely messy scene, between them both, sits two flowers in a small glass vase.

"No blood splatter," Cal says quietly, motioning to the bright pale pink flowers. "How is that possible?"

"Because they were placed there *after* the murder," I nod, covering my face to snuff out the strong stench of death that permeates the room. "This was a hit. And *that* is a message."

Hours later I sit alone in my darkened penthouse, staring at the gas fireplace with a bottle of vodka in my hand. Caesar lays at my feet, napping peacefully.

The events of the day still don't feel real.

However, the news confirmed for me that the bomb at Alberto's was real. And so was the massacre at his mistress's house, which surprisingly had come to police's attention just a few hours after Cal and I had discreetly left the premises.

And yet, neither of these things are nagging at me as much as the uncomfortable thought that perhaps this wasn't all just an "unfortunate incident," or home invasion gone wrong, as the newscasters were saying on television tonight.

No, on some level, I know that that bomb at the restaurant today had been meant for one person: *me*. And it was unsettling.

Perhaps it's because I didn't see this coming, and being who I am, I make every effort to not just be in the know, but to stay ahead of it. It's not enough for me to just know this city's dark and dangerous secrets, I need to see them coming a mile away.

Cal and I hadn't said much on the way home, but we did discuss the possible motives behind such a violent act. Al wasn't just a Michelin-rated chef, or a longtime friend. He was a high-ranking representative for the Sicilian mafia.

While many assume New York's long and bloody history with the various factions of the Italian mafias is a thing of the past, those of us still involved in the underground know different. They still have a seat at the table, even if the balance of power has shifted to be an ongoing battle between us and the Irish.

The issue is that my relationship with Al was what had tied the Sicilians into *our* side of the war. And given that Cal and I were unable to find Al's phone in the apartment, I have to at least entertain the idea that Al and his mistress were murdered before the bomb at his restaurant…because they knew exactly when I would be there.

And now, me fleeing the restaurant with Abby mere minutes before the bomb went off could look incredibly suspicious to the Sicilians, who obviously take revenge to a new level.

Now the only thing I could hope to do was get ahead of those suspicions and meet with the rest of their leadership.

Or things could, and would, get very messy, very quickly.

And then there was Abigail Wayne. My little fox.

Of course, I was probably in the hole with her for teasing her with world-class food, only to practically drag her out of there when I realized something was off. But something was off with her too. And today's almost-lunch confirmed it.

Before the "date," as she had so eloquently put it, had gone to shit, I had her talking.

…But something she'd told me today had been a lie.

Almost immaculately, Abby had weaved a story about her past that was uneventful, peaceful, and dull. However, what had triggered my alarms was when she had briefly talked about her husband. Her ex-husband.

Who I knew to be *dead.*

I'd trust Anastasia's background file more than I would from NATO themselves. And if asked about a deceased partner, most available single women would openly share the fact that they were *widowed,* rather than deliberately making up some fictitious story about how their marriage had dissolved and he had moved overseas. Which is what Abby had told me.

Whether or not the reason is innocuous, it just confirmed for me that my clever little fox is hiding something.

She lied to me.

And yet, for some reason, I'm more turned on by her secret than disappointed, or even angry.

Is this the "edge" I sense about her?

My thoughts are interrupted, however, as I hear the key card lock unlatch. Instinctively I'm on my feet, aiming my gun directly at my front door.

But as it swings open, I learn that the unexpected intruder is only my very intoxicated brother.

"Pasha," I growl, quickly throwing the safety back on my gun and putting it back in my trousers. "I almost blew your fucking head off."

"Well, that would save me a hangover," he chuckles.

He takes two steps, and promptly trips over the step in my foyer, landing hard on the marble tile.

"Ow," he groans, but as I walk toward him.

Caesar rushes over to greet him, licking his face profusely and causing him to burst into a fit of laughter.

"Jesus Christ," I sigh, rolling my eyes helping him to his feet. "Why are you here? You do realize your penthouse is just below mine, right? Did you get lost?"

"No," he says, as I dump him onto the nearest couch. "I just got lonely."

"What no bikini model tonight?"

"Nah, bro," Pasha chuckles, kicking off his shoes and settling into the couch, draping his hand over his eyes. "I fucked her earlier. I even got out of taking her dinner because Alberto's had a fire or some shit like that."

"Yeah, some shit like that," I repeat, downing the rest of my vodka.

"So," Pasha says, peeking at me from beneath his arm. "Your new assistant is a hot little number."

"She's off limits," I snap immediately. "So don't even get any ideas about trying to stick your dick—"

"Relax, Ro," he chuckles. "I know she's yours."

"What? No…she's not mine…she's just…" I start to explain but find myself struggling to formulate sentences.

"Yeah, she *is*," Pasha says, draping his arm back over his face. "And no, we don't have to talk about it. I'm kinda tired anyway."

I should explain that Abby isn't *technically* mine. I should explain that I now think she has some secret she's deliberately keeping from me. I should explain the events of the day, and how they may or may not have a massive impact on how things proceed. I should explain a lot of things. But I don't.

Instead, I just stand there, trying to muster a response, but unable to concoct one, because the mere mention of her has me remembering the inexplicable effect this woman has on me.

"Sleep well, little brother," I say, turning on my heel and walking out of the room. "We have a big day tomorrow."

ANTONOV

CHAPTER SIXTEEN

Abby

Leaning against my kitchen counter I glare at the greenhouse replaying the day's events.

Roman caught me researching *Conium maculatum* for the greenhouse on company time.

Luckily men usually have zero idea what they are looking at when it comes to flowers, they simply see the colors and think it's just another white flower. But, no, *Conium maculatum* is known as poison hemlock, a species I haven't added yet to my collection. All parts of this plant are poisonous to both humans and animals.

There's a number of reasons I haven't added it to my collection, the first being that it can grow up to eight feet tall. It also isn't exactly the pretties of plants, and would likely stand out like a sore thumb, among all the flowers. Its stems are also hairless with purple spots, making it very easy to identify.

I was so focused on my research that when Roman randomly materialized behind me, he actually scared me.

He rarely comes to my desk, and has never once told me that we are leaving the office together. He never takes me anywhere, which ironically *would* make my job a lot easier if I could attend some of these meetings with him, just so I can make sure I am doing my job properly.

Both of my jobs.

The longer I'm here, the more names I add to my list.

Just this morning I added the office mean girls to it. Not because I think they are bad people, but more so because they're just mean, and love to make my life difficult whenever they can.

They also love to remind me that they've had Roman in ways that would get a nun banished, which ironically makes my blood boil, even if it shouldn't.

Because Roman is on the list too.

Fuck, no, he *is* the fucking list.

I suppose it's pretty telling that our first excursion away from the office ended with the damn restaurant exploding.

A bomb.

Roman took me for lunch, and there was a bomb.

Who is this man? And why wasn't he even phased by a bomb? There's clearly more going on with him, and this company, than what meets the eye.

However, if I'm being honest, I didn't care about the bomb as much as I cared about the fact that Roman Antonov took me for lunch.

Yes, I know. I'm heartless.

My obvious attraction to this man, who could very well be a killer, is becoming an issue. He's becoming a distraction. One that I cannot afford to have. Even now I fear I'm getting sloppy, considering he caught me researching poisonous plants.

A sigh escapes me, as I lean my head back.

Lily bumps her head against my leg, forcing me to bend down and stroke her soft fur.

"What do I do, Lilibug?" I ask, and she meows in response. "It's not as if I could just go to a bar and pick up a guy. Well, I could, but the problem is that most of them don't know how to use what's between their legs anyway."

She bows her head and bumps her head against my hand, her purr vibrating loudly in the quiet kitchen.

"I want a man who can use his dick as a weapon. Someone who's power compels me to submit to him, and who isn't afraid to get a little rough with me."

Upon saying it, however, I laugh.

"God, I'd be a therapist's wet dream, wouldn't I?" I giggle, my voice higher than normal.

Still chuckling to myself I stand, opening the cupboard behind me to grab her bag of cat treats. The moment Lily smells them sprinkling onto the counter she jumps up excitedly. I pat her little head and walk toward the stairs.

I bet I *would* be a therapist's wet dream.

In my journey toward healing, I've heard all sorts of advice, the strongest of which being that in order to fully move on, I need to rediscover who I am, and reclaim my power.

Well, I reclaimed power by killing my husband, and killing other abusers.

A therapist wouldn't know whether to arrest me, or to treat me, and lord knows a typical man would know even less than that.

That's the reason I know that any man I might pick up and bring home, would likely leave me unsatisfied.

That, and the fact that most of the time, I need it a little rough to get off.

My late husband used to give it to me rough, but that had little to do with my satisfaction, and more so because that was just another form of abuse. He got rougher each time, crossing each and every line I set. Looking back, I sometimes wonder if that's *where* the abuse started.

But my mind wanders.

How rough would Roman be?

I can tell he likes to take control, and he seems like the type who would like submission in the bedroom.

No, not like…*need.*

He needs submission, and not just from the people who work in the office, but from everyone in his life.

My insides clench as images flash in my head. Images of Roman, his head thrown back, ramming into me, his neck flexing as a bead of sweat rolled down his perfect abs.

God, I bet he would dominate me. And fuck, I'd let him.

The heat is replaced by anger as I remember the way some of the girls at the office look at him, or say hello to him. Alison and Jenny try relentlessly, but the worst offender is the blonde bitch from accounting.

Heather.

The same Heather from the story idiots one and two were telling me the other day, who had sucked him off in his VIP section.

I'd nearly forgotten about it until she strolled on to the floor yesterday and shamelessly flirted with him.

The way she'd seductively rolled "Mr. Antonov" off her tongue, her eyes glued to him, before not-so-subtly descending to his crotch. Each time she batted her fake eyelashes at him, I wanted to tear them off her eyes, and scratch her eyes out.

For no reason whatsoever, I'd almost wanted to mark my territory. Yet it was like something about Roman practically demanded I did.

Ugh. Stop it Abigail. Focus on the mark, not the man.

There was a lot of information to unpack from this lunch, and the more I learn about him, the more I feel like I might be slightly out of my depth here.

Obviously, the big thing was the bomb, but the other significant feature of interest was his comment about loving torture.

Who does he torture? And why?

He also seems a bit…paranoid.

The moment someone other than the owner came to the table to take our order he lost it. Poor Trevor looked petrified, stumbling through the rest of our entire interaction.

And speaking of our interaction, Roman went from being charming, and dare I say flirty one minute, to confrontational and flighty.

Then there was the timing. He'd marched us out of the building so fast I nearly got whiplash. And the bomb goes off *conveniently* just after we leave, and the man isn't even fazed?

He gave me some bullshit explanation, but I couldn't help but feel like it didn't really fit with who Roman is, nor did it do anything to quell my suspicions.

Today has confirmed one thing for me though: attractive or not, Roman Antonov is a bad person.

And bad people don't live very long around me.

Roman glides onto the floor like a phantom, the air around him crackling as I bend down to grab the stapler.

"For fucks sake…" I hear him grumble. "Abigail! How many fucking times do I have to tell you that your skirt is to fucking short! I can see your cunt from here!"

I immediately straighten.

Who the fuck does he think he is?

I turn my head slightly to glance at him over my shoulder, seeing his massive frame practically vibrating.

"Is my skirt distracting you again, Sir?" I say, raising an eyebrow at him.

Roman glares at me, his eyes locked on my ass. Out of the corner of my eye, I see movement behind him, and that's when I happen to catch Oleg standing just off to the side, biting his lip.

Watch him love this.

Raising it in the air, I gingerly hold the stapler between two fingers, before deliberately letting it fall.

"Oops, my bad, I'm so clumsy sometimes!" I smirk, covering my mouth with my hand playfully. "But I do have a lot of paperwork to do today, *Boss*."

I turn, bending down to pick it up slowly, as I hear him growl behind me.

"Oleg! Office. Now."

"Yes Boss." He squeaks, darting around him into Roman's office and slamming the door closed.

Roman steps toward me, his eyes narrowed.

"You are asking for trouble, Foxy. Do not test me."

"Or what? You'll fire me?" I laugh, "Fat chance of that really. Your schedule has never been more organized, and I'm pretty sure all your Department Heads like me better than you."

His jaw flexes.

"You know as well as I do, Roman, that you'd never get any work done around here without me," I say, my voice smooth and seductive.

He growls in response, clenching his fist as he turns, muttering to himself about skirts and women as he walks toward his office.

However, just as he opens the door, he turns to me once again.

"I didn't have time to get my coffee. Go to Roast and fetch me one." He says, walking toward me again, "Oh, and while you're at it, go ahead and buy yourself a pair of pants."

He reaches into his pocket and pulls out his wallet, tossing a black American Express on my desk in front of me.

"Consider it a bonus."

And with that, he walks into his office and slams the door closed behind him.

Honestly, I don't even know how the door is still attached to the wall at this point.

But if Roman Antonov thinks for a second that I'm going to buy a pair of pants, then he is sorely mistaken.

My shopping bags swing in the breeze as I walk down the city sidewalk.

His card took a beating, and I'm so looking forward to seeing his face when he sees the little leather skirt I bought, that is far shorter than the one I wore to work today.

Roman wants me to wear pants? Hah!

I head toward his preferred coffee place on the corner, Roast. When I googled it, it said they are well known for their 'high quality coffee beans'.

Even though he never asked me to fetch him a drink before, I still know what his order is.

Coffee, black with no sugar.

Bitter just like him.

It suddenly occurs to me that this is the opportunity I need, my chance to finally be able to put down another monster.

Yet I find myself hesitating.

The thrill that I normally feel before I take someone out is a high. I love the ride, but this time there is no high. Just a sinking feeling in my stomach as I order his drink.

And even as I covertly drop the Widowmaker in, using a packet of sugar as cover, the thrill still doesn't come.

Shrugging, I pop the lid back on the warm little cardboard cup and glance around, taking a deep breath.

Time to go put down another monster.

The slow melody of the elevator music fills my ears as I step inside, the doors slowly closing behind me. I watch the light flashing as it ascends upwards, passing each floor.

I rub my sweaty palm down my new skirt, feeling my heart racing and the leather sticking against me. I glance at myself in the reflection of the door.

Roman is going to hate this.

…Which makes me happy.

If I twist it slightly you can almost see the black lace thong that I have on underneath.

I don't know why I put it on, Roman will be dead by this evening yet I still want to piss him off. The rise I get out of him matches the thrill I get from killing a man.

And I don't know why.

As the elevator approaches his floor, my eyes focus on the twentieth-floor button. Part of me has always wondered what Roman's penthouse looks like above us.

The elevator dings, and the doors open. However, as I step out onto the floor, I notice that all the lights are dimmed in the office.

That's strange…it's only quarter to eleven?

"Roman?" I yell through, peering around the corner of the hall.

"Office." He yells back.

Shakily, I walk forward, wobbling a little in my six-inch heels as I head toward his voice.

Jesus…I wasn't this nervous when I killed my husband.

Roman Antonov has a dark side to him, one that was probably never balanced in the first place. I never know what move I'm going to make that will cause him to go off the rails, and I have no idea what he's going to throw at me next.

But I *like* that about him.

Peering into his office, I see that his desk is still piled high with paperwork and his hair disheveled. He stands, his long legs bringing him directly in front of me as he reaches for his coffee, his fingers gently brushing against my hand, sparks ignite, and I feel the shock course through me.

My eyes watch his trail down my body to my skirt.

"Abigail," he says, his voice deadly calm. "What the fuck is that?"

"You said it was a bonus, so…." I smirk, my throat dry. "Thank you."

It thrills me to see the glare reflected in his deep blue eyes way more than it probably should. Something about him feels familiar, safe.

Like how I imagined *home* would.

He bites his lip, his eyes darkening as he walks back to his desk, placing the coffee down in the center of the paper piles, my eyes lock onto it.

He's going to drink that. And then he's going to die.

He turns, walking around me, circling me like a lion would appraise his prey. He stops behind me, his breath warming my cheek as he whispers.

"The lace doesn't cover a single thing, Abigail."

His voice is dark and gravelly.

"It…it…" I clear my throat, "It was too cold to wear nothing at all."

How does this man, this infuriating man, manage to fluster me? Every. Single. Time.

"Honestly Roman, you shouldn't even be looking. It isn't professional."

"Fuck professional, Foxy, you haven't been professional this entire time."

"Foxy?" I ask, scrunching up my nose. "Why are you calling me *Foxy*?"

"Because you, Abigail, remind me of a fox. Elusive, cautious, even jumpy at times. And yet there's something in the way you move," he says walking toward me slowly, his eyes holding me in place. "Something darker on the fringes, that's cunning and dangerous. Like a predator that innocently disarms their prey before delivering that deadly blow."

His voice is low and lethal as he stops so close to me, I can smell his cologne. He leans in to whisper, his lips practically touching my ear lobe.

"Your actions are deliberate and calculated, little fox. So, it begs the question as to why you walk into the lion's den every day, dressed like *that*. Do you have no self-preservation? Or are you trying to be devoured?"

My eyes fall closed, trying to get a handle on my sporadic breathing, my heartbeat running wild in my chest.

Can he hear it?

My eyes flutter open as I feel the heat of him against my back, he walks in front of me, my neck straining to look up at him. Reaching forward, he plays with a strand of my hair, rubbing it gently in his fingers before tucking slowly behind my ear. I shudder as a shiver runs down my spine.

I have no idea what to even say in response to that.

He smirks, walking away from me as he heads back to his desk. I watch as his suit jacket strains over his muscles as he leans across the desk to pick up his coffee.

His coffee.

This is it.

My heart pounds as I see him lift the cup to his lips…

"Fuck you, Roman." I spit, unable to keep myself quiet.

"What?" he says.

"You heard me, you act like you're so high and mighty all the fucking time, constantly coming at me for what I'm wearing. I do everything you ask, yet all you constantly bitch about is my skirt. My *skin*. It's my skin, that you seem to despise."

"That's not true—" he starts to say, his eyes flashing.

"I can wear whatever the fuck I want to wear, whenever I want to wear it. If I want to come to work fucking naked, I will!"

"Fuck no you won't," he spits, stepping toward me.

What am I doing? Why am I saying any of this?

"My body. My choice." I throw back at him.

"My money, my choice." He smirks, "Considering I fucking paid for it apparently."

"I'll pay you back for it!" I snap, my chest is heaving as he stops in front of me, staring down at me with a look in his eye that threatens to set the whole executive floor on fire.

He smirks, shaking his head, before raising his coffee to his lips again.

That's when I feel it happen.

I snap, my hand darting out and knocking the coffee clean from his hands, I watch it seep into the rug, slowly turning it dark brown.

Oh shit.

All I can hear is our breathing as we both just stare at the coffee on the floor.

Roman's mouth opens, and without thinking I slap him straight across the face.

My hand burns.

The imprint is already visible on his defined face. I didn't think, I just reacted. His head turns to me slowly, his eyes dark, glistening, a dangerous rage held within them.

It's a look I've seen only once before…

He's pissed.

His body stiffens, and I know what's coming. The anger. The pain. My heart stops.

And then he pounces.

His hand wraps tightly around my throat, slamming my back into the door behind me. My lungs heave, trying to regain the air he slammed out of them, but I can't. His fingers twitching in time with my pulse racing.

Can he feel it too?

Instinctively, I raise my fists, preparing to use my claws if I have to, only for him to grasp them with his free hand, locking them almost painfully above my head.

I wanted this reaction. Fuck, I needed it.

But I *shouldn't* want this.

My pulse racing and my body is vibrating with a need I've never experienced. What is this electricity that's sparking between us?

No man has ever made me feel so…*alive.*

I kill men like him. I kill men who hurt people. I kill men who hurt me.

But not *him.*

I can't hurt him…and I don't understand why.

"Why do you do this, Abby?" He growls, stepping into me. "Why do you constantly push and push?"

I can feel the hard lines of his body pressed tightly against me. As if I don't know where I end, and he begins.

"Because… I fucking can," I murmur, my eyes focusing on his lips. "And you know you *like* it."

His eye twitches.

"Don't ever do that again," he smirks, touching his nose to mine. "Or I'll have to punish you."

"*Punish me*?" I laugh. "Like hell that's happening."

He laughs, such a rich sound, one that vibrates through me and instantly puts me on edge.

He knows. I mean, he *has* to know? Right?

My eyes dart down to the spilt coffee soaking into the rug.

Along with the poison that was meant for *him*.

His knee slides between my legs, pressing against my heat, sending shockwaves through my body, rattling me to my very core.

"I can feel how wet you are for me, Foxy. Fuck, you're practically soaking my leg."

"No, I'm fucking not!" I snap, my cheeks heating.

"Yes, you are," he grins darkly. "I bet you regret wearing this skirt now, don't you? I told you what would happen if you kept disobeying me." His knee presses harder, causing my head to drop back against the door with a thump. His fingers clench around my neck as he pushes himself away from me.

"Now be a good little slut…and bend over my fucking desk."

My breath hitches in my throat.

Roman Nikolai Antonov was supposed to die today.

…So why do I find myself walking over to his desk?

ANTONOV

A
ANTONOV

CHAPTER SEVENTEEN

ROMAN

I've never been one for restraint.

I'm very proud of the opulence and indulgence in the life I lead. It's far from a secret, and practically public knowledge. And given that lifestyle, and the fact that I'm the one and only Roman Antonov, the favorite son of New York City, and the same man that Jaxon Pace refers to as the *Russian Rooster,* I don't have to bother with stupid bullshit like restraint.

I'm a monster, and my only drive in life is to acquire, consume and destroy anything and anyone in my path.

So, where Abigail Wayne is concerned, my exercise in restraint should probably qualify me for sainthood.

I lusted after her for years, but never acted on it.

I lusted after her at the club, but never acted on it.

I've lusted after her since I hired her, but never acted on it.

…Until today.

Today the invisible line that I told myself I shouldn't cross has been obliterated, the moment she smacked me.

My cheek stings as I watch her shaking legs obey my command and walk over to my desk. Her dark brown eyes find mine, and I watch with bated breath as she slowly bends over.

The little fox has wandered into my den…and now I'm going to devour her.

My heart is hammering in my chest, and my cock is throbbing in my pants as I take a step towards her.

But just as I do, the elevator dings behind me. Immediately, my head whips seeing Jenny and Alison come into view as the doors slide open.

I turn, deliberately blocking Abby from their view, not wanting their nosey prying eyes to taint this moment for me.

"Go the fuck home!" I snap at them both, before they even have a chance to step off the elevator. "If you're not gone in five seconds, you're both fucking fired!"

"Erm…yes, Boss!" Alison yelps, her eyes wide as she frantically hits the elevator button repeatedly, causing the doors to close.

As I turn back around, I pull out my phone, opening my text thread with Cal. Locking eyes with Abby I press the voice record button.

"I'm to be undisturbed for the rest of the afternoon," I say into the phone. "If anyone sets foot on this floor, I will have their head."

Abby, who is still bent over the edge of my desk with her head resting on her hand, inhales deeply.

Yet she doesn't *move*.

Why? Because deep down, despite pretending otherwise, she knows as well as I do, that she actually wants this. She wants *me*.

And she will have me.

…But first, I'm going to spank the fuck out of her.

My eye catches one of the large decorative vases in the window, filled with fake reeds of pussywillow.

How convenient. And slightly ironic.

But I want my *hands* on her first.

I walk toward her, unbuttoning the cuffs on my dress shirt and slowly rolling them, without breaking eye contact with her. Reaching forward I cup her gentle face in my hand, running my fingers along the base of her jaw.

"You," I growl softly, "have been a very, very, bad girl, Miss Wayne."

"I…I know," she whispers back, swallowing hard.

"So, you understand that you must be punished," I say gently, tipping her chin up to face me. "And you know how I'm going to do it, don't you?"

She nods, but I shake my head.

"No, no," I say firmly, pulling her bottom lip down with my thumb. "I want to hear you *say* it."

Her pupils dilate, and I can hear her rapid breathing.

"You're…going to…spank me."

"Yes," I growl. "Yes, I fucking am."

"Is it," She asks, biting her lip. "Going to hurt?"

I grin.

Slowly I walk around to the edge of the desk on which she leans and take a seat, running the tips of my fingers along the inside of her thigh, making her gasp.

"Yes," I snarl, grabbing the edge of her impossibly short leather skirt and pulling it up.

The moment I see her black thong riding up the slit of her perky thick ass, and the matching black lace garter belt holding up her stockings, my chest heaves.

Fucking hell she's hot.

Abby is like every vice, every addiction, and every Achilles heel rolled into one, and I want her more than all of them combined. Desperately.

I hook my finger inside her little G-String and pull it down, hearing her moan as I trail it down her leg.

"I'm afraid it *will* hurt," I run my hand along the soft skin of her ass cheek, until I reach the place where it meets her thighs, feeling her legs start to shake. "In fact, when I'm done, turning your little rump as red as a cherry, it might even hurt to sit down later."

"Oh God!" She groans, feeling me now slip my hands inside of her thighs, brushing the lips of her pussy with my thumb.

"Little fox," I whisper viciously. "After the stunt you just pulled, flaunting this in front of me, even God can't help you."

Without warning I suddenly pull my hand away, and bring it down hard against her ass cheek, making her yelp.

"But I think a good spanking is exactly what you deserve," I say as I rub the spot I just struck, squeezing it. "No, actually, it's not what you deserve. It's what you *need*."

Again, I bring my hand back, this time striking her other ass cheek.

"Eek!" She cries out, burying her head on my desk as my hands rub over the rapidly reddening flesh.

"Now, now, I don't want to hear you," I laugh, darkly. "You're the one who wanted to play your dangerous little games. So now you get to reap the reward you've sewn here."

Wrapping my arm around her waist to keep her firmly in place, I repeat the process several more times, each time alternating which side I strike, and immediately rubbing some of the soreness away. And with each slap of my hand, I can feel Abby's thick legs shaking beneath me, and hear her stifled little moans, making my already swollen cock throb.

"As I said," I grin, bringing my hand down hard once more. "I bet this has gotta be so hard for you, knowing it's so easy for me to just slip my hand up here and have access to such sensitive little parts."

As I say this, I place my hand between her legs and run my fingers along her slit.

Jesus fucking Christ. She's soaking wet.

Unable to resist, I slip a finger barely inside her pussy lips, feeling her arousal dripping down my hand.

"Oh my Goddddddd!" She moans loudly, her voice hitching.

Turning slightly, I pull her face up to mine.

"Bet you regret wearing that sorry excuse for a skirt now, don't you?" I hiss in her ear, sucking on her earlobe.

That's when I feel her stiffen.

"No," she breathes defiantly shifting from the pain. "I fucking don't."

"Not yet," I grin, biting my lip. "But I've only gotten started."

I bring my hand down again. And then again. Each time allowing the sting to resonate just long enough that I hear her gasps and grunts, telling me that Miss Wayne is struggling.

Only when she finally whimpers at my soft caress, do I know she's reached her breaking point, and I instead slip my hand between her thighs and stroke her soft bare pussy.

"Oh fuckkkkk!" She moans, as this time I don't waste my time teasing her and instead push my fingers deep inside her.

She tosses her head back and I wrap my other hand around her neck as I swirl my fingers around inside of her.

"Filthy little fox," I growl, pulling in and out of her aggressively. "Your cunt is dripping."

I bring my fingers to my lips and when her eyes meet mine, I suck her cum off of them.

"Delicious."

With my hand still around her throat, I pull her upright and grab the front of her blouse, ripping it open straight down the seam sending the ivory buttons trickling to the floor.

"My top!" she gasps, her perfect breasts heaving in her black lace bra.

"Bill me."

And without another word I grab the back of her hair and crush my lips to hers, shoving my tongue into her mouth. She moans, kissing me back.

I bury my face in her neck, biting and sucking, tasting the salt on her skin as I make my way down to her breasts. Using one hand, I unlatch the clasp in the back, freeing her tits from the delicate fabric.

She reaches for me, fumbling with my belt and frantically freeing my cock from my pants.

"I'm not finished with these tits yet," I growl on her lips, gripping her breasts in my hands, and squeezing them hard. I bend down, wrapping my mouth around each of her nipples sucking hard, hearing her whimper.

But that's not enough for me.

"Argh!" She groans, as I nip it with my teeth.

Perfect.

"I told you not to make a sound," I hiss, my voice low and raspy as I grab the back of her hair again. "Maybe you need something to fill that sassy mouth of yours."

Forcing Abby to her knees, I grab my cock with my other hand and stroke it slowly, watching as her eyes widen.

Oh, Miss Wayne, I'm going to have fun fucking you.

"Open wide," I whisper darkly.

For a second, she hesitates, staring at the massive length of my cock, and the smallest part of my brain wonders if perhaps this is too much for her. But then I see the wicked grin spread across her face, and I realize that her hesitation isn't reservation…it's desire.

"Yes, *Sir*," she winks at me, deliberately accentuating that word before opening her red lips and sticking her tongue out.

Releasing my fistful of her hair I push the tip of my cock into her mouth and lean down to whisper in her ear.

"Go on then, be a good slut and show me what you've got."

Abby accepts my challenge, immediately wrapping one hand around my leg, grabbing my balls tightly with the other, before taking my entire erection down her throat. She swallows me, looking up at me with her deep brown eyes as she does.

Holy fuck.

Pumping me several more times, I struggle to stay standing. Gently, I place my hand on the back of her head, while stretching the other back behind my head, catching my reflection in the window.

I said I'd never fuck in my office, yet here I am on the twentieth floor, getting blown by the sexiest woman I've ever laid eyes on.

God, it's good to be me.

She pulls back and swirls her tongue around the tip and my entire body shudders.

"I take it you like that," she chuckles arrogantly, deliberately doing it again.

Oh no, I'm not having that.

I grip her hair and yank her head back, exposing her neck and collarbone.

"If you're talking, then you're not working hard enough," I snarl, before shoving her head down, forcing my cock back down her throat, making her choke.

I repeat the process, before letting her up for air. She coughs, water forming in her eyes.

"Caught your breath? Good."

Again, I shove her head down on my cock, fucking her mouth until once again her face reddens. This time I release her and she collapses back on her feet, gagging and gasping for air.

But I'm not done with her.

I grab her by the shoulders and pull her up, bending her over my legs and spanking her ass again, making her yelp. Reaching over, I yank one of the fake pussywillow reeds from the large vase so forcefully it sends it crashing to the floor, the pieces shattering all over my now coffee-stained Persian rug.

Having caned more than a dozen partners in the past, I know exactly where to strike the reed across her backside, and that I don't need to use the same amount of power. Even still, when the reed comes down on her perky ass, she shouts loudly, wincing in pain.

"Aw, is that too much for you, bad little girl?"

"Fuck you!" She fires back defiantly.

"Oh, I will, but only after I've given you something to remember me by."

I smack her bottom again, hearing her sharp intake of breath. And then again.

"Arrgh!" She cries, as I deliver a fourth blow, squirming on my lap.

"I think one more for good measure," I whisper, biting my bottom lip before whipping her a final time.

"Fuck! That stings!" She whimpers.

"It's supposed to," I say, picking her up in my arms. "Perhaps if you wore clothes with a bit more coverage, this wouldn't have been so bad. But you wanted to be a little slut, so now you're paying the price."

I spin her around and lay her on her back, sending the majority of the shit on the top of my desk crashing to the floor without so much as a second thought.

Abby winces, likely from feeling the cane marks on her ass. But I'm about to distract her from the pain.

Stepping up to the edge of the desk, I pull open her knees and hook my arms around her thighs, pulling her down to the edge. She moans like a whore the instant I press my lips to her beautiful pussy, slipping my tongue vigorously inside of her.

"Oh my Goddddd," she shouts, throwing her head back against the desk and thrusting her hips against me.

Pressing down on her stomach, and tightening my grip around her shaking legs I devour her, sucking and swirling my tongue around her clit, tasting her delicious cum. I keep her firmly in my grasp as I shove my long index finger back inside of her.

Fuck my life, she's so tight.

I've never felt anything like it.

"How's that feel, baby girl?" I growl, the taste and scent of her pussy driving me absolutely mad.

"It's…it's…" she stutters, her whole body convulsing. "So good. Please, don't stop."

"Have you learned your lesson, Miss Wayne?" I ask, pulling out and slipping another finger inside of her, this time pressing upwards directly against her swelling G-Spot.

"No. I mean…yes…I…I…Oh, God, fuck, I don't know!" She breathes, as I work my fingers even harder.

"I'm afraid I'm going to need an answer," I grin, now rhythmically flicking her clit, feeling her muscles contracting around my fingers.

"Oh shit! Shit! If you keep doing that then…then…I'm going to cum, Roman!"

"Not yet," I growl pulling out of her and rubbing her arousal all over my now throbbing erection. "I want it to be on my cock."

"Oh fuck! Yes!" She says, gripping my shoulder so hard I can feel her nails digging into my skin.

"Tell me how bad you want me to fuck you, Foxy," I growl, rubbing the tip of my cock between her lips. "Say it for—"

But her hand comes down hard across my face once again, stunning me momentarily.

"Will you just shut up and fuck me?" She snaps angrily. "Stop talking and fuck me!"

That does it.

I ram into her hard, taking her breath away, and forcing myself inside of her impossibly tight pussy and immediately grabbing her throat.

"Slap me like that again, Miss Wayne," I snarl at her venomously, thrusting into her over and over as her eyes roll back into her head. "And I swear to God, I will fuck this pussy of yours so hard that I'll put your ass in a coma."

I lean in, biting her earlobe slamming into her again.

"...And *then* I'll fuck you whenever the hell I please."

"Holy shit!" She gasps, her jaw dropping.

Over and over, I plow my cock inside of her, as her whorish moans echo throughout the office. Without pulling out, I grab her ass and pick her up, walking her over to the glass wall of my office and slamming her body against it.

And then I continue fucking her.

"Ro…Roman," she groans, her eyes clenched shut. "I'm going to cum."

"Cum," I command, my own orgasm building. "And you better make sure I can feel it dripping down my leg."

"Yes, *Sir*," she breathes, and I feel her shudder and her arms wrapping around me tightly as she climaxes.

Unable to resist the sensation of her pussy clenching around me, I empty myself inside of Abby, certain that I have never felt so alive…and that I am finally home.

"They're ready for you, Boss," Cal says, as we walk down the hallway of my Chelsea Pier warehouse. "I think we've extracted as much information as we possibly can."

I say nothing, pulling on my leather gloves as he opens the door, and we step inside the room in what we affectionately call *The Block*.

This place is my fortress. My castle. My refuge. And essentially my back-up plan if any and all hell breaks loose in the city, and we need a place to retreat to.

I bought the massive building not only because it was in a prime location at Chelsea Pier, just off the harbor with direct access for freight off-loading, but because it's also a four-story warehouse that was used to house drilling and construction equipment.

And it's built like Fort Knox.

I started calling it The Block because the security this building provided is unparalleled. The floor is one gigantic concrete slab, and instead of wood or aluminum walls, which are standard for most New York shipping warehouses, mine are actually reinforced concrete. The building itself is near impenetrable, having withstood tornadoes, at least one hurricane and even the occasional earthquake, I was fairly confident that only a nuclear blast could make a dent in this beast.

That's why I keep my central command team here, as well as my main armory. Equipped with a massive generator, there's also a kitchen, storage, and even some basic, but relatively small living quarters in the upper levels. On top of that there was a helicopter pad on the roof, and escape tunnels that led underneath the road to a fleet of small boats in the harbor. This provided me with multiple escape routes, which is something that's always important to a mafia don.

But to me, the main benefit to this warehouse isn't the security, accessibility, amenities, or even the escape routes.

It's the animal rendering plant next door.

As a don, sometimes we require a discreet, swift, and relatively clean way to rid ourselves of a body or two.

With a monthly payment to the man who runs the facility, he's willing to allow us to add our occasional "trash" into his grinder and look the other way.

When I step into the main room, and see two men tied to two rusty metal chairs placed directly above the sewer drain, I know that *they* know, this little interrogation will only go one way: *Mine*.

"Well, this is certainly an interesting reunion," I say, walking around the first man in the chair and crossing my arms in front of my body. "It's good to see you again, *Trevor*."

The terrified waiter from my ill-fated date with Abby at Albertos looks up at me. His face is bruised, and both his nose and lip are bleeding profusely.

Cal silently carries a second chair forward and sets it down in front of Trevor.

"That cut looks pretty nasty," I say, motioning to his busted lip. "What happened?"

"They broke my…" He says, looking up at me briefly.

However, as he does, he also makes eye contact with one of my "extractors," Jacques standing behind me. Jacques's main job is to interrogate our prisoners before I arrive, by any means necessary… providing he keeps them alive.

And knowing the sick shit that Jacques and his clueless little brother Noah are into, it looks like they took it easy on Trevor tonight.

"Sorry, Boss," Jacques says, wiping blood off his hands. "The last guy took us longer than we thought. We were just getting started with this one."

That explains it then.

"I asked you a question," I say quietly.

Trevor swallows hard and looks down at the floor.

"I mean *I* broke my tooth," he says, his voice trembling. "And it cut my lip."

I smirk.

Most people in his position would likely out the man who just beat the living shit out of him. After all, Trevor and the terrified man next to him have to understand that the probability of them leaving this place in one piece is slim to none.

However, the beaten and battered Trevor, just chose to keep his mouth shut. It's a gamble that's unlikely to pay off, which is why I find that kind of awareness and bravery in the face of terror intriguing.

"Oleg," I snap, holding out my hand.

He opens his switchblade and a trembling Trevor flinches at the sound, screwing his eyes shut, and clenching his jaw as Oleg places the knife in my hand.

Appraising him carefully, I walk around him and cut the zip ties on his hands, freeing him.

But Trevor isn't stupid enough to run, likely aware of how many guns are pointed at him at the moment. Instead, he pulls his sore arms in front of him, rubbing his wrists and looking up at me. Stepping forward I sit down on the cold metal chair in front of him, handing him my handkerchief for his bleeding lip.

"Now, what have you told my men?" I ask.

"Boss, he told us that—" Noah starts to say, but I immediately hold up my hand, and glare at him.

"If I wanted to hear from you," I snap venomously. "I would've fucking asked you. So shut the hell up, or you'll go in the grinder with the rest of them."

"Yes, Boss," Noah nods, lowering his eyes to the floor and stepping back into the crowd that now encircles us.

"Go on, Trevor," I say with a smile. "I'm anxious to know how out of all the people who died in the explosion at the restaurant that day, *you* somehow made it out?"

"As I told them, Mr. Antonov," he says quietly. "I *was* hired by Cillian McCleary."

"Hired to do what exactly?" I ask, narrowing my eyes at him. "To kill me? To just drop a bomb in my *Cacio y Pepe* and then run for the door?"

He shakes his head, his eyes wide.

"Oh God No, Sir!" he says, swallowing hard. "He only asked me to let him know when you arrived. All they wanted was for me to call them if you showed up for your reservation."

"Well, you had to know about the bomb," I scoff softly. "Because how else would you have known to leave before it went off and killed people?"

"I swear to you, I didn't know anything about any bomb! I swear on my mother's life! After you left, I…I…" He says, his eyes falling from mine.

"Go on."

"Well, I went straight outside to smoke, and have a bit of a freak out," Trevor says quietly. "I thought for sure I'd done something to piss you off, and like you're…*you*. I mean, you're Roman fucking Antonov, and I was terrified that when Alberto found out I'd upset you, he was going to be furious with me, and fire me. So, I was outside in the back having a mental breakdown when the bomb went off."

I have to stop myself from smirking, my eyes finding Cal's who nods, silently confirming that he believes Trevor is telling the truth.

"And what about Alberto?" I ask, scanning his eyes. "Did Cillian McCleary tell you about his plans for *him*? How he, his girlfriend, and all their house staff were going to be brutally murdered with their throats slashed open?"

"Oh my God, no!" He gasps, covering his mouth. "You don't understand, Mr. Caruso was a *mentor* to me! He was helping me pay my way through culinary school. I would never, ever, betray that man! He was like a father to me. If I had any idea that he was in trouble or that I was going to bring him trouble…I…I…"

Trevor starts to hyperventilate, coughing and gagging loudly, panic written on his face.

"Oh my God," he gasps, trying to breathe. "Cillian used me. He…he…set me up! All over two-hundred fucking dollars that I didn't even get!"

"Two hundred dollars," I repeat, shaking my head, glancing up at Cal. "I suppose it's pretty easy to promise money to a kid that you think will die in the explosion. But that's how they do things."

"I can't believe this!" Trevor cries, his hands shaking. "I didn't know! I swear to God I didn't!"

"He's lying!" Jacques shouts from the crowd.

I tilt my head toward him.

"You know, I got to be honest, kid," I sigh. "They have a point. That's a hell of a story."

"Kill him! He's a snitch!" Boris yells in the back of the crowd, followed by the cheers and murmured agreement.

"I'm not! I promise!" Trevor pleads, his voice cracking. "I thought it was a strange request, but they offered me money when the job was done. And you know, I don't make much money as a waiter and—"

"Shoot the snitch!" Another voice calls from the rowdy crowd. "Kill him!"

"Oh, God," Trevor cries, burying his wet face in his hands. "I get it! I know now I fucked up, but if you're going to do it just, please do it quickly."

The crowd around me is like a pack of wild dogs, hooting and hollering for this man's demise. It's what makes them terrifying soldiers in my little army.

But it's also what makes them *wrong*. And in my experience, feral mobs rarely ever make the right choice.

Once again, I raise my hand in the air and the room around us goes silent. I stare at Trevor, before clicking my tongue in my mouth.

"Here's my dilemma, Trevor," I say quietly, leaning in and placing my hand on his shoulder. "As you can see, my men, well, they're very loyal to me. So, I can't just let you go, because then they won't be satiated without seeing you receive some sort of punishment, because they feel that what you did was unforgivable."

He whimpers, folding his shaking hands together.

"But the thing is," I grin. "I don't *have* to listen to any of them. Because as you said yourself. I'm Roman fucking Antonov. And around here, well, I'm *God*. I'm the one who makes the rules. And if I decide to spare your life, not a single one of them can touch you."

His eyes widen.

"Please!" He begs. "I'll do anything you ask! Literally anything. I promise!"

"See, I believe you," I smile at him. "But here's the thing. I'm going to need some sort of confirmation that your promise isn't just some heat of the moment thing. You know that you're not going to say one thing to my face, and then go running back to Cillian. Or the police. Because that would be just bad business."

"Please, Mr. Antonov," he begs. "I have no intention of ever going back to the McCleary's, and I'm no snitch. I made a mistake, but I know I can be of use to you. I...I'll join you! In whatever this...this *thing* is! If you just give me a chance, I promise I won't let you down. I'll be your man for life."

"For life, huh?" I ask as I stare at him, weighing the option in my mind. "That's a big promise, you know."

"I mean it," Trevor says, his eyes finding mine.

"Alright, kid," I say. "I'll give you one chance to prove yourself. But it's going to be here, and now."

Trevor nods excitedly.

"Come," I command, my voice echoing in the silent room.

Obediently, Trevor limps along behind me as we walk over to the other prisoner in the room, who sits a few feet away with a bag over his head.

"Cal," I say, staring at the man as he appears beside me. "Who the fuck is this?"

I kick the foot of the prisoner, and his muffled screams begin to echo against the warehouse walls.

"Boss, this is Todd Steinbeck," Cal says plainly. "He's a Wall Street Investor, for Steinbeck & Associates, which is Cillian McCleary's wealth management firm."

"And why is he here?" I ask, already knowing the answer but deliberately asking so Trevor can hear.

"As I understand it, he's the man who is in charge of the majority of Cillian's mutual funds and stock exchange investments. The same funds he's leveraging as collateral for the Walston Street deal." Cal explains.

"Steinbeck & Associates, huh?" I ask, rubbing my chin. "Any chance they are associated with *Stein & Co.*, the holding company for the Walston Street property?"

"That's what Ana thought, Sir," Cal nods. "Turns out they're distant cousins. Cillian probably thought he was being smart."

"But Ana was smarter," I grin. "As always."

"Yes, Boss. She said she wanted us to get the passcodes and transfer information," Cal whispers so that only I can hear him.

"So she can make that collateral disappear," I nod, suddenly understanding her motivations. "And disqualify him from the purchase."

Clever girl.

"Did she say what her intentions were with him?"

"I think," Cal says, raising his brows. "She intended for you to let him go if he gave us what she was after."

"And?" I ask. "Did we get them?"

Cal smiles.

Slowly, a wicked grin spreads across my face, as I stare at Cal, watching as my intentions slowly register in his eyes.

"Alright kid," I say, turning to Trevor next to me. "You said you wanted to prove your loyalty to me, right?"

"Yes!" Trevor says earnestly, glancing nervously at the mob still encircling us with their weapons drawn.

"That you'd be my man, loyal to me, for whatever I need, whenever I need it, correct?"

"Yes, Mr. Antonov," He nods, his eyes wide. "Whatever you need."

"Good. Kill him." I say, pulling my gun from my holster and handing it to Trevor. "*Now.*"

It's nearly quarter past two when I finally crawl into bed back at my penthouse.

But it's also when I receive the first text from Abby.

Little Fox
2:15am: Just to be clear, what happened today was a mistake. It won't be happening again.

I chuckle to myself, realizing that given the time of this text, she's likely been stewing on it for hours, wondering what I've been up to all night. Maybe even wondering why I haven't called her.

Though she would probably lose her shit if she knew.

Me
2:15am: Oh, it definitely will. But it's adorable you think that.

Little Fox
2:16am: I was hired to be your assistant, not your slut, Mr. Antonov. It's royally unprofessional.

Me
2:17am: Unprofessional or not, I can still smell your pussy on my cock. And I like it.

Little Fox
2:20am: Gross. And I'm serious, Roman. That was a one time thing. It's not going to happen again.

Me
2:21am: Yeah, you keep telling yourself that, little fox. Now go to bed, well-fucked ASSistants still have work in the morning.

As I lay back against the covers, I can't stop the wicked grin on my face.

A
Co
ANTONOV

CHAPTER EIGHTEEN

With a scream I throw my phone across the room, hearing the distinct sound of the screen cracking as it hits the wall.

Fuck.

What was I thinking?

I knew, I fucking knew that me submitting to Roman was going to be a mistake, probably the biggest one I've ever made. I knew the moment I had him once, I'd want him again and again. I can still smell him on my skin, I can still feel him between my legs.

Mr. Asshole
2:17am: Unprofessional or not, I can still smell your pussy on my cock. And I like it.

A shudder runs down my spine, because I can still taste him on my fucking tongue.

He was everything I expected him to be, and more. My God, he was fucking everything.

He should've died today. I should've ended him today.

But no, I slapped the coffee from his hands, watching it slowly seep into the expensive rug that lined his office floor. The first opportunity I had to end the monster, and I fucked it up…then let him fuck *me*.

I don't know what came over me, it was like I was possessed. I certainly felt possessed. My demons intertwined with his, twisting and bending until there wasn't a him and me, it was just *us*.

We came together like pieces of a puzzle, slotting into each other and completing an unachievable jigsaw.

My jaw pops.

I let him come inside me. I've never let a man, other than my husband, finish inside me.

Throwing my head back against my pillows I stare at the ceiling, my eyes drawn to a flaking piece of paint just by the light fixture.

"Alexa, lights off," I sigh, and she chimes a reply as all the lights dim, plunging my room into darkness.

I always think better in the dark.

A bitter laugh escapes me, at least I don't need to worry about Roman's spawn arriving in nine months, but I do need to worry about whether or not he's infected me with some disease, given the number of bitches he's stuck his cock into.

What happened today can never happen again.

Maybe I should actually quit, like I'd originally planned before the monster meeting in his conference room.

But since I just broke my phone, I can't do that either. Turning on my side, I close my eyes, only for Roman's face to fill my mind. The way his eyes narrowed as he watched his cock thrust in and out of me, is a memory that is seared into my brain like a brand.

It was like he couldn't quite believe that it was happening.

Neither could I really.

Never have I lost control like that. I swore four years ago I would never give a man that amount of control over me, even if I craved it. Yet today, in his office, I did.

And if I'm honest, I want to again.

However, *because* I want to, I know I can't. The taste of Roman was like a fucking drug, one that I refuse to get addicted to.

He was so aggressive.

I mean, I still have bruises on my ass from where he whipped me. By all accounts, I should hate him for that, and for being so rough with me.

But I don't.

I should hate him for destroying my blouse.

But I don't.

I should hate how he felt inside me.

But I don't.

And I should really hate him for not pulling out.

But I don't.

I squirm in my blankets, squeezing my legs around the pillow between my legs as I think about his seed dripping out of me. I could feel it as I ran out of his office, wrapped up in his coat…which now sits beside me on the bed.

It smells like him, and I find myself intoxicated by it.

When the fuck did this get so out of control?

I'd planned to kill him today, and ended up fucking him instead. But even if he learned of my deadly intentions for him, I'd still feel how I do now.

My eyes fall closed, as I take in a slow and steady breath, inhaling the scent lingering on his coat.

Roman feels like home, and for once, home feels pretty safe.

The pounding on my door wakes me, Lily jumps off the bed, her ears pressed back against her head, and a soft growl emanating from her small form at the intrusion. Sitting up, I wince, before sliding off the bed, my knees hitting the floor as I crawl over to my door, using it to stand.

Oh God…my ass is so sore.

Walking over to the mirror, I lift my dark green silk nightdress, feeling the cool material slide against my skin. Turning, my eyes widen at the sight of my ass, each cheek red, with a distinct handprint on the left cheek. Slowly, I poke a single finger against it, shuddering as pain ripples through me. Shivering as pleasure follows, as I watch it turn from white to pink as my blood flows back into the area.

The pounding at my door continues, louder this time, followed by a shout.

Who the fuck is here right now?!

Rolling my eyes I drop the dress back down, before flinging my bedroom door open and storming down the stairs.

I yank the front door open just as the man standing outside raises his fist to pound once again. He freezes at the sight of me, his eyes widening, before falling straight to the ground.

I know him. He's the man from the restaurant who waited on Roman and I. Or the man who *tried* to anyway. But he looks much different than when I saw him last. His skin is pale, a large deep bruise spreading across his face leading from his split lip.

What was his name? Todd? Tim?

But it occurs to me that no one knocks at my door. Not even my delivery drivers or mailman. So somehow, I know that Roman has something to do with this.

"Hello, Miss Wayne," he says, his voice rough, tired and void of any emotion.

"Good morning! Who are you?" I say cheerily.

"I'm your driver," the man says gently.

"Okay, but that still doesn't answer my question," I ask, still smiling sweetly. "*Who* are you?"

"I'm Trevor, Miss Wayne."

Cocking my head slightly, "Weren't you at the restaurant the other day? Albertos?"

"Um…yes," he mutters, his spine straightening, the more I stare at him, the more uncomfortable he looks. "Mr. Antonov sent me to fetch you because, well, um, you're late."

"I am? What time is it?" I say, cocking my head to the side as I appraise the man in front of me, one that still refuses to raise his eyes to meet mine.

"It's ten, ma'am," he says shortly.

Well… fuck.

I sigh, straightening my posture, waiting for him to look up at me, but as the minutes tick by the silence becomes deafening.

"I'm up here, darling, not on the porch," I snap.

Clearing his throat, his eyes slowly meet mine, as sweat runs down his neck.

"I…Mr. Antonov said—"

"I do not care what Mr. Antonov said, you will look at me when you speak to me," I finish for him, cutting off his stumbling as I glare at him, continuing I say, "Mr. Antonov is not here, so if you wish to talk to me, you will look at me, and show some fucking respect."

"Yes, Ma'am," he says, looking up at me briefly, smiling weakly.

"There we go," I grin. "Now, what is it you want?"

"Mr. Antonov sent me to collect you, as you didn't arrive as you were scheduled to. For work."

"Yeah," I say sheepishly, running a hand through my hair. "I broke my phone."

"Excuse me a moment," he says with a nod.

Without moving from his spot, he pulls out his phone, before quickly bringing it to his ear.

"Boss, all is well. She said she broke her phone...yes...no Boss...of course, Boss."

I open the door wider, causing Trevor to gulp, before casting his eyes down again. I can hear Roman yelling down the phone, tapping my foot, I interrupt the stumbling man before me.

"You can come in, you know."

That causes more yelling from the phone in Trevor's hand, and I have to fight the smile tugging at my lips.

Trevor flinches away from the receiver before shaking his head. "I'm sorry, Miss Wayne, I am instructed to remain outside."

Grinding my teeth, I glare at him.

"You will come inside, and sit on that couch," I say pointing behind me. "I need to shower, dress and get something to eat."

"But Mr. Antonov said—"

"I do not care what Mr. Antonov said. You either come inside my house, and wait, or leave without me. I can always go back to bed."

He silently stares at me, listening to whatever Roman has to say on the matter, before nodding his head and stepping forward.

"Excellent!" I clap my hands together, before closing the door behind him.

"Miss, Mr. Antonov would like an ETA on your arrival," he says, his eyes apologetic.

"Tell him I'm not sure," I shrug, turning for the stairs. "I'm moving slow, because I'm feeling a bit *tender* this morning."

After my shower I step into my walk-in closet, pondering what to wear. After my skirt yesterday getting me fucked on Roman's desk, maybe I should dress more... *conservatively.*

Pulling out a pair of dark gray pants, which I pair with a black long sleeve blouse I drop them onto my bed, before grabbing a pair of flats.

After tugging the pants on and buttoning up the blouse I stare at myself in the mirror, my eyes staring at my curves, and how the pants emphasize my ass, which feel tight against my sore skin.

But…I kind of like the pain.

"In fact, when I'm done, turning your little rump as red as a cherry, it might even hurt to sit down later."

He *had* given me something to remember him by.

No. I'm not going to go an entire day wincing every time I move, forced to think about *him*. I'm not giving him the satisfaction of that. Or feeling like he's won.

I don't reward bad behavior.

Flicking my hair over my shoulder, I pivot, turning back to my closet, tugging the pants down, and kicking them to the side haphazardly. Roman doesn't get to dictate what I wear, even if it means I have to fight off his actual dick, as well as my traitorous pussy.

I want to fuck him, but I also hate that I want to fuck him.

So, I won't.

But, if I can't, I can still have the thrill of this man wanting me and hating my skirts. Grabbing the shortest skirt I own, I slide it up my legs, fastening it at the side, before grabbing a pair of stockings and suspenders. With how short this skirt is, they are going to be visible every time I move.

Smiling, I giggle knowing this is going to piss Roman off more than anything else I've worn.

I intend to flaunt what he can't have and remind him how good that one time was. By the end of the day, the man will be salivating for me.

Walking over to the mirror, I quickly throw on some eyeshadow, deciding on a smokey eye. After adding my eyeliner, and making sure they are even, I coat my lashes with mascara. Satisfied, I quickly run my fingers through my hair, opting to let my waves cascade down my back.

As I step back, I admire my reflection, noticing how bright my eyes look today.

The truth is, I haven't felt this alive for a very long time.

With a bounce in my step, I walk down the stairs, before bending down and grabbing a pair of six-inch heels from the shoe rack.

A cough sounds from behind me, glancing over my shoulder I see Trevor, covering his eyes with his hand, and leaning his head back on the couch.

"You know, I'm assuming Mr. Antonov told you that you're not allowed to look at me, right?" I ask, throwing my hand on my hip.

Trevor says nothing but peeks out from behind his fingers.

"But it's going to be awfully hard to escort me to the office, if you can't see," I grin. "So, in order to make this easier, how about you lower your hand, and this stays between us?"

He pauses a moment, but then slowly, puts his hand back in his lap with a respectful nod.

"I'm just going to grab something to eat then I'm good to go." I call to him as I walk into the kitchen, hearing footsteps following behind me.

"Miss Wayne, could we get something from Roast?" he says, a note of nervousness in his tone.

Closing the cupboard, I glance at him, as he averts his eyes once again. He runs his hand down the front of his black pants, before quickly looking at me with a small smile.

It's then that I realize he's terrified. And as much as I enjoy torturing Roman, I don't want to torture Trevor in the process, who is innocent.

And fuck, it looks like he's already been tortured.

"They do have the best Panini's," I say, my voice soft.

He nods, before turning and heading toward the door.

As we get to the car, he turns quickly. "There's a new phone on the back seat for you, from—"

"Mr. Control Freak," I snort, rolling my eyes as I climb inside, distinctly wincing as my ass touches the seat.

We roll to a stop outside of Roast, which is bustling with customers.

My hand grips the handle, tugging it open as the car's central locking disengages. Before I can step out into the cool crisp air, Trevor calls out to me.

"Miss."

"Hmm?" I murmur, looking over at him, my eyes draw to his face, his skin paling.

"Please don't be long," Trevor says, staring forward in the car. Following his line of sight, my eyes focus on Jacques, who works a few floors below mine.

And he's on *The List*.

"Trevor?" I ask softly, but he doesn't respond, he doesn't even turn to look at me.

Leaning forward, I gently rest my hand on his shoulder, making him flinch and pull away.

He turns, the apology on the tip of his tongue, but I hold my hand up to stop him.

Nodding to his face, I ask, "How'd that happen?"

He shakes his head softly, "I… umm…fell down some stairs."

Once again, I notice the way his nervous eyes fly back to Jacques, who's chatting to a petite blonde while waiting for his order.

My heart stops as I glance back at Trevor, his eyes looking anywhere but at me as he picks at the stray lint on his jacket.

I remember *my* stairs.

Suddenly I'm pulled from the present to a memory I've successfully repressed…

My heart is pounding as I fly out the door, running from my monster. I hear him roar as he realizes before his footsteps pound down the hall behind me.

Oh fuck. Oh fuck. Oh fuck.

My hair whips across my face as I turn, slamming into the elevator door. Pounding my fist against the button, praying it comes before he does.

But it doesn't.

The monster appears in the hall, charging toward me.

I can feel the sweat trickling down my back.

I have to get away.

As I push away from the metal door, I scream in terror, flying straight for the emergency stairs. But just as I fling open the door, his body slams into my back, forcing me through the door into the stairwell.

His shouting echoes against the concrete walls, deafening me, and making his words indecipherable. Another scream escapes my lips as my eyes dart behind him, hoping and praying that someone, anyone, will appear and save us.

Tearfully my head shakes as I stare up at him, holding my stomach as I whisper pathetically, bracing myself against the metal railing. "Please."

His face is red, every single vein in his neck straining against his skin as he continues to spit venom at me. Sweat drips down his temple, and his eyes that look black in the fluorescent stairwell lights, bulge from his skull.

He brings his hands up to my shoulders, yanking me away from the wall.

For a second, I breathe a sigh of relief, thinking he's going to relent, and take us back to the penthouse.

But then his fists clench, pulling me further away from the door, backing me towards the stairs.

Time freezes as a singular word leaves his mouth.

"Whore."

"Abigail?" Trevor asks, turning toward me, and unknowingly pulling me from my memory. "Are you okay?"

It takes me a few seconds to remember what we were just discussing.

Stairs.

And the fact that Trevor's comment is almost certainly related to whatever abuse he's sustained at the hands of Jacques who continues to shoot venomous glances over at us.

"That's happened to me before too," I say quietly, glaring at Jacques. "Hopefully your *stairs* get some swift karma."

Luckily for Trevor, karma's my middle name.

His eyes meet mine in the mirror again, a look of recognition reflects back at me. It's interesting when someone realizes what I *actually* mean by that. Most people look at me differently, but Trevor looks at me with understanding.

With a nod, I step out of the car.

"Wait," I ask, turning back to face him. "How do you take your coffee?"

"Oh, Miss Wayne, I can't," he insists firmly, shaking his head.

This just makes me grin.

Nodding, I walk into the busy coffee shop, sighing only when I see that the line is nearly out the door.

Luckily, because the owner Chloe knows me, and knows who I work for, she immediately looks up from her tattered smutty alien romance and jumps to her feet, waving me over to a separate register.

"Miss Wayne," she says politely. "Mr. Antonov's usual?"

I smile.

"Actually no, Chloe," I say, pulling out Roman's black credit card. "I believe Mr. Antonov is in the middle of a strict colon cleanse at the moment. Doctor's orders."

Her eyes widen.

"Oh…I see," she says, blinking profusely. "Well, what would you like?"

"Two ham and cheese paninis, one small espresso," I say, rubbing my chin as I glance up at the menu. "And a double caramel Frappuccino, with whipped cream, and extra drizzle."

"Coming right up!"

She bounces away to start my order, and I move off to the side, inhaling the comforting scent of freshly brewed coffee, glancing up at Roast's famous "bean-pipe" roasting system.

Unlike anywhere else in the world, this coffee shop puts their roasting process on display for their customers to see.

Thick plexiglass tubes stand tall like the pipes of a church organ, reaching all the way to the ceiling. Custom-built heaters slowly orbit around the length of the pipe, keeping the raw beans inside rotating and cooking until they have reached the ideal state of roasting. They are then filtered down into the grinding machine behind the registers.

When a customer orders a coffee, the barista selects the size and grind, and the machine dispenses the exact amount of *freshly* roasted beans. It's then perfectly ground to the customers specifications, making for the most individualized cup of coffee in all of New York City.

No wonder Roman likes this place. It's almost fancier than he is.

As I stand there waiting, the beans above me reach their cooking time, and suddenly a loud beeping echoes through the café, signaling that they are ready to be moved.

But it is *that* beeping, steady and monotonous, that suddenly thrusts me back into my memories…

Beep… beep… beep…

Everything feels heavy, my arms, my legs, my chest as if I've been buried alive.

But I am alive…right?

The harsh smell of bleach is overwhelming, like I'm taking a bath in it. The smell is a clear indicator that I'm in the Hospital…or the morgue.

Hospitals always smell like the dead.

My eyelids are gritty, feeling as if they are glued down.

I will myself to blink, and am instantly overwhelmed by the bright lights above me. I pinch my eyes closed before trying again, forcing them to adjust, as I slowly look around.

The room is gloomy, and so very white, with only a pale blue accent on the walls. The bedding beneath me is scratchy and irritates my skin.

The more I move, the more the pain is noticeable. My face feels tight, every breath I take burning in my throat, making me whimper.

I'm powerless.

But this is my fault. It's always my fault.

"Oh, Mrs. Adams, you're awake!" A man says, bending to collect my medical chart. "I'm Dr Downing. How are you feeling?"

My mouth opens but no words come out. The doctor continues speaking to me, as my world starts spinning.

What the hell happened?

But I know the answer: Garrett Adams pushed me down the fucking stairs.

Why do I let him do this to me?

I don't deserve this…do I?

That's when I hear him say the only thing I truly care about.

"…Unfortunately, Mrs. Adams, we couldn't save the pregnancy."

Jumping back into the car, I lean forward, handing Trevor his panini. His eyes widen as he stares at me through the rearview mirror, but makes no move to take it, so I shake it slightly in front of him.

"Take the panini," I say firmly.

His eyes find mine again, and I can see how tired this poor man is. As we drove across the city, I'd caught him shaking his head, and sitting up straighter in his seat, desperately trying to stay awake.

"I can't…" He trails off.

But even from the backseat I can hear his stomach rumbling.

"Just take it."

Finally, he relents, and reaches for it, grabbing it from my hand. The moment he turns back to the wheel, I casually slip the small espresso into the cupholder next to him.

"That's for you too."

"Miss Wayne—"

"They got my order wrong, and I didn't want it to go to waste. So, it's yours now."

I can't be sure, but I almost see the faintest trace of relief flash behind his eyes as he slowly reaches for the cup.

"Oh, and I'm eating this before I go into the office," I grumble, changing the topic before taking a bite of the delicious panini. "If I go in there without carbs, I can't be held responsible for my actions against the bitches in there."

Trevor laughs, before tearing into his, grumbling as a piece of cheese drips down onto his shirt.

A giggle escapes me as I watch him struggle to clean the stain, and before I know it, we are both laughing. However, it comes crashing down around us as Cal knocks on the window, a scowl on his face as he looks at Trevor,

Trevor gulps, putting his panini down before rolling down the window, a stifling tension filling the car as Cal starts muttering about how Mr. Antonov is growing impatient, and something about how heads are going to roll.

Balling up my trash, I lean forward, patting Trevor on the shoulder.

"Thank you for being such a great driver, and making sure I had sustenance before my workday," I say with a smile. "As I'm sure Mr. Antonov would want his assistant to be ready for her day, with plenty of *energy,* right?"

I glare at Cal as I open the car door, slamming it behind me.

Out of the corner of my eye, I watch Jacques, taking a last gulp from his coffee cup, before grimacing and throwing the cup on the ground.

With a smile, I walk into the Nikotech lobby. As I do, I can feel all eyes on me, their intrusive stares making me feel as if bugs are running all over my skin.

A shiver runs down my spine, and goosebumps erupt on my arms as I step into the elevator.

This skirt is going to get a reaction from Roman.

…And I'm excited for it.

With a ding, the doors open to the executive floor.

My giddiness is immediately halted when I come face to face with the only bitch in this office, I can't stand more than Alison and Jenny: that insufferable cunt from Accounting, *Heather.*

Her eyes scan my body, silently judging me, before locking on mine. But I simply step onto the floor with my head held high, carrying the box with my new phone.

Heather opens her mouth, but before she can say anything, Roman's voice echoes through the floor.

"Abigail! Office! Now!" He thunders.

"Gotta go," I say, with a wave.

Dropping my bag on my desk, I walk into Roman's office, shutting the door behind me.

He stares at me, his chest heaving as his eyes caress my thighs, stopping briefly on my suspenders, before continuing up to my chest, where my blouse barely contains my cleavage.

With a growl he pushes away from his desk, looking over the top of his glasses as he hits the privacy glass, cutting the two of us off from the people outside.

"What are you wearing, Abigail," he states, not really wanting me to reply.

"Clothes." I huff back.

A laugh escapes him, coated in darkness as he continues to devour me with his eyes.

"That's not clothes, Abigail," he gestures forward, before running his thumb over his lip. "You know, if you wanted a repeat of yesterday, you could've just asked."

His smirk is arrogant, and it instantly infuriates me.

"As I said in my text last night, Mr. Antonov," I say, narrowing my eyes at him, while trying not to inhale his intoxicating scent. "It was a one time thing, and it cannot happen again. It *will* not."

"And as *I* said last night, Foxy," he whispers, stepping forward, closing the small distance between us. "You can keep telling yourself that."

"I mean it, Roman, it isn't happening again."

He takes another step, causing me to back up into the wall. Pressing his hand against the wall behind me he pins me there, and I can hear his ragged breathing. He licks his bottom lip, his eyes darkening as he reaches forward and gently caresses my neck.

"Why?" He growls, his voice low.

The moment his warm skin touches mine, electricity ripples through me, and my breath catches in my throat, threatening my resolve.

"Because I said *no,* Roman," I whisper, hating how breathless I sound as I fight every traitorous impulse to kiss him. "Or does the word *'no'* mean nothing to you?"

He recoils as if I've slapped him, his hand dropping from my neck as he steps back from me. He stares at me, the seconds passing slowly, feeling like a small eternity as my heart thumps loudly inside my chest.

Admittedly, a part of me, a very small part, almost regrets what I just said to him, seeing the undeniable look of pain written on his face.

"Fine," he finally says, his voice quiet as a whisper.

He flicks the switch on the wall, immediately returning the glass to its clarity before turning and walking back to his desk.

"Then we have work to do today, I need the financial reports from accounting, as well as all my meetings for tomorrow canceled. Oh, and email Cal to make a few phone calls and find me a contact for the people handling the Walston Street deal. Rumor has it their current contracted buyers aren't going to have the funding to solidify the deal, and I want them to know we are interested."

Is that it? Did I just…win?

"Yes, *Sir,*" I say with emphasis, grinning as his eyes dart to mine.

He shakes his head before snatching his fancy letter opener off his desk and stabbing it into the wood.

"Go get some work done, Abigail."

Hours later I sit twirling on my seat, playing with my new phone, and installing all of my favorite apps.

Suddenly, an unfamiliar noise chimes, indicating a notification has come in.

My brows furrow as I hunt for the culprit, only to discover that it's an *email* notification.

FROM: RomanAntonov@Nikotechinvestments.com
TO: AbigailWayne@Nikotechinvestments.com
SUBJECT: You're welcome.
Glad to see you're acquainting yourself with your new phone. Heard you broke yours last night.
Figured it was about time that you had a company one. Your emails, calendar and contacts have been synced for you.
For your convenience.
Roman Antonov.
CEO of Nikotech Investments.

No. Fucking. Way.

I stare at the phone, disgust flooding my veins as anger swells inside me. Hitting "reply" my nails audibly tap against the glass, my fingers flying over the screen as I type furiously.

FROM: AbigailWayne@Nikotechinvestments.com
TO: RomanAntonov@Nikotechinvestments.com
SUBJECT: No.
Are you kidding me? A company phone? So now when I go home I can't escape this building? Absolutely fucking not.
You can take this phone back.
Abigail Wayne,
Executive Assistant to Roman Antonov, CEO of Nikotech Investments.

I resist the urge to throw this very expensive phone at the nearest wall as I see that it automatically signs the email off with a digital signature.

FROM: RomanAntonov@Nikotechinvestments.com
TO: AbigailWayne@Nikotechinvestments.com
SUBJECT: Professionalism.
I must remind you Miss Wayne, that all communications within the company are monitored.

While we are on the subject of professionalism, I have also attached the company policies regarding the Nikotech dress code for you to read. Since you clearly require a refresher.

You are in direct violation of article 6.1.3.2

Please make the necessary adjustments to your wardrobe.

Roman Antonov.

CEO of Nikotech Investments.

FROM: AbigailWayne@Nikotechinvestments.com

TO: RomanAntonov@Nikotechinvestments.com

SUBJECT: RE: Professionalism.

You can take that 'attached pdf' and shove it up your ass.

I'm glad to hear that these emails are monitored.

While we are on *that* subject, who do I reach out to regarding a sexual harassment issue that I'm currently experiencing within the office?

Abigail Wayne.

Executive Assistant to Roman Antonov, CEO of Nikotech Investments.

FROM: RomanAntonov@Nikotechinvestments.com

TO: AbigailWayne@Nikotechinvestments.com

SUBJECT: RE: RE: Professionalism.

Someone is harassing you?

Who?

Give me a name.

Roman Antonov.

CEO of Nikotech Investments.

FROM: AbigailWayne@Nikotechinvestments.com

TO: RomanAntonov@Nikotechinvestments.com

SUBJECT: RE: RE: RE: Professionalism.

You.

Abigail Wayne.

Executive Assistant to Roman Antonov, CEO of Nikotech Investments.

FROM: RomanAntonov@Nikotechinvestments.com

TO: AbigailWayne@Nikotechinvestments.com

SUBJECT: RE: RE: Professionalism.

Hmm.

I would take it higher than HR.

But that would be me.

Roman Antonov.
CEO of Nikotech Investments.

FROM: AbigailWayne@Nikotechinvestments.com
TO: RomanAntonov@Nikotechinvestments.com
SUBJECT: RE: RE: RE: RE: Professionalism.
You can't see it, but I'm rolling my eyes right now.
Abigail Wayne.
Executive Assistant to Roman Antonov, CEO of Nikotech Investments.

FROM: RomanAntonov@Nikotechinvestments.com
TO: AbigailWayne@Nikotechinvestments.com
SUBJECT: RE: RE: RE: RE: Professionalism.
Actually, I can see that very well.
Roman Antonov.
CEO of Nikotech Investments.

Turning my chair to face Roman, I glare at him, resisting the urge to stick my finger up at him.

I decide that since I have his attention, now is probably the best time to ask him.

FROM: AbigailWayne@Nikotechinvestments.com
TO: RomanAntonov@Nikotechinvestments.com
SUBJECT: RE: RE: RE: RE: RE: Professionalism.
Regarding our impromptu private afternoon meeting yesterday, I was wondering if that is something that you do regularly with all of your assistants?
Specifically, I'd like to know if I need to seek an appointment with a professional regarding the…end result?
Abigail Wayne.
Executive Assistant to Roman Antonov, CEO of Nikotech Investments.

Immediately after pressing send, I feel the heat rush to my cheeks, and immediately turn my chair away from Roman.

FROM: RomanAntonov@Nikotechinvestments.com
TO: AbigailWayne@Nikotechinvestments.com
SUBJECT: RE: RE: RE: RE: Professionalism.
Feel free to seek a professional for your *own* peace of mind, but I can assure you mine is…immaculate.

Happy to provide any documentation you require.

And no, yesterday was an exception. That's not something that I do…I usually pull out.

Roman Antonov.

CEO of Nikotech Investments.

I turn back to my computer, feeling myself blushing.

I was Roman's exception.

"Nikotech Investments, Mr. Antonov's office, Abby speaking, how may I assist you?"

"Hello Abby, this is Detective Hevon. I'm hoping to speak with Mr. Antonov. Is he available?"

My eyes widen as Roman rounds the corner, a stack of papers in his hand.

"Erm, one moment please." I say sweetly, before placing the call on hold and staring up at Roman who's now standing directly in front of my desk, his face red, and that vein in his neck throbbing.

Dropping the stack of papers, he smashes his hand down on a particular page.

"As you refused to look at article 6.1.3.2, I printed it out for you. Read it."

Choosing to ignore him, because it's clear he's trying to get a rise out of me, I nod my head toward the phone.

"There's a call for you."

"I don't have anything scheduled today." Roman replies, back into business mode.

"Yeah, okay, let me just tell Detective Hevon that."

As I reach for the phone, Roman grabs my hand, pulling it away from the receiver.

"What does he want, Abigail?" He glares at me, his eyes full of suspicion.

"To speak to you," I say, rolling my eyes. "I didn't quite get that far before you dumped this ream of paper on my desk."

"Fine, patch him through," he states, adjusting the buttons on his sleeve before walking away and into his office. "And get reading."

He walks into his office and closes the door.

My eyes track his movements, curiosity filling me at the idea of the police reaching out to Roman.

As he sits down at his desk I grab hold of the receiver once again, taking Detective Hevon off hold.

"I'll transfer you through to him now!" I inform the detective brightly.

"No need. I'm in the lobby," he replies before ending the call.

My stomach drops, and my heart stops, dread filling me as I jump from my chair and dart toward Roman's office.

"Abby, I said to transfer him," Roman sighs, running his hand through his hair.

"He's…he's down in the lobby."

"What?"

"Down…in the lobby, Roman." I mutter, trying to catch my breath, feeling my heart thundering in my chest.

Roman scrunches up his face.

"Why are you so flustered?" He snorts. "He isn't here to see you."

But I can't explain to him why I'm flustered.

The truth is, I recognize that name, and I know that Detective Hevon is someone who could reveal things that I have kept buried.

"The…the restaurant," I breathe, trying to explain away my panic. "The *bomb*."

For the first time today, Roman's face softens. Silently he stands, walking over to me and taking my hands in his.

Once again, the feeling of his skin touching mine heats my blood within my veins, and I look up at him, staring into his beautiful face as my heart thumps loudly in my chest.

"Relax, Abigail. It's alright. I'm sure this is just a procedure. After all, we were witnesses. We were there before it went up in flames."

His voice is soft and tender, so different from how he's spoken to, and acted around me all day. If I didn't know better, I'd say there was genuine concern in his eyes, seeing my uncharacteristic response.

"Okay," I breathe quietly.

"Go take a seat. I'll take it from here, okay?"

"But…I should go and get him, right?"

Roman grips my chin, tilting my head up so that I'm forced to look at him. I know that my face right now is an open book, but I don't care.

Gently he rubs his thumb gently over my lips as he leans forward.

"No, I'll greet him myself."

And taking my hand, Roman leads me back to my desk, before squeezing, "And don't worry, I'll keep your name out of it."

He turns, walking away from the corridor and into the waiting elevator. Gradually my muscles relax as I sit and stare aimlessly, waiting for him to return.

A few minutes later, just as I'm dumping Roman's dress code in the trash can, the elevator chimes, opening to reveal Roman, and Detective Hevon, following behind him.

Aside from the fact that he looks older, Hevon hasn't changed much since I last saw him. His dark mahogany skin has a few more wrinkles, and his hair has grown lighter, speckled now with flecks of white.

I try desperately to hide my face, but as the two of them walk past, the detective makes eye contact with me and his face lights up immediately.

"Mrs. Adams! How lovely it is to see you again!" He says, genuine joy filling his features.

Roman stops, glaring at him.

Standing slowly, I smooth my skirt down my legs.

"Detective, I go by Miss Wayne now," I correct him, ignoring the feel of Roman's eyes burning into the side of my face.

"Ahhh, yes, I was sorry to hear about your loss, losing a life partner at your age is truly sad." He says, shaking his head.

"I—"

"A life partner?" Roman whispers, drawing my eyes to his, forcing me to swallow my words.

Shit.

"Yes, it was tragic." The detective continues, nodding solemnly. "Hearing that her husband died of a heart attack so young is almost unheard of these days, especially in a man who used to be a professional athlete."

As I nod my head, my eyes are still locked on Roman.

"Yes. Very sad," I say, trying to hide the disgust in my voice, hearing how even now people are still idolizing my monster.

"Anyway," Roman interrupts, still staring at me but gesturing to his office, "Shall we, detective?"

With a nod, Detective Hevon walks forward.

As they walk into his office, Roman closes the door, and just before the privacy screen coats the glass, I catch him winking at me.

ANTONOV

CHAPTER NINETEEN

ROMAN

"You sure about this, Boss?" Boris says, looking up at me warily. "You really want me to just drill this…directly into the desk?"

"Did I fucking stutter?"

"No, Boss," he says, shaking his head. "You didn't."

The whirring sound of the drill echoes through the empty office floor. A hole is bored straight through the desk. And then another. And another. That's when the welder steps up to the plate.

Closing my office door with my coffee in hand, I walk around to the desk and sit down watching the construction scene before me…a smile growing on my face.

Oh, Abby is going to love this.

With the early morning team of professionals I've assembled, they finish in just under an hour. On top of that, they've cleaned up their mess, put everything back where it was, and have cleared the building before Abby even steps on to the floor.

Perfect.

Throwing my airpods in my ears, I begin my day, mapping out my meetings, and answering emails.

The first is from Ana.

FROM: AAntonov@Nikotechinvestments.com
TO: RomanAntonov@Nikotechinvestments.com
SUBJECT: Three Questions
Detective Hevon came to see you. Fill me in.
And I heard through the *grapevine* you took Abigail Wayne to lunch at Albertos that day, even though we discussed this.
Did he talk to her?
Should we be talking about her?
Are you a dumbass?
Anastasia Romanov
Chief IT & Operations Officer, of Nikotech Investments.

I snort.

Only Ana gets to talk to me like this. But it's clear that she's nervous about the detective, and rightly confused by the fact that I was at Albertos with Abby. I know she's already hacked the police department's server, so her comment about the *grapevine* is likely just her way of covering our asses in the event of any situation in which we might be required to submit email transcripts.

Detective Hevon claimed that he was only stopping by as a courtesy, and from what Ana learned from hacking the police department email server, the cops didn't actually *have* any security footage from the street cameras that showed me there with Abby. If not for the register of reservations that day, they wouldn't have even known that I was there.

Which would've been preferred, but I'm not worried.

However, Ana's question regarding the detective asking about Abby is interesting.

Because it did strike me as odd that he remembered Abby's husband's death.

And now she knows that I know, that she lied about him.

The look on her face was priceless though.

The other interesting part was the missing footage. Obviously, the Detective hadn't divulged that information, but from the email chain between the Detective and his sergeant we learned that the street cameras were conveniently down the day of the bombing. The email between them also stated that even though Albertos had cameras on the inside, as well as on the front and back of the building, they too had been disabled that day and the footage from inside the restaurant was severely corrupted.

Cal was right. This was *professional.*

Someone not only knew how to hit Albertos, but they also knew how to make that hit effectively disappear. And so even though there was a giant crater where Albertos used to be, proving that a bomb *had* gone off, there was little visual proof.

But there was something else.

Those are steps that *we* take to cover *our* hits, and skills I have specifically fostered.

Few organizations in the world are set up like mine, with men trained to do what mine are trained to do: make "messes" look like accidents.

When Polina married Igor, part of our tradition was for Igor's father to gift my father something "valuable." And at the time, because of the business we deal in, that gift could only be one thing: *men.* And I learned from Dimitris and Jaxon Pace that having more boots on the ground than your enemy is what gave mafia families the advantage.

So, on Igor and Polina's wedding day, our family mafia grew by a hundred strong men, sent to us from Igor's hometown of Moscow.

These new troops were just a bunch of young, naive orphans and misfits, who were just eager to belong somewhere. But I saw their potential. I saw them as ripe for molding into whatever need our family had. And because my father died shortly after their wedding, I soon had the power to dictate which direction our new manpower would be applied.

Because the FBI and the CIA were developing all kinds of tracking and monitoring systems that were making our industry harder, I felt that to combat the powers that be, espionage and cybertechnology was going to be a skill *my* men needed to have. So, I set about training them to do what the rest of the underworld does…only *better.*

And with Ana by my side, we've been excelling above and beyond our "competition" for years.

But unlike my diversified portfolio, Cillian McCleary's "clean income," is significantly smaller, as he has less resources than I to launder it. And because dirty money can't pay for clean men, his mafia is younger and far cruder. The men he attracts are inexperienced and volatile, so instead of cleaning up the messes they make, they just make more messes to cover them up.

Cillian's team has never had the tech, or the technical intelligence of people to know how to stitch up a job this immaculately.

However, now it seems they *do.*

And they want us to know it.

I choose not to respond to Ana's email, deciding that if Cillian has the brainpower to get past any of our firewalls, I don't need him getting his hands on emails that could potentially incriminate me, or the company.

Pulling out my phone, I dial my digital sister, but am greeted immediately by her voicemail.

I guess it's pretty early, considering she's usually up til late.

"Call me when you get this, but don't send any other emails regarding Detective Hevon," I say into her machine. "And I'm sure you're already working on this, but I'm going to need you to decipher that interior footage. It's imperative."

As I set the phone down, I run my hand through my hair.

That footage is going to be necessary when trying to meet with the Sicilians. This warrants my second phone call, to Lev, who I know will be awake and at the gym, per his usual routine.

"What's up, Bro," he says, grunting into the receiver.

"This a bad time?" I ask.

"Nah, you got me on leg day," he huffs. "So hit me."

"I need a meeting with Giovani Ricci."

"When?"

"As soon as possible," I say, taking a sip of my coffee.

As I do, my eyes fall to the stain on my rug where Abby had slapped it out of my hand the day that we…

Stop it. She said no. Focus.

"Can you set that up for me?" I say into the phone, trying to get the images of Abby with her legs spread atop my desk out of my head.

"Sure thing," he grunts again. "I'm almost finished here, so I can stop by the Tap Room on my way back from—"

"No, don't go yourself," I say firmly, cutting him off. "We need to get ahead of this whole situation with Al, but I'm not sure where they're at with the whole thing. So, we need to be cautious until we know who they are pointing the finger at."

"You mean pointing their *guns* at," Lev chuckles, the loud sound of weights crashing behind him.

"Yeah. I need to make sure that it isn't at us," I grumble. "So, until I talk to Gio, I don't need any of you idiots putting yourselves in the line of fire, understood?"

"You got it, Ro," Lev confirms. "Anything else?"

"No, I think that's—"

"So, what's the deal with your new assistant?"

"What?" I ask. "What have you heard?"

Fuck, did someone see us the other day?!

"Well, Pol was bitching," he snorts. "But Pasha said she's cute and that you might have a thing for—"

"Just get the meeting set up," I snap irritably, immediately ending the call.

Coincidentally, as I look up, I happen to see Abigail walking down the aisle toward me….Unsurprisingly wearing yet another short skirt, like the defiant little instigator she is.

After setting her purse down at her desk, I notice her scrunching up her nose.

Probably confused by the scent of wood and fresh welding.

Conveniently, as she turns to make her way back to her desk, my cell starts buzzing and I glance down to see that Cal is calling me.

"Morning," I say, taking a sip of my coffee. "Tell me some good news."

"I just heard back from the representative from Stein & Company," Cal says. "We have the greenlight for negotiations."

"Who's our contact?"

"Solomon Stein. You have an appointment on Tuesday morning at ten next week to discuss the Walston Street deal."

"Excellent."

"Also, the Pace Transport cargo will be here in the morning," Cal continues. "Would you like me to make the transaction?"

His question makes me pause. On one hand, I know that if Cal handles this, there's no doubt in my mind that things will go down without a hitch. However, I've been toying with another idea.

"Actually, Cal," I say, taking a deep breath. "I might want to go in a different direction with that. But let me get back to you. Just make sure our warehouse is ready to accept it, and—"

"What the fuck?!"

Abby's voice suddenly echoes through my office.

"What is…oh my God! Are all of these…Holy fuck!"

"…Just keep an eye on the shipment and standby for updates," I say with a grin. "I'll connect with you later."

"Roger that, Boss."

I'm setting my phone down on my desk just as Abby comes storming into my office.

"Did you do this?" She demands, her face red.

"Good morning, Abigail," I say with a smirk, casually taking a sip of my coffee. "I trust you had a pleasant evening?"

"Did. You. Do. This?" She says, accentuating each word.

"I'm afraid you're going to have to be a bit more specific."

"Did you *bolt* all of my things to my desk, Roman?!" She practically shouts. "My computer, my phone, my tape dispenser and my stapler are all fastened directly to the fucking desk!"

"No, actually," I say, shaking my head. "I didn't."

"What?" She asks, now thoroughly confused. "But…they are all…I mean, my stuff is all—"

"*I* didn't do anything," I say, unable to stop the wicked smile that spreads across my face. "But then again, when you make as much money as I do, you don't *have* to get your hands dirty just to complete a little welding job."

Her jaw drops, and for a good three seconds she struggles with what to say.

"But…how? I mean, no, *why?*" She finally stammers. "Why on earth would you actually go through the trouble of attaching all of my stuff to my damn desk?"

"Because," I say, leaning back in my chair and putting my hands behind my head. "It seems as though your supplies were having such a hard time actually staying *on* your desk, and not on the floor, that I decided to help things be a bit more stationary for you. More…grounded."

She stares at me, scoffing loudly before looking back at her desk.

"And plus, I didn't want you to hurt your back," I wink at her. "Especially since you seemed to be bending over. *A lot.*"

"Oh my God," she whispers, narrowing her eyes at me. "That's why you did it. You did it because you're pissed about me wearing miniskirts, aren't you?"

I grin, staring back at her growing frustration, and feeling nothing but selfish satisfaction.

"Well, I did tell you about a dozen times that your skirts are too fucking short," I growl. "And I can't have my men up here, staring at your damn cunt all day, so I had to come up with a solution."

"You fucking bastard," Abby laughs sarcastically, shaking her head in disbelief. "You petty, fucking bastard."

"At your service, Miss Wayne," I smirk.

"You do not get to choose what I wear every day!"

"Actually, yes, I *do,*" I smile at her. "And it seems that your entire wardrobe is in direct violation of our dress code. So, either I had to fire you, or I had to improvise."

She purses her lips but says nothing.

"Now, as much as I would like to continue this riveting conversation, I do have work to do. I just spoke to Cal this morning and he confirmed the Walston Street deal is on. So, I need you to work with him and reach out to the people from Stein & Co. to get the specifics of the presentation they will need for the meeting on—”

"No," she interrupts, folding her arms suddenly across her chest. "Actually, you know, I think I'm feeling sick today."

"Oh really?" I say, tilting my head and narrowing my eyes at her. "With what sickness exactly?"

"Your *bullshit*."

And without another word, my assistant storms out of my office.

"Abigail," I yell after her, but she ignores me, grabbing her purse and stepping on to the elevator before I can even muster up an excuse or command to make her stay.

Well shit…that backfired.

"Where did she go?" I ask Cal.

"We don't know," he replies. "I alerted security to catch her in the lobby like you asked, but she took the elevator to the second floor, went out the fire exit, and caught a cab."

Clever little fox.

"Tell Trevor I want to see him," I say through gritted teeth. "Now."

I sit in my office staring at her desk, wondering if maybe I took our petty little game too far. Of course, I anticipated Abby being pissed, but I didn't anticipate she'd storm out of here like a bat out of hell. And now no one knew where she was.

Well…technically. I could know. Right now. If I wanted to.

Biting my lip, I pull up my phone and open the tracker I personally had installed on her new company phone.

I picked this app specifically because it covertly doubled as a weather app, which is constantly tracking the phone's GPS location anyway. So that meant there was a minimal chance that even a suspicious Abby would ever discover it.

Clicking on her pin, it shows me that she, or at least her phone, is pinging at the Black Cat Lounge, a dive bar about a mile away.

Should I…go there?

My thoughts are interrupted however when Trevor gets off the elevator.

"You wanted to see me, Boss?" He says.

I smirk.

On some level, I have to admit I'm impressed. The kid has assimilated faster than I thought he would.

The once trembling and terrified waiter had passed the initiation test, and was now standing in front of me like a veteran who's been part of our organization for years.

Even Cal said that he'd surpassed *his* expectations.

"Trevor," I say, folding my arms across my chest. "You've been driving Miss Wayne for a bit now, correct?"

"Yes, Sir."

"And tailing her?"

"Yes, Boss."

"I assume she was curious about how you came to work for me?" I ask, swiping the Antonov Dagger off my desk and spinning in my hand.

"Yes, Boss, she did ask about that," he nods.

"And what did you tell her?"

I look up at him, twisting the knife in my hands.

"I told her that you'd felt bad about our interaction the day of the bombing, and about my loss of employment, so you offered me a position with your company, Sir," Trevor says, his eyes briefly falling to the dagger in my hands before immediately looking away. "I expressed how grateful I was for your… generosity."

I grin, nodding.

"Impressive."

I really do like this kid.

"Tell me what you've learned about her," I say with a nod. "What are her activities outside of here? Who is she hanging around with? Where is she going?"

He stares back at me, considering his answer, which is something I've learned that I appreciate about him. He never asks me to repeat myself, or pretend he didn't understand my question, and always gives me straight concise answers.

"She's quiet, Boss," Trevor says slowly. "She sticks to herself mostly. She's mentioned going to The Studio and the Black Cat Lounge on occasion, but from what I've seen it's not excessive."

"Does she…have a boyfriend?" I ask, trying to sound as disaffected as possible. "Or male visitors that come over?"

"No, Sir, not to my knowledge," he says, shaking his head. "And I haven't seen *any* visitors to her home. Male or female. As I said, she's pretty quiet, and it seems she prefers to be on her own."

"Anything else?"

Trevor opens his mouth, but then immediately closes it, biting his lip.

"Tell me," I say firmly. "What is it?"

"That's the thing, Boss," he says, with a sigh. "I'm not sure it *is* something. She made a comment to me the other day that made me wonder if perhaps she'd been in a…*bad* relationship."

"Bad?" I ask, narrowing my eyes at him. "How bad?"

"Well, she said something about falling down a set of stairs," he says quietly before looking at the floor.

"What do you mean? How did she…I mean why would she bring that up? With *you*?"

Trevor swallows hard and shakes his head.

"I don't remember the context exactly, Boss," he says softly. "But she kind of just zoned out for a few minutes, staring out the window. I don't know, I guess it just felt like she was referring to something like *that*."

"Why?" I ask. "What made you think *that's* what she was referring to?"

"Just a hunch," he says, shrugging. "And given the fact that she mostly likes to stay at home with her cat, it can't be a current boyfriend, so I guess I just got the impression that maybe someone had hurt her in the past."

The very thought of anyone hurting Abby, in the past or present, makes my blood boil.

And then another feeling creeps in. A twinge of guilt maybe? Or perhaps regret for how aggressively I had fucked her in my office just a few days prior.

Was I too rough with her?

And yet, I distinctly remember the way she'd deliberately provoked me, and goaded me the entire time. I mean, she actually smacked me.

My mind is still racing when I realize that Trevor is still standing in my office while I sit and rub my chin, lost in my own thoughts.

"Thank you," I say, clearing my throat and standing to my feet. "Go home for the day. You've done well, Kid."

And for the first time since I met him, I see the faintest traces of a smile tugging at the corners of his lips.

"Thank you," he says excitedly, before correcting himself. "I mean, Boss."

After he leaves, I swipe my phone from the desk and walk over to the windows overlooking the city, replaying the information he just gave me.

Abby was an anomaly I didn't quite understand. A contradiction that screamed to be noticed. She was far too observant, too clever, and too intentional, to just be the meek, innocent, naive assistant she was masquerading to be.

Was she running from someone?

Or hiding from something?

Did she just not want to be with me?

I'm not sure.

But I *am* sure that I've wanted her more than anything I've ever wanted in my entire life. And as I look down at her location pinging on the app, I know that if I just let her go, I'll regret it for the rest of my life.

No, I know exactly what I need to do.

I need to track down a fox.

"Kinda irresponsible," I say softly. "Being out and about in public. You know, considering how *sick* you are. You're practically a leper."

"Jesus Christ, are you deliberately stalking me now?" Abby groans, looking up from her drink long enough to glare at me. "Or just determined to drive me insane?"

"Both," I say, yanking the chair back beside her, and sitting down next to her at the bar.

"Never thought of you as the desperate type," she says, rolling her eyes. "But hey, I guess I've been wrong before."

I chuckle, licking my bottom lip.

Ohhhh, this sassy girl.

"Whiskey," I say, waving to the stunningly pretty dark-skinned bartender, with long purple hair.

"Brand?" She smiles, her eyes canvasing my body slowly.

"Whatever's the most expensive," I wink. "You pick, sweetheart."

"Okay!" She giggles.

Abby suddenly chokes on her martini.

"You alright there?" I ask, fighting the smirk that tugs at the corners of my lips.

Of course, I'd immediately noticed the menacing glare she'd shot to the beautiful girl behind the bar, who was now overpouring my shot, while shooting me another smile.

"I'm fine," she says, clearing her throat again. "Just planning how I'll word my next email to HR about my ongoing workplace harassment situation."

"I'll be sure to forward that on," I say, glancing up at the football highlights playing on the bar's television. "Give it plenty of dedicated attention. Will be good late-night reading. You know, to help me fall asleep."

"What do you want, Roman?" Abby sighs, but then stiffens, noticing the bartender approaching with my shot.

"Thank you," I deliberately grin as she places a napkin face down on the bar top, putting the drink on top of it.

"You're welcome!" She smiles, blushing.

As she walks away, she glances back at me once more, prompting me to flip the napkin over.

"Oh, would you look at that," I chuckle. "Is that…is that her *number*?"

"What?" Abby asks, looking down at the napkin.

"Not bad for a *desperate* man," I shrug nonchalantly. "Considering I barely said ten words to the girl."

"Jesus Christ," Abby snorts.

"Is there a problem, Miss Wayne?" I ask, turning to her and taking a sip of my drink. "I mean, it's not like you care, right?"

"Not a bit. It's just amusing what a shameless whore you are, Mr. Antonov," she says, shaking her head.

"So, I'm a whore now," I say, nodding slowly. "I thought you just said I was desperate. Forgive me, you're a bit…*confusing*."

I stare at her, watching as her eyes find mine. She opens her mouth to say something, but then changes her mind. Biting her bottom lip.

Gotcha.

"What do you want, Roman?" She finally says.

"I want to know *why*."

"You know exactly why," she scoffs. "You literally bolted my shit to my desk and—"

"No, not why you left today," I say firmly, interrupting her. "I want to know why you *lied* to me, Abigail."

My tone is dark and heavy, as is my stare.

What happens next is incredibly interesting.

Abby makes no visible movement, her posture and facial expression unchanging. However, I know my question has her immediately on the defensive, and her eyes are all the confirmation I need.

It's easy for a person to lie, but their eyes cannot.

I watch in real time as Abby's widen and her pupils dilate ever so slightly. And in the silence shared between us, it's almost as if I can see her weighing the options of her lying to me, against giving me the truth I seek.

"I lied because I don't like talking about my ex-husband," she says finally, lowering her eyes to her glass.

"You mean *late* husband," I correct, waiting for her to look back up at me before continuing. "For the record, that's usually how people talk about their dead husbands. But I gotta say, I feel like that would be even more reason to tell me that he died, not tell me you just split up."

"You know, I don't really want to talk about this—" Abby says as she starts to push her chair away.

"Sit. Down." I growl, so forcefully that Abby jumps and instantly collapses back against her seat. "I want a straight answer out of you. And don't fucking lie to me Abby. Because I promise I'll know if you do."

She swallows hard, before turning to the pretty bartender.

"I'll take another one of these," she says, shaking her empty glass. "I'm going to need it."

"Sure thing, hon," the girl says, before turning to me. "And you, dear?"

"No," I snap, without moving my gaze off Abby.

"Oh…well, okay then," the dejected girl says. "I'll be right back with that martini."

"If you're not careful, you're going to give that girl whiplash," Abby says, biting her lip.

"Good, that will make two of us," I fire back. "Now quit stalling and answer my question."

"Can I get my drink first?"

"No," I hiss, grabbing her chair and turning it to face me.

"I didn't…I mean, I don't…well I don't talk about it," she says, sighing heavily. "It's not something I talk about."

"Well, here's something *I* don't talk about," I say, narrowing my eyes at her. "I *knew* your husband."

"What?" She asks, shock blanketing her face.

"I knew who you were. You might not know this, but we were in the same circle at one point in time, Miss Wayne," I say, watching as her jaw drops. "And I have to say, you seemed pretty content on his arm at all the parties and Galas. So, I guess I'm just having a hard time understanding why you'd be out here spreading a lie about him still being alive and—"

"He…wasn't a good person, okay?" Abby suddenly snaps, closing her eyes.

"What?"

She stares at me for a long moment, and then takes a deep breath.

"Look, I loved him, and I'm sure it appeared that he loved me. I'm sure it looked like we were this incredibly happy couple, because that's exactly what he *wanted* everyone to think. But behind closed doors, he was…he was just different," she sighs, playing with her fingernails. "I don't expect you to understand."

I hear the bartender set Abby's drink down on the bar, and I hear Abby thank her, but I still refuse to tear my eyes from her.

"Try me."

She scoffs quietly to herself.

"Why did you marry him?" I ask, hating the way my chest tightens at the thought of her picking anyone else. "If he was mistreating you?"

"He didn't start out mistreating me," she says softly.

She takes a deep breath, rolling her eyes and sitting back in her chair.

"I'm not sure what you're looking for here, but it's not that unique of a story. He was something, I was nothing, and I was just grateful that he picked me. He got a football scholarship, and I followed him to school. But then he tore his ACL and couldn't play anymore, he started drinking, and started partying. I don't know. He just changed. And so did the way he treated me."

"Tell me," I ask quietly. "Did he…*hurt* you?"

But says nothing.

"Abigail," I whisper darkly. "Did he hurt—"

"Who cares if he did?" she suddenly laughs sarcastically.

"I fucking do," I growl. "And I care about whether his parents knew about it and—"

"He's *dead*, Roman," She scoffs, throwing her hands in the air. "What are you going to do? Dig up his coffin and beat up his corpse? No, you're not. Because it's done. It's over. Good, bad, or indifferent, there's nothing anyone can do to fix the past. But in my future, you know, the one I'm still responsible for? I don't have to think about him anymore, so I *don't*. That's my peace."

She takes a deep breath but narrows her eyes at me further.

"And yeah, I lied to you about him, and yeah, I probably shouldn't have. But in that particular moment, I guess telling you he was an ex, and not my dead shitty husband felt like what I wanted to do. And you know, after spending years under someone else's thumb, I make it a point to only ever do what *I* want to do," she scoffs, chuckling softly and rolling her eyes. "So, there you go! Whether you accept my explanation or not, I don't give a fuck. At the end of the day, I don't really know you, or trust you, and I don't have to tell you anything about anything. I might work for you, Roman Antonov, but I don't owe you a damn thing and—"

"Okay," I say firmly, holding up my hand.

"Wait…what?" Abby asks, confused.

"I said okay," I say, softly. "You're right, you don't know me. And you don't owe me anything."

"But…" she scoffs, once again opening her mouth as if to say something, only to instantly close it again.

The two of us fall silent, and if my mind was spinning before, it's a fucking hurricane now. Abby's words felt like yet another slap in the face, with this revelation feeling like daggers plunging straight through my chest.

Trevor's assessment over the last week had been correct.

And my assessment over all those years…had been wrong.

While I was fantasizing and coveting her from the sidelines, Abby *hadn't* been happily married to the man of her dreams. She'd more or less just told me that she'd actually been married to a monster in a human suit. And if I *could* dig up her bastard dead husband, and make him face my justice, I'd flay him alive for whatever he did to her.

But on that point, I don't actually know what he did to her, because she's not ready to talk about this with me. And why should she be? She's right. She doesn't know me.

Even if she did…am I really any better than him?

I'm certain that I'd never hurt her, but I know that I hurt others. Every day. Hell, it's part of my job. Which would probably seem even more fucked up to her.

"I'm sorry," I say quietly, no louder than a whisper.

"Don't be," she says, shaking her head. "It gives him power. And I stopped allowing that a long ass time ago."

She shrugs, taking a drink.

"Besides, I did lie to you. You just caught me in it."

I stare at her, trying to think of something to say, but feeling utterly and completely lost in her eyes.

"Well, I should probably get going," she sighs, pulling out her wallet, and her credit card. "If I'm going to make use of the one sick day I'll have for the next three weeks, I don't want to spend it all here."

"Wait…you're coming back to me?" I ask, my mouth suddenly going dry. "Er…I mean, to *work* for me, that is?"

The faintest of smiles flits across Abby's face.

"Well, I guess that's up to you," she says, batting her lashes at me. "I suppose it depends on whether or not you can find a way to forgive me."

"Well," I grin wickedly. "I'm sure I could—"

"…While not expecting me to sleep with you," she says, raising her brow at me. "Because I *am* serious about that. I'm really not interested in you like that."

I snort, raising my hands in defense.

"Fair enough, Miss Wayne."

Suddenly my phone rings on the bar top.

Cal.

That's not good.

He knew I was here and wouldn't be disturbing me unless it was urgent.

"What is it?" I say, quickly answering the call.

"Boss," Cal says, his voice riddled with concern. "I thought you should know, but Jacques…well, he's…dead."

"Dead?" I breathe incredulously. "What do you mean Jacques is dead?"

Out of the corner of my eye, I see Abby raise her hand to her mouth, clearly shocked.

Fuck, I shouldn't be having this conversation in front of her.

"Actually, Cal, I'll call you back in a minute," I snap, ending the phone call.

"Apologies, I have to run," I say, aggressively snapping my fingers at the bartender.

"Everything okay?" Abby asks innocently. "Did I hear you say that Jacques is…dead?"

"Yes," I say, clearing my throat. "He is."

"What a shame," Abby says, taking a final sip of her drink.

"Mmhmm," I say, realizing I should probably divert this conversation, and distract her.

"Are you leaving?" The bartender says as she walks up to us.

"Yes," Abby nods, trying to hand the woman her card.

However, I stop her, putting my hand on top of Abby's and throwing a $100 bill on the bar top.

"Oh, I've got hers," I say with a smile, watching as the girl immediately smiles back at me, my earlier moodiness apparently forgotten.

"And I don't need change, honey," I say with a wink. "After all, I've got all I need right here, don't I?"

I slide the napkin with her phone number out from under the glass, and put it in my pocket, making Abby's polite smile instantly disappear.

"Hehe, I guess so," the bartender giggles, biting her lip. "I hope I'll hear from you then."

"Perhaps you will," I wink back at her.

Abby stiffens, a bright shade of red now flooding her cheeks as she glares at the bartender once more, telling me it's the perfect time to go.

Let her sit in it.

"Well," I say, standing to my feet, and tapping Abby on the shoulder. "I do hope you feel better soon, Abigail. We will certainly miss you at the office."

Turning on my heel, I do my best to stifle my smirk as I head quickly toward the door, leaving an obviously frustrated and flustered Abigail standing there.

However, as I touch the handle of the door I turn back around, snapping my fingers.

"Oh, I almost forgot! I will need you to get better by Friday," I say, watching as Abby turns her murderous glare to me. "Because I'm taking you to a Gala. Professionally, of course, so don't worry, I'll respect your wishes and won't cross any boundaries. But you will need a dress. An evening gown preferably. Not a tennis skirt."

"A what?" I hear Abby ask behind me, but this time I slip out into the street, unable to hide my laughter any longer.

"He didn't show up for work this morning at eight," Cal says to me from the driver's seat. "Noah went by the house and said that he had to kick the door in."

"Do they know how he died yet?" I ask, nonchalantly checking the app and seeing Abby's little dot speedily making its way toward Forest Hills.

She's going home.

"Not yet, Boss," Cal sighs. "But he wasn't shot, and Noah said he didn't see anything recreational. He just passed out on the couch, clutching his chest."

"So…another heart attack?"

"Looks that way," Cal replies. "But we'll know as soon as we get the coroner's report."

I say nothing, but then again nothing needs to be said.

Cal knows as well as I do that something about this seems highly suspicious, but it doesn't change the fact that two of my men are dead.

And I have no idea why.

A
ANTONOV

CHAPTER TWENTY

Abby

That infuriating man wants me to attend a gala with him.

"Professionally."

That's what he said, but I fight the urge to roll my eyes.

To be honest, nothing about my relationship with Roman Antonov has been professional.

But a gala? I fucking hate galas.

And I hate rich people. Especially *fake* rich people.

I thought I'd escaped them forever after I escaped my old life. I was sure I was done mingling with old crusty aristocrats and dusty tycoons, shaking hands, smiling, pretending to care about whatever bullshit they're going on about.

But apparently, I thought wrong.

Wishful thinking, I guess.

So here I am.

Instead of enjoying my lunch hour, which for the most part is a working lunch, I'm shopping.

I like shopping as much as the next girl, but *not* for a high-class function that I have no interest in attending.

While these events were always for charity, there was always an alternative motive lurking behind the scenes.

The men do business, while the women sit there, sipping their expensive champagne judging everyone around them, taking bets on how many zeros their competition has in their bank account.

Parasites.

"Won't be long, Trevor," I call over my shoulder as I walk into the quaintest little boutique I've ever seen. After spending all morning looking for one, I gave up and asked Trevor if he knew of anywhere that could be of any help to me.

Without hesitation his eyes lit up and he told me about a coworker of his that talked about this nice little shop on the outskirts of the city. Apparently, the waitresses at Albertos said that the owner of the boutique was rumored to be a 'witch,' because with one singular look, she knew exactly what dress would work best on you.

Something that I was keen to experience myself.

Shopping is an art, one that you have to be in the mood for.

Which I am not.

Pulling the door open, I'm immediately hit with the sweet smell of fresh Jasmine. And my soul relaxes a bit.

Surveying the collection of dresses that line the walls that seem to go on forever, my eyes catch on a flash of red, conveniently covered by a drape.

"Hello!" A cheery voice calls out to me, her head popping up from behind the counter.

"Hi! I called ahead," I say back, giving her a small wave.

"Oh yes, Miss Wayne, right?" She nods, darting out to greet me.

"I just go by Abby," I say with a polite smile.

"You said you needed something formal, right?" She continues, pulling dresses from the racks.

"Yeah, it's for a charity event, I was told it needed to be formal and *classy.* But—"

"I know the perfect dress already," she interrupts, before she basically evaporates in front of me.

Dropping down onto the dusty pink loveseat, I throw my bag down next to me, before shaking my head.

She flies back into the room, garment bags thrown over her arm as she starts hooking them onto the rail. Throwing a quick smile over her shoulder, she unzips the first bag, revealing a baby blue silk piece.

My nose scrunches at the color.

She takes in my expression, before frowning and unzipping the next one, a ruched velvet yellow.

Now, the style of the dress would highlight my curves, as well as showing off my shoulders, however with *that* color, and that fabric, it's a hard no.

She reaches for the next bag.

Yeah, this isn't going to work at all.

Sighing heavily, I stand to my feet.

"I'm sorry, I didn't catch your name?" I ask politely.

"Oh god! I'm so sorry. I'm Mimi." She says, twirling around on the spot, "the owner!"

"They call you a 'witch', right?"

"Ha! You bet they do," she says, rocking on the balls of her feet.

"Look, I need you to be the biggest baddest witch for me today, I don't want this," I say, gesturing to the dresses she currently has out for me to try on. "While they're lovely, they aren't quite right. For *me*."

She goes to respond but I hold up my hand.

"What I need is something that suits *my* needs for this event."

"Oh…okay," she says, swallowing loudly, "What is it that you need?"

"I thought you were the biggest baddest dress witch in town?" I say, crossing my arms. "Work your magic."

With a grin, she nods, darting back out of view.

"Miss Wayne," she yells from the back, "Could you help me with this?"

Following her voice, I step through the drapes as I navigate the messy backroom, stepping over boxes and garment bags as I go.

Suddenly, a door marked 'authorized personnel only' flies open, and Mimi's head pops out from behind it. Glancing round, she gestures with her head to come inside.

This is weird.

"Miss Wayne, I feel like I should be honest with you. A man called just after you did," she whispers, closing the door. "He said you had to have one of these four dresses as well as all accessories, and that he would come pay for it later. He said he'd be watching."

Oh no he did not…

"Did he leave a name, Mimi?" I ask, keeping my tone measured as my blood pounds in my ears.

"Mr. Antonov," she whispers, making herself as small as she can.

"Did he say which dress he wanted?" I snap back, before taking a deep breath.

"The yellow one."

"You mean the mustard dress which would make me stand out like a sore thumb?"

She looks up at me, her eyes wide as a frosting of tears begin to form.

"You don't like my dresses?" she asks, her voice small.

Fuck.

"Shit, I'm sorry," I say, walking toward her, "I didn't mean it like that."

I pause, my mouth opening and closing as I try to think of the words to explain.

"Look, the truth is, Mr. Antonov can be quite…*opinionated*. And pushy. It's almost like he enjoys getting under my skin. And when he's buried deep in there, well, let's just say I'm not the best at handling my reaction."

"Oh, I see, are you two…" She wiggles her eyebrows, sniffling slightly as she wipes her eyes. "You know, together?"

"I have no idea," I laugh.

She hums in response, nodding her head slowly as understanding slowly creeps into her eyes.

"I don't like men who try to dress up women like their own porcelain dolls," she says, a tinge of bitterness lacing her tone.

"Yeah, me neither," I mutter.

Maybe there is still hope for this excursion.

"Mimi, your dresses *are* amazing. You clearly have skill," I say, touching her shoulder gently. "And something tells me you wouldn't be called a 'dress witch' for nothing right?"

She nods.

"I'm looking for something a little different," I say, biting my bottom lip. "Something that makes him stop and pay attention, while also telling him, fashionably, to fuck off."

"Oh, Miss Wayne," Mimi grins. "I think we can definitely make that happen."

"That's what I like to hear," I smile back at her. "But please, call me, Abby."

"Okay, Abby."

"How about we put on a little show for my driver outside? Since I'm sure he's reporting everything back to Mr. Antonov."

After a few minutes, I step back onto the store floor, catching Trevor visibly relax against the side of the car.

My jaw clenches, Roman is clearly keeping tabs on me, and is using Trevor to do it. Which pisses me off, especially after what happened to his face.

For some reason, I feel oddly protective of him.

"I think this one would be perfect for you my dear! I have the perfect shoes and little clutch to go with it as well," she looks at me, clearly pretending to still be on Roman's team. "Hmm, yes, yes this is the one!"

Mimi continues pulling out all the accessories for the yellow dress, which is still revolting. However, once accessorized, it wasn't that bad.

But still, it was *mustard* yellow.

Staring at the monstrosity in her hands, I must admit, I appreciate how well she is holding up this act.

"Mimi, no."

"No?"

"No, I want *that* one," I say, pointing to the bright red dress hanging off to the side.

"Unfortunately, Miss Wayne, that isn't available." Mimi states, sheepishly biting her lip.

I love how committed she is to our little ruse.

Pulling the dress off the rack I walk it over to Mimi and hang it on the rack on the wall.

"Oh! This is stunning!" I sigh, bending my knees slightly to look closer to it.

 Mimi really was a witch, the detailing on this dress is exceptional.

Some women fall in love with handbags and shoes at first sight, that rush of serotonin forcing them to buy them, and even hoard them.

However, ever since my husband died, I've let myself buy whatever clothes I want, or whatever I find pretty. And coincidentally that included a lot of formal dresses.

I sort of *collect* them, the same way I collect pretty plants for my greenhouse.

In truth, I have no need to buy a new dress for this Gala, because I have plenty in my closet at home I could wear.

But I have Roman's plastic…so why not?

"Mimi, can I ask you a question? And I want you to be completely honest with me."

"Of course, you can," she replies, her hand running down the front of her black dress pants.

"Is there a reason you've only shown me these *specific* dresses?"

"What?"

"Did someone call ahead?"

"Well…"

"Did a Mr. Antonov call?" I ask, crossing my arms.

"Um…"

She fidgets nervously.

In truth, we've already discussed this entire conversation, and I told her my plan to make Roman feel like an asshole, while also protecting *her* from his wrath.

But we have to put on a good show.

"Mimi, you said you'd be honest with me," I say, tilting my head with a pout. "You're known around town for being the best at your craft. It's why I came here, because I trust your judgment. But I want to know, are you recommending these dresses to me because you honestly think they would suit me…or because someone else told you to recommend these dresses to me?"

Mimi says nothing, but dramatically glances behind me as if someone is listening to us. Exactly as planned.

Because we both know someone *is*.

I turn in the direction of her gaze and that's when I see it. In the corner I notice a little red-light flashing on what appears to be a portable video camera. I feel the corner of my lips twitch.

That little fucker.

Roman is keeping tabs on me. On *camera*.

I look directly into the red flashing light before giving it a little wave and flipping it the bird.

Since my interview, it feels as if Roman and I have been locked in a game of chess, each move we make getting one step closer to checking the other.

Technically, it's a game I should've already won, with the help of my Widowmaker. But I chose to skip my turn.

…And the bastard doesn't even know.

Since then, each move has escalated. I taunt him with my skirts, and he responds by welding my desk down.

Deep down I wonder if the end result of this game is one where neither of us are going to win, no matter how much power we each think we hold.

He's petty, possessive, and persistent.

But so am I.

An idea forms in my head.

He told me he wanted me presentable, and that this gala *is* business related.

But I will not surrender the control of my wardrobe to a man again. And certainly not so that Roman can look like some big powerful business CEO, shaking hands with the rich and awful…with some prized piece of candy on his arm.

A business CEO with demons.

My CEO.

No. Stop that.

If I'm being forced to go to a snobby gala, then it won't be a repeat of how it was with my husband. I won't go as a ghost who isn't seen or heard.

I refuse to just be his arm candy.

Instead, Roman will be the candy on *my* arm.

Winking at the camera, I turn back to Mimi.

"I'll take the red one."

"Miss…"

"I'll take the red dress, or I'll take nothing." I state firmly, leaving no room for discussion. "Mr. Antonov requested I find a dress. And I have. If he doesn't like it, I can go naked. Or he can go *alone*."

Mimi chuckles softly.

"Would you also like the matching…support items?" She asks, wagging her brow and smirking at me.

"Support items?"

Mimi blushes.

"Lingerie, Miss Wayne."

A deliciously wicked grin skates across my face.

"Oh, I think I need all of that as well."

"Lovely!" She says, clapping her hands. "I think you will love it, it's all sewn custom to support each individual dress, so no one will ever see it, or know you're wearing anything at all!"

Excitedly she dashes back behind the curtains as I deliberately turn back around, facing the camera.

"So that no one will ever see it," I say firmly, narrowing my eyes at the little red dot. "What a fucking *shame*."

As Mimi reappears, carrying a few boxed items, I pull the black card from my wallet.

Roman's card.

"And you can charge them with this card," I say with a smile. "It's Mr. Antonov's and will save him a trip down here to pay for them."

"Of course, Abby."

Game on Roman.

Dropping down at my desk, I take a minute to catch my breath. I was nearly an hour late back from lunch, and I didn't even eat a single thing.

Which makes me grouchy at the best of times.

Clicking into Roman's schedule I see that Boris is due onto the floor at any minute. My stomach clenches as I remember what he said in that monster meeting.

…And the fact he was willing to go after someone's wife and children to get whatever they wanted.

Children should be protected at all costs. After all, they're the only purely innocent thing left in this world.

And yet, this monster was more than willing to… I don't even know what he was or wasn't willing to do.

And I don't want to know.

What I do know, is that two years ago he was accused of raping three separate women, who were related to Nikotech's biggest competitor.

It didn't go anywhere, as there was no hard evidence, no DNA, just the word of three women, who were later accused of being junkies. All of them eventually withdrew their accusations and the case was dropped.

I looked into them too, and while addiction might be easy to hide, the signs are always still there if you know what you're looking for.

But these girls were clean, had perfect GPA's, and graduated in the top one percent at Columbia. They worked for the same company and had relatively normal lives.

…Until Boris entered the equation.

It's interesting that one of his accusers hasn't been seen since the report was filed, and the other two moved out of state somewhere.

The problem with Boris is that since the "incident," he's a bit of a recluse. He doesn't go to The Studio, or anywhere really. At least anywhere that's noticeable anyway. It's as if he just goes to work and then he disappears until the next morning.

With how dedicated he was to this corporation; I wouldn't be surprised if he slept here.

Speaking of the monster, I watch as Boris strides toward me, his head held high as his tattooed knuckles clench.

"Don't worry, I'm on his schedule." He snaps at me, strolling right past me and into Roman's office.

Guess I should go be a good little assistant.

Standing, I walk over to Roman's office, and lightly tap my fist against the dark oak door, before stepping inside.

Roman immediately looks up at me over the top of his glasses, smirking softly.

Boris, on the other hand, is outright glaring at me.

"Can I help you, Abigail?" Roman asks.

Smiling sweetly, I clear my throat.

"I was just checking if you needed anything," I say, pointedly ignoring Boris as his eyes burn into my skin.

"No, Abby, we are all set here." Roman replies, slightly confused, as I never just ask if there's anything he needs.

"You sure? I was actually thinking of getting a drink from Roast, and wanted to see if you wanted a coffee?"

I smile sweetly, batting my lashes at him.

"No, I'm fine," he says, still staring at me quizzically, taking his glasses off.

"She could get *me* a drink." Boris states, his accent thick. "We are going to be here for a while."

Roman immediately glares at Boris, the vein in his forehead becoming more and more pronounced as the seconds tick by.

"Um, never—"

"Oh sure! I can do that!" I intervene, my voice slightly higher in pitch. "No problem!"

"No, Abigail…" Roman starts.

"Really," I smile at him, before turning to Boris. "I don't mind! What do you want, Boris?"

Boris looks at Roman, who glares at him before giving a frigid nod.

"Medium iced matcha green tea latte," he mutters, his cheeks tinting red.

"Coming right up!" I say, before turning to Roman expectedly. "You sure you don't want anything, *Boss*?"

He smirks, shaking his head.

"You know my order."

After waiting more than fifteen minutes for Boris's Matcha, I slowly make my way back into the office, glancing down at the offending green drink in my hand, I realize the power I have right in front of me.

My heart pounds as I stop quickly at the benches and set the drinks down before quickly unclasping the necklace from my neck.

Quickly, I glance around, before grabbing the straw and swirling it around.

"Fuck it," I whisper, dropping the Widowmaker in, before stirring it, making sure there's no telltale signs.

Holding my chin high, I scoop up the drinks, heading straight toward the elevators. With my free hand I smash the button, before using my employee badge.

Okay, so I'm really doing this.

At the office.

In *front* of Roman.

Slowly the elevator climbs, floor by floor. And with each beep my heart rate increases with it.

This is more than just risky; this is fucking stupid. And I know it. But as the doors open to the executive floor, my body floods with adrenaline. High on the endorphins, I walk briskly over to Roman's office, hearing his voice echoing down the aisle.

"McCleary can't get away with this," Roman seethes.

"Don't worry boss, he won't." Boris replies darkly. "I've got guys on the ground already and they will—"

Without knocking I walk straight in.

"Sorry!" I chuckle as they both stare at me.

Lifting the drinks up, I give them a small shake.

"That took longer than it should have."

Roman clicks his tongue.

"Apparently, the barista was new, and hadn't had someone order an iced matcha green tea latte," I ramble, deliberately leaning over the desk to place Roman's black coffee in front of him, and catch him staring right down my top.

"So, they had to get someone back off their break and yeah..." I ramble before trailing off.

I hold the matcha out for Boris, staring back into his cold gaze. He reaches out and grabs the drink, before leaning forward to place it down onto Roman's desk.

No. I want to see it happen. I need to know.

"If you don't mind, could you try it? The lady said that they'll redo it for you if there's any issues," I say, twisting my hands together as I intentionally lean against the desk, my back to Roman.

I know that he would see my demons, wrestling in their restraints as Boris brings the drink up to his lips.

At first, he takes a small sip, clicking his tongue inside his mouth, before nodding and taking a second much larger one.

Unable to stop myself, I bite my lip, watching him down nearly half of it, before nodding.

"It's fine," he rumbles.

"You got…a little something, right there…" I gesture to my lips, watching him copy my movement before wiping his matcha mustache off.

A cough sounds behind me, making me jump.

"If the two of you are quite finished with your little taste test," Roman snaps irritably. "We have fucking business to discuss."

"Absolutely! Let me get out of your way!"

And without another word, I walk out of Roman's office, closing the door behind me.

A twisted smile forms on my lips as I walk back to my desk.

Bye Boris.

ANTONOV

CHAPTER TWENTY-ONE

ROMAN

The next day at the office is incredibly busy, and even with Abby's scandalous outfit, I barely have time to notice.

Well, I do *notice*, but if she's going to deliberately wear that shit in front of me, while also pretending to not want to be with me, then I can pretend I don't.

In reality, I nearly had to go wank one out in the apartment upstairs because I couldn't fight my cock chubbing up every time she walked to the bathroom.

"Good morning, Sir," she says, knocking on the door to my office just after nine.

"Morning, Abigail," I say without looking up.

"*Abby*, Sir," she chuckles, setting my Wall Street Journal on my desk. "How many times do I—"

"I'm extremely busy this morning," I interrupt, looking over copies of Cillian's bank statements that Cal added to my report this morning. "So, please hold all calls that aren't from the approved list."

"Of course, Sir, I can—"

"And I need to meet with Cal at one, and I need Lev and Pasha to be here at five. Remind Pasha not to be late," I say, pushing a pad of paper in her direction. "Do you need to write this down?"

"No, I've got—"

"Good," I say, continuing on. "And then lastly tell Heather I need to see a full financial rundown of our portfolio by three this afternoon. I also want to see the numbers for the presentation. She'll likely need to reschedule her meetings for the rest of the day."

"Sure," she says, sounding far less enthusiastic about that direction. "Is there anything else that I can do for you?"

"No, that will be all, *Abigail*."

She lingers for a moment, as if she doesn't know how to handle my cold and disaffected tone, before quietly shutting the door. And yet the moment she does, I have to fight my smirk.

Her little dress shopping experience proved that Abby is *enjoying* the frustration she brings to my life. She was getting off on dangling her gorgeous flesh in front of me, knowing I want her, all the while claiming she doesn't want anything to do with me.

And while yes, there was a small, dark part of me that had briefly considered snatching her off the street and keeping her as my prisoner until she eventually learned to love me, I knew that wasn't really what I wanted.

I wanted her to be mine, on *her* terms. Because I knew that with a girl like Abby, anything less wouldn't be enough. It wouldn't be *everything*, and I want everything.

So, I've resolved to respect Abigail's wishes, even if they frustrate the fuck out of me.

…Because I know I can be just as frustrating.

If Abby wants to play games, she better play to win.

Just after ten I gave her a list of properties to review and put into one combined document for me. I waited a good ten minutes before texting Jenny to go and get my coffee from Roast. The look on Abby's face when she saw Jenny sashaying down the aisle with the shop's distinct blue cup was mildly entertaining to see the least.

I did have to shoo her from my office as soon as she dropped it off, however, as the bitch apparently thought me sending her on this quest meant I wanted her attention for some reason. But it still accomplished what I hoped it would: it got under Abby's skin.

By eleven she was fidgeting with everything on her desk. I watched her getting increasingly more frustrated every time she'd go to pick up her stapler or tape dispenser, only to remember that everything was bolted directly into the surface.

And by noon she'd probably refreshed her coffee half a dozen times, likely just to walk up and down the row of desks in an attempt to lure my attention with her pin-stripe tights.

But I stayed buried in my work.

Or at least I *appeared* to be.

What my sexy little assistant *didn't* realize was that as our Chief Executive Officer, I could pull up the security camera footage on my computer. And that while I appeared to be so preoccupied with those executive duties that I couldn't acknowledge her existence; I was actually watching every little glance she shot my way.

And for a woman who claims to not be interested, she sure couldn't keep her eyes off of me, and also couldn't stand when mine weren't constantly on her.

But perhaps the cherry on top of the entire day was requesting Heather to meet me…*in* my office.

Heather was one of the most beautiful girls at Nikotech. Second only to Abby, of course.

She was slender, with long blonde hair, and perfectly shaped fake tits. There wasn't a man on my team that wouldn't sacrifice their left nut to sleep with her. But unlike Jenny and Alison, who had already opened their legs for me, as well as a handful of my men, Heather was aroused by power…which meant she only had eyes for *me*.

And Abby knew it.

So, at three, when the elevator doors open, and she steps onto the executive floor, in her bright red chiffon blouse, matching red-bottom heels, and tight black pencil-skirt, it feels as if the temperature drops five degrees.

And this time it *wasn't* me fiddling with the thermostat.

My plan almost backfires on me, however, as I find Heather to be exhausting.

Her company is boring, her personality vapid, and her lust for relevance is pathetically obvious.

Strangely there's also a part of me that hates the way she glides past Abby's desk, prematurely drunk on a fake sense of superiority.

Abby is far above you, Miss Jenson. Watch your step.

But I know there's a purpose for her visit, and I have to play along if I want it to be effective.

"Afternoon, Mr. Antonov," she says, batting her lashes at me. "Is this still a good time for you?"

"Yes, Miss Jenson," I say, forcing a smile. "I've been looking forward to it."

I'm not, and her voice already annoys me. But I press on, because this little meeting is *intentional*.

I've noticed the way Heather stares at Abby, likely sensing my attraction to her. And I've noticed the way Abby glares at Heather, likely sensing that the slut has had my cock shoved in all of her little fuck holes.

Women were observant like that. Almost as if they can smell when another woman has been on you…or when they're a threat.

And today I'm going to leverage that threat.

After all, I could've just asked for this portfolio analysis to be emailed, not delivered in *person*.

I also could've left the privacy glass off. But I knew it would make Abby jealous, especially knowing what she did with me, in that very office.

So, with the flick of the switch, I light the fuse.

Taking a seat back behind my desk, I allow Heather to drone on about financial gains and trades that I already know by heart, discreetly watching my little fox squirm on my monitor.

She taps her pencil against the desk.

Rearranges her desk drawers.

And walks to and from the water cooler at least a dozen times, trying to catch wind of any portion of our conversation.

And here I thought she didn't care.

As five o'clock nears, I decide to compliment Heather on her outfit, making her giggle loudly.

"Do you have dinner plans tonight?" Heather says, biting her lower lip. "If not, you could come by my place tonight, I'm sure I have something you can…*eat*."

I chuckle.

"I do in fact have dinner plans," I say, walking her to the door, and switching the privacy glass off. "But I'll likely be going to The Studio tonight. If you're free, you should come."

"Mmhmm," she giggles just as I open the door. "I would very much like to do *that*."

She reaches for me, but I motion her out the door, aware that Abby can now hear everything we're saying.

"I need the transfer completed by tomorrow," I say stoically. "Make sure I'm sent the confirmation number."

"Absolutely, *Sir*," she says, smiling and pressing her files to her chest. "Anything you say. As always."

She winks at me before walking back down the row. As she presses the elevator button, it dings, bringing my brothers up to the floor, surprisingly on time.

I wonder what Abby said to actually make Pasha punctual.

"Rooooo!" Pasha says, laughing with Lev as they walk down the row of desks toward me. "You ready for dinner?"

Rolling my eyes, I step back into my office to close up shop for the day.

"Lev says there's a new steakhouse that opened up in Times Square, has these tomahawk steaks," Pasha continues, wagging his tongue. "I'm starving."

"You're always starving," Lev laughs, before turning to Abby. "Well, hello there, you must be Abigail."

"You would be correct," she says, smiling up at him. "And *you* are?"

"Oh, I'm just another Antonov brother," Lev jokes leaning on her desk. "Don't feel bad if you can't remember me, there's like a dozen of us so I'm pretty forgettable."

"That can't be true," Abby says. "Who could possibly forget you?"

She glances up at me briefly, chewing on her pencil and intentionally batting her lashes at Lev, sending my heart rate skyrocketing.

This is her payback for denying her attention all day.

…And, of course, for having a two-hour private meeting with Heather.

"Well, I—" Lev chuckles, but when he looks over at me, his smile instantly fades. He clears his throat and takes his hand off of Abby's desk as if it is on fire.

"Let's go," I snap coldly, motioning for the elevators. "I don't need Pasha wasting away on me. Especially since I have a job for him."

"Oooh!" Pasha says excitedly, clapping his hands together. "Ro's giving me a job, dinner, and a brothers night at The Studio? Is it my birthday, or something?"

"No, it's a Tuesday," I snort, stepping up to Abby's desk. "You two idiots head down and call Niko. I'll be right behind you."

I wait until the boys have disappeared into the elevator before turning to my assistant.

Who looks pissed as hell.

"I emailed you the completed excel sheets," she says, shoving stuff in her purse angrily. "And your meetings are all confirmed for next week. And the week after."

"Good," I nod, rubbing my chin to hide my amusement at her obvious jealousy. "But that red dress you bought, isn't appropriate. So, you're going to need to get another one."

"No, I don't," she says, slamming my black credit card down on the desk. "I've decided I'm not going,"

She slides it aggressively toward me.

"Oh really?"

"Yes," she snaps, glaring up at me. "I'm busy that day."

Why do I like it when she's angry?

"Then I guess you'll have to cancel your plans," I shrug, putting my hands in my pockets. "Because, unfortunately, it's part of your job."

"I don't recall seeing it as part of my *job description*," she fires back, crossing her arms across her chest. "And if it's not part of my job description, I'm not doing—"

"Actually, Miss Wayne, it *is*," I interrupt, narrowing my eyes at her provokingly. "Now it wasn't in the *posted* job description, but that's usually a vague list of the general daily duties, which is pretty standard for the industry."

"What?" She gasps, her eyes widening.

"However, the document you signed during your onboarding said, and I quote, *'the executive assistant will attend any and all business and/or social events as required by the executive.'*" I say, a wicked grin spreading across my face. "I know it's in there, because I wrote it myself."

Abby glares at me before yanking a drawer open, and pulling out a file labeled *Onboarding Docs*. She slams it down on her desk and rips it open, frantically flipping through pages. When she finds the copy of her signed job description, she begins running her finger down the length of the document.

"Fifth paragraph, I believe," I whisper. "I remember I really liked the placement."

"Shh!" She snaps at me without looking up. "I'm reading."

"Didn't you read it when you signed it?" I snort sarcastically. "You know, it's a dangerous habit to sign things you don't fully understand. Can get you into some sticky situations I'm afraid."

I watch with satisfaction as she slumps back into her chair, gripping the paper so hard it crumples.

"So, as I said," I say, licking my bottom lip. "You'll have to cancel your plans. Because I do require you that night. *Solely* for a business event."

Abby purses her lips together, her adorable pale cheeks turning red with frustration.

"But from what I can tell, you *still* need the appropriate attire," I say, sliding my card back across the desk to her. "So, get a different fucking dress, Abigail."

And without another word I leave my speechless sulking assistant where she sits, and head off downstairs.

"Tell me once more," a slightly excited, and slightly hammered Pasha says from the back seat of the Cadillac.

"Dude, he's told you like ten times," Nikolai snorts in the passenger seat. "How many more times do you need?"

"A lot!" Pasha bellows, laughing to himself. "Roman, just say it again. Do it for me. Come on! Because you love me."

"No," I sigh, rolling my eyes. "You know exactly what you need to do, and what I expect. Just make the transaction with Pace's man, without any fuckups, and we're golden."

"Oh my God!" Pasha exclaims, shaking his head. "I just can't believe you're giving me a job like this. With Pace's people too!"

"Jesus Christ, Pasha," Lev laughs. "It's just a job."

"Maybe to you, fucknugget," Pasha fires back. "But it's my first assignment. And it's guns! I love guns! Do you guys even know how much I love guns?"

"Yeah, we do," Lev rolls his eyes. Because you've been raving about it for the last two hours."

"Psssh," Pasha laughs playfully. "Just because I'm not a masochist who likes getting my face kicked in every night in some underground fight club, doesn't mean I can't find a little pleasure in what I like to do."

"Yeah, just don't find so much pleasure that you accidentally cum on Roman's leather seats," Niko chuckles beside me. "Or your next job will be setting *his* car on fire."

"Alright, alright, you assholes," I say, waving my hand as we pull up outside The Studio. "Get your shit together. Remember, we don't talk business at the club, got it?"

I hear their murmured replies as the bouncers begin to clear a pathway through the massive crowd of people in line, just before midnight.

After making our way inside and up to the VIP section, the night proceeds with the way our few Antonov brother nights usually start: Vodka. And lots of it. Tatum, Pasha's best friend shows up, and the two of them compete with Lev and Niko for best tale of stupid younger man adventures.

We've probably been here for an hour, when I feel my phone vibrate against my leg. Pulling it out, a grin spreads darkly across my face.

I have very few push notifications enabled on my phone. But one of them is a notification that tells me when Abby's little red pin…is within fifty feet.

She's here. My little plan worked.

Abby might've heard me inviting Heather to The Studio, but she couldn't have missed Pasha mentioning it before dinner.

Which means she came here of her own desire. For me.

That is also the reason I deliberately took the boys to another club before making our way back here.

But while I *know* she's here, from where I'm sitting, I can't actually see her in the crowd. For protection reasons, my chair is situated in the corner of VIP farthest from the stairs, next to a secret fire escape. So, if any clubbers with nefarious intentions, or the police, ever come looking for me here, I have plenty of time to slip away.

I'm debating whether or not I should walk over to the railing and go look for her, when Pasha makes the decision for me.

"Roman," he grins, leaning against the glass railing. "Guess who's hereeeee?"

Unable to resist, I walk over to him, but turn around, leaning my back against the banister.

"Where?" I say, sipping the drink in my hand.

"Over by the bar to my left," Pasha says leaning in. "Looks like she's talking to the bartender. Do they know each other?"

I find her in the crowd, smiling as she sits down, talking animatedly with Lizzie.

"Aw, shit," Lev says, hitting me on the shoulder as he and Niko join us. "See, I told you Ro had a thing for that girl."

I try to shoot him a glare, but my brother is far too drunk to care if I'm mad at him right now.

Not wanting to give them satisfaction or any sort of explanation, I set my drink on the nearest table and make my way downstairs, cutting deliberately across the dance floor in an effort to bury myself in the crowd of people.

Any part of me that's unsure if Abby actually has come here for me, evaporates the minute I catch her discreet glance up to VIP. Her discreet *lingering* glance, that I just so happen to interrupt, stepping up behind her.

"I'll take a vodka tonic," I nod to Lizzie, who immediately drops her current order to start making mine. "Double."

"Oh God," Abby groans beside me.

"Miss Wayne! What a surprise to see you here!" I say, tilting my head to the right, and narrowing my eyes at her. "You're not stalking *me* now, are you?"

"Keep dreaming, Mr. Antonov," Abby sighs, rolling her eyes. "You're the one who likes following me, remember?"

"Well, see, I would give you that, but tonight you're kind of at *my* club," I say with a sarcastic shrug. "Soooo…"

Abby throws her head back and laughs before leaning into me so that I can hear her over the club music.

"For your information, I'm actually here to *see* someone," she smiles at me bitterly. "His name is Teddy. So, for you to assume that me being here has anything to do with you is just comical, and kind of narcissistic."

"Teddy, huh? That's a very unique name. Not too many of those around here," I laugh. "Please tell me that you're not referring to Teddy the *bouncer*, are you?"

"And what if I was?" Abby says, her smile fading. "Teddy's great. And he's a *man*, so he's my type."

I snort. "A man who's a bouncer."

Abby laughs, shaking her head.

"God you're such a prick!"

"Yup," I shrug. "Forgive me, but I just feel you could do a hell of a lot better than him."

"You mean *you*," she says, licking her bottom lip and looking away from me. "Because you seem to think you're hot shit and better than everyone else."

"Nah," I say, shaking my head. "I know you don't want to be with me. And I respect it."

The arrogant smile on Abby's face drops, and her eyes find mine.

"You respect it?"

I nod, taking a sip of my drink.

"I'm a lot to handle," I wink at her. "I could see how that would be intimidating for…some women."

"No, this has nothing to do with—"

"There you are," a seductive purr comes from beside me, and a woman's arm slides into mine. "I've been looking all over for you."

While I do enjoy watching the smug smile evaporate from Abby's face, I still have to fight the urge to push Heather off me, as she reeks of desperation and cheap body spray.

But I'm playing a specific card tonight.

"Why hello, gorgeous," I say, slowly canvasing her body. "Wow, don't you look stunning."

"I was looking for you in the VIP," she says, shooting a side-eye glance over at a very annoyed looking Abby. "I thought that's where you said you'd be."

I smile.

Good job, Heather, tell Abby I invited you.

"I apologize," I say, wrapping my arm around her. "Little miscommunication is all. Would you like a drink?"

"No," she says, pressing her body against mine. "I think I want to dance first."

"Well, I don't want to be rude, but I was talking to Miss Wayne here," I say, leaning in close to her ear. "You two know each other, don't you?"

"Yes," Heather says, plastering a fake smile while glancing over at Abby. "We're still…getting to know each other."

"Yeah," Abby growls, clicking her tongue. "Something like that I suppose."

Heather smiles at her again before placing her hand on my chest.

"Come dance with me, Roman," she says, loud enough for Abby to hear. "I'm dying to feel your hands on me…*again.*"

"I guess you'll have to excuse me, Abby," I say, shrugging as Heather bites her lip and intertwines her fingers in mine, pulling me out toward the dance floor.

And just like that, I leave Abby standing there, glaring after us both, while clutching her drink so hard her knuckles go white. Admittedly there's a tiny part of me that feels the slightest bit guilty, but I have to remind myself that she's the one insisting she doesn't have feelings for me.

And she said she's here to see Teddy? The fucking oafish bouncer who's always smiling? That wang wouldn't even know what to do with a girl like Abby.

Hell, I barely do.

Heather pulls me on the dance floor and immediately her hands are all over me. Grinding on me and rolling her hips against my crotch. And while my desire to fuck her fizzled after the first experience, I do kind of enjoy watching other men lust after her.

And I *really* enjoy watching Abby at the bar, chatting with Lizzie, occasionally glaring over at Heather and I.

That is until that meatloaf brain Teddy gets off his shift and scrambles over to her like a puppy, inserting himself into her conversation. Even still, as he stands there lumbering over her, I notice her conveniently shielding herself behind his massive frame, while discreetly keeping a clear line of sight in my direction.

Then she strikes back.

Using the coked-out gyrating Heather as my diversion for my own stolen glances, I watch Abby take Teddy's elated hand, and drag him onto the dance floor.

My blood boils as I watch his giant hands slide down her body, as she grinds her hips against him, almost as explicitly, while shooting a pointed look my way.

Ohhh, she is asking for it tonight.

But I'm Roman Antonov. I'm a God.

…And a dickhead.

I flag down one of the bartenders that float around the dance floor taking drink orders and give her my request.

And my instructions.

When she returns a few minutes later, I grab Heather by the arm and force her to look at me.

"When I tell you," I growl in her ear. "I want you to put this shot between your tits."

"Oooh! Okay!" She giggles ecstatically.

The DJ transitions songs, and that's when one of the floor lights above us illuminates, putting us in the spotlight.

Heather obediently puts the shot between her perky breast implants, as the crowd around us cheers.

With all eyes on us, I proceed to lick down her tits slowly and seductively, gripping them firmly in my hands as I take the edge of the glass in my lips and throw it back.

Heather laughs, as I find Abby's face in the crowd.

Her absolutely *furious* face.

But I don't stop there.

With my eyes locked on my sexy assistant, I deliberately shove my tongue down Heather's throat, kissing her repeatedly.

If I thought Abby looked pissed before, it's nothing compared to her face the minute I kiss Heather. Her small arms crossed tightly across her body, she looks as if she wants to poison me…or slice me into tiny little pieces.

Yeah, okay, tell me again that you don't want me, Abigail.

But then Abby does the only thing I'm *not* expecting her to do: she leaves.

And it's not like she just casually walks away, no, she bolts for the backdoor, abandoning a very confused and dejected looking Teddy standing in the middle of the dance floor.

Shit.

Pushing Heather off of me, I immediately follow after Abby, shoving anyone in my path out of the way as I chase her out the heavy metal backdoor, and into the cold fall air.

"Abigail" I call after her.

"No!" She shouts back.

"Abby! Just wait a moment," I call, catching up with her.

"You know what," She hisses, whirling around to face me. "Go fuck yourself."

I have to stop myself from laughing.

My entire plan to prove she *does* have feelings for me, played out as perfectly as I hoped it would.

"You don't mean that," I smile.

"Yeah, I fucking do," she snarls, storming toward me. "Go fuck yourself. Or go fuck Heather. Go fuck whomever the hell you want because I don't—"

But before she can finish her sentence, I cup her face with both hands and crush my lips to hers, silencing her.

She protests momentarily, pushing against me and trying to hit me, but I kiss her again, forcing my tongue into her mouth.

And then she kisses me back. *Hard.*

Her tongue is in my mouth, and my hands are in her hair, my body consumed by the taste of her lips, and the softness of her cheek under my fingers.

My entire body is instantly electrified, heat flooding my veins as everything around us fades away, except the feeling of her lips moving passionately in tandem with mine.

But as quickly as we collided, we are suddenly ripped apart.

"Roman? What the hell?"

Heather's frustrated scoff sounds behind me and Abby rips away, covering her mouth in embarrassment as she steps away from me.

No. No. No.

"Heather, go back inside," I growl, taking a step toward Abby, only to have her step farther away from me, still refusing to look back at me.

"What the fuck? Seriously? You ask me to come tonight, and then you—"

"I said go the fuck back inside!" I thunder, whipping around to glare at her, making her jump. "Can't you see I'm in the middle of something? Or are you as blind as you are stupid?"

"Doesn't seem like you're in the middle of anything anymore," Heather glares, narrowing her eyes at me before switching her gaze to Abby.

Well, she *would* if Abby had still been standing there. However, in the five seconds I spent yelling at Heather, Abby apparently took off, at lightning speed, and now is nowhere to be found.

God fucking damnit! How the hell does she do that?!

"Get. Out."

This is all I can say to Cal.

Thankfully, he obeys and silently lets himself out of my apartment.

He came by to tell me that Boris was found dead in an alley uptown. No wounds, no injuries, and according to the doctors at the hospital, it appeared as if his heart had just…stopped.

Boris was one of my longest-serving men, having been with me for nearly a decade. He also was a health fanatic. The kind of guy who worked out every day, drank green smoothies and watched his cholesterol.

To hear that he had multiple blood clots in his coronary artery, doesn't fit the profile.

It should concern me.

But it doesn't.

Nothing concerns me right now, other than the fact that Abby won't return a single call, text or email.

Everything today went according to plan. I'd riled her up and got her to show that she wants me the same as I want her.

But then she left, and now she won't talk to me, and I can't escape the crippling feeling that maybe I pushed her too far.

And for all my bright ideas, I have no idea how to fix this.

I fucked up.

CHAPTER TWENTY-TWO

Abby

My blood boils as images from last night of Roman and Heather flash through my mind.

The way her eyes lit up, and the way she curled her body further into his. The way his tongue licked up her neck while his eyes burned into mine.

He *wanted* me to see. He *needed* me to see.

Twirling Roman's beloved letter opener in my hands, that I swiped from his desk this morning, I glare at his office door. He's had it closed since he walked in, with the privacy glass on. Indicating to me that he doesn't want me to see what he's doing in there.

Fuck him. I don't care.

When I eventually turned my phone on this morning I had a dozen text messages, two voicemails, and an email from him, all begging for the opportunity to speak with me.

I ignored them all.

Sure, I'd briefly thought about quitting, or at least calling off today. But I know if I did either of those things, his pestering would only get worse, and he would only get more persistent. And what's more, I would be giving him the confirmation he's so desperately seeking.

Confirmation that I *do* care about him.

After all, that's what last night was all about. Roman wanted a reaction from me.

A smirk fights its way across my face, knowing that while I gave in a little when he kissed me, he still ultimately failed.

It only served to further confirm my resolve.

So, today, I refuse to acknowledge what he did, even if I want to. He doesn't get that from me. Roman and I are nothing. And we will remain nothing.

I'm his assistant, and only his assistant. And until I have ousted all of the monsters, I find at Nikotech, I'm going to continue with my work like nothing happened.

However, the moment I hear a particular familiar cackle sounding down the hall, getting louder as it approaches, my entire body tenses, the echo setting my teeth on edge.

Heather.

My jaw tenses, and I take several deep breaths, attempting to think happy thoughts, while also trying to control the raging urge to smash her stupid botoxed face into the nearest wall.

God, the mess it would make. Her blood everywhere.

I snort to myself, realizing how dark my thoughts have turned. It feels as if the more time I spend in this building, the more my demons riot, testing my restraint every day.

In an attempt to distract myself I look down at the letter opener in my palm. My little souvenir.

If he happens to wonder where it went, he'll have to ask me.

The whalebone handle feels cool in my hands, so as Heather slithers her way over to my desk, I focus on all the tiny details, and how they feel under my fingers.

The light shines off her long hair cascading down her shoulders in smooth waves, as she stops in front of my desk.

"Roman needs *these*," she snaps as she drops a stack of papers in my bin. "I'm sure he'll want them all copied and then hand delivered to each department head. Which is something you can handle, right?"

I say nothing, simply staring at her.

"After all," She continues, arrogantly folding her arms across her chest. "That's *your* job,"

Don't do it Abby. Don't lose control.

Looking down again at the letter opener I run my thumb along the cool obsidian blade.

"Did you not hear me? These are urgent and—"

"Okay," I say, interrupting her, smiling up at her sweetly, and imagining her getting eaten alive by an escalator. "Anything else, *Miss* Jenson?"

I deliberately choose to put the emphasis on the "miss" part, reminding her that she is neither my boss, nor Roman's wife, but simply just another employee.

Like me.

For a moment she just stares at me, her eyes wide before quickly turning and heading straight for Roman's office.

She doesn't knock, she just steps inside.

I wait, expecting to hear him yelling, or snapping at her to get the fuck out of his office…but he doesn't.

Well, I guess his door is open to anyone but me today.

Dropping the letter opener on my desk, I wince at the audible thud the intricate handle gives.

Impulsively, I open Roman's schedule.

I don't know why I'm even looking. I shouldn't even care, but I need to know if Heather had a scheduled appointment with him today, because I know I didn't make one for him.

Smashing my finger down aggressively on the mouse button, I pull it up on my screen.

No. He has a clear day. Not a single thing scheduled.

My head smashes into the back of the chair as I glare at the screen, somehow even more infuriated that he just…let her walk into his office.

Unlocking my phone, I stare at Lily.

Maybe I should've called out and stayed at home today.

The only noise on the executive floor right now is the whirling of the computers and my rapid breathing.

Something bangs in Roman's office.

My hands clench into fists, my nails stabbing into my palms, leaving little crescent shaped indents. Leaning forward I grab the letter opener off the desk, hoping that fidgeting with something will distract me.

The phone rings, and I glance up.

Holy shit…It's *Roman*. Calling from his office.

My entire body heats as anger begins to flood my veins.

Why the fuck would he phone me when he has her there? Does he want me to get coffee for the two of them? Or is he calling just to rub their little *fucklationship* in my face?

So much for those apology texts, Roman.

Seeing red, I jerk forward and grab the receiver, slamming it immediately back down.

A sharp prick draws my eyes down to my finger, which has blood pooling from the cut the obsidian blade has accidentally made, the crimson replacing the red haze of my vision.

Fuck I barely even felt that.

Realizing I'm about to get blood all over my clothes and desk, I reluctantly stomp my way over to the bathroom, holding my hand away from my body and leaving drops of blood as I go.

Behind me I can hear my phone ringing again, but I don't give a shit.

I hit the door with such force it flings it open, slamming into the wall. My breathing is still ragged as I lean over the sink and set the letter opener on the counter beside me. My dark red blood glints up at me from the blade, and drips from the wound on my hand into the sink below.

How fucking careless of me.

Turning the faucet on, cold water flows over the cut, running red as it swirls around the white porcelain bowl.

But as I stare at my reflection in the mirror, I don't care about the pulsing pain in my finger.

My demons are right there, staring back at me, screaming to be let out.

My fragmented heart tries desperately to calm itself with each breath, only to stutter and accelerate as an uncomfortable realization dawns on me.

I'm angry at him, but not just him.

I'm angry at *Heather* too.

Roman used her to make me jealous. To prove to me that I do want him as badly as he wants me. And he knew that of all the bitches in the office, Heather is the most condescending and rude, and therefore would bother me the most.

And yeah, it was his plan, but Heather knew what she was doing. She loved the part he asked her to play in his little game. She loved flaunting Roman in front of me.

It's somehow ignited a fire in my chest and now all I really want to do is smash her fucking face in.

But that too would give him the reaction he wants.

I close my eyes, drawing in a trembling breath, and holding it, trying to put all these feelings back into the box, so I can process at a later date.

A *much* later date.

But before I can do that, the door creaks open.

The click of her heels echoes on the tile floor, and an overpowering scent of cheap synthetic floral perfume invades my nostrils.

Opening my eyes, I see Heather standing behind me, a smirk on her lips.

"Little Abigail Wayne," she chirps with a laugh. "Guess you're not so special after all."

My fingers twitch, balling into fists.

"Nothing to say? Hmmm what a pity," she sighs venomously before continuing, "I suppose I should head back. Now that the business is concluded, I think I might have Roman show me how skilled he is with his tongue. Well, you know, *remind me*, anyway."

My jealousy bubbles in my chest, even though I know that all this bitch can do is taunt me.

At least Polina, seemed ready to put her hands on me when she was confronted. She might be a bitch, but at least she was brave enough to back up the shit she wanted to spew at me.

Heather isn't. She's weak. Pathetic.

She doesn't deserve Roman.

A man like him deserves someone who can handle a little pain, someone who can fight their own battles. Someone whose demons will dance with his. Not some slut who wants to sleep her way to the top.

But as I watch Heather turn, time suddenly slows.

I hear her arrogant little chuckle, her heels tapping on the floor, and the jiggle of the handle as she reaches for it.

Then everything goes red.

I'm on her in a heartbeat. Gripping the back of her head by her hair I slam her face into the door as hard as I possibly can. She instantly drops to the floor, the weight of her body nearly knocking me over too.

With my chest heaving, and my pulse pounding in my ears, I stand over her unconscious body.

Fuck! I really just did that.

I've never been this foolish. I've never reacted impulsively, no matter how much I've wanted to.

But then Heather starts whimpering, and I realize I have to do something.

"Shut up and let me think," I bark, but she moans, louder this time.

It's going to draw attention.

Honestly, there's no way for me to know if her absence has drawn attention already. And if anyone comes in here and sees this, I won't be able to cover it up.

I need *time*. Time to think of what I'm going to do, how I'm going to sort this fucking mess sorted out.

Stepping over her, I quickly click the lock on the bathroom door in place, my brain struggling to process everything I just did.

Heather moans louder, attempting to roll over.

Nope. Can't have that. I need to restrain her.

But…with what?

Then an idea comes to me.

Setting the blade on the floor I pull up my skirt, shimmy my tights off, followed by my panties. Straddling Heather, I grab her hands pulling them behind her back and wrap my tights around each wrist, locking them behind her back.

I roll her back over, she stares up at me, her eyes wide and disoriented as they dance around the room.

"Surprise, bitch, it's me."

We stare at each other in silence, before the sound of a door opening outside catches our attention. Heather draws in a breath before opening her mouth, a scream building in her throat. But, before she has a chance I shove my panties in her mouth.

"Humph!" She screams, a tear leaking from her eye.

Running my finger down the mascara stain on her cheek, I wipe it before placing it on my lips.

"Shhh," I whisper, cocking my head. "You've got to keep your voice down."

She thrashes her head back and forth, her entire body visibly trembling as she lays there.

"You think you deserve him?" I mutter, smoothing her hair from her face, "You think you can *keep* him?"

She shakes her head again, her feet kicking underneath me. Reaching over her I grab the letter opener from the tile. Heather's eyes instantly go wide the moment she sees the obsidian blade, one she must've seen a hundred times… on Roman's desk.

"Humph! Humph!" She grunts.

In the cold fluorescent lights of the bathroom, the bright red ruby on the hilt sparkles, and for the first time I can see how detailed the ring that encompasses this gem actually is.

It truly is immaculate craftsmanship.

Unlike *this* slut underneath me.

There's nothing immaculate about this cheap knockoff Malibu Barbie bitch.

Slowly my fingers flex against the smooth cool handle.

"You know what you are?" I whisper, leaning in close to her, savoring the look of her bloodshot eyes blinking up at me, sweat coating her brow. "*Stupid.* He used you; you know that don't you? He used you to get to me, to get a reaction. You mean absolutely nothing to him."

I trail the blade gently down her cheek, watching with satisfaction as the first layer of skin flays under its touch. It's not deep enough to make her bleed, but enough to leave a faint line behind.

God, this blade is sharp.

Dissection was always my favorite part of class, something I excelled in. It was like muscle memory, knowing exactly how much precision and pressure needed for a clean cut.

I should stop, I should help Heather up, tell her to keep her mouth shut and leave…but I don't.

"How does it feel? To not be so special after all?" I spit, throwing her words back at her. Running the blade down her neck to her blouse.

She thrashes her head from side to side, her muffled pleas falling on deaf ears.

This is as much her own fault, as it is Roman's.

She suddenly stills as she sees me lower the blade closer to her skin. Slicing through her blouse it falls open, exposing her chest to me.

"I really should let you go." I mutter, shaking my head slowly. "But this is way more fun."

Screaming, she flails frantically as she kicks beneath me, using her hips to try and buck me off. I twist my legs under hers, locking my ankles and preventing her from moving.

I lean forward, my cheek rubbing against hers.

"And everyone deserves to know what you are."

With one hand over her mouth, I press the knife to her skin, slowly carving her chest.

A blade like this doesn't need that much force, the knife cuts so easily, so smoothly that it feels like an extension of me.

Heather's eyes are rolling into the back of her head by the time the first letter is done, and snot is running down her face.

I'll admit the "S" looks a little wonky, but my attention is pulled to the blood pouring down the side of her boob. I trail my thumb over it, feeling the hot raised skin.

The cut is clean and precise, but the letter isn't perfect.

I can do better.

Adrenaline pumps through my veins, and her screams are muffled beneath me, covered by my hand and my maniacal laughter.

The blade passes through layers of skin like they are paper, and the next letter looks so much better.

So much cleaner.

I carve the next, and then the next, the high and euphoria from slicing her skin making me almost feel dizzy.

Eventually I finish, signing my artwork with a simple X.

"Perfect," I grin up at her. "X marks the spot. Or I guess it marks the *slut* in this case."

She sobs beneath me, her makeup streaking down her cheeks, mixing with the blood on the floor.

"Now listen to me, Slut," I start to say, but Heather just continues wailing.

I grab her hair, smashing her head against the concrete and making her screw her eyes shut.

"If you," I hiss, "continue throwing yourself at Roman, you'll find yourself like everyone else who has crossed me: dead before dawn."

My eyes fall to her chest, entranced by the way the blood trickles and pools in the cuts.

However, when I glance down at my hands, everything catches up with me and the reality of what I've just done hits me like a slap in the face. I was so lost in the moment that I didn't really think about my actions.

Heather is covered in blood. I am covered in blood. It's on my hands, under my nails, it's fucking everywhere.

What the fuck have I done?

Pushing off her, I walk backwards until my back hits the opposite wall, staring at her laying there, her bloody chest heaving.

The words become a mess of blood, but my branding is clear:

SLUT.

I carved *slut* into Heather's fucking chest.

My nostrils flare as I stare at the mess in front of me, out of the corner of my eye, I catch sight of myself in the mirror, my eyes dark. A sinister grin stretched across my face. Blood smeared across my forehead running into my hair.

I'm covered in *her*.

Shooting forward I dart toward the sink, throwing the tap on. Water splashes everywhere as I scrub the blood from my hands and knees.

Eventually I turn back to Heather, who is sobbing quietly on the floor, and bend down to her level.

"I'm going to untie you, you're going to cover that up," I gesture to her chest, "and then you're going to fucking leave. Am I making myself clear?"

She nods frantically, moving forward I grab the blade and roll her over, smearing more blood over the white tile floors. After slicing through my tights binding her hands, I step back and let her up.

I keep the letter opener firmly pointed at her, just in case she decides to come at me. But she doesn't, and instead she dashes to the door, unlocks it, and bolts out of the bathroom.

Okay, so it doesn't look like a massacre here anymore.

I've cleaned the blood from the floors the best I can, but I couldn't get it out of the grout between the tiles, the red tinge is still visible if you look closely enough.

Bracing myself, I walk from the bathroom, the letter opener tucked in my sleeve and my chin held high.

The floor is silent, and I breathe a sigh of relief as I round the corner toward my desk. But just as I'm about to sit down, the privacy glass on Roman's office changes, giving me a clear view of what's going on behind it.

Roman is sitting at his desk, glaring at me as a hysterical Heather sobs from one of the chairs, and Cal stands behind her.

Well shit, the little slut sang like a canary.

Ignoring the scene in front of me, I sit down, opening my emails and going on with my day.

My face burns as I feel Roman's gaze. I hate that I know when he's staring at me, it's like an itch I can't quite reach. My entire body vibrates with the need to turn around and stare back at him.

A molecule of regret bubbles in my chest as I hear her sobbing, her cries getting louder and louder the longer she's sat there. I know that an obsidian blade like this, against the sensitive breast tissue, will leave a scar, one that will likely be carved into her chest forever.

Still, it felt so fucking good.

It felt better than anything I've ever done before. I could probably go skydiving tomorrow and the rush wouldn't even be able to touch this.

The phone to my left rings, and I jump, grabbing the receiver and bringing it to my ear without hesitation.

But before I can utter a word, *his* voice comes through.

"Get in here. Now."

Before I even have a chance to respond, the line goes dead. Yet I can still feel his eyes lingering on me in the silence.

Well, shit.

Rising from my desk, I stand, smoothing my hands down the front of my skirt before heading over to his office. Taking a deep breath, I push open the door, only for the calm to be interrupted by Heather jumping up as she screams.

"Get her the fuck away from me, she's fucking crazy!"

"Sit down, Heather!" Roman snaps, leaving no room for Heather to argue. Reluctantly she obeys and takes her seat. Leaning against the doorway I stare at Roman, cocking my head to the side.

"Oh, Heather, what happened?"

"You crazy fucking bitch! You did this to me!" She screams, before lunging out of her chair at me.

Roman stands, but Cal is closer, quickly stepping in front of Heather and grabbing her arm, pushing her back to the chair.

"He said sit!" He says firmly.

"I have no idea what you are talking about," I reply, my voice flat.

"Look at it!" She screams, gesturing to her chest, the blood drying on her skin. "I'm going to have this for the rest of my life!"

"Oh gosh," I say sweetly, placing my hand dramatically over my mouth. "You really should get that checked out, Sweetie. You wouldn't want that to get infected."

"Arrrgh!" She screams, once again lurching toward me, and once again being stopped by Cal and shoved into the chair.

She turns her angry glare on Roman.

"You're going to let her get away with this?!" She seethes, her bloodied chest heaving.

But Roman is ignoring her, his gaze locked on me.

"Heather," he finally says after what feels like a small eternity. "Go home."

"Excuse me?" She replies, completely bewildered.

"I said," Roman says darkly. "Go home, Heather. Or maybe to a doctor. Either way, you're done for the day."

Heather scoffs.

"You're joking," she whispers, her jaw slack.

"No, I'm not," Roman says, his voice soft but firm.

"You're actually taking *her* side?!" She snaps her voice shaking. "The side of a woman who…who…"

She snatches her bag from atop Roman's desk and pulls out an envelope.

"Here," she snarls, throwing it onto his desk.

It's then that I notice that this envelope has "Mr. Antonov" written on the front, in my clear, cursive, and very distinctive handwriting.

There was only one envelope I'd addressed with his name:

My resignation letter.

A letter that I'd specifically shredded after attending his little meeting with his monster friends. Except that clearly someone had specifically fished it out of the bin, taped it back together, and held onto it. For such an exact time as this.

My heart stops beating, and I stop breathing, realizing that I'm fucked.

Roman's eyes scan over the tattered cross-stitched document, darkening with every breathless second that passes. When he finally looks up at me, I want to evaporate on the spot, paralyzed by the haunting rage reflected in his face, restrained only by his $3000 suit.

Heather turns to me, a smirk playing on her lips.

"You see? She was going to quit. The bitch doesn't even want to be here. And after this?" She gestures to herself, "She shouldn't be. She's a monster!"

Roman glares at me, his blue eyes now dark and cold. The only sound in the room is Heather's shaky breathing and the crinkling of the paper slowly crumpling in his hand as he closes his fist, his jaw tensing.

From the moment I started at Nikotech I've wondered how deep Roman's darkness *could* go. Wondering what would happen if he just snapped his restraints one day, and let it exist, untamed and *free*.

Hell, one could argue I've been pushing him there myself.

However, now seeing the terrifying look in his eye, aimed directly at me, I've suddenly changed my mind.

…And I wish I could take it back.

My mind begins racing, remembering the rumor Jenny and Alison told me about what had happened to Roman's *last* assistant after she had betrayed him.

Exactly as I just have.

"Cal?" Roman finally whispers, without taking his frigid stare off me.

"Yes, Boss?"

"Escort her from the building."

Shit. Shit. Shit.

"Hah!" Heather gloats triumphantly, jumping to her feet.

That's when Cal steps forward.

…And grabs *Heather's* elbow.

ANTONOV

CHAPTER TWENTY-THREE

ROMAN

"Seriously?" Heather gawks at me. "You're going to just send me home? After she did this to me?"

"Well, let me ask you this," I ask, rubbing my chin, and glancing briefly over at Abigail who is trying, and failing, to contain her grin. "Do you have any proof *she* attacked you?"

"Of course! I…I…" She mumbles, glancing down at the blood-soaked towel in her hand. "But she…she did…"

Sighing heavily, I fold my hands together and tilt my head toward her.

"I'm going to take that as a no," I click my tongue.

"There's cameras!" Heather says defensively.

"Not in the bathrooms. That would be highly illegal," I say, shaking my head. "So, since you have no proof that it was Miss Wayne here that attacked you, but you *were* clearly attacked, go home."

"But, I…I know *she* did this!" Heather whines. "You could check her for the weapon! It was a black blade with an ivory handle."

Guess that explains where the Antonov dagger went.

"As you well know, unlawful workplace searches aren't something we condone here at Nikotech, Heather," I purse my lips with a shrug. "But you are clearly in need of medical attention, and I don't need you bleeding on my fucking rug, as it's worth more than you make in a year. So, as I said, go the fuck home. And understand that I won't be asking you again."

Heather's jaw drops.

She glares at me, then at Abby, before kicking the chair back and storming to the door.

"Oh, actually, Heather," I call, causing her to turn around and immediately drop the scowl on her face.

"Yes?"

"You can leave the tights."

This time I can barely contain smirk tugging at the corners of my mouth.

Setting her jaw, Heather storms back over to my desk, and throws the bunched-up pair of bloodied tights and panties at me, hitting me in the chest.

If she were a man, she would die right here for that offense. And I'd be using her salary to buy a new rug.

However, Abigail is grinning wickedly, confirming for me that she definitely is responsible for the carving of Heather's chest. And what's more, her motivation for doing so is incredibly clear: *Me.*

I'd have pity for Heather if I didn't know for a fact that she enjoyed making Abby jealous.

But also, as a mafia don, I don't allow myself to feel pity, just on general principle. It's dangerous, distracting, and detrimental to my business that needs to run free of emotion.

So, instead of yanking my pistol from my desk and shooting Heather in the back, I simply let Cal escort her out of my office. Once the elevator doors have closed, I stand and walk around the desk to my jealous secretary.

"You," I snap, making her jump, and causing her grin to evaporate instantly. "Let's go."

"What? Where?" Abby scoffs, incredulously, but refusing to move. "And what if I don't *want* to go anywhere with you?"

I snort, rubbing my jaw.

Oh, this girl...

I grab her chair, and violently spin it to face me. Bending down, I place my hands on either side of her, pinning her in her seat.

"Perhaps you misheard me. You can get the fuck up on your own," I growl, leaning in close enough to hear her draw a shuddering breath. "Or I can drag you out of that chair by your fucking hair. Makes no difference to me Abigail."

"*Abby,*" she hisses. "I've already told you I prefer that."

"I don't give a rat's ass what you prefer," I seethe. "You just sliced up one of my employees, which is going to cost me something to bury."

"You don't actually know if I—"

With a knee jerk reaction I snap, grabbing the back of her hair, and twisting it in my hand, making her yelp as I pull her up on her feet.

"Fuck!" She winces, glaring up at me.

But then she smiles. And not in the normal way that people smile. No. This is dark and dangerous.

"Oh my God, do you think I actually *want* you?" She chuckles viciously. "Or do you think that I'm *afraid* of you? Because I assure you, Mr. Antonov, I'm really fucking not."

Her words sting, landing like a dagger in my chest.

No, I felt her glare last night. And I felt her kiss.

No one can make Abby do anything she doesn't actually want to do. And she wouldn't have done what *she* just did to Heather if she didn't want me the same way I want her.

I release her, but before she has a chance to escape, I press my shoulder into her stomach, and toss her over my shoulder.

"Roman!" She gasps, as I head for the door.

"Yes, Foxy?" I ask, slapping her ass hard while swiping her undergarments off the desk and shoving them into the top drawer.

"Put me down!" She squirms, beating her fists against my back.

But I hold her fast.

"No, I don't think so," I say, carrying her past the empty desks toward the elevator. "But you go right ahead and wear yourself out, Abigail."

"You're going to show everyone my ass and I'm not wearing any—"

"*Panties*?" I say with a smirk. "Now that's interesting. Wonder how you lost those? Also, bet you wouldn't have this issue if you'd worn a pair of fucking pants."

Once inside the elevator I slam the button for the rooftop penthouse.

"Roman, if you don't put be down, I'll—"

"Do what exactly?" I say, slowly running my hand up the smooth skin on the back of her now bare calves, hearing her gasp. "Scream? Go ahead. No one will hear you. Hit me? Honey, I've had worse."

I move my free hand up her leg to her inner thigh, and slip my fingers between her trembling legs, deliberately brushing her pussy lips with my thumb.

She groans.

"But if you *didn't* want me to fuck this pussy," I growl doing it again and hearing her shuddering breath. "Then you shouldn't have allowed it to get so very wet when you were carving up Heather…over *me*."

The elevator dings, opening to the penthouse, and instead of setting her down, I carry her straight into the bedroom and toss her on my bed.

She scrambles backwards toward the headboard on her elbows, breathing heavily. Without hesitation I grab her ankles and yank her toward me before climbing on top of her, pinning her body beneath mine.

But then I feel her press something against my throat. Something cold… and sharp.

The Antonov Dagger.

She did have it. And she *kept* it.

Clever little fox.

"If you're going to use that, Abigail," I growl, leaning in closer, pressing the blade harder against my own skin, watching her eyes widen. "I suggest you do it now."

I know that if I wanted to, I could disarm her, and take it from her before she even knew what I was doing.

And I also know that based on what she just did to Heather, with sickening satisfaction, my throat would already be sliced if she really wanted to.

Or felt like she needed to.

But it isn't.

Instead, her pupils dilate, and her breasts struggle against her blouse, rising and falling in an increasing rhythm.

She does want me. Badly.

"I…hate you, Roman Antonov," she hisses breathlessly, her eyes fluttering as I move my knee between her legs rubbing it against her sex.

"That's fine. Hate me, or love me," I say, slowly reaching for her shirt. "As I said, I don't care, Miss Wayne."

Slowly I start unbuttoning her top from the bottom.

"Because I have wanted you, for a very, very, long time."

"You…haven't…known me…for a long time," she says, her voice trembling, but her hand on the dagger still holding firmly against my neck.

"I have, Abigail," I say, unfastening the last button instantly exposing her perfect tits. "It's just, you weren't mine to *want* back then. So, I didn't let myself want you."

Her expression softens, and for just the slightest second, she lowers the blade.

But that moment is enough for me to snatch her hand in mine. Pressing firmly on the pressure point in her wrist, I force the blade into my hand.

Her breath hitches, as now she realizes that she no longer has her protection. And her entire body stiffens as I lower the blade toward her chest.

Savoring the look on her face, I slide the terrifyingly sharp blade beneath the front of her bra and yank upwards swiftly, slicing it open and exposing her naked tits.

I toss the knife across the room.

"But now," I say, wrapping my hands around them, kissing her nipples and sucking sensually on each one as she throws her head back and moans. "I will not stop until I have you."

Slipping my hand between her thighs I run two fingers along her slit, watching her shiver before I shove them deep inside of her. She gasps as I immediately twist them upwards and press directly on her G-Spot.

"Oh, fuckkkk," she moans, arching her back on the bed as I continue my rhythm using my other hand to yank her short little skirt upwards around her waist, exposing her completely.

Fuck. Me.

Unable to stop myself I press my face to her pussy, pressing the backs of her thighs back toward the mattress.

"Holy Shit!" Abby gasps.

I swirl my tongue around her clit, still using my fingers to strum her from within.

Her body convulses, and squirms beneath me, but I hold her tightly, my cock starting to swell. Within minutes of my relentless onslaught, her breathing quickens, and I can hear her nearing her orgasm.

And just when she mumbles about being ready to cum, I immediately stop everything.

"Wait…wait! No! Don't stop!" She whines running her hand through her hair.

Her cheeks are flushed, her lipstick is smudged, and there are tiny beads of sweat forming on her breasts, as her mostly naked body writhes on the bed.

"What do you want, Abby?" I growl, feeling my cock throbbing.

"You know what I want," she whimpers.

"Tell. Me."

Her eyes find mine and threaten to undo me right here.

She sits up in the bed, and immediately starts to unbuckle my pants. As she slowly, ever so slowly, pulls my zipper down she presses her lips gently against mine. I lean in to kiss her deeply, but she pulls back, a wicked grin spreading across her face.

"Roman," she says, taking a deep shuddering breath as she frees my erection from my boxer-briefs, taking her time squeezing it end to end. "I want you…to show me why I shouldn't just go home and use my vibrator."

My jaw slacks, and I scoff.

Oh, you bold little bitch.

I snap, grabbing her jaw in a flash and pulling her sassy lips to mine, kissing her hard.

"Say it again," I growl against her swollen lips, emphasizing each word.

"I want you—"

"No," I whisper darkly, still holding her chin. "Say my fucking name."

"*Roman.*"

The moment Abby utters my name, I release her, sending her crashing back on the bed. Without hesitation, I grab her left leg, and swing it over her body, flipping her on to her stomach and smacking her ass.

Her yelp is followed by a sassy little giggle, and so without any fucking warning, I shove my cock deep inside of her, and grip her hips hard, so my hands are full of her soft flesh. I ram myself into her, over and over, leaving my fingerprints on her fine ass with every swat.

"Oh, my fucking God! Yes!" She moans whorishly, as I feel my own orgasm building.

Without pulling out of her, I place my legs on either side of hers, and press my chest into her back. Wrapping my hand around her throat, I pull her face to the side as I thrust deeper and deeper inside her tightening little slit pinned here beneath me.

"Hear me now, little fox," I growl in her ear as her moans get louder. "You can't get rid of me now. If you run, I will chase you. If you hide, I will hunt you until the ends of the earth. There is nothing that can stop me from having you, Abigail. Nor will there ever be. You are *mine.*"

"Roman…" The way she whispers my name, and the feeling of her climax squeezing my cock pushes me over the brink and I empty myself inside of the sexiest woman I have ever known.

…And the only woman I've ever fucked *twice.*

My promise to fuck Abby into a coma sort of came to fruition as she passed out shortly after we fucked.

However, between the two of us, the outfit she wore to work is completely destroyed. And given that the fall temperatures in New York were getting colder every day, I texted Cal, and asked him to pick up a new outfit for Abby.

Something with *pants*.

But as I lay here, with her naked and asleep next to me, I can do nothing but admire how beautiful she is. Her long brown hair lays messily around her face, her eyelids twitching as she subconsciously snuggles closer to me.

Who *is* she? And why does *she* have this hold on me?

Abigail Wayne makes no sense to me.

The woman I'd seen all those years ago, on the arm of her fuckhead of a husband, had seemed so quiet, so demure and almost shy. She almost looked as if she wanted to disappear into thin air.

And yet, the woman who lays in bed next to me now is far from the shadows of that creature. She is feisty, and sassy, and witty…and possessive. Scarily possessive.

Why does that part turn me on so much?

Ana found nothing out of the ordinary about Abby.

According to her, Abby was as pure as the driven snow, at least as far as a criminal rap sheet was concerned, and she had no affiliations to the Irish, or even the Feds. She was just an ordinary girl, living an ordinary life in Forest Hills, in a house she was gifted after husband's untimely death.

But Abby isn't ordinary.

When she walks into a room, she eclipses all other women, without question. I've never wanted someone like this before, as if deep down some fragmented part of my soul is convinced that only she can calm the rage within me.

…Or make it worse.

And for some reason, that only makes me want her *more*.

Cal arrived with fresh clothes for Abby a few hours later.

However, any high I felt from the blissful few hours we'd spent together naked, evaporated the moment he called Trevor to take Abby home, ominously requesting to speak with me…in private.

"This can't be good," I sigh heavily, my chest suddenly feeling tighter than it was just a few minutes prior.

"It's not," he says quietly, setting the laptop down on my marble kitchen island. "And I didn't want to bring it to your attention until I had something to back it up. But I think I've finally got a lead on who killed Igor, Jacques and Boris."

"Really?" I say, blinking. "That sounds like good news to me!"

But my stomach twists the moment I see the look on Cal's face, and I know that I really am not going to like whatever he says next.

However, instead of saying anything, he turns the laptop to face me, and presses play.

"This is Jacques at Roast," he says quietly, as I watch him walking in and out of the coffee shop.

"Am I supposed to give a shit that he's getting coffee?" I say sarcastically.

Cal presses fast forward, and that's when I see her.

Abby walks into frame next to him, but because another patron of the cafe walks in behind them, I can't see exactly what interaction happens at the counter.

"So, he was there the same time she was," I snap irritably. "Why does that make her a suspect exactly?"

"It doesn't," Cal replies matter-of-factly. "But this does."

He takes the computer, closing the file and opening another one. I immediately recognize the footage from The Studio.

"The next two clips are on the nights that Abby was spotted at the club."

Pressing play, I watch the two thirty-second clips. The first is blurry and too hard to identify, but the second is very clearly Abby sitting at the bar with Igor. The footage in the dark club is admittedly poor, but I can clearly see the distinct tattoo that sits between her shoulders of the snake and the flowers.

It's her alright.

And I can also see where Oleg came to get Igor, presumably to answer my phone call, where I told Igor to keep an eye out for *her*.

Fucker conveniently didn't mention she was already there.

Honestly, I'm glad Igor's dead. I hated him anyway.

"This doesn't show much Cal," I growl, trying to convince myself with my words. "It's clear she operates in the same circles as we do."

Cal's stare drops from mine, and that's when I know.

He has more evidence. Damning evidence.

"I went through all the tagged posts for The Studio's social media accounts on both nights," he says quietly. "And, well…"

Sighing heavily, he minimizes the current video and presses play on another.

It's posted by a woman claiming to be a regular, and in the time-stamped video, I watch as Igor leaves the bar, and Abby waves her hand over his unattended glass.

Fuck.

"If you zoom in on the video," Cal says cautiously. "You can see the ring on her hand a little better. From what I can tell, it might be an old pillbox ring. They were pretty popular in the 80's club scene, for cocaine."

"Is that what you think she gave him?" I ask, without meeting his eyes, instead watching the looping image of Abigail drugging Igor. "What did the coroner say?"

"They retested him, per your request," Cal shrugs. "But nothing came up."

"Then…she *didn't* drug him?" I ask, confused.

"There's really no way for us to know," Cal says with a shrug. "The coroner said that certain aspects of decomposition on his body could potentially indicate poisoning, but if there isn't a test already out in the world for the particular type of poison she used, then we'll never find it."

"What?"

"There are thousands of different poisons, Boss."

My jaw spontaneously clenches, and I take a deep breath.

"Boris," I say softly. "She volunteered to get him coffee. She could've…"

But my voice trails off, knowing I don't even have to finish that sentence as I watch Cal nodding at me.

This definitely could explain how my men have kept dropping like flies around me, but I still don't understand why.

Somehow, I both have answers, and new questions.

"Boss," Cal says quietly. "If you'll allow me?"

I don't want to allow him.

I want to hit him.

Not because of anything *he* did, because the man was just doing his job. But because I can feel my chest tightening at the very thought of Abby betraying me.

…And what I'd have to do about it.

Realizing that Cal is staring at me while I continue to silently spiral out of control in my own personal hell, I nod.

"Even with what I'm seeing here, I still don't think she works with the Irish," he says as gently as he can manage.

My eyes find his briefly before he respectfully lowers them to the ground.

"And…why is that?" I ask.

"She doesn't fit the profile, and this isn't their MO. And frankly, Boss, if she was sent to kill you, she would've done it by now. There's no reason for her to risk exposure by prolonging her time as a mole."

There's a slight ringing in my ears and I can feel my heartbeat pounding within my chest.

"But…why then?" I ask, my voice low. "Why target Igor? Or Boris? Or Jacques? Or any of our men?"

Cal shakes his head.

"I don't have an answer for that. But the Irish aren't our *only* enemies. Igor had quite a few, and more than a few jilted mistresses in his past. But this," he nods, pointing toward the looping video of Abby slipping the drugs into Igor's drink. "Tells me that this is not her first time doing this. I can promise you that. It's too smooth."

He's right.

The way Abby's body movements coincide with her hand discreetly waving over Igor's glass are so discreet, they would be virtually undetectable unless you were specifically looking for them. It's so smooth, it's damn near professional.

Abby is a professional…killer? As in, a serial killer?

Immediately my thoughts drift to her husband.

Her conveniently *dead* husband.

She'd said he "wasn't a good person," and nearly admitted to me that he put his hands on her.

"I'm just suggesting that you think on it," Cal says, clearing his throat. "We've been so focused on Cillian, that perhaps we're trying to see a motive that fits *our* objective, instead of an objective that fits *her* motive. Perhaps there's more to this than you think."

Looking up at Cal I can see the brave sincerity in his eyes.

He knows that I could break his jaw for saying something bad about Abigail, and yet he'd still say it if it were the truth. That's just the type of man he is, and has always been. Loyal. Trustworthy. And keenly observant.

And I know that if he truly thought that Abby was a threat, he wouldn't be telling me to think about it.

…He'd have killed her already.

ANTONOV

CHAPTER TWENTY-FOUR

How the hell did this happen?

How did I catch feelings?

Feelings that have pushed past the point of being just attraction. Roman has become more than a mark, and it happened the moment I hesitated.

The moment he felt like home, was the moment my plans changed irrevocably.

I still can't believe I allowed him under my skin. And not just under my skin, but into the marrow of me so deeply that I lost control, and carved Heather.

And even after being faced with what I'd done, or what I'd tried to do with the resignation letter, he didn't punish me. Instead, he threw me over his shoulder like a caveman, and took me to his penthouse to fuck me.

And my God did he fuck me *well*.

After our romp, I woke sore, in all the *right* ways. Minus that leg cramp, that even now still sends a spasm through my body, randomly making me shiver.

He didn't make me admit my jealousy, and he didn't ask me why I cut

Heather. He didn't even ask me about the letter opener that I clearly stole from his desk.

What he did do, however, was send me home…with his cum still dripping from my pussy.

A long, relatively restless sleep followed, wishing that he had come home with me.

But when I showed up this morning, Roman acted as though the events of the day before hadn't happened. All in all, it was a relatively normal day.

…Until he sent me shopping at lunch.

"You can run, and I will chase you."

His words still linger in my mind annoyingly as I spend the rest of the afternoon testing the limit on Roman's card.

I spent forty grand in Mimi's, twelve grand on greenhouse necessities, and ten grand on some new art supplies.

And then of course there was the five grand donation I made online to the "New York Widows and Orphans Fund," while I was waiting in line.

I'm sure Roman will love that one.

But as I stroll out of the last boutique, I see Trevor waiting for me beside the blacked-out SUV. He opens the back passenger side door, but not for me.

…For Roman.

He steps out of the car in his black suit, and matching aviator sunglasses, with an arrogant smirk.

"Having fun, Miss Wayne?" He asks me as I approach.

"Ahh Roman! Fancy seeing you here? Don't you have a meeting in fifteen minutes on the other side of the city?" I say sweetly, batting my lashes at him. "Because if you do, I think you're going to be late!"

"Get in the fucking car, Abigail."

"Well, aren't you in a fine mood this morning?" I say, rolling my eyes, my shoulders sagging. "Couldn't you lighten up a bit? It wouldn't kill you, you know."

He sighs, his hand running through his hair. "Just get in the car."

My arms cross across my chest, bumping the bags together as I stare at him, "Manners?"

"Please?" He asks between gritted teeth.

Out of the corner of my eye I see Trevor's eyebrows jump as he listens to our conversation, and Roman Antonov saying *"please."*

It isn't like him to cave so quickly, or even politely.

"Okay, okay." I mutter with a shrug before raising my arms that are weighted with bags, "What do I do with these?"

Trevor steps forward, his hand outstretched for me, "I'll take them, and put them in the back for you."

However, as he reaches for my bags, I notice the gun attached to a harness under his jacket, and then another tucked into his waistband. I pause, my eyes widening as I stare at him carefully putting my items in the car.

Trevor glances over at Roman, whose eyes are meticulously scanning the street around us.

What's going on?

Roman slides across the seat to make room for me.

Running my hands down the front of my skirt I walk forward, closing the distance between us and slide into the seat. The leather is still warm from where he was sitting.

From out of nowhere, Cal appears, whispering something to Trevor and pointing him toward another car. He then jumps into the driver's seat of our car, and instantly his eyes find mine in the rearview mirror.

I can't explain it, but something about his stare feels procedural, and calculating.

Eventually he tears his gaze from me and back to the road as he pulls away from the sidewalk.

The silence is deafening as Roman stares at the side of my face, willing me to look at him. After a few seconds I finally cave, and turn to face him. I watch him appraise me the same way Cal did, almost like I was a puzzle he needs to crack.

"Did you enjoy your little shopping trip?" Roman says. "On my dime?"

Laughing, I dig out his card, holding it out between my fingers for him to take, "Of course."

"Keep it," Roman states, waving me off before looking at Cal through the mirror.

"What?"

"Keep it," he repeats, looking back at me with a smirk. "Besides, I happen to look forward to seeing *you* in whatever you purchased."

My cheeks flush in response, and I look out the window to hide my face from him.

"I do have a question for you though," he says, but doesn't finish.

Turning back to him, I look up at him expectedly.

"What exactly did you buy from Arts Fortune?"

"Just a few sketch books, and pencils," I say, tucking my hair behind my ear.

"A few… Abby, you spent nearly ten grand," he laughs.

"Well, I wanted the best."

"What for?"

"People commission me for tattoo sketches every now and then," I shrug. "And since it's art that goes on your skin, they need to be precise, and detailed."

"Seriously?" He scoffs, his tone judgmental. "And you need ten-thousand-dollar pencils for that?"

"Yeah, I do," I nod with a playful grin.

"What tattoos have you drawn?" He snorts.

"Well, you know the one on my back?" I say, flirtatiously batting my lashes at him. "The one that you had your mouth all over, and said you liked while you were thrusting inside me?"

He suddenly clears throat loudly, shooting a pointed glare at Cal in the mirror, as if silently telling him to forget he heard me say that.

"Yeah," I say, raising my chin proudly. "I drew that."

"Hmm…maybe you should draw me one," he says, rubbing his chin. "You know, since I paid for the ten-thousand-dollar pencils."

"What would—"

"Did you kill Igor?" He suddenly states, interrupting me.

His tone is flat, and his jovial attitude and expression has evaporated in an instant, nearly giving me whiplash.

My heart stops, and I stare at him, my jaw hanging open as I laugh quietly to myself, feigning surprise.

"What?"

"Did you, or did you not kill Igor Ivanov?" He states again, his eyes hard as he reads my face.

Holy shit.

Why is he asking this? Does he know something?

"No, Roman, I didn't," I scoff, turning my body toward him, intentionally forcing my muscles to relax as I simultaneously try to imagine how an *innocent* person would respond to this question. "What the hell? Why would you even think something like that?"

He copies my movements, twisting his body toward mine, as his eyes burrow into my soul.

"Well, I checked the CCTV footage from The Studio for that night. *You* just so happen to be the last one to speak to Igor, before he died a few hours later," he says, his face blank as he narrows his eyes at me. "So, I will ask you again…Did you kill my best enforcer?"

Wait, Enforcer? Shit. Shit. Shit.

The genuine surprise of his unforeseen interrogation causes my jaw to slack, and my wide eyes to blink profusely. Attempting to keep a lid on my reaction, I school my face, and scoff loudly.

"I can't believe you'd think that, Roman," I say, shaking my head and folding my arms across my body. "And what the fuck do you mean by "enforcer?" Am I supposed to know what that means?"

"Abby… I'll ask you one more time. And do *not* fucking lie to me," he growls, ignoring my question. "Did you kill Igor?"

As I stare into his eyes, I see his demons reaching forward, straining to escape and to dance with mine.

I have to touch him.

Reaching forward I gently place my hand just above his knee, locking eyes with him as I soften my face, attempting to look both hurt and honest at the same time.

"No," I say quietly, my voice barely above a whisper. "I did not kill Igor. And for the record, I didn't approach him that night, he approached me. We had a short conversation, then he left for a phone call. But while I waited for him, I contemplated how rude he was to Lizzie, and changed my mind. So, I left. That's all that happened."

He looks up at Cal in the mirror before nodding.

"Okay. I just…had to ask," he says quietly.

My heart is pounding as Roman reaches forward, his fingers running down the side of my cheek.

But then all of a sudden, he snaps, and grips my chin firmly. Tilting my face up to his, he leans in, slowly closing the distance between us.

"But I promise you," he whispers, his voice low and gravelly. "If I find out you've lied to me, Abigail, no one will ever find you."

My nose twitches as I lean into him, his cologne wrapping round me, clutching my heart in its grips.

"You'd miss me though," I whisper against his lips, quickly pressing our lips together before I pull away. Leaning back into the chair, I sigh, staring out the window.

We sit in silence for the next twenty minutes, as I watch the autumn trees fly past us enroute to my house. I frown, glancing back at Roman.

"Seriously though, you did have a meeting today, and you're going to miss it."

He shrugs, smirking at me as he rubs a finger over his bottom lip.

"Guess you'll just have to reschedule it for me."

"Roman, it took me three days to get you this appointment!"

"Oh well. Get me another one."

He reaches into his suit pocket, and as my eyes can't resist following the movement, I happen to catch sight of the same harness that Trevor was wearing.

Roman is carrying a gun as well.

He pulls out his phone, nonchalantly tossing it over to me and forcing me to catch it.

I swallow hard, cradling the device in my hands.

"Um…okay. I'll need the—"

"It's 9817," he says with a nod down to the phone's password prompt.

Quickly I type in the code, watching as the screen unlocks to show his very organized display.

I do, however, find it kind of endearing that this scary gun-carrying CEO's wallpaper is his dog, Caesar…and he's wearing a bowtie.

"Awwww," I coo, holding the phone up toward him with a wave. "He's so cute."

"Don't let him hear you say that, or he'll go soft." Roman chuckles, the sound being the most normal thing I've ever heard him do all day.

I feel my cheeks heat as I stare at him.

As I continue to stare at him, I notice when he smiles, he gets a little crease in the corner of his mouth, his demons retreating ever so slightly.

I'm certain he's never laughed like that before, and it makes me wish he did it more.

His smile fades slowly, his brow furrowed as he nods to me, "Are you going to reschedule my meeting, Foxy?"

"Right, yeah, sure," I say, shaking my head as my fingers fumble over the keys. "I'll do it now,"

But just as I'm about to press the call button, a text message pops up.

Lev
11:46 a.m.: Pasha's going rogue Ro, he's insisting he try out the guns before we make the final sale with Wesley.

All the blood in my veins freezes instantly, and my heart stops beating in my chest. I glance over at Roman, finding that he is staring at me. Intently.

The phone vibrates again.

Lev
11.46 a.m.: Seriously Ro, you better fucking deal with him. He's now drinking vodka. Around heavy artillery.

My brain attempts to process the words in the sentence I've just read.

Guns. Sale. Heavy artillery.

But before it can, another message comes through.

Pasha:
11.46 a.m.: Hey big, Ro! I know you're the head of the family and all that mafia jazz, but guns are MY passion. Just let me deal with it. Tell Lev to fuck off.

Mafia?

My vision of the car around me suddenly turns hazy, and my mouth dries as I breathe in through my nose. I bite my lip, slowly moving my jaw back and forth as I lock the phone.

Holy. Fucking. Hell.

Mafia?

Everything starts clicking into place. I've had the pieces of the puzzle for months, each one practically hand fed to me as I worked and listened to the chatter in the office.

How was I so *blind*?

Roman is in the Mafia.

And not just *in* the Mafia, but according to Pasha's text, he's the head of it. What's more, the monsters in that meeting that day in his conference room, were all in the Mafia too.

"How did you kill my best enforcer…"

Roman's words ring in my ears.

Fuck…I killed a mafia enforcer!

No wonder Igor always had fucking men with him. He was just like Roman, who always had even *bigger* men with him. Big, scary, grandma-killing monsters who do his dirty work.

Well done, Abby, you wanted monsters. And you found them.

My brain feels fuzzy, the synapses now flawlessly connecting all the dots I've missed.

Roman has access to whatever he wants, however he wants, and his business is clearly more than just corporate investments. He carries a gun, as do all of his men. Even his SUV is outfitted like a tank going into an active war zone.

His demons make more sense now, as does the darkness I see in him.

I've read plenty of books on the mafia, most of them detailing how men in his position are usually born into this life, raised to be ruthless, merciless, savage.

Born to be monsters.

The power this man commands isn't because he's rich and successful. It's because he's dark and dangerous, maybe even deadly. And everyone knows it.

Everyone but me apparently.

And I realize now that if he finds out I killed his men, I'm dead.

I need to get out of this car and regroup.

My brain is overloaded and bursting with all this new information that I know that if I stay round Roman much longer, I'll fuck up.

He's always been five steps ahead of me, and I had no idea.

And while yes, I may have thought I was getting in bed with the devil, it turns out I didn't fully know that devil at all.

Smiling up at him, I pass him back his phone.

"You know what, I just remembered they'll be heading to lunch soon." I say, my eyes looking past him and out the window, seeing that we have pulled up to my street. "I'll just call them later, and get it rescheduled."

"Okay," he shrugs.

The car rolls to a stop outside of my house and I gulp.

"Thanks for the ride." I say, gripping the handle of the door as I push it open. "And the clothes and, um, art stuff."

"Foxy."

"Yes?"

"Tell me, one last time, that you didn't kill Igor."

I do my very best to hide the fact that once again my heart stops, and my stomach twists, realizing that I'm going to have to lie to Roman Antonov, head of the fucking mafia, once again.

"I didn't kill Igor, Roman," I say, shaking my head. "Honestly, I don't even know why you're asking me that? It's kind of disturbing."

He says nothing, his eyes scanning me like a hawk.

"Let's be real for a second, do you really think of me as the type of person who would kill someone?"

"You carved *slut* into Heather's chest, Abigail," Roman snaps back, raising a brow. "And I never thought you'd do something like *that*. So, yeah, I'd say the consideration is there."

Shit. He has a point.

"Okay," I say, swallowing hard. "Tell me this then, how exactly would I have killed him, Roman? I barely spoke to him, the man was twice my size, and I was long gone when he died."

But as the words leave my mouth, I immediately realize I fucked up.

I might not have said I killed him, but I just gave the man a bone. And I suspect he knows *something* that he's not telling me, probably more than I realize, because he's at least suspicious of me right now.

"Long gone when he died, Foxy?" He says, with a nod, his eyes narrowing again.

"I…er…just mean he died at The Studio, right?" I say with a shrug. "That's what Oleg told me, and I think I read about it in the paper."

But somehow, the look in his eye confirms that we *both* know that's not what the paper printed at all.

He stares at me in silence, and for a minute, I wonder if he can hear my heart thumping in my chest as I sit here, waiting to know if my hasty improvisation has worked to cover-up my slip. The quiet seconds tick by slowly, chipping away at my resolve.

And just when I consider cracking and confessing to everything, in hopes that he will understand and not kill me right here in front of my townhouse… he smiles.

"Of course. You're right. That's ridiculous," he says, shaking his head with a grin. "I'll pick you up at seven for the Gala this evening. I look forward to seeing your dress."

"Mmhmm," I chuckle nervously.

And without another word, I dart from the car, finding some of my shopping bags already sitting on my top step.

Looking over, it's then that I see Trevor has hopped out of the car behind us, which has apparently been following us the whole time. He's carrying the rest of my bags to the door when I look at Roman, who is still staring at me from the backseat.

I turn on my heel and bolt up the cobblestone path to my door.

"Thank you, Trevor," I say softly, and he nods silently before walking back down the path to the cars.

I dig for my key in my purse, with each passing second my heart rate increases, as I slowly struggle to breathe. Piece by piece I can feel my composure crumbling as I finally find my keys, but nearly fumble them.

After I jam the key into the lock and twist, I throw the door open, hearing it bang off the wall as I lean down and grab the bags. I practically throw them in the walkway, narrowly missing Lily as she darts to greet me.

The door closes behind me, but just before it does, I catch Roman, now leaning against the side of the SUV, and staring up the path at me… *grinning*.

ANTONOV

CHAPTER TWENTY-FIVE

ROMAN

Got you little fox.

Perhaps I might've missed the way her pupils dilated when I asked if she killed Igor. Or the nervous way she shifted and looked away from me, tucking her hair behind her ear. Or even the way her cheeks turned the brightest shade of crimson.

But there's no way I could've missed her little slip of the tongue before she got out of the car.

"…I was long gone when he died."

Indeed, she was. And how convenient.

"Where to, Boss?" Cal asks me, as I stare up the walk towards Abby's little Tudor style house.

"Chelsea Pier," I say, rubbing my chin. "I suppose we have to go handle this Pasha situation before he fucks up my shipment with Jaxon Pace."

I take one last look, certain that I see the curtain moving, as if someone has just sheepishly ducked behind it.

"Trevor," I say as I open the backseat door. "Stay behind and keep an eye on my little fox. I don't want her slipping off into the woods or anything."

"Yes, Boss," he nods.

My phone buzzes in my pocket.

Lev
12:21pm: Hello???

Jesus Christ. How bad could it be?

But as Cal pulls away from the curb and I call my brother, I have no idea I'm about to learn exactly how bad.

"They did *what*?!" I thunder at him.

"They…got drunk, and…and…went down to the…dunes," Lev says, panting heavily.

"Are they still at the dunes?!" I say, my eyes registering with Cal's in the rearview mirror, silently instructing him to head in the direction of Long Island.

"Y…yes…" Lev replies. "Aw, fuck! My ankle!"

"What?" I ask, confused. "What's going on Lev? Why are you so out of breath?"

"Because," he continues, gasping for air. "I've been trying to keep up with them. They just took off running across dunes talking about playing a game."

"What game? What the hell?"

"I don't fucking know, Roman!" Lev thunders back at me. "It all happened so quickly that I didn't catch the details!"

I sigh, closing my eyes and pinching them together.

Today is the day that I'm going to murder my little brother.

Of all the days he decides to be an idiot, he picks today.

I can't believe he would pull this shit, when I specifically instructed him not to embarrass me in front of Pace's representative.

"Seriously, what is wrong with this kid," Lev pants. "And how the fuck is he so fast? Why are they both so fast?"

"Lev, they are grown adults," I say, rolling my eyes. "More or less anyway. If they want to—"

"They have *guns*, Roman!" He shouts into the phone.

"*What*?!" I roar. "Why would they do that? And who gave them guns? What the fuck is going on there Lev?!"

"Everything was going good until Pasha invited Wesley to test out the guns," Lev says defensively. "Then they got drunk."

"How much did they have to drink?"

"It's not how much they had, Roman, it's *what* they had," Lev snaps irritably. "Tatum brought a bottle of absinthe and--"

"You let Pasha do absinthe?!" I thunder at him, feeling the car accelerate as Cal steps on the gas.

"Hey, I didn't *let* him do anything!" Lev yells back at me. "As you said, he's a grown adult and—"

"He's a not an adult, he's fucking moron!"

"Oh shit," I suddenly hear my brother say. "Oh fuck, oh fuck!"

"What? What's wrong now?" I ask, my blood pressure immediately spiking.

"Oh fuck! What is that? Is that…*blood*?" He shouts to someone that isn't me. "Holy shit! Is he shot?!"

"What?!" I shout into the phone. "*Who*? Who got shot?! Lev? Lev!"

But the call goes dead. And all I see is *red*.

"I just have one question," I snarl menacingly to the young man staring up at me, his eyes wide with fear. "Have you lost your fucking mind?"

"Um," he hiccups, leaning slightly to the right. "I…I don't think so, I just—"

"And what the fuck happened to all of your clothes?"

"Um, well, the sun was really hot, and I just thought—"

"You weren't supposed to think," I hiss. "You were supposed to obey. That was my instruction."

"I know," he says, hiccupping again. "But I thought—"

"There's that word again," I snap. "See you *thinking*, Pasha, is the problem here."

There's a shuffling behind me and Lev approaches carrying a handful of clothes. Angrily he slams them down on the sand in front of me, glaring at Pasha.

"Noah is gathering the rest, but now that you're here Roman, I'm going home to ice my ankle."

"See if the guys working on Wesley have an ice pack before you go," I bark at Lev.

He rolls his eyes before begrudgingly limping over to the ambulance that has driven out to meet us.

Thankfully, the bullet my idiot brother drunkenly fired at Wesley had missed any vital organs, hitting him in the ass cheek instead.

But it has still hit him, meaning that he was injured, and now I have a royal mess on my hands.

I glare down at my brother, who sits with his legs crossed in the sand in front of me, his hand covering his genitals.

"Look, I know that you're mad," Pasha says, squinting at me in the blazing sun. "But do you think that maybe I could put on some clothes now? I'm kind of getting sand up my ass."

"I don't fucking care!" I roar at him. "Did I not explicitly tell you exactly what I wanted you to do, and exactly what not to do?"

"Yes, but—"

"This was supposed to be a simple fucking transaction, Pasha! Just one!" I roar. "So please explain to me little brother how that instruction translates to two fuckheads drinking absinthe and playing fucking war games on the dunes with the man you're supposed to be buying guns from?"

Pasha opens his mouth several times but says nothing.

"Answer my fucking question!"

"Well, I'm confused because to be fair, you've asked me more than one question, Ro," Pasha says, lifting his hand to block out the blazing sun.

He smiles at me, probably hoping that like so many times before, I will forgive him simply for being my little brother.

But no. Not today.

I kick him straight in the balls, sending him toppling over, coughing into the sand.

"You're a fucking idiot!"

"Look, Roman, I…I'm sorry, okay? I didn't mean—" My terrified brother says, as he sits on the ground next to the ambulance.

"Sorry? Oh, you're sorry. Oh, well, what a fucking relief!" I say sarcastically. "Well, I guess if you're sorry, then I guess that makes everything all better then!"

"Really?"

"No, you moron!" I shout at him, spit flying from my mouth. "I gave you one job—one fucking job to do, Pasha! You were supposed to meet with the guy from Pace Transport, and make the transaction—now he's sitting in a fucking ambulance with a bullet in his leg!"

"Actually, Sir, it's not in my leg," Wesley says, looking up from the stretcher. "It's actually just my ass cheek that—"

"You shut the fuck up!" I hiss at him, shooting him a look.

"Yes, Sir. Sorry, Sir," he says nervously, immediately putting his head back down.

Pace's munitions "expert" can't be much older than my brother, and lays on his stomach on the stretcher as two of New York's paramedics, that I have paid handsomely to not report this incident, work to remove the bullet fragments from his right ass cheek.

Glaring between Wesley and Pasha, I'm not sure who to be more pissed with, but I'm leaning toward Pasha, who looks exponentially guilty.

"You shot one of Jaxon Pace's men," I snarl at Pasha. "Do you even realize what that means? It means that if he wanted your head in retaliation, there would be little to nothing I could do to prevent him from killing you!"

"I promise I won't say anything!" Wesley calls from the stretcher. "To be honest, I'd probably be in a lot of trouble anyway for—"

"I said shut the fuck up!" I snap at him.

"Sorry, Sir," he says apologetically. "Again."

I see the realization of what could have happened register in Pasha's eyes, and he immediately hangs his head.

After staring at him for a few seconds, I finally sigh, and bend down so that only he can hear me.

"Do you have any idea what your death would do to me?" I ask, imploringly. "It would break me, Pasha."

"I'm sorry, Roman," he says quietly. "You're right, I was an idiot. I didn't mean to be so selfish. And stupid."

The tone in his voice and inability to look at me tells me that my brother is finally understanding the gravity of his actions.

Placing my hand on his shoulder I open my mouth to say something, but I'm distracted when I hear someone else walking up behind us. Rising I whip my head around, only to be greeted by Noah, who is carrying more clothes he found scattered on the dunes.

"Boss…here is the rest of…" he says breathlessly wiping his sweaty brow.

However, that's when I notice that he seems to be sweating far too much for these temperatures, and even in the bright sun his skin looks sallow and pale.

"Noah?" I ask, watching him clutch his chest. "Are you al—"

But I don't get to finish this sentence before Noah just collapses face down in the sand in front of me, making me jump backwards.

"What the fuck?!"

Despite the paramedics' efforts there was nothing they could do to save Noah's life. He died right there in the sand.

But even before they loaded him up, and took him to the morgue for a formal autopsy, I already knew what the coroner was going to find as his cause of death.

It was going to be a heart attack.

How did I know this? Because after recalling the events of the morning, I realized that Noah had been the only member of my team to ask Abby for a coffee in our early morning briefing with Pasha before the Pace deal.

The only one besides me.

Yet I felt fine. In fact, I've never felt better.

And it only further supports the idea that Abigail Wayne does in fact have something to do with my men dropping like flies around me.

While I am irritated that men I've trained and mentored keep finding their way to the morgue, I don't value my men as much as some Dons value theirs.

But I don't operate the same way most Dons do.

My father taught me from a young age that power resides in fear, and that having my men fear me, and the consequences of disappointing or angering me was far more effective than trying to earn their love.

Why your men respect you isn't as important as the fact that they do in fact respect you.

The loyalties and love of men are easily influenced, and can be easily swayed, especially where power and money are concerned. Should a new opportunity arise, or someone promising them more than I'm willing to offer, they could be tempted to betray me.

However, their fear keeps them tethered to me at the hip. Or the fear of what could happen to their loved ones.

A lot of my men have relatives back in Russia that they send money home to every month. Should they leave, the payments I make to keep their kin above water would stop. And should they fuck up, well, the people they love might just go missing.

And then there's my system.

Unlike Jaxon Pace, who is land-locked and therefore chooses to outsource trained professionals from all over the world, I prefer to work with what I've got. And in an international melting pot like New York City, I have one thing in abundance: people.

With over eight million residents, NYC is inundated with potential recruits, and that's not even counting the sixty-million visitors a year. I decided to work with the system, not against it.

Over the last decade, I've spent a lot of time building a team of people who build people.

It means that I could take any man off the street, and within a matter of weeks, turn him from a raw recruit to a ruthless trained killer. It also means that my men constantly seek my approval, and aim to perform every task assigned to them to the very best of their ability…because they know what's at stake if they disappoint me.

They know they are all replaceable.

Yes, I should perhaps be pissed that my foxy brunette is killing my men. And perhaps I should confront her, and even punish her for it.

But I won't.

Because while my men are replaceable, Abigail Wayne is *not*. And she's worth a hundred of them.

And as I stand in the mirror, buttoning the dress shirt on my tux, preparing for my date with a potential serial killer, I can't fight the smirk that is tugging at my lips.

Of course, it would be her.

I've avoided relationships because of the nature of what I do, and I never thought a woman would be able to even face my darkness, let alone wrestle my demons. Because no woman I've ever met has been able to keep up with me.

Until *her*.

And Abby might just have bigger balls than all of my men combined.

Every day she works a stone's throw from the most dangerous man in New York City and shows absolutely no fear. No matter how terrifying, arrogant, or downright unbearable he can be, she always stands her ground, and even defies him whenever she feels like it. What's more, she's systematically taking out his trusted men…right under his nose.

Well, technically, I don't know that for certain yet.

The deaths of Igor, Boris, Jacques, and Noah certainly follow the same pattern and they've all had direct contact with Abby just before they kicked the bucket.

But I still don't have any *conclusive* proof.

And a part of me wants to see her doing it.

No, I *need* to see her doing it.

So, instead of retaliating, I will wait for my curious little fox to fall into my trap…because then she will be mine forever.

It's my own fault.

I should've known better than to tell a woman what to wear. Or more specifically what *not* to wear.

Especially one like Abby.

Because doing so is like baiting a tiger…It's never going to go the way you plan.

I sent Abigail shopping for a dress, watching her through the store's security cameras the whole time.

But somehow, she still manages to walk out of the house in something that barely covers anything at all.

Now I find myself fighting the urge to rip the eyes from the skulls of my entire security detail for staring at her, as it would get blood on my favorite tux.

I'm also now fighting my desire to skip the Gala completely and spend the entire night hearing her scream my name.

As the two of us step into the ballroom it's immediately evident how stunningly beautiful she is. And as we mingle between the attendees, I watch as all eyes turn to her.

But, unfortunately, that includes my sister, Polina.

"Roman, darling," she sneers as she glides over to us in her silver sequined full-length gown. "Sleeping with the *help* now? Tsk tsk."

Abby's lips smile politely, but her eyes do not. Eyes that tell me she would love to have her hands on the Antonov dagger and carve something into Polina as well.

Admittedly that would be interesting to watch.

"Polina, you joined us," I say, rolling my eyes as I take a sip of my champagne. "What a disappointment."

"And surprising," Abby says with a smile. "Considering I was sure I mailed the invitation to the wrong address. *Intentionally.*"

I cough, choking on my champagne.

Her eyes scan Abby's body, as she clicks her tongue inside her mouth.

"You're an interesting little thing, aren't you?" She sneers, narrowing her eyes at Abby. "You think you belong here, with us, simply because you flashed a bit of skin and—"

Knowing Polina's affection for physical altercations, I see the moment she decides to reach for Abby before it happens and I'm able to snatch my sister's arm before she touches Abby.

"Lay a hand on her, sister," I growl menacingly. "And you'll be buried *with* your husband. Have I made myself clear?"

Polina yanks her arm away from me.

"Well, then at least you'd be doing something about it!" She hisses at me, her voice low. "Instead of just sitting on your ass while my husband's killer is out there, somewhere, free!"

"So sorry for your loss," Abby taunts, with a vicious grin. "I bet he was quite a standup guy."

"You don't get to speak to me, you working-class, bitch—" Polina snaps, once again reaching for Abby.

This time I grab her, and pull her into a tight hug.

"Walk away, Polina," I whisper. "This is your last warning."

My sister mutters a curse in Russian as she pulls away from me. She glares at Abby once more before turning around and storming away from the two of us.

My heart is pounding in my chest, my rage taking over my body.

She's getting far too fucking bold. I'll have to fix that.

I'm tempted to go after her, put her in a car, and have one of my men take her home, until I'm ready to deal with her myself. But when Abby presses her body against me, and smooths the lapel on my tux, I forget about Polina entirely.

"Let's dance," Abby says suddenly, taking the glass from my hand and setting it on the nearest table.

"What?"

"Dance?" She says, raising her brows at me. "And no, unlike *Heather*, I don't require a tequila shot."

The snippy little way she says it, paired with the way her eyes narrow at me, makes me chuckle.

If she only knew how angry I am right now…

But I don't want her to see that. So instead, I take her hand, and lead her out onto the dance floor, spinning her into me in tandem with the music.

"Your sister seems *really* nice," Abby chuckles, tilting her head and batting her lashes at me.

Somehow, it's her sarcasm that pulls me back from my spiral of anger.

"Nah, Polina is actually a huge cunt," I snort, looking down at the mysterious creature in my arms. "No one likes Polina."

"I mean, someone *did*," Abby shrugs.

"What was that?" I ask, raising my brow.

Did she just admit to it? Right here?

"Well, I mean she was married to Igor," Abby says, her cheeks flushing. "But then again, even the devil likes company I suppose."

I grin.

"Funny, that part is true actually," I growl, leaning in to whisper against her ear. "I do enjoy company."

"Are you saying you're the *Devil*, Roman Antonov?"

"I could be," I reply, clicking my tongue. "Why, are you afraid, Abigail?"

A wicked grin spreads across her face.

"No, but you should be."

"And why is that?"

"Because," she says, biting her lip. "I want your *job*."

I don't know if it's the look in her eyes, or the terrifying remorselessness with which she says it, that turns me on so much, but I'm convinced I have never wanted her more.

"You know, you might be the most fascinating woman I've ever met," I say quietly, spinning her around as the tempo in the song picks up.

"If you're expecting me to self-deprecate all over this expensive dress that you paid for, Mr. Antonov, you should know that I personally think I'm adorable."

"Oh, I don't disagree."

"Good, then—"

"But you're a *liar*, Abigail," I say, dipping her. The arrogance evaporates from her face instantly.

"Now you have a choice," I whisper, pulling her back up and into my arms before spinning her again. "You can either play coy, or you can come clean. The choice is up to you."

Abby stares at me, blinking rapidly. But just as she opens her mouth to respond, she's interrupted…by Cal.

"We have a problem," he whispers to me. "Cillian isn't here."

My stomach immediately drops.

"But he was confirmed on the list?"

"He was," Cal nods. "But he hasn't shown, and I just heard from the host that he called an hour ago and removed his name from the silent auction. And said he wouldn't be attending dinner."

"He's erasing his trail," I growl, my heart starting to pound.

"Is something wrong?" Abby asks, her brow furrowing.

"We're leaving," I say, taking her hand. "Now."

"What?" She asks as I drag her off the dancefloor with Cal in tow. "But we just got here?"

"My sister?" I ask Cal.

"She left after placing her bids," he says before muttering into his earpiece for the team to bring the car around.

"Mr. Antonov!" A man says, stepping in front of the three of us as we head for the exit. "So glad you could join us tonight—"

"Move!" I bellow, as Cal practically shoves him out of our way to the door.

"Uh, at what point are you going to tell me what's going on?" Abby asks. "I got all dolled up for tonight, at your request, we just got here, and now we're just leaving?"

But I say nothing.

My mind is spinning.

The fact that Cillian isn't here is concerning. And the fact that he took his name off the guest list and his bids for the silent auction, could be a sign that he wants no association with this event...in case something goes down.

"What?" Cal says, pressing his hand to his ear. "What do you mean they won't let us pull the cars around front?"

Tossing our tickets to the boy running the coat check I glare at him for good measure, prompting him to quickly find and hand us our coats.

"Boss, we need to take the back exit," Cal grumbles. "The cars are waiting for us there."

"What the fuck?"

"There's a press event out in front."

"So?" I hiss.

"Channel 4 is outside," Cal says as he opens the door to the back stairwell that he knows leads outside to the parking lot.

"Whoa, whoa, whoa," Abby says, stopping dead in her tracks. "I'm wearing a ballgown and five-inch heels. I'm taking the elevator and I'll see you in the lobby."

She tries to reach for the door, but I stop her before she can.

"Oh no you don't," I say, snatching her jacket from her hands and tossing it to Cal before grabbing her around the legs.

"Wait! Roman!" She shrieks as I throw her over my shoulder. "Oh my God!"

"Keep your voice down," I bark, immediately starting down the stairs and unbuttoning my suit coat to give me access to my gun.

"Right but you're making my tits pop out of my dress!" She huffs, fidgeting behind me, presumably adjusting herself.

"Which as I recall, wouldn't be a problem had you gotten an appropriate dress," I quip sarcastically. "And not one that shows off every single *ass-et* you have."

"Funny," Abby fires back immediately. "I didn't see you complaining when you were adjusting your little chubby all night, Mr. Antonov."

I purse my lips, barely resisting the urge to slap the fuck out of her perky behind now shoved in my face.

I'll make her pay for that comment in front of Cal later.

Floor by floor we make our way down the steps, with Cal going ahead and making sure the doors leading to the stairwell stay closed until we've passed.

When we finally set foot on the ground floor, I gently set Abby down, and take her coat from Cal, holding it open for her.

"Well, I hope you're not too winded," she says with a taunting smile, slipping her arms inside of it. "I was going to invite you back to my place."

She reaches back and her hand immediately grabs my crotch, squeezing hard. A bit *too* hard.

Oh, this girl...

Cal opens the door for us to the parking lot, but before I let Abby step outside, I pull her back and pin her against the wall by her throat.

She gasps just before I crush my lips to hers, shoving my tongue into her mouth.

She kisses me back, her hands pressing gently against my chest as I suck hard on her bottom lip.

"Don't worry, Foxy," I whisper as I pull away. "I was already planning on it."

However, the flash of sincerity in her eyes that bat up at me, before settling back on my lips, softens my aggression ever so slightly, and I release my hand from around her throat.

Of course, there's a part of me that wants to ravish her, right here. And of course, I love manhandling her around and taking her breath away.

But what she said to me that day at the bar still gnaws at the corners of my mind like an earworm.

"Let's just say my ex wasn't a good person..."

The vague words sent me on a small quest down a minute rabbit hole, looking for answers. But I couldn't find much. Her dead husband may have been a douche, as so many aristocratic men often are, but his business dealings were either very clean, or very well hidden.

Which has left me to wonder if her comment is in reference to something he did to her *physically.*

I never saw any marks on her, whenever I'd see them out in public together. But I did see the extensive list of small "accidental" injuries reported in her medical file as minor bumps and scratches.

The idea of anyone laying their hands on Abby makes me immediately murderous…while also making me second guess how aggressive I should be with her.

Because I know how aggressive I *can* be.

Taking a deep breath I step back, and extend my hand, which she accepts without hesitation.

As we step into the city night, our two cars wait for us down the sidewalk, the heat from the exhaust turning to steam in the cold fall air.

"So why did we—"

"Death to Antonovs!"

Abby's question is interrupted by a man's shout, followed by rapid gunfire to my left.

With a pistol in his hand a short skinny man wearing a ski starts running toward Abby and I. And just as one of his bullets grazes my left arm I push her behind my body, yanking my own gun from my belt but unable to get a shot off.

Thankfully, Cal's aim is impeccable.

He fires two shots directly into the man's chest before landing the last one right in his forehead, sending his brain matter scattering all over the parking lot.

"Boss!" Oleg pants, racing up to me. "Are you alright?!"

"We're fine!" I snap, pointing to Abby. "Get her to the car now!"

"No!" Abby protests, her lip trembling as she clings to me. "I want to stay with you!"

"Abby, I will be right behind you," I say reassuringly, grabbing her shoulders. "I just need to make sure the threat is dealt with. Go with Oleg!"

"Please, Miss," Oleg says, pulling her toward the car as I turn around.

"Roman!"

However, before I can say anything, I hear another man screaming, charging at me from behind. Another shot echoes through the air, and as I turn to look, I find the man already dead and on the ground.

…And Abigail holding Oleg's gun.

CHAPTER TWENTY-SIX

I'll never forget the life leaving his eyes.

I've killed my fair share of men, but I'd never actually seen them… *die*.

I enjoyed the waiting.

That was the best part for me, not seeing them die, going home and waiting for there to be a news report, scrolling through the obituaries, hunting down the death certificates.

The thrill kept me going, it was like a surprise.

But the only surprise I see right now is the look on Roman's face as he stares back at me, his jaw slack.

He whipped his head round so fast toward the sound of the gun firing that he didn't even register it was me that pulled the trigger.

His gun is pointed directly at me, as are the guns of his men. He jolts, the pistol in his hand dropping just as fast, before tucking it away.

"Lower your fucking weapons!" He yells, and his men follow the command. My eyes glance down to the gun in my hand, still pointed at where the attacker stood, watching it shake.

Why is it shaking? Do they do that? Do guns shake?

It only gets worse as I realize it's not the gun that's shaking…it's *me*.

"Fuck!" Roman exclaims, his hand roughly tugging its way through his hair. "How the fuck did this even happen?"

"Boss…" A man to my left starts, but it fizzles out as I stare forward, my eyes blurring as everything shifts out of focus.

Drawing in a deep breath, I feel the air fill my lungs, as I hold it, before releasing out my nose.

After a moment my eyes start to focus again, only to see the blood pooling around the dead man's head, staining the concrete as it tries to seep into the earth. With each beat of my heart his blond hair turns crimson.

The gun drops from my hand, the sound echoing through the alley as all eyes dart back to me again.

Roman curses under his breath before turning back to his men.

"You!" He points to the man to my left who's burning a hole into the side of my face with his gaze. "Get the fucking shells."

Roman slowly walks forward, looking past me, at another one of his men, who is also staring at me.

"Someone clean this up! Now!" He hisses, venom pouring from his mouth.

"Yes, Boss."

"We were never fucking here. Abby was never fucking here!" He thunders, glaring at each one of them before stopping in front of me.

He gently takes my hand, which is still shaking, and still outstretched, frozen in place.

"Foxy…" He sighs, my name sounding like a prayer from his lips.

"I killed him," I mutter, my voice flat.

"I know."

"He was going to shoot you in the back… I shot him… I killed him… Roman… I want…" I trail off, my voice quiet.

"I know, Abby. I know," he murmurs, pulling me toward him.

My body feels heavy, and my knees buckle as the weight of what I did hits me in the chest.

I've killed before, but I've never *seen* it.

Roman catches me, trying to stop me from sinking to my knees, but they hit the cold concrete making my bones ache.

"What the fuck are you standing around for?! Get to work!"

"Yes Boss!" Oleg barks. "You heard him! Fan out, get scrubbing."

"Where the fuck is my car?"

The sound of muttering and feet scuffling on the ground follows as the men start moving around me as Roman crouches down next to me, his eyes locked on mine.

Oleg steps round us, walking up to the body.

"It's okay, Abby, you did what needed to be done," Roman tries to reassure me, I feel my head nod in agreement. But I can't look away as Oleg grips the guy's shoulders, flipping him onto his back. Lifeless, empty eyes stare blankly toward the sky. His skin was already tinting gray, in contrast to the blood pouring onto the ground.

"It's okay, you're okay," Roman continues, whispering into my hair. My eyes close, as his thumb rubs soothing circles on my back.

Roman's reassurances fall on deaf ears.

Because the truth is I'm not upset that someone died by my hand tonight. I'm at war with my thoughts and feelings over how much my demons enjoyed it.

I can hear the body being dragged away, likely to be swept under the rug and forgotten.

Deep down I know that I should feel some remorse, regret… guilt. I should feel anything other than what I'm feeling right now, but I can't find any reason to.

He was going to kill Roman, so I had to kill him.

But…I *wanted* to. And I would do it again.

Fuck. I want to do it again.

We stay in silence, Roman sweetly trying to comfort me, and protect me at the same time. His body is practically wrapped round mine like a shield. He whispers that everything is going to be okay, and that I did nothing wrong. All the while my demons riot and roll, fearing that I'm going to cage them once again.

I hear feet shuffling towards us and I twist, glancing up at Oleg over my shoulder.

"What?" Roman barks crudely, causing Oleg to jump and stand a little straighter.

"I—sorry, Boss," he clears his throat, trembling as he does so. "We—I, we need the *gun.*"

"Fine," Roman snaps, untangling himself from me, leaning forward to grab the gun.

"No." I say, my voice clear.

The alley falls silent as everyone turns to me once again, Roman leans back, leaving the gun exactly where I dropped it.

"Miss Wayne," Oleg says, quietly wringing his hands together as his eyes ping pong between me, Roman and the gun. "It's a murder weapon, it *has* to be disposed of."

"No," I repeat, narrowing my eyes before turning to Roman. Somehow,

I know that he will understand, even if he isn't aware of what I need him to understand.

"I want it," I say softly.

"Abby, this ties *you* to his death," Roman says, his head tilted slightly, appraising me.

Can he see it? The demons rolling beneath my skin, wrestling with my soul. Can he see them staring back at him through my eyes?

He grabs the gun in his hand, standing to his full height, leaving me seated on my knees.

The gun clicks once, twice, the magazine sliding out of the grip. Twirling them both in his hands, a smirk gracing his lips as he looks down at me and extends his hand.

Glancing up from beneath my lashes I take his hand, and he squeezes it before pulling me to my feet.

"No one will know what happened here. The weapon won't tie you to anything, Abby, I'll make sure of that."

His large hands grip the barrel of the gun as he hands it to me, the veins in his wrists pulsing.

With a nod, my fingers flex as the grip settles into my palm, as if it was made for me, the weight filling me with a strength I didn't know I've been missing. Gently, I run my fingers lightly over the barrel, feeling the cold metal nip at my skin. Twisting the gun in my hands, I quickly tuck it away in my clutch, the weight heavy on the strap.

My lips twitch, a smile fighting to break free as a laugh bubbles in my throat.

It's clear to me now that Roman was indeed cut from the same cloth as me. His demons dance with mine, to a tune that neither of us fully understand.

Yet here we are.

I was going to kill him. Part of me had regretted my impulsive decision to knock that coffee from his hands.

But now I no longer regret anything.

I don't want Roman to die at all.

Swallowing, I glance back up at this man, feeling him staring at me.

"Can we go?" I murmur.

He gestures toward the front of the Alley, smiling.

"After you, Foxy."

The city blurs past me in black and white, lights shining and glittering as we sit in comfortable silence. He didn't ask how I was; he didn't reassure me again. Not because he didn't care, but because he knew he didn't *need* to.

Never have I seen a mark go down like that, but I suppose *he* wasn't a mark at all.

Just someone trying to take what's mine.

I glance over at Roman who is furiously texting on his phone, his jaw tensed.

"Where are we going?" I ask, stopping that thought from continuing.

"Home."

Turning slightly, I stare at him. "Home?"

"The penthouse."

"That's not my home, and that's work," I state, crossing my arms over my chest.

"Not *that* penthouse."

My spine stiffens, "You have more than one fucking penthouse?" I roll my eyes.

"Yes."

"Where?"

"You don't know? Abigail, you lived in that building."

What the fuck.

"Roman, I just want to go home," I glare at him.

"You are going home." He replies, his answer short.

"That's not my home Roman." I shake my head at him, as he smirks back at me.

"It used to be," He says, his eyes sparkling as he stares at me, "is there a reason you don't want to go there?" He probes, trying to pry something from my lips.

"Bad neighborhood," I reply with a shrug, brushing off his question before looking back out the window. "And I just don't like it there."

"Fine," he sighs, relenting. "But first, I need to check on something at the penthouse."

I fight to resist the urge to cave and give in to his wishes. But instead, I scoot silently across the backseat toward him, resting my head on his shoulder as his arm wraps around me, pulling me ever closer.

"Thank you," I whisper in response, my body tired after dancing all evening, and my feet aching as my heels finally claim my toes as their victim.

With his other hand, Roman reaches across, and places it on my knee before giving it a squeeze. Warmed by his body, I close my eyes, letting sleep claim me.

The sound of a door slamming drags me from my slumber.

"Fuck!" He rumbles in my ear.

Groggily I look around, blinking the sleep from my eyes.

"Hey, sleeping beauty," Roman murmurs quietly, rubbing his hand down my arm. "You can stay in the car."

"How long was I asleep?" I ask, my throat dry.

"An hour."

"It doesn't take an hour to get from the gala to here," I say, straightening, my bones cracking as I flex my spine.

"We may have circled a few times," he says quietly, clearing his throat. "I thought you could get some sleep. It's been... a night."

Rolling my eyes, I shake my head.

"I'm not a delicate little flower, Roman, I'm fine."

He scoffs quietly to himself, a soft smile on his lips. Lips that are so perfect, that I find myself leaning in, electricity crackling between us as I stare up at him.

He leans forward, his lips ghosting over mine, kissing me softly, but setting my body on fire at the same time.

"Shall we head up?" I breathe, watching him smile.

Without saying a word, he exits the car, the door slamming closed behind him, but before I have a chance to open my own door he's already there, extending his hand to me.

Sliding out of the car I glance up toward the massive building, staring at the place where I once lived.

My pretty prison...that nearly killed me.

This building is a reminder of all that I lost, not just myself but my child too.

I never thought for a second that I would be back here, I hadn't even considered how it would make me feel.

After my husband died, I never returned, and had no desire to ever do so. I hired men to empty it.

Oleg walks past and gets whacked in the back of the head by Roman.

"That's for slamming the door, you shit."

"Ouch, shit, fuck, sorry. Won't happen again. I didn't mean to wake her," he says, rubbing the back of his head with a sheepish look on his face.

"It better not."

A giggle escapes me, causing both men to look at me.

"So, what are we here for?" I ask, trying to distract myself from the towering prison before me.

"Pasha."

This is all he says as he pulls me toward the entrance.

As we step inside the glass doors, I take in the interior once again, hating how even now it's still familiar, and that once upon a time I called it home.

But, home has never been a place for me.

It's a person, or in my case, a cat.

My heels echo across the expensive marble floor as we cross the foyer toward the elevator.

Oleg follows behind, stopping short before clearing his throat awkwardly. "I'll, uh, take the stairs, Mr. Antonov."

A shiver rolls down my spine, grateful that Roman doesn't want to take the stairs too. Even though I've healed from everything that I've experienced here, this building is imprinted with nightmarish memories for me, and I wish the whole thing would burn down into the ground.

I swore I'd never return. Yet here I am…because of the man holding my hand: Roman Antonov.

The elevator dings, revealing the polished mirrored walls, and the lights shining out of it like a beacon. Roman doesn't respond to Oleg, he just walks into the elevator, his eyes fixated on me.

Straightening my spine, I follow, the elevator moving slightly as I step inside and finally release the breath, I didn't realize I was holding.

Without a word the doors close, and we begin to ascend.

He steps up behind me, his chest flush against my back, warming the chill that has crept into my bones.

"What's wrong?" He whispers into my hair, causing goosebumps to rise along my arms.

"Nothing."

"Don't lie to me, Abigail… What's wrong?"

I shake my head slightly, as I lean against him, borrowing some of his strength.

He sighs, reaching past me and hitting the emergency stop.

Gripping my shoulders he spins me round, pressing my back into the mirrors behind us.

"What. Is. Wrong." He repeats, each word firmer than the last.

"I killed someone," I spit out, the lie rolling off my tongue like butter to try and cover my truth.

Roman stares at me for a second, his eyes scanning mine, as if trying to gauge whether or not I'm being honest with him. Just before I'm about to cave, he sighs, lowering his head with a slight nod.

"He deserved it," he replies, before pressing the emergency stop button again, the elevator jerking as it resumes its climb.

I just lied to Roman Antonov. *Again*.

I could've told him. I could've told him how this building reminds me of everything I lost, but I didn't.

My fear is that it would leave him with so many questions. Questions that I don't particularly *want* to answer.

It's not that I think Roman couldn't handle the truth, but more because I know that it could potentially raise suspicions about how his men keep dying. Which could lead to me having to explain how and why I killed them…and that I'm going to kill another.

Perhaps one day I will tell him.

And perhaps one day this building will burn.

I'd love to watch it crumble, until there is nothing left. And then, maybe, it'll be rebuilt, just like I was, and will become something better.

Just as I did.

The elevator dings, the doors sliding open to reveal a softly lit foyer of a penthouse, the layout completely different from the one I used to live in.

The colors are dark, exactly like Roman.

Usually, dark color schemes like this make the room feel smaller. But this? This somehow makes the room feel bigger.

Or maybe it *is* bigger.

My eyes glance around, drawn to the windows. The penthouse I had didn't have windows like this. The entire outer wall is made of floor to ceiling glass planes, providing a breathtaking view of New York City at night.

Allowing its King to watch over his kingdom.

"Do you—" Roman starts to say, but is suddenly interrupted by a loud bang, coming from the other side of the penthouse.

He looks up, listening intently.

There is another bang, followed by a muffled shout.

Roman quickly pulls his gun, before looking at me.

"Stay here," he whispers forcefully before he turns toward the noise.

But just as he is about to round the corner, Caesar suddenly appears at his side.

"Who's here, boy?" Roman asks, looking at the dog in confusion.

As strange as this interaction is becoming, it occurs to me that the first thing any intelligent intruder would do would be to restrain the dog…or take him out completely.

And as Caesar doesn't appear injured or even on high alert, something about his behavior makes me feel slightly less anxious about this whole situation.

But apparently Roman disagrees, as he continues to stalk the hallway. I lose sight of him as he silently steps around another corner, his gun still drawn, and Caesar loyally by his side.

As more bangs echo down the hall, I can't help but take in the credenza in front of me. A family picture in a gold frame draws my attention.

Gently I pick it up.

In the center is a well-dressed man and woman. She is tall, thin, and blonde, with soft, almost sad features. In her arms she holds a blond-haired, blue-eyed toddler, who smiles broadly.

At their feet sit three brunette boys, and a girl. A fifth child stands slightly off to her mother's side.

This is Roman's family.

He sits at his father's feet, with the tall dark-haired man's hand resting on his shoulder. His father looks cold and stoic, with deep wrinkles around his eyes and mouth.

Lev and Nikolai, the identical twins, sit on either side of what can only be a young Ana. And unsurprisingly the grumpy looking child standing to the side is unmistakably Polina.

"What the actual fuck!"

Roman's voice startles me, thundering from across the penthouse, followed by Caesar barking.

"Woah! Chill!" A familiar voice shouts defensively. "Chill!"

"What the fuck are you doing here?!" Roman snaps. "And what are *you* doing here?!"

"Pasha said it was cool!" Another man shouts.

Setting the picture back down, I stroll forward, heading toward the commotion.

"Why the fuck are you locked in the bathroom?!" Roman bellows, followed again by Caesar barking. "What the fuck are you both doing in your *boxers*?"

As I round the corner, I see Pasha, and a man I don't recognize crawling out of the bathroom with their hands raised in the air…wearing just their boxers.

"Answer me!" Roman barks, still pointing his gun at them both.

"Sorry, Mr. Scary Russian Man," the strange man hiccups. "We were just in here looking for…erm…"

"Looking for *what*?"

"Condoms." Pasha finishes for him.

Slowly, Roman lowers his gun.

"*Condoms*?" He asks, confused.

"Yeah, for the girls…"

"What fucking girls?"

"Oh…aren't they out there?" Pasha asks, confused, straining his neck trying to look around a towering Roman. "They were just sitting in the living—"

"There's no one out here!" Roman snaps. "What fucking girls are you talking about?"

"Um," Pasha clears his throat, rubbing the back of his head. "The girls… we ordered…from Jewel Rose."

Roman mutters something in Russian running his hand through his hair before turning to see me, smirking, and leaning against the wall watching the shit show unfold.

"Put on some fucking clothes," he hisses at them both. "There's a lady present."

"Really? Where?" The unknown man says, excitedly looking around Roman. "Oh! Hello there, Miss—"

"Wesley!" Pasha snaps, elbowing him in the ribs.

Wesley's smile fades the moment Roman steps forward, blocking me from view, and muttering something under his breath that makes Wesley sit back on his heels and lower his head submissively.

"Yes, Mr. Scary…erm…I mean, Mr. Antonov," he whispers quietly. "My apologies."

"Get. Fucking. Dressed."

Roman's tone is terrifying as he steps away from them both and turns to me.

As he walks down the hall, Caesar bolts forward excitedly, licking my hand with his tail whipping around.

"Caesar!" Roman shouts, clicking his fingers.

With a whine, the obedient pup runs to his bed, and lays down, staring at me with his beautiful eyes wide.

Roman motions silently to the large open living room.

Pouting, I step into the room and sit my ass down on the couch with a thump.

The three of us sit in silence, waiting for Pasha, and the guy called Wesley to return. When they finally emerge, they approach sheepishly, with a limping Wesley stopping slightly behind Pasha, looking incredibly pale.

"Explain yourselves."

"Well, erm… you see—" Wesley stammers, rubbing his arm, looking tentatively at Pasha.

"We, I mean… *I* hired some girls from Jewel Rose," Pasha interjects. "It's that top tier escort service."

"They're like the best of the best!" Wesley pipes in, before immediately biting his lip.

"Yeah, it wasn't cheap," Pasha nods, hiccupping again. "But that's like, the point, you know?"

"Never heard of them," Roman snaps irritably. "But I've never had to *pay* for sex before."

Well, that's a relief.

"Well, like," Pasha says quickly. "Neither have I. But Tate said—"

"Fucking Tatum," Roman growls, clenching his fist. "I'm going to strangle that fucker the next time I see him."

Pasha gulps, and licks his lip before continuing, his voice shaking slightly.

"Yeah, well, erm, he recommended them. He said they were the best, and like super discreet. And because you told us to stay off the streets, we were trying to be discreet and—"

"Wayyyyy discreet!" A visibly drunk Wesley chimes in, only to get elbowed by Pasha once again.

"Yeah, I'd fucking say so," Roman hisses, his jaw flexing. "So discreet that they managed to lock you two drunken idiots in the bathroom and leave."

Neither of the men say a word, their eyes lowered to the floor.

"How much did you have to drink?" Roman demands.

"Oh just a few," Pasha snorts, waving his hand.

"Glasses?"

"No! *Bottles!*" Wesley interjects. "We found a bunch of them in your wine cellar."

Even from where I'm standing, I can hear Roman growl.

"Hey…Pasha," Wesley suddenly asks inquisitively. "Wasn't there a painting there?"

And that was when all hell breaks loose.

Roman is screaming.

Pasha is screaming.

And Wesley is creeping as far away from the pair of them as he can, while Caesar barks at the scene in front of us.

"Come here, boy," I call to the dog, who whips his head around and follows me jovially to the kitchen, likely to escape the noise.

After my impromptu nap in the car my throat feels drier than the Sahara Desert.

Seeing some organic dog treats on the counter I open the bag and Caesar wags his tail.

Of course, Roman would have organic dog treats.

"Here you go buddy," I say to the pup, who is expectantly offering me his paw.

I bend down to shake it and pet his head, before rising to my feet. Still thirsty, I begin opening cupboards until I find a glass, and turn to the refrigerator looking for something to drink.

I wonder what Mr. Antonov eats when he's not in the office.

However, my curiosity is disappointed when I find it empty. Well, apart from a singular can of cheap beer, which somehow, I suspect isn't his.

Rolling my eyes I head over to the black marble sink, filling my glass.

Taking a deep breath, I lift the glass to my lips, but pause as the smell of flowers suddenly fills my nose. Turning I look for the source of the smell, hunting until my eyes land on two singular roses just laying on the kitchen island.

Immediately I recognize the flowers, and my jaw drops.

What kind of monster leaves *this* type of rose drying on the counter?! Why didn't they put them in water? Do they have any idea how fucking expensive they are?

Actually, that gives me an idea.

Gently picking them up I take them over to the counter by the sink. Placing them inside the glass in my hand I immediately grab some paper towel and run it under the faucet. As I wring it out in the sink, Roman comes storming into the kitchen, with Pasha close on his heels.

"I cannot believe you paid to get your dick wet, and somehow get your ass locked in the bathroom while those bitches robbed my penthouse."

"I know, I know, this is bad."

"*Bad*?!" Roman roars. "Pasha! Bad doesn't even cover it you fucking idiot!"

My eyes jump between the pair of them, noticing that Wesley is absent from the conversation, having conveniently managed to creep away.

Probably wise given the mood Roman is in, and the lethal glare he was shooting at him earlier.

Opening the nearest drawer, and then the one beside it, finding what I was looking for: the *knives*.

Grabbing the biggest sharpest blade I see, I close the drawer and turn around.

"Woah!" Pasha yells, throwing his hands up, his eyes wide.

Roman glances from Pasha to me before cocking his brow at the knife in my hand.

"Abby, I know you just shot someone…But how about you put the knife down?"

"She did *what*?" Pasha exclaims.

I shrug, and roll my eyes, ignoring them both and grabbing the wet paper towel from the sink. I swipe the glass with the flowers and settle onto a stool at the kitchen island.

Removing a rose from the cup, I lay it gently on the cold marble and gingerly cut straight down the bottom, careful not to slice all the way through.

"Abby…"

"Do you know how expensive these are?"

"I'll buy you whatever flowers you want."

"No, Roman, you don't understand, these are Juliet Roses, they can only be found in one place and tha—"

"The UK." He finishes, the rage in his eyes evaporating as they now fall to the flowers in my hand.

"Oh!" I say, excitedly, smiling broadly. "You know about flowers!"

Roman shakes his head, his cold stare now locked on the roses.

"No, but Polina does."

ANTONOV

CHAPTER TWENTY-SEVEN

ROMAN

I wish I could say that the minute I got the two fucking morons out of my penthouse, and locked away in Pasha's penthouse, that I ripped off Abby's dress, and fucked her rotten.

But given Abby's dislike of the penthouse, and the evening that we've had, I decided that it would be best for us both that we went to the *office* penthouse.

Besides, my brain is far too preoccupied for sex, which is definitely a first for me.

However, in my defense, the last twelve hours had been more than a whirlwind.

Pasha had tried to kill Wesley.

The Irish had tried to kill me.

And I'd witnessed Abigail *actually* kill someone.

Despite how absolutely stunningly beautiful she looked tonight, and how little we got to enjoy the gala, her dress was also covered in forensic evidence, and needed to be disposed of as quickly and professionally as possible. And, despite Ana telling me that she wasn't going to be around for any more of my late-night requests, I sent her on a mission to find new clothes for my life-saving lady friend.

Thankfully, she happily obliged, and showed up within an hour with three different outfits, as well as some small toiletries for Abby.

"I look forward to hearing the story of how you saved my brother's life," Ana smiles at Abby as she lays the garment bags on the bed. "But, I figured you'd probably appreciate a shower first and a fresh set of clothes."

"Thanks," Abby grins. "That's very kind of you."

She quietly takes the small leather bag off the bed and heads into my bathroom, closing the door.

I wait for the shower to start before ushering Ana outside onto the balcony.

"What the actual fuck?" she snaps, dropping her polite smile the moment the sliding glass door closes. "The Irish issued a hit on you? At the Children's Benefit?! That's bold even for them."

"I know," I say quietly.

"And what the hell was Pasha thinking?!" she continues, flailing her arms about angrily.

"I know."

"Drinking absinthe with Pace's man? Is he a complete idiot? Did he ever stop to think about the repercussions of—"

"Ana," I cut in, somewhat irritably. "I realize that all of this is new for you, but I've been living in this disaster all day. I don't need you to reiterate it for me."

"Sorry," she shrugs apologetically before shaking her head. "I just cannot believe how stupid he was. And then to invite hookers back to your…sorry, again. You just said you didn't want to talk about it."

"Actually," I say, licking my bottom lip. "That is the part I actually want to talk about."

"You said on the phone that you think Polina is involved somehow?" Ana says, raising her brow. "I don't understand, though. How?"

I shake my head.

"I have no idea. All I know is that Pasha said that the hookers they hired tonight were from this company called *Jewel Rose*. Apparently, their specialty is discretion. Their signature calling card is that the girls are sent to a client's house with a rose, and are told to utter a particular phrase in order to identify their client for the evening."

"Okay…" Ana says, furrowing her brow. "Not that I have much experience with hookers, but that seems standard?"

"Perhaps, but the fact that when *Abigail* happened to see the flowers the girls brought with them tonight, she recognized them as Juliet Roses, and stated that they are an incredibly rare breed of roses," I cross my arms tightly across my chest, glancing back through the glass door to ensure that Abby is still in the bathroom. "Who do we know that keeps Juliet Roses, Ana?"

"Polina," she breathes, her eyes going wide. "But…I…I don't understand. What purpose could that serve Pol?"

All I can do is stare back at my sister, because I have no idea how any of this ties together.

…I just know it *does*.

Ana was gone before Abby emerged from the bathroom.

However, when she finds me sipping a drink in the living room, she's wearing my bathrobe.

"Did the outfits not fit?" I ask, raising a brow and looking at her over the rim of my glass.

"No," she shrugs, biting her lip. "This just looked comfier."

I snort, taking another drink.

My robe is loose on her curves, and my eyes settle on how the lapel lays tauntingly down her breasts as she sits down on the couch next to me.

The room is quiet, the static in the shared air between the two of us feeling as if it too is alive.

Cal showing me that Abby was conveniently spotted with four of my men, who are now *dead,* weighs heavily on my mind as I stare at my little fox, with one thought superseding them all:

Can I trust her?

On one hand, she saved my life tonight.

On the other, she's potentially killing my men.

At the very least, she knows more than she's letting on.

Most of the time, I can smell a rat a mile away. One of the only valuable skills bestowed on me by my prick of a father.

And yet Abby doesn't *feel* like a rat to me.

I didn't tell Ana about how far things have gone with Abby, although I suspect I don't have to. And even though Ana herself procured Abby's file, and I chose *not* to tell her about Cal's discovery this afternoon, I know there's a part of Ana that has to at least be concerned that Abby might be another plant by the Irish.

Abigail clears her throat, pulling my attention back to her, and out of my spiraling thoughts.

"Look, Roman," she says quietly, crossing her arms tightly across her body. "I don't want to fuck tonight."

I nod, unable to think of anything to say in response.

"But," she continues. "I also don't really want to be alone."

What?

"Would you mind if I just crashed on the couch? Or I don't know, maybe in one of the many guest bedrooms you have here?"

I stare at her, trying to put my thoughts together. However, despite all of the crazy things I witnessed today, the only thing I can't quite put my finger on is Abby herself.

Miss Wayne has a secret. Of that I have no doubt.

But the look on her face when I accused her of being a liar wasn't what I expected it to be. Well, I should say it wasn't *only* what I expected it to be. Because there, mingling with the surprise in her eyes, and the way her breath hitched in her throat, there was another emotion I never anticipated: *relief.*

Obviously, I couldn't be sure, but Abigail looked as if she'd been *waiting* for me to discover her secret, as if I'd been stumbling around in the darkness and had finally found some hidden treasure buried deep within her soul…or perhaps her closet full of skeletons.

And now, as I sit here, inches away from her, staring her down and considering her request to stay here in my penthouse with me for the night, I don't know what to think. I feel as if I am trying to reconcile two very different perspectives.

Of course I *want* her to stay.

I've lusted after Abigail for years. She's the only woman I've slept with more than once, and as much as I don't want to admit it, I know that if I thought there was any real possibility she'd say "yes," I'd have asked her to marry me already to soothe my aching heart.

But my heart isn't the only part of me screaming for acknowledgement. My brain is throwing quite a tantrum too, saying that Abby is far too clever, far too deliberate, and far too risky for me to even consider "wife-ing" up anytime soon.

Cal's observational research and analysis reports are the most reliable information I have. And so as much as I hate to admit it, I have to accept that there's at least the possibility that she's the invisible killer that's been stalking us in the shadows for the last few weeks.

And if she did have something to do with Igor's death…

I shudder, reflecting both on Abby's provocative exchange with my sister at the gala tonight, as well as my intimate knowledge of Polina's insatiable desire for revenge.

She wants the person responsible, so that she can torture them. And in any other circumstances, I'd be happy to comply with her request.

But if it's Abby…

I breathe in deeply, taking another drink.

No. I can't think about that.

"Are you okay?"

Abby's soft voice pulls me from the haunting visceral mental images flashing behind my eyes. Gently she reaches forward and places her hand on my knee.

I snort.

She's the one who shot and killed someone tonight, saving *my* ass, and here she is, asking if I'm okay.

My little fox is definitely a mysterious puzzle I haven't quite figured out. Like a mirage in the desert, luring desperate men farther into its deadly clutches, Abigail Wayne could very well be tempting me into the quicksand of my own ruin.

And perhaps the real problem is…I'd let her.

Without another word, I stand and turn toward her, offering her my hand.

"Of course, you're welcome here." I whisper as I pull her up and into my arms. "But if you choose to stay the night with me there's only one place you'll be sleeping."

"Which is?"

"With me."

Abby blushes, tucking her hair behind her ear.

"There is one slight problem," she says, wincing playfully.

"Which is?"

"I need someone to stop by my place, and feed Lily."

"Who's Lily?" I ask, raising my brow. "Do you have a kid I don't know about?"

"No," she says flatly. "Lily is my *cat.*"

I pause a moment, before pulling out my phone and dialing a number.

"Yes, Boss?" Trevor says sleepily. "What can I do for you?"

"I need you to go feed a cat."

"Now?" he asks, confused.

"Yes," I say darkly. "Now. Miss Wayne is staying with me for the night and her cat needs to be fed."

"Sure thing, Boss," he yawns. "I'll get right on it."

"Tell him I'll text him instructions," Abby says in the background, pulling out her own phone.

"You have his number?"

"Of course, I do," she snorts. "We talk about you all the time."

"Is that so?" I ask, raising my brow again.

"No! Boss!" Trevor says quickly on the other end of the line. "It's not what you think!"

"Miss Wayne will be texting you instructions," I say quietly. "We can discuss the conversations later."

And then I end the call.

"You asshole," Abby snorts, shaking her head. "You know the poor kid is going to panic now and probably rush over there."

"Yeah," I shrug with a wicked grin. "But your cat will be grateful."

Abby lays with her head on my chest, wearing nothing but an old t-shirt of mine. The two of us have been laying in my bed silently for the last half hour, as a soft rain patters against the windows of the penthouse, and Caesar sleeps quietly in the corner.

"I feel like we should talk," she says softly. "But I'm not exactly sure where we should start that conversation."

I know where I'd like to start it.

But somehow, I also know that would be a mistake.

"What do you want to know?" I ask, slipping my hand up the back of her shirt and running my fingers along her soft smooth skin.

"You're in the mafia," she says, more as a statement than a question. "I… accidentally saw it on your phone earlier today."

I smirk, biting my bottom lip.

"It wasn't an accident," I whisper, kissing the top of her head. "I wanted you to see it."

She says nothing, and breathes in deeply, her chest rising and falling as the beat of her heart thumps against my skin.

"Why?" She finally asks.

"Why what?"

"Why did you want me to see it?"

This time it is me who inhales deeply, pausing as I contemplate my next words carefully.

"Because it's who I am, Abigail," I say, swallowing hard. "It's who I've always been."

There's no stopping my pulse from accelerating, realizing that this conversation may be a turning point in my relationship with the woman I have wanted for so very long.

It may also be my undoing.

But I know there's no way around it, and I also know there's no hope for any kind of future with her without it.

"I've already told you that I've wanted you from the moment I laid eyes on you," I say quietly. "I told myself I shouldn't desire you, because you belonged to another man. And when you disappeared, well, I thought that was the universe's way of telling me it wasn't meant to be."

I feel her moving, and for a moment I freeze, terrified that she might get up and want to leave, right as I'm about to bare my soul to her.

But she doesn't. In fact, she lays her hand across my chest, gently running her fingers along my abs.

"But then you came back into my life," I continue. "And now…well, I want different things."

"Different things?" She asks, her small frame stiffening ever so slightly in my arms.

"I *want* things to be different," I clarify. "And I know that starts with me being honest with you. About *who* I am."

She turns, twisting her body so that her chin rests upon her hand on my chest.

"What does it mean," she asks, her brow furrowing. "To be in the mafia?"

If I thought my heart was pounding before it's nothing to how it hammers now.

"It means I do bad things, with bad people," my tone is hoarse and raw.

"Do you…kill people?" She asks.

I'm not sure if it's the fact that she's barely reacted to the fact that I just told her I'm in the mafia, or if it's the intensity with which her eyes scan mine as she asks this question, but it nearly paralyzes me in place.

Softly I tuck a strand of her hair behind her ear.

"Yes, I have," I answer. "I've killed people."

She stares at me a moment longer.

"Do you kill *innocent* people?" She asks quietly.

"None of us are truly innocent, Abigail."

"I mean…what about women?" She says, her breath catching in her throat.

I consider her question, and it doesn't escape me that perhaps her past is her motivation for asking.

"I won't lie to you and say I'm some cinnamon roll when it comes to women, or even a gentleman," I snort.

But when I see disappointment flood her face, and her eyes fall from mine, I reach up and gently grip her chin, lifting her gaze back to me.

"However, I don't beat up women, or ruthlessly slaughter people for kicks. I'm a *businessman*, and unfortunately, I run a ruthless business. If someone fails me or betrays me…well…sometimes there's just no other choice. And when that happens, their gender doesn't matter to me. Only the offense they've committed."

Abigail's eyes burrow into mine, searching them for any fraction of dishonesty. But after what feels like a small eternity, I slowly watch her nod before she lays her head back against my shoulder, snuggling closer to me.

"Continue," she says quietly, her fingers gingerly tracing patterns on my chest. "Tell me about what your life is like. You know, in the mafia."

I'm grateful that in this particular moment she can't see the genuine shock that is plastered across my face.

I've just told this woman that I've wanted her for years, that I'm in the mafia, and that I've killed people, and she has barely batted an eye.

What I said to her tonight at the gala is true. Abigail Wayne *is* quite possibly the most interesting woman I've ever met.

She feels like one of those Russian Matryoshka dolls mother used to keep, that stack inside of each other. Just when I think I know all I can about her, she opens another layer, and buried inside is another version of her.

And something tells me that even after all this time, and all we've been through together, I've only just scratched the surface of who *she* truly is.

The next morning, Trevor drove Abby back to Forest Hills and I found myself sitting on my balcony, replaying our conversation the night before.

We talked until we fell asleep, with Abby asking anything and everything she could think of. And contrary to my usual policy of keeping civilians at a distance, I told her things about my life that I never intended on telling anyone.

She seemed genuinely interested in what kind of business I ran, outside of Nikotech. She asked how many employees I had, and what their jobs entailed. She asked about the Irish, and the men who attacked us outside the gala.

She even asked about my old assistant.

But no matter what I said, she didn't flinch.

Nothing seemed to shock her, no matter how macabre or gruesome my answer was. In fact, she said that in some weird way, a lot of things made more sense now.

Like my comment about Igor being my "enforcer," or why I had reacted the way I did about the bomb at Albertos, and the fact that all of my men seemed to carry guns.

And then she fell asleep, right there on my chest, as if nothing I said was shocking or earth shattering.

Admittedly, it had felt like a relief to unburden part of my secret double life to her, and even better to feel like she wasn't threatened or intimidated by it.

But although I'd confessed my secret.

Abby still hadn't confessed *hers*.

She'd opened up a little about her husband, telling me what an actual monster he'd been to her when no one was looking. And it took everything in my power to remain calm and collected, while simultaneously wanting to track down his parents and strangle them both with my bare hands.

I still might.

However, despite cracking the door enough to give me a glimpse of her past, she still hasn't told me what I'm actually dying to know: whether or not she's the one who has been killing my men. And *why*.

But in the end, I'd ultimately decided not to broach that topic. At least not yet.

I'm not entirely sure why I hadn't pushed it, but I suspect it's because on some level, I can sense she isn't quite *ready* to tell me.

Cal knocks on the glass door to the patio, distracting me from my thoughts.

"Morning, Boss," he says, stepping outside. "You wanted to see me?"

"Yes," I ask, taking a drink. "What did you think about my conversation with Abby last night? I trust the Bluetooth caught it all?"

"It did," he nods slowly. "She took that…rather *well*."

"She really did, didn't she?" I say, rubbing my chin.

"Almost…too well."

"Yeah, my thoughts exactly."

"I have a theory," Cal says, rubbing his chin. "If you'll allow me."

"Go on."

"All of the men who have died were in your Walston Street meeting."

"No," I say watching Cal's brow furrow. "You forgot about Igor. He was the first to die, and technically Abby's resume was on my desk, well, on Ana's desk, days before he died. Which was weeks before the rest of the men started keeling over."

"True, but perhaps Igor was an isolated incident? Because when I think about the men she's targeted—"

"*Potentially* targeted," I growl, pointing at him. "We don't know for certain."

"Yes, Boss," Cal nods. "But Boris, Jacques and Noah may have worked together, but they didn't actually *like* each other. They didn't associate outside of the office. So, I was trying to think of places or instances where they would've all been together, and I remembered that meeting."

I rub my chin.

"I invited her to that," I say quietly. "Even though I stressed the fact that she wasn't to discuss it outside of work."

"Right, but she was *there*. With all of them. And heard everything they said. And what if Igor was just a—"

"Catalyst," I finish for him.

"Right," Cal nods. "What if he was the first? What if she applied for the job to get close to him? And then, separately, what if Boris, Jacques, Noah were targeted because of that meeting."

My finger taps along the armrest of the wicker chair I'm sitting in as I consider her theory.

"That's a possibility," I finally say.

"We just have to figure out what her motivation for killing them is," Cal says, sitting down across from me. "That's the only thing we have yet to understand."

Trying to remember what we discussed at the Walston Street meeting, my mind is immediately drawn to the notes Abby took.

Boris—wants to know if there's grandmas he can kill.

Jacques—will "extract" information.

Noah—will help his brother "extract" information.

At the time, I remember thinking they were quite comical when she had typed them up and put them on my desk. But now, they seem to scream her motive.

"Actually," I say slowly, the pieces slowly slotting into place. "I might."

Cal looks at me tilting his head.

"She had an abusive ex. What if that's somehow her target? Men who hurt people?"

"Well, Boris did have those three girls who accused him of rape."

"He *did* rape them," I say, shooting him a look. "He just made sure none of them talked."

"Well, if she's after men who hurt people," Cal says, blinking rapidly. "We're fucked. Because the only three people left from that meeting are you, me, and Oleg."

"No," I say, shaking my head. "If Abby wanted to kill me, she would've done it already. And she's had access to you nearly every day."

"Which just leaves *Oleg*," Cal says, the smirk spreading on his face echoing the one on my own.

"Sounds like bait to me," I grin watching him nod.

There's no way for Cal to know, but I'm desperate to catch Abby in the act. As morbid as it sounds, I have this insatiable desire to see how she's been systematically killing my men for the last few weeks.

…And I have no idea *why*.

"I have a plan," I say quietly. "And I think it could work, but I need to sort out some details first."

Cal nods before taking a deep breath and closing his eyes.

Oh shit…what now.

"There is one other piece of business I need to discuss with you," he says cautiously. "But you're not going to like it."

"I haven't liked any of this," I sigh, instantly clenching my jaw. "But what is it?"

From his suitcoat Cal produces a small white envelope with my name on it.

"This was delivered to your office this morning," Cal nods, handing it to me. "I've already opened it."

Flipping up the envelope flap I realize that it contains three pictures.

"There was no note," Cal says quietly, "No fingerprints either."

"Another professional?"

"Seems like it."

But the moment I pull the photos out and look at them, my blood runs cold. Because there in my hands are three photos…of Pasha.

One of him on his date with the social media chick.

Another of him getting out of the car.

And the last of him at The Studio VIP section…with me.

Cal motions for me to flip the photo over, and there on the back are five words, scribbled in red ink.

"Are you your brother's keeper?"

"Now this feels more like the Irish," Cal whispers. "They always go straight for the jugular.”

My chest tightens around me, strangling the air from my lungs.

The Irish have just marked their next target: *my brother.*

No. Not Pasha. I cannot allow this.

Immediately my brain kicks into action, and I start formulating a plan.

“Where is he now?” I ask, my words strangled in my throat.

“Still at his apartment,” Cal replies with a nod.

“Keep him there. Get Giorgi on the line, and tell him that he’s to go to Pasha’s, and I don’t care if he has to tie the fucker to the bed and feed him by hand. He is not to leave that apartment under any circumstances, understood?” I growl, pointing at him.

“Yes, Boss,” Cal agrees, pulling out his phone.

“Which reminds me,” I sigh, taking mine out of my pocket as well. “I need to make a call.”

“Have you…told *him* yet?” Cal asks quietly, looking up from the text he’s furiously typing.

I shake my head, hearing the receptionist on the other end pick up.

“Yeah, it’s Roman,” I say quickly to the polite woman on the phone. “I’ve got a code 5-0-5, and I need to speak to him.”

“Copy that,” she acknowledges, immediately patching me through to another number.

“Hello?”

“Hey, It’s Roman,” I say to the man on the other end of the phone. “I need to speak with him. It’s urgent. Yeah, that’s fine, I’ll hold, Ethan.”

ANTONOV

CHAPTER TWENTY-EIGHT

My eyes drill holes into the ceiling as I resist the urge to look at the gun that is laying on my dresser.

The gun that I fired. The gun that took a man's life.

I wanted it so that I could have my souvenir. Roman would bury what happened that night, there would be no public record of the death. Which meant there would be no obituary. No news reports.

So, I needed my souvenir.

My leg bounces up and down, as my demons flex against my mind. A small warm body curls up against my leg, trying to soothe me.

I have the itch. God, do I have the itch.

My skin feels like it's crawling and constricting my bones. I can feel every movement, every breath I take, every brush of the cotton sheet against my skin, and it's driving me up the wall.

I've never spiraled like this. I can feel the control slipping through my fingers every time Roman tugs on it.

And he tugs on it all the damn time.

Storming over to the gun, I snatch it off the dresser, the weight in my hand flooding my body with heat. I throw open the walk-in closet doors, heading straight to the back where I keep the box.

I drop down onto the floor, placing the gun to the side and slide the box toward me. My fingers run over the lid before I lift it off.

My chest heaves as I see the death certificates of every man I've ever killed. I don't think I can describe the sensation of seeing the contents of this box, and how it fills me with a lightness that makes me feel like I could just float away.

I grin to myself, my fingers smoothing the edges of Igor's newspaper clipping down.

Sighing, I grab the gun, placing it inside the box before throwing the lid back on and shaking my head. I run my hands down my legs as I stand, walking backwards away from the box, and closing the closet door behind me.

Stepping away from the temptation that sits inside it.

"It means I do bad things, with bad people."

Roman's words have replayed on a constant loop since he said them.

He said that he doesn't kill the innocent, but no one in this world is truly innocent.

I should've had more reservations about Roman and him being in the mafia, but I couldn't find it in me to care.

I want him.

No, it's more than that, I *need* him.

But, I know that deep down, if I let him in, his demons will caress mine, forcing them out into the open and tempting them to break our code.

A code that I live by, one that I don't stray from.

I do not kill unnecessarily.

I do not kill impulsively.

I do not…

I could.

I *want* to.

And that scares me right down to the very marrow of my being.

It's always been there, that fear.

The violent urges I had since I was a child always worried me, so I harnessed them in order to prevent them from taking over my life.

But now, it feels as if they're running my life.

Only this time, I like it.

I want them to.

Ever since I killed the man who attacked Roman, I've been slowly retreating deeper and deeper inside my own demons, and I have no desire to climb back out. I feel them surrounding me, filling me with strength.

They are like a warm hug on a cool winter's day.

Comforting, and refreshing.

But somehow, I've lost who I was.

Or have I gained who I really am?

I glare at myself in the mirror.

Who am I?

I punish men who abuse women. Women who can't defend themselves. But Roman said he doesn't do that, that he doesn't do it without reason. What he does doesn't apply to my code.

So, is Roman truly a monster?

And if Roman is a monster, am I?

Ever since that day in the office, the day I stopped myself from killing him, something clicked into place.

I knew it. And I tried to run from it.

Unsuccessfully.

But something changed inside me, an impulse that's been lurking deep beneath my skin, buried so deep that I didn't even feel it there…until now.

My demons were starving, suffocating in the prison of my own mind and limitations. They've been rioting, screaming for their next feed, and work did nothing to quell their chaos.

The next week at the office was hell.

The office sluts were on another level. It was like they knew exactly what was happening between Roman and I, and decided that they would torment me until I either caved, or quit. Everywhere I went they followed me, testing my teetering patience.

Honestly, it was a miracle I made it to the end of the week without killing anyone.

My brain threw violent images at me, taunting and teasing me, until I finally stormed out around three, resulting in Roman scolding me via email for walking out of work early.

But he didn't understand. He couldn't.

I left because I needed a *fix*.

Exactly *what* fix I required was still unclear. Whether that be Roman, or a drop of Widowmaker in a bad man's drink.

I flop back down on the bed, bouncing as my hair covers my face and with a sigh I reach for my phone, snatching it off the charger.

The only way I know how to wrangle my demons is to feed them, and it just so happens that I still have a mark left from The List.

And I've been toying with a plan to scratch off that name all day, trying to talk myself out of it, but to no avail.

So, without further hesitation I press the call button, lifting the phone to my ear.

As I slide onto the stool, I feel my phone vibrate against my thigh. I don't even have to open it to know it's Roman.

It's *always* Roman.

That man outside the gala would've killed him had I not intervened. But even though I saved his life, it feels as if the King of New York has somehow become more suspicious of me.

His eyes follow me everywhere, and when they can't, it feels as if he has *other* pairs of eyes watching me. Always.

To escape them, I called Lizzie, who sits down on the stool next to me with a smile.

I knew she doesn't work Sundays, and so I asked if maybe she wanted to have a girls' night and come get a drink with me. Thankfully, she was more than happy to come, and could barely contain the surprise and excitement that practically danced through the phone.

Sundays at The Studio are different from normal days. The party really starts after midnight, but beforehand the music is lower, allowing people to mingle and actually talk to each other before the festivities start.

I have no idea what is on deck for this evening, and I would've normally checked, but I was in such a rush to get out of the house and escape my rioting demons, that it didn't even cross my mind.

I place my wine glass down on the table, pulling out my phone. The screen lights up as I open my messages.

Roman
10:57 p.m.: Should you be here on a work night?

Abby
10:58 p.m.: Didn't I tell you? I'm taking the day off tomorrow.

Roman
10:58 p.m.: No. You are not.

Abby
10:59 p.m.: Yes. I am.

Sighing, I put my phone back into my clutch, my eyes catching a grinning Roman up in the VIP section, before I quickly look away.

Of course, he's here. Where else would he be? This infuriating man is everywhere I don't want him to be.

I overheard the office sluts complaining about not being invited tonight, especially after finding out that all department heads were invited.

This meant that Oleg *would* be here. My last mark.

Which would be perfect if I didn't have Mr. Mafia looming above me in the VIP lounge sipping his drink, looking far too perfect and godlike.

Lizzie stares at me as I lift my glass to him, and I watch as she follows my line of sight straight to him.

"Shut the fuck up!" She hisses, her eyes wide. "Is that Mr. Antonov?!"

I was worried that maybe this would be awkward.

Lizzie gave me her number months ago, and I've never texted her, nor called her. I only ever saw her at the bar when I came in. Yet here we are, talking like we've been friends for years.

"Mmhmm," I hum, clicking my tongue as she raises her wine glass to her lips, gulping it down. "My *boss*."

The wine flies from her mouth, as she slaps her hand over her face.

"Are you fucking shitting me right now?" She splutters. "He's your boss?!"

I nod.

"Well...is it true what they say about him?" She says, wagging her eyebrows suggestively.

"What?"

"You know... *dick* for days?" She sings.

I blink at her.

"Lizzie, he's my *boss*..." I chuckle, rolling my eyes.

"You can fuck your boss, you know. I mean, *I* did," she shrugs, then grimaces. "Yeah, on second thought, it's probably best you don't actually."

From the occasional chats we've shared at the bar, I know Lizzie's history of partners isn't exactly a list of people you'd take home to meet the family.

Luckily, I've not needed to kill any of them...yet.

As I understand, she's had a few not so nice guys, and if the bar wasn't inconveniently good at getting busy, and cutting our conversations short each time, they'd probably be dead.

I smirk at her over the rim of the glass.

There's always been something about Lizzie that makes me want to tell her all my secrets.

Well, all but *one* of them.

She's charismatic, and full of life, not a demon in sight.

I could never tell her that I live to kill people. I wouldn't want her to be terrified by my demons, or worse…infected by them.

Plus, I'm pretty sure she took an oath to save people, not end them.

Before I can dwell on it any longer, Lizzie continues.

"Anyway," she laughs. "Are you excited for the *festivities* tonight?!"

"What are the festivities exactly?"

"It's switch night."

"Switch night?"

"Yeah… The ladies pick their man for the night," she wags her brows.

Oh.

Switch night sounds like the perfect night for Oleg, almost *too perfect.*

It's interesting that this place would have a night where they openly give *women* the power, considering how much it caters to their misogynistic members most of the time.

"So, we could pick anyone?" I ask, leaning forward on my elbows. "That's how that works right?"

Smirking, she twitches her nose, "Yep! The men can't approach us at all, they can't even talk to us. They can only sit and wait till a woman approaches *them*. And only then can they shoot their shot."

She jumps up and down, her hair bouncing with her, "Oh! And the VIP isn't off limits. They open it to everyone. So, we can go up there," she grins. "And maybe you can have Rooooman."

"No," I state.

This is sounding better and better.

This might be the perfect opportunity to approach Oleg tonight and finish him once and for all. I twist the ring round my finger, relief filling me.

"Fiiiineeee, got your eye on anyone?" Lizzie asks.

"Umm, maybe."

Lizzie smirks, her eyes flashing up to Roman before darting back to me, a grin splitting her face.

"Absolutely not. He hates me," I lie with a giggle. "Every time I go into work in a skirt, he yells at me."

"Girl, if he stares at you anymore, he'll set you on fire."

A laugh bursts from my chest.

Glancing up to VIP, I see Oleg leaning against a corner booth. But just as I do, Roman Antonov once again, steps into my line of sight, sipping his glass and staring at me. I can practically feel the heat of his eyes on my skin.

How does he do this?

This man drives me fucking crazy.

But no matter how possessive, how impossibly overbearing, and how infuriatingly sexy he might be, tonight he's a distraction from my work.

"Why don't *you* go for, Roman?" I ask, silently smothering my demons as they riot, my heart trying to overthrow my head.

"*Roman*?" She gasps. "No, I couldn't…"

"Why not?" I say sweetly, hiding behind my glass.

As much as I hate the idea of anyone getting close to Roman Antonov, I need *him* distracted tonight. Because even with it being switch night, I still know there isn't a chance in hell I'll be able to take out Oleg with Mr. Over possessive watching me like a hawk.

"Why not? Because you and him…" She trails off, her hands tapping against the stem of the wine glass.

"There is no me and him," I lie, swallowing past the growing lump in my throat. "There can't be."

But yet, my heart screams a single word:

Mine.

The music pounds, the bass vibrating as bodies grind against one another on the dance floor. My shoulder bumps into a couple as they devour each other right there in front of everyone. I quickly flick my eyes away from them, feeling the heat in my cheeks, remembering the way that Roman had devoured me.

Stop it. Stay focused.

The moment midnight struck the music cranked up, and a flood of curious basic bitches, who would normally never be allowed to set foot in the VIP Lounge, practically trample each other trying to score one of *its* inhabitants for the night.

It takes less than ten minutes for the bouncers to start limiting how many people can be up there at the same time, simply for the weight limit allowed by the suspended glass floor.

However, I remain in my seat sipping my Rose Martini as Oleg slowly makes his way down onto the main floor.

And suddenly an idea comes to me.

"Lizzie," I say, turning to her with a smile. "I need your help."

"Oohh!" She says, throwing back her third drink before leaning in excitedly. "With what?"

"So… I lied. I *do* want Roman," I say, trying to appear bashful. "But I don't want him to know it. And I don't want to approach him outright. You know, since he's been such a dick to me at the office."

"Okay…"

"I have a plan," I playfully scrunch up my face. "And I want to make him a little jealous,"

"Yessss!" Lizzie giggles, clapping her hands together and biting her lip.

"So, my thought is, what if *you go* and talk to him, just to distract him for a little bit," I say, biting my lip. "So, I can approach a different guy, and well… we'll just see how Mr. CEO reacts."

"Ooooh! Oh my God!" She squeals excitedly. "I love that!"

"Can you do that for me?" I ask, pressing my hands together in a prayer pose.

"Of course, girl!" Lizzie says, slamming her hand down on the table, before jumping up and giving me a finger salute. "I've got you!"

Without another word, she turns and heads toward VIP, even if she wobbles a bit on the way there.

And just as I suspected, the gatekeeping bouncers let Lizzie past the line of eager hopefuls and open the rope for her.

Admittedly, my stomach lurches watching her walk up the stairs, and my mind screams to stop her, repeating once again that Roman is *mine*.

No. I can't get distracted. I have work to do.

I make my way through the throngs of people on the dance floor, being pushed and pulled left and right. I've never been to a *switch* night at The Studio before, and honestly, I never want to come to one again.

The energy is a lot different tonight, darker even. This usually wouldn't bother me, but the mounting sexual tension is fueling my restless demons, tempting, and taunting them.

Oleg has been sitting solo at the bar for the last fifteen minutes. A few girls have approached him, but he's waved them all off, which is a bit unusual for a ladies man like him.

Maybe he's just not feeling it tonight.

I would've already approached him if not for Roman's eyes on me the entire night, everywhere I go, the burning sensation drilling into my skin.

But my plan to send Lizzie his way and distract him, has apparently failed, as I now see her drunkenly straddling a friend of hers.

Well, clearly that didn't work.

However, glancing around, I don't see Roman anywhere, and coincidentally, I no longer feel the burn of his eyes on my skin. He seems to have just… disappeared.

Perhaps he had mafia business to attend to.

But that just means this is my window of opportunity.

Slowly I make my way off the dance floor and find a spot on the wall with a good view. Leaning against it I feel the coolness on my bare back. I take a few deep breaths, inhaling in and out, trying to ground myself before approaching my mark.

It's now or never.

Oleg is still alone, his shoulders hunched as he leans his elbows on the bar.

So, after taking a deep breath, I make my way toward him.

Grabbing the attention of the male bartender was easy, as all I had to do was lean forward on the bar, and his eyes were instantly drawn to my chest.

With a smirk he walks over, before resting both hands on the bar, caging me in as he runs his nose over my cheek to yell in my ear.

"Pretty lady, what can I get ya?"

"Whatever he had," I yell back, biting my lip and nodding my head toward Oleg.

"Coming right up, sweetheart."

Before I know it, he's slid a glass of amber liquid across the bar, a sphere of ice filling nearly the entire glass.

Clicking my tongue, I smile sweetly at him.

"Could you take the ice out?" I ask, batting my lashes.

Ice is my archenemy, as my Widowmaker would stick to it, stopping it from dissolving in the liquid and giving me away. It also waters down dosage, and if it isn't just right, it could allow my mark enough time to get treatment.

Which is the opposite of what I need.

"Sure, sugar!" He says, his southern accent more pronounced.

He returns with a new glass, I mutter a quick thanks with a nod. before he turns to serve someone else.

Quickly, I pull the glass close to me, twisting the ring open and dropping the Widowmaker in. I swirl the glass in my hand before walking over to Oleg and slide the glass along the bar to him.

"Tough day?" I ask.

He stares at me, his eyes wide, and I'm almost sure he's not breathing.

"Uh…" He says, glancing around nervously. "Does the Boss know you're here? On *switch* night?"

"Roman isn't my keeper," I smirk sarcastically, nodding toward the drink.

"Take it, you clearly need it."

"Thanks," he says, throwing me a quick smile.

He grabs the drink, pulling it toward him with his hand. But his smile fades, and he once again lowers his gaze, looking just as defeated and depressed as before.

My brows furrow as I stare at him, and my stomach knots.

Truth be told, Oleg didn't necessarily *do* anything wrong.

If anything, he is one of the better guys lumbering around at Nikotech Investments. Sure, he might make minor mistakes, like slamming a car door, but he's always been a gentleman to me, and always treats everyone with respect.

The only reason I have for killing Oleg is that he could potentially connect me to Igor's death. This wouldn't normally be a problem, as I usually stay away from anyone connected to my mark once they've been put down. However, given that Oleg and I work together daily, it increases the likelihood that a suspicion could arise.

Swallowing down the lump in my throat I step closer to him.

"Wanna talk about it?"

He looks up at me, before his eyes cast down again.

"I thought coming here tonight would be a nice distraction," he says softly before tilting his head toward me. "There was this girl…"

His trails off, sadness filling his eyes.

My knees weaken, and I sit down on the stool next to him, my body hyper aware of everything going on around it. The music feels louder, almost deafening, as blood pounds in my ears, and regret bubbles in my stomach.

"Oh yeah?" I ask, biting my lip. "Why don't you tell me about her?"

"Well… She's the prettiest girl I've ever seen, but we can never be together. It's the twenty-first century and arranged marriages are still a thing." He pauses, his hand tugging at his hair. "We had one weekend together, and that's all we can have, and I guess, if I had more pull, I could fix it, I could save her. But I can't."

My stomach drops.

"*Save her?*"

"Yeah. The guy she's gonna marry, well, let's just say in my line of work, I know a lot of unpleasant people, but him…he's a monster."

Monster.

Staring at Oleg, my heart splits in half.

What am I doing? He doesn't deserve this.

He didn't do anything to justify the death I've just handed him.

Oleg lifts the glass to his lips and suddenly I stop breathing.

"Oleg, I—"

"Don't drink that," barks Roman, his hand slamming down between us.

Oleg flinches away from him, dropping the glass down on the bar, and spilling the contents everywhere.

Momentary relief fills me as I stare at the amber liquid dripping down from the edge.

"Boss! She approached me!" Oleg stutters, his eyes flicking to mine. "I swear, I didn't touch her or—"

"I'm well aware," Roman states, the look on his face murderous.

Fuck, he knows.

A
ANTONOV

CHAPTER TWENTY-NINE

ROMAN

"Roman," Abby gasps, her eyes wide as Oleg scrambles away from her at the bar. "I…I can explain, I swear—"

"Oh, I'm sure you can, Abigail," I hiss glaring at her. "I'm sure you have a whole story lined up and ready to play at a moment's notice."

I lean in close, smelling the sweet floral perfume on her neck as I whisper in her ear.

"But I'm not going to let you kill any more of my fucking men."

Her breath hitches, and in contrast to the confident facade she's painted for me over the last month, she looks genuinely surprised.

Good.

"Oleg," I say, without taking my eyes off of Abby. "Miss Wayne needs a ride home. Now."

"Yes, Boss," he quips, scurrying out of my sight to get the car.

"Roman, I—" She starts to say, but I raise my hand.

"No," I whisper lethally. "Not tonight. You're going to go home, and you're going to stay there. And if anything should happen to Oleg on the way home, I will hunt you to the ends of the earth. Do you understand me,

Abigail?"

She gulps, her breath shaking as she looks between me and Cal who stands to my left.

"Do you," I say slowly, "*understand*?"

Abby nods without saying a word.

"Her tab is closed," I say to the bartender, slamming a hundred-dollar bill down on the counter before turning back to Abby.

"Let's go."

She bites her bottom lip and scoops her purse off the bar. I place my hand on the small of her back and move her toward the door. As we step outside, I can hear the murmur of the club crowd standing in line as I open the back door of one of the two Cadillac SUVs waiting.

"Roman, it's not what you think," Abby says as I help her into the car.

I smirk.

"Abigail," I snort coldly, putting my hand in my pocket. "You have no idea what I think."

She flinches, telling me silently that my appearance and demeanor has not just rattled her…it's *wounded* her. This is only further confirmed when she folds her arms across her chest and looks away from me.

She's hurt.

For a brief second, my resolve waivers, and I consider climbing in with her, and hearing her tell me the truth.

But I already *know* the truth.

And despite what she may think, this icy interaction is more for her benefit than mine. Because Polina will not give a flying fuck about Abby's justifications for killing Igor, and still demand blood for her late husband's death.

Abby's blood.

After all, that is the tradition in our family.

My protocol requires me to hand Abby over to Polina and allow my sister to exact whatever revenge she desires, in whatever gruesome manner she prefers.

But I won't do that. I can't.

As inconvenient and possibly insane as it is to admit, I care deeply for Abby. Probably more than I should.

However, if Abby's actions come to light, combined with the fact that I both knew and didn't immediately give her to my sister, the fallout could be catastrophic. And deadly.

I need time to figure out a plan, and my next steps, without having to worry about something happening to Abby.

…And I also need to make sure that Abby doesn't "happen" to any of my men.

Closing the door, I tap the top of the car twice, and Oleg drives off.

Now I'm off to my second task of the night:

Dinner.

A little over an hour later I sit across from one of the wealthiest billionaires in the world…and one of the *deadliest*.

Jaxon Pace, the Don Supreme of Chicago's underground crime syndicate is my platonic date for the evening.

He's also my oldest friend.

Well, he's technically my only friend, outside of Cal, who was sworn in service to me when we were kids.

Jaxon and I, on the other hand, go back nearly a decade. The two of us have a long backlist of chaotic debauchery, which is why I decide to finally unload my situation with Abby.

"…So let me get this straight," he says, taking a drink and then pointing at me with his wine glass. "You've had a thing for this woman for years, even back when she was married. She disappears one day, shortly after her husband's death, only to show up for a job interview at your company. You hire her, and fall for her, only to find out that she's the same woman who killed your brother-in-law."

"Yep," I say into my own glass. "That about sums it up."

"And she's the same woman, who is also potentially killing more of your men," he leans back against the booth.

"I'd say it's a bit past *potentially* at this point," I cough. "We're up to four at the moment. And that's just my men, not any others that she might've… *disposed* of."

"You think she's been targeting men for some time?" He asks. "As in, before the two of you got together?"

I nod, cutting off a bit of my prime rib and swirling it around in the juice on the plate.

"So…she's a killer," he whispers, although his quiet tone appears more from shock than from any reasonable worry that someone could overhear our conversation.

"Yeah," I sigh, popping the steak into my mouth. "Seems that way."

Jaxon stares at me intently for a few seconds before raising his brows and shaking his head.

"Huh," he snorts, leaning in and taking a bite of his food.

"What?"

"It's just a bit funny," he says, chuckling as he wipes his lip with his napkin before tossing it on the table.

"What's funny?"

"You are," he scoffs before taking a drink of his wine. "If I recall correctly, weren't you the same guy who had a policy about not fucking the same girl twice? Who said monogamy was a made-up concept of misery, and who swore he'd never settle down with one woman?"

I chuckle.

"I was," I say nodding, leaning back against the leather booth wall. "But to be fair, *you* also said you'd never settle down. How'd that ideology work out for you, old man?"

"Careful there," Jaxon laughs, smiling while cutting himself a bit of his steak. "I'm still young enough to kick your ass."

"Well, I'm guessing it didn't age too well, judging by your shiny new wedding band and the tattoo on your left hand," I say, sarcastically. "Which by the way, thanks for the wedding invitation."

"We sent you one," Jaxon shrugs. "Your sister Ana declined on your behalf, saying something about you being in the middle of a hostile takeover or something?"

"Semantics," I roll my eyes, waving him off. "I trust you weren't that devastated, and just busy impregnating the girl with the first of many heirs?"

"Yeah, something like that," he snorts.

"Even still," I smile. "You caught the monogamy too."

"Hey, at least I chose a wife who has her head screwed on. Leave it to you to fall for a crazy bitch."

I shrug with a chuckle.

"What can I say? I like a challenge."

Jaxon shakes his head, grabbing the bottle off the table and pouring us both a drink.

"And besides, aren't all women a little crazy though?" I say, picking up my glass of Cabernet and waving it around the table. "You know, if the mood strikes? Or, I don't know, every fucking full moon?"

"A *little* crazy?" Jaxon says, dipping his head. "Yes. Absolutely. I'll argue that any woman can be a little crazy for the right reasons. Sometimes they have to be. Especially where her loved ones are concerned."

"Well, there ya go—"

"But you just said Abigail isn't just a *little* crazy, in fact, you said that she's actively picking off your men," he continues, pointing at me as he rests his arm on the back of the booth. "Including your brother-in-law."

"Yeah, well, I never cared much for the prick anyway."

"But even still," Jaxon says, taking a sip of his wine before narrowing his eyes at me. "If that's true then unfortunately she's not just a little crazy, Roman…She's a serial killer."

He's blunt, but that's his nature.

Like Cal, Jaxon Pace has never been the type of man who would beat around the bush, or tell me what he thinks I want to hear just to appease me. He simply states the facts as he sees them, which is also why I enjoy his company, and his wisdom.

Even if I wouldn't overinflate his head two sizes by telling him as such.

A few years my senior, the successful, and *singular* Pace Family Mafia heir might not have siblings as I do, but he did have a very similar upbringing, with Jaxon being groomed from a young age to shoulder his family's legacy and intimately understanding the same pressures of leadership.

It was also Jaxon who taught me the importance of assimilation, having integrated dozens of his legitimate businesses with aspects of his darker and occasionally "shadier" ventures.

My father and his father formed an alliance nearly a decade ago, putting us in touch with one another. Since then, we've combined forces on multiple projects, and reaped the mutual benefits. As it stands, he provides me with shipping pipelines and contacts around the world, as well as supplying non-serialized weapons for my organization.

In turn, I provide him a disgustingly low price on high-quality Russian steel contracts for his luxury hotels, the first being his crown jewel, The Jefferson, located back in Chicago.

But all in all, he's probably the only man alive I trust to have this conversation with.

"Yeah," I nod slowly, inhaling deeply. "You're right. Abby is very likely a serial killer."

I grin, bringing my wine glass to my lips.

"But she's hot as fuck though."

Jaxon snorts loudly, shaking his head.

"Does she know that you're in the mafia?"

I nod, setting the glass down on the table.

"And how did she take that?"

"Remarkably well, actually," I shrug.

"Do you think…" He pauses, narrowing his eyes at me. "She's tried to kill…*you*?"

"No, of course not," I scoff, waving him off.

"Are you sure?" He presses. "I mean, you just admitted she's a serial killer, and that's kind of what they do."

I grin.

"She wants me," I say smugly. "Besides, she defended me the other night."

"…And killed someone else in the process."

For some reason, his words seem to poke a tiny hole in the unwavering belief I have about Abby.

"She hasn't tried to kill me," I say, playing off the gnawing sense of doubt that threatens to creep into my mind. "I'm sure of it. She feels the same way about me as I do about her."

Jaxon stares at me for a moment, almost as if he wants to say something, but then changes his mind.

He concedes with a shrug.

"Who would've thought," he scoffs, clearly amused. "That the ol' Russian Rooster, and famous one-night bed-hopper, would get his heart snatched by a femme fatale."

I sigh, my eyes falling to the table.

"Not me, that's for sure."

"So now what?" Jaxon says, asking the very question that's been bouncing around in my brain.

All I can do is shake my head.

"I don't know," I whisper quietly. "I mean, I obviously can't let her run around my ranks, offing my men. And if Polina, or anyone close to Polina found out…well, I'm sure you can imagine how that would go."

He nods silently.

"By that logic, the smartest thing to do would be to send her far away from this place, and hope that Polina finds some new little fuckboy to distract her," I sigh.

Even though there is truth in my words, I hate every single one of them, as they feel like knives plunged into my chest.

"But…" Jaxon says slowly, his eyes falling to the table. "You can't stand the idea of being parted from her."

I watch as a subtle, knowing smile spreads across his face as he spins his wedding ring on his finger.

"Yep," I say, clicking my tongue in my mouth. "What do you think I should do? Do I take the risk?"

"Well, unfortunately I don't have experience dating a serial killer," Jaxon says, taking a deep breath. "However, I have learned a few things while dating a very feisty nurse, who I guess technically *has* killed a couple of people."

"Ooh," I grin playfully. "Something tells me I'm going to like this one. But go on."

"You know as well as I do that nothing in this life is guaranteed. Everything is a risk. We're cutthroats, and monsters, and assholes who have to fight for every morsel we can't steal. Our very existence teeters on the edge of a knife, and every day we gamble with our lives for money, or power, or respect. But no matter what bullshit we have to wade through, we press on, because we have no other choice."

He smirks to himself, once again looking down at his wedding band on his ring finger, and the tattoo beneath it.

"But of all the stupid, selfish reasons we have to gamble with our lives, love is perhaps the only one that's actually worth the risk. And the *fight*."

I'm not sure if it's what he says exactly, or *how* he says it, but his words resonate with me, and it feels as if some forgotten chord plays within my soul.

But realizing how uncomfortably deep this conversation just suddenly became, I clear my throat.

"Thank you," I chuckle, taking a drink. "I'll have to file that away in the Jaxon Proverbs."

This makes him laugh.

"All I can say is that I'm sure that hearts are breaking all of New York tonight."

"...As I'm sure they did in Chicago when you actually tied the knot with your own lovely paramour," I smile, narrowing my eyes at him. "Whom I'm dying to meet by the way. I hear she actually came with you on this trip. Don't tell me that you two are *still* in the honeymoon phase, Mr. Pace?"

"No, my wife just wanted to keep her bodyguard in one piece. She was worried I might push Wesley out of my moving plane on the way home," he growls, his frustration evident. "Because truth be told, I might've."

This time I chuckle, waving him off.

"It's fine."

"No, it's unprofessional," Jaxon seethes. "He's lucky he only ended up with a bullet in his ass."

"Nah, it wasn't his fault. At least not entirely," I snort. "Pasha is a hard man to refuse, especially when fucking absinthe is involved. But rest assured, if I ever get my hands on his little bitch of a best friend, I'm going to remove his testicles and keep them in a jar on my desk."

Jaxon closes his eyes and shakes his head, his tone darkening.

"I still cannot believe they did that."

"Yeah, neither can I, actually," I groan. "But while we're on that subject, there is something else I'd like to discuss with you…"

A
ANTONOV

CHAPTER THIRTY

Abby

The look on Roman's face replays in my mind. He knew, and he caged me instead of killing me. Well, there was still time for him to kill me.

Plenty of it.

His face was murderous, that rage aimed directly at me.

Not that I can blame him, I've slowly been picking off his men during my time at Nikotech. Honestly, I'm surprised I've gotten away with it for this long. I wasn't planning each kill out like I normally did, I simply went for every opportunity that presented itself to me, with no hesitation.

But I did hesitate with Roman. And my body clenched with regret for Oleg. Without realizing it, he humanized himself in a way that had my knees buckling. The pain in his voice over the woman he loved being trapped in an arranged marriage with a *monster*, whispered to my demons, making them pause before he even took a sip of our deadly concoction.

The relief that flooded my body and soul when the glass shattered, seeping that deadly liquid everywhere, was soon replaced with dread when I realized it was *Roman* who was interrupting us.

But he didn't even give me a chance to explain. He silenced me.

I'm so sick of being silenced.

He's right, I did have my story ready to go. But it wasn't a story, it was truth and not lies that I was ready to throw at his feet.

Yet, when he whispered in my ear, he'd hunt me to the ends of the earth a shiver trembled through my body, and my demons rolled over in submission.

It wasn't fear I felt at that moment. No, it was heat, pure fucking heat.

A part of me wanted him to hunt me, so much so that for a second, I even considered running…just so he would chase me.

Silence fills the car as I stare out the window.

A flutter of relief fills my chest as we pass the little bakery I'd often visit before my "book club" meetings at the library.

Oleg is taking me home instead of my grave.

Closing my eyes, I inhale deeply as my shoulder sag. When I open them, I catch Oleg staring at me in the mirror.

I clear my throat softly.

"I'm sorry," I mutter, shame filling me.

"What?"

"It wasn't personal," I whisper, refusing to elaborate.

He winces, dropping his eyes from mine as his face glows green from the lights changing.

He continues driving in silence and I return to looking out the window once more. After a few minutes of suffocating in the heavy silence, my guilt has festered, pooling in my stomach and rising in my throat.

"I…I hope you save her," I say.

He barks a humorless laugh, shaking his head softly.

"What just happened Abby?" he asks, ignoring me.

"I'm sure Roman will fill you in, but as I said, just know, I'm sorry, it really wasn't personal. It was self-preservation and all that."

Pulling up outside of my Townhouse, I jump out, running toward my door, only to freeze and run back to the car. Leaning in through the open window, I meet Oleg's wide eyes, as they dart between mine still trying to piece the puzzle of me together.

"Truly, I'm glad Roman turned up when he did. I'm sure you'll save your girl," I nod, pushing off the car and turning away leaving him alone in the dark.

Being under literal house arrest is infuriating.

Roman has locked me up in my own fucking house as if he is my warden.

I could be doing anything else with my fucking time, instead I'm sitting in my living room, in the dark with Lily curled up and purring on my lap. She understands too.

Am I just supposed to wait here until he decides to free me?

But I already know the answer to that.

Yes. Yes, I fucking am.

My phone lights up, vibrating so suddenly that it almost falls off the cozy recliner. With a sigh, I swipe my thumb over the screen, opening the new message from Roman.

Roman
4:18 a.m.: I want to see you. I'm on my way.

Me
4:23 a.m.: Sorry. Not home. I went back out.

Roman
4:23 a.m.: Abby, I know you didn't.

I roll my eyes.

Deciding to fuck with him, I gently push Lily off my lap, before switching on the TV. After a few minutes of scrolling, I find the perfect video. With a small laugh I run into the kitchen, sliding to a stop as my socks lose their grip on the tiles.

I grab a glass, throw in a piece of ice, and skip back into the living room. With the glass in hand, I stand in front of my TV recording a video of The Studio in the background. I watch it a few times making sure that it looks okay before heading back over to my recliner. I snuggle my shoulders into the comforter and send it to Roman, giggling to myself.

Me
4:30 a.m.: Attached Video.

The instant reply doesn't come, causing a smile to stretch across my face. The urge to stand up and dance flies through me, but I push that thought aside, as I kick my feet against the chair, bopping my head to the bass through the TV.

Take that Mr. You-Will-Stay-Home-And-Not-Kill-Anyone.

My phone vibrates in my hand, causing my racing heart to stop.

Roman
4:40 a.m.: Pretty little LIAR, look outside your window.

Shit.

Look outside my window? What does that even mean?

I tuck my phone into my bra, and slowly walk toward the front of the house.

How creepy does this man want to be?

I take a deep breath and inch the window curtain open. I scan my yard and see nothing. Just as I let the curtain fall, I see movement out of the corner of my eye.

Tearing the curtain back from the window once more, I glare directly at Oleg, who stands dutifully by my front door. He meets my glare with a shrug of the shoulders, giving me a salute.

Grinding my teeth, I stride toward the back of the house, only to open my backdoor and find another man standing watch. He stares at me, his eyes focused on my exposed thighs before rising to my chest. Every second he stares at me causes my blood to boil.

"You should go back inside and shut that door, honey," he says darkly, a smirk on his lips.

I slam the door shut before throwing each lock on it.

Standing in my dark kitchen, my chest heaving as my heart races, I yank my phone out of my bra.

Me
4:44 a.m.: Are you fucking serious right now?

Me
4:45 a.m.: Fuck off Roman.

With a sigh I head back to the living room, watching that little chat bubble indicating he's typing.

Roman
4:46 a.m.: You're mine.

I throw my phone at the recliner with a scream, scaring poor Lily half to death.

Fuck this. Fuck him. Fuck everything.

He thinks he owns me? No.

No one will ever own me.

Slowly, I shimmy out of my skirt and panties, before sitting down on the floor.

Reaching onto the recliner I grab my phone, before letting my legs fall open. Unlocking the screen, I quickly snap a picture before I open the text message thread.

Me
4:49 a.m.: Take a good hard look, Mr. Antonov. This is the last time you'll see it.

Hitting send I throw my phone to the side again, before quickly putting my clothes back on.

My phone immediately vibrates but I ignore it.

Fuck no. I'm so done with this crazy piece of shit.

ANTONOV

CHAPTER THIRTY-ONE

ROMAN

Jaxon had just finished telling me about his ongoing battle with his ex-girlfriend's brother Michael, and the devastating loss of his unborn son, when he got a phone call from his wife. That's when the two of us realized that it was after four in the morning.

"My apologies, we lost track of time," he says with a smile. "I'll be back soon, Αγαπημένη."

After a brief argument over the check, which I win, I settle our tab and the two of us go our separate ways.

"Take me to her," I say to Cal, closing the door to the back seat of the Cadillac.

I know it's late, and I know from the texts I've exchanged with Abby that I'm likely to catch far more hell than Jaxon, by showing up at her house at this ridiculous hour, but I don't give a shit.

Ridiculous is on par for Abby and I.

And I need to see her. Now.

As Cal navigates the relatively deserted New York City streets I replay the conversation I had with Jaxon.

"Do you think she's tried to kill you?"

Something about his question hasn't exactly sat right with me since he asked.

I watched Abby slip something in Igor's drink on camera. I don't know what she used, I only know that my brother-in-law was dead a few hours later.

So was Boris. And Jacques. And Noah.

And as I think back through my interactions with Abby, I keep thinking back to that day in my office where she slapped the coffee out of my hand.

Had *that* been poisoned? Had she tried to kill me?

But then, at the same time she's gotten me coffee dozens of times since then.

If she really wanted to kill me, she's had plenty of opportunities to do so, and she would've had no reason to save my life when that man tried to gun me down outside the gala.

Jaxon had a fair point when he said that it is the nature of a serial killer to kill. But something doesn't add up.

I need to know.

I need to ask her.

I need her to help me to understand *why* she does this.

A message comes through on my phone, lighting up the backseat of the darkened car, and I chuckle to myself.

She tried to convince me she was at the club. How cute.

But just as I'm about to respond to her latest message, my phone suddenly starts ringing. Only this time it's not Abby.

It's Ana.

Shit. That definitely can't be good.

"Roman," she says as I answer the phone. "What the fuck happened with Heather?"

"Who?" I ask, slightly confused.

"From Accounting?" Ana snaps.

"Oh, *AccountTits*," I say, before I can stop myself.

Shit. I may have had a glass too many this evening.

"What?!"

"Nothing, what about her?"

"Apparently, she stormed into your CFO's office, with a massive bandage on her chest and quit on the spot. She didn't even give two weeks notice. I've only just had time to read the email."

"Okay…and?" I scoff. "Why is that my problem?"

"It's your *problem*, brother of mine," Ana seethes on the other end of the phone. "Because she claimed that you were the one who maimed her, and she said that she wanted to file a police report about it."

"Oh shit, really?" I snort, but immediately regret it when Ana starts yelling in my ear.

"What the fuck did you do to her chest, Roman?!"

"Nothing! It was an accident," I say, trying to choose my words carefully so as not to implicate Abby. "She just had a little accident."

"She had the word *slut* carved into her chest, Roman!" Ana continues shouting. "I understand if you want to do your scary mafia stuff outside in the real world, but Nikotech is supposed to be set above that shit. It's supposed to function legitimately, which means you can't just go carving words into whomever you feel like slicing up!"

"I didn't!" I snap back. "It was one of the office girls."

"Who?!"

Shit.

"Um, fuck, I don't know, you know I'm not good with names."

"Roman," Ana growls. "I have worked so damn hard to build Nikotech and keep it above brow."

"I know you have," I nod. "And I support you in this—"

But my words are completely ignored as Ana continues on her furious tirade.

"...And I'll be damned if I let you tarnish the reputation I am so carefully building because you feel like branding whatever bitch you're currently fucking!"

"Watch it, Ana," I growl darkly, my fist tightening. "I just told you that I didn't carve up Heather. That should be enough for you."

"Alright," Ana scoffs. "Then you need to figure out who did and bring them to justice."

"I will look into it," I lie, sighing deeply. "But for the time being, I have a few other more pressing issues on my mind, and I don't give a shit if that bitch doesn't work for me anymore."

"Yeah, well you should," Ana snaps back at me. "Because she's gone to Polina."

Her words instantly make my blood run cold within my veins.

"What?" I whisper. "Wh…How?"

"*You* told me to monitor her closely," Ana hisses. "So that's what I've been doing. I've had one of our men posted at her house for the last twenty-four hours and he just sent me a picture of Heather's vehicle pulling up at Polina's gate."

"I…don't understand," I say, shaking my head, struggling to form complete sentences. "Why would she…she doesn't even know Polina. They don't run in the same circles. The only interaction she would've ever had with her would be casually observing Polina coming into the office a handful of times. What the fuck could they possibly have in common?"

Ana snorts sarcastically before cursing in Russian under her breath.

"You really don't get it do you?" She laughs coldly. "The thing they have in common is their hatred of *you*. Both your ex-employee, and your disgruntled sister now are bonding over their hatred of you, and who the fuck knows what they are planning. But considering Heather knew that you and Polina were on the outs, and immediately went running straight to her, I'd say she's a bit more observant than you think, and things are a bit past casual now."

"Ana, I—" I start to say but she simply hangs up the phone, leaving me stunned and seething in the silent backseat.

Fucking hell.

In the middle of my chaotic little spiral, the car suddenly comes to a stop on a quiet street.

"Boss, we're here," Cal says, clearing his throat. "What would you like to do?"

What would I like to do?

The question is simple, but the truth is not, and I realize now that I have no idea why I even told Cal to come all the way across town to Abby's house.

A serial *killer's* house.

However, as I sit here, debating my decisions, a text comes through... from Abby. When I open it, I find that staring back at me is a picture of her perfect little pussy.

I ball my fist, biting it with my teeth.

Ooh this fucking girl.

And just like that I've made up my mind.

I may have a lot on my plate right now. Between the turf war with the Irish, and the rapidly developing problem with Polina, I probably have more open-ended questions than I have answers, all of which require my attention.

But you know what? Fuck it. Fuck it all.

So much of my life is spent growing my family's dynasty, and relentlessly working to ensure its safety and survival.

Tonight, however, I just want to be selfish.

...And fuck the sass right out of Abigail if it's the last fucking thing I do.

"Cal, stay here," I say as I step out of the car.

My heart pounds in my chest as I make my way up the cobblestone path to her porch, finding Oleg waiting for me.

"Has she said anything?"

"Not much," he shrugs, furrowing his brow. "But she did apologize."

"What?" I ask. "She…apologized?"

"Yeah," he says, shaking his head. "She said something about it being self-preservation?"

Oh.

As strange as it might be, hearing that Abby had some remorse gives me a bit of relief.

I raise my hand to her solid wooden front door, and knock politely.

But there is no answer.

Shit, did she go to bed? I mean, it is nearly five in the morning.

However, when I press my ear to the door I can hear shuffling inside, and what sounds like Abby muttering to herself.

I knock again. This time louder than the first.

"Go away, Roman," Abby suddenly snaps from the other side. "I don't want to speak to you."

"Yes, you do. Let me in."

"No!" She shouts back. "Leave!"

"Abigail," I snort, shaking my head and biting back the instant frustration her stubbornness invokes in me. "We both know that's not true. Now open the door."

"It is true! I don't want to see you ever again, you possessive, chauvinistic, egotistical, asshat! Oh, and I quit!"

"No, you don't," I bite back, her tone grating my patience which is only exacerbated when I notice Oleg and the other men that I had posted up outside her house, looking over at me standing here…getting rejected.

"I just want to talk to you."

"Fuck off! And take your men with you!"

"Abby, stop being difficult and just open the fucking door," I growl. "Don't make me ask you again."

"Oh, I'm not making you do anything!" She laughs venomously. "I'm *telling* you to go the fuck home because I don't want to see you."

Her continued obstinance causes my rage to boil in my veins. I cannot believe the utter audacity of this woman.

Does she have any idea who the fuck I am? And what I could do to her? Especially for killing off *my* men, a crime that would earn anyone else a one-way ticket to a slow and painful death?

I briefly debate just telling my men to kick down her stupid wooden door, but at the same time I realize that course of action likely won't win me any points with her.

However, as I raise my fist, intent on rattling her front door off its hinges, I'm immediately reminded of my conversation with Jaxon just a few hours ago.

"But of all the stupid, selfish reasons we have to gamble with our lives, love is perhaps the only one that's actually worth the risk. And the fight."

I pause, unclenching my fist and instead pressing my hand to the door as I take a deep breath.

Godfuckingdamn it. He's right.

While I'm completely unsure of how exactly I'm supposed to win the love of the girl behind the door, who is deliberately refusing to open it and let me inside, I do know that smashing it into her foyer certainly isn't the answer.

And no matter how much I try to fight it, and no matter the fight I might have on my hands to be with her, or even how insane it is to say any of this out loud, I know *exactly* how I feel about her.

…And what I'm willing to risk to have her in my life.

Everything. Every. Single. Thing.

Closing my eyes I take a deep breath, and try the only thing left I have left in my arsenal.

"Foxy, baby," I say softly. "Let me in."

ANTONOV

CHAPTER THIRTY-TWO

"No," I spit, completely and utterly done with this man.

He thinks he can control me?

That he can *own* me?

I'm a person.

I was controlled once before, and even though in my bones I know this is different than it was with my husband, it still makes me feel like I'm suffocating.

But then, at the same time, a part of me *demands* I throw open the door and fly into Romans arms.

"Foxy, open up," he repeats, his dominating frame casting a shadow through the glass.

"Why should I? You've locked me in my house! Why? So you could control me like I'm some pet?!"

"That's not why I did it, Foxy," he says slowly. "You know that. I just can't let you kill any more of my men."

"Your men," I scoff. "You mean rapers and abusers! Exactly the kind of people who deserve to die!"

Angrily I kick over the umbrella holder by the door, as I notice that I've slowly crept forward, gravitating to his presence.

"Foxy, you know if I let you kill any more of my men, I can't save you from them." I see his hand run through his hair, sweeping it back from his forehead. "Just… let me in, baby."

A sharp laugh bubbles out my mouth, which turns nearly maniacal as I struggle to understand my own emotions warring within me.

"Why, Roman? Why? What will that achieve? Then I'll just be locked in here… with *you.*"

I slam my hand against the door, my eyes stinging with tears as I glance toward the ceiling.

"Would that be so bad?"

"Yes!" I snap, turning to stomp my way up the stairs.

"Abigail!" Roman yells out again, stopping me in my tracks. "Just…tell me *why* you kill them."

My breath hitches in my throat as I tighten my hand on the banister.

He wants to hear it from me. He wants to know *why* I kill them?

"I know everything else about you, Abby," I hear him sigh, seeing his hand press against the glass. "Before you came to work for me, I had Ana put together a file on you. I know where you went to school, your parents, your employment history, about your fucking…*husband.*"

The disgust in his voice is evident even through the door.

"I know what you do," he says firmly. "And I'm not here to punish you. I just want to know why you became a killer."

I hear a thud as something hits the door, but I'm already on my way back down the stairs, my eyes taking in Romans intimidating frame hunched behind the glass, his head resting against it. I press my forehead to the door, the mirror of his as my lip's part, my breath steaming the cold glass beneath it.

"I just want to understand you," he says softly, an ache in his voice. "To know what happened to you that made you decide to kill men. Who did this to you, Foxy?"

"What does it matter?" I mutter, but he still hears me.

"It matters to me, Abby. Who drove you to this point?" He curses. "You didn't wake up one day and decide to kill people."

"What does it matter to you who started this, Roman? This is who I am! I'm exactly who I want to fucking be!" I snap, wiping my eyes. "Why do you care?"

"I care because I'll fucking kill them for hurting you," he growls lethally. "Anyone who made you feel like you have to kill—"

"They didn't! That's what you're not getting!" I fire back. "You kill people all the time, Roman, why is it a problem when I do it? And why is it so hard to understand that this was my decision and it's who I *am*?"

"Foxy… just let me in," he pleads. "Explain it to me."

My fingers shakily reach out, grabbing hold of the bolt as I slide it across, my other hand grips the handle and I swing it open.

Roman stares at me, his face flushed with unreadable emotions churning in his eyes.

My arms drop to my sides as I sigh, stepping around the door as I bend down to pick up the pair of boots. Wordlessly, I tie the laces, securing them to my feet.

"I killed my husband first," I say emotionlessly, staring straight into his eyes.

I've never said it out loud before.

"Why?" He questions, the tone of his voice lowered as he still blocks the doorway. Almost as if he's worried, I might bolt before he gets his answers.

"He abused me, tormented me, and killed my unborn baby to name a few things," I shrug, grabbing a cardigan from the coat rack.

Stepping backward, I silently gesture for Roman to come in as he eyes me with curiosity.

"He didn't *make* me this way, Roman. He controlled aspects of my life, but when his life ended…he set me *free*."

I smile, feeling the power of the words rush over me.

Roman is silent for a few seconds, and when he finally opens his mouth, I already know what he's about to ask me.

"I should probably show you how."

"Show me?" He replies, puzzled.

"Yeah…" I trail off as I walk through the kitchen to the back door.

As I pull open the handle, I find the same creepy man still grinning at me as before and licking his lips.

However, the moment he sees Roman materialize from the darkness of my house, looking absolutely murderous, his sleazy smile drops and he pales in the moonlight.

"Fuck. Off." Roman growls darkly.

The man doesn't need to be told twice, hightailing it quickly around the side of the house to the front yard.

My scary mafia CEO then follows me out into the garden, pausing to stare at me when the greenhouse lights flicker on, illuminating the bright flowers within. I can almost feel the heat of his body as he shadows me.

The tension in my shoulders releases as I take a large gulp of air, feeling it calm me as it releases through my nose.

I grab the handle, pressing it down to open the door. When I look back at Roman, I see that he's still staring at me, waiting for me to make the first move.

I tilt my head.

"After you."

His freshly polished shoes cross over the doorway, and I realize this is a first for me. I've never had another person in this greenhouse, my safe haven.

A part of me feels exposed… *vulnerable*.

Roman's hands tuck into his pants pockets as he slowly takes in the length of the greenhouse, turning around slowly on the spot as I shut the door behind us, with a resounding *click*. I pick at the hem of my cardigan, twisting my hands in it until I feel it indenting the skin. My entire body is tingling all over, as I stare at him, the only thing I can hear is my pounding heart.

"Abby, this is very pretty…" He trails off, breaking the silence as he runs a hand through his hair.

He turns, strolling down one of the rows of flowers, running his hands over the pansies and marigolds as he goes.

"But how is this *showing* me?"

"I poison them," I state, ignoring the slight waver in my voice as I finally voice the biggest secret that I've hidden in plain sight for years.

"With…flowers?" He questions, his voice thick with confusion.

I point to the middle bay, his eyes following my finger as he moves around the greenhouse, until he stops in front of my deadly *collection*.

"The one that has pale yellow flowers with purple, that's henbane, next to it…" He points at the white bell-shaped clusters, causing me to nod with a smile, "Lily of the Valley. Behind that is Morning Glory."

"And this one?" He gestures to the pinkish purple flower.

"My personal favorite. Foxglove. Each one of them is deadly in their own way. Combined they are unstoppable."

"Your husband died of a heart attack…"

"Yep," I nod, clicking my tongue.

I step toward my delicate beauties with confidence.

"Together they make a deadly concoction that brings about a heart attack. I labeled it my Widowmaker," I say quietly. "My husband was my first victim. Granted, it took me a while to buck up the courage to actually do it, and I left so I wouldn't have to watch it happen. But the coroner labeled it a heart attack, and thankfully no one questioned it."

Roman nods slowly. "And Igor? How did you kill him?"

"The same way, I put the Widowmaker in his drink when he was hitting on me at the bar." I smirk.

"What do you mean they can bring on a heart attack?" He asks.

"All of these plants attack a different vital function. When mixed together, with the right dosage, they cause the heart to either increase or decrease rapidly, effectively replicating a heart attack."

His eyes darken as he glances at the flowers.

"Brilliant," he whispers.

He steps toward me, his head tilted to the side as he assesses me, like the predator he is. I shiver, the hair on my arms standing up as electricity ripples down my body.

"And me, Foxy?" He growls. "How were you going to kill *me*?"

"The same way."

I watch as the realization hits him, as his eyes widen slightly.

"The coffee…" He grins darkly.

I nod, humming my agreement.

He steps toward me, forcing me to take a step back, and then another as he advances on me.

My back hits the door, my hands fumbling as I try to find the latch. My eyes haven't left his for a second, as he steps into me, molding his body to mine.

"But," he whispers. "You couldn't do it, could you, Foxy?"

My eyes drop closed as my breath shudders out of me, I lean into him as I feel his fingertips running along the side of my face as they trail down to my jaw.

He grips my chin, tilting my face up to his.

"I want an answer," he whispers in my ear, his teeth nibbling along my ear lobe. "You couldn't do it, could you?"

The warmth from his breath on my cheek sends a jolt straight to my core.

"No," I say breathlessly, my thighs clenching.

"Why?" He says huskily, his thumb rubbing circles along the pulse point in my neck.

Straining up onto my tip toes, running my nose along his jaw I whisper.

"You make me feel *alive*."

Suddenly, his lips smash into mine, electricity sparking between us. My hands grip the lapels of his suit jacket, pulling him closer.

His hand snakes round to the back of my head, fisting my hair tightly and tugging, causing me to moan against his mouth, as his tongue caresses mine. My back arches into him, my breasts crushed against his chest.

His attention is demanding, my body under his control.

Just like me, under house arrest.

The realization hits me, and I push against his chest, forcing *him* to take a few steps back.

My chest heaves as I take him in.

The way that his suit is disheveled, his hair ruffled and wild, and the look on his face is laced with the same darkness and desire that floods my veins.

I lunge at him, my body crashing into his.

He catches me with a grunt, my legs wrapping around his waist to steady myself as my hands tug his hair, forcing his head back as I lick up his throat, nipping sharply at his jaw causing him to hiss as he squeezes my ass.

My hands run across his chest, feeling his muscles bulge and clench beneath me as I explore him. My nails claw at his jacket, forcing him out of it as I throw it behind me while he walks us toward the workbench, planting me down roughly.

His hands run along my thighs, squeezing as he pushes the rest of my skirt, bunching it at my waist. His cock rubs against my lace covered pussy, my hips grinding against him, chasing the delicious friction.

"I hate how much I want you sometimes," I whisper my lips ghosting over his, I feel his lips quirk as a smirk forms.

"Fuck me like you mean it then, Foxy."

Leaning back, I hook my fingers into his belt, spreading my legs slightly as his fingers brush my slit. His eyes shoot to mine as he discovers how wet I am for him, and I feel his knuckles brush across me. His fist clenches as he forcefully tears my lace panties from me. The fabric burns across my hip as he pulls it free, exposing me completely.

Locking eyes with me, he lifts my panties to his nose, inhaling deeply as he groans before tucking them into his suit pants pocket.

"*Mine.*"

His finger runs down my wet slit, gathering me on his finger before he pops it in his mouth, sucking it clean, causing my lips to part.

"So fucking mine," he growls, making my pussy clench with need.

His hands grip my cardigan, forcing it off my shoulders, as he runs his hands down to the hem of my shirt, tugging it up and over my head exposing my nipples to him.

Roman's large hand wraps around my throat before he smashes our lips together, biting me softly. He pushes me onto my back and squeezes my neck as he leaves a trail of kisses against my jaw, continuing his path down my neck.

My body is on fire, every nerve ending misfiring as he overloads my senses. I can feel the path of destruction his eyes have left behind as he reaches my breasts, turning me into a quivering mess. He sucks my left nipple, biting down and making me moan. Impulsively my back arches from the sweet pain, thrusting my breasts into his face. Sucking harder, he suddenly pulls back and blows, causing my hands to flail around me trying to find something to grip.

"You look so good like this, Foxy, all flushed and needy, I want to mark your flesh, so everyone knows your mine."

His teeth continue to nip at me playfully and painfully, sucking the sensitive marking and sending waves of pleasure through me with the possessive act.

I jerk upwards, needing to touch him, to taste him.

I hook my fingers into his waistband, pulling him to me as I reach down, and run my hand over his hard length, squeezing him firmly.

Roman holds my hand against his throbbing cock as he grinds against me, his fingers back between my thighs. His hands explore, rubbing and squeezing my thigh before he sharply grabs me, pulling me to the edge of the workbench, slapping a hand against my pussy.

I gasp, as the shock from such a painful pleasure shoots through my core.

"You like that, baby?" He slaps again, causing my hips to jerk as my head tips back on a moan.

"Oh fuck!"

"That's right, such a good fucking girl," he growls, as he rubs against my clit. "So fucking responsive."

I tug at his dress shirt, wanting to feel his skin beneath mine, as he slowly presses a finger inside me, curling it gently.

Distracted by the ecstasy, my fingers fumble the buttons, and with a growl of frustration, I tear his shirt open.

He inserts another finger, and then another, working them in tandem, his pace increasing as I feel myself getting closer and closer.

"More," I gasp, my thighs quivering as I feel my pussy clench against him. "I want more."

"You want my cock?"

I nod, "Yes."

His fingers curl, hitting that sweet spot inside me, "where do you want it?"

Fuck. Everywhere. I want it everywhere.

I want him in my mouth, I want to taste him on my tongue… but my need to have him inside me overrides that, his thumb pressing down on my clit, my brain short circuiting.

"My pussy," I shout, feeling lightheaded.

"Take it out, Foxy," he breathes, his own voice trembling.

Yanking his zipper down, I slip my hand into his waistline, gripping his erection in my hand.

His cock is smooth, the veins defined under my palm. I pump him once, then twice as my other hand tugs his clothing down, hearing him groan.

"Holy fuck," he mutters under his breath.

Feeling him shaking under my hands, his legs clench tightly as he tries to steady himself. I lean forward, locking my eyes with his as I intentionally let my spit drip down onto the head of his cock. He groans louder as I continue to pump him, my other hand rubbing up the center of his chest, feeling his heart pounding.

And then, without warning, I stab my nails into his pec, scratching my way down, feeling him wince as his cock jerks in my hand.

His control snaps as he grabs my hand on his cock, his other wrapping round my neck, slamming me back against the workbench. He steps further into me, knocking my knees open as he rubs the head of his cock against my clit. My body trembles, as his eyes lock on mine, his hand tightening around my throat.

As I feel the head of his cock at my entrance, I run my hand across his hip, my nails scratching as they go, leaving another mark on his beautiful skin.

"Go on, Roman," I smile, biting my lip. "Fuck me like you mean it."

ANTONOV

ANTONOV

CHAPTER THIRTY-THREE

ROMAN

I grip Abby's hips, thrusting into her hard.

Possibly *too* hard.

"Fuck!" She cries, as I pull out and ram into her again.

I know I should calm down, but I can't.

I'm tired of playing nice.

She breathes in sharply with every thrust of my cock. Her eyes are closed, and her hands grip my shoulders, as if she is holding on for dear life.

Leaning in I kiss her neck, swirling my tongue against her sweet skin and feeling her shake as I continue to relentlessly slam into her.

"You may hate me, Abigail," I growl, kissing her earlobe. "But your body fucking *loves* me. I can feel you dripping down my leg like a bitch in heat."

She takes a shuddering breath, her perfect tits heaving against me.

"I…I…can't help that," she whispers.

"No, you can't." I grin softly, biting my lip before kissing her deeply. "Because no matter how you fight it, you want me as badly as I want you."

"No!" She winces, shaking her head. "I could never!"

But her words do not match the look in her eyes, which are filled with unbridled desire. I further test her statement by slowing my rhythm and pulling out of her.

"Wait…no…what are you doing?" She whines breathlessly.

I smile.

"Thought you didn't want me, little fox?"

Her ragged breathing hitches and her face instantly turns red, her brown eyes darkening.

"You know what? Fuck this!" She snaps, hopping off the bench.

But I'm already ahead of her.

I grab her arm and pull her to me aggressively, slamming her against my chest and pinning her against the workbench. She struggles for a moment before I slide my hand over her tits, squeezing them hard and burying my face in her neck.

She gasps as my hand slips down to her dripping pussy, and I firmly rub my finger along her slit.

"Oh, baby girl, fucking *this* is exactly what I had in mind," I growl darkly, before forcing her legs open.

And then, without warning I grip my cock and shove it back inside her.

"You know," I sneer, thrusting into her, hearing her moan like a whore. "It used to bother me when you'd say that to me."

I press down, causing her to arch her back and allowing me to push deeper inside of her.

"But now I see it as a *challenge*."

I smack my hand hard on her ass, making her yelp before gripping the flesh on her hip and slamming my cock in and out of her.

"Oh fuck…" Abby groans as I thread my fingers in her hair.

"This, right here," I whisper, slipping my other hand around her, rubbing her clit. "Is *mine*."

"Shitttttt," she yelps, jolting violently as I swirl my fingers around.

"You can bitch and whine all you want, and tell me you don't want me. But nothing is going to stop me from doing as I please with these filthy little fuck holes of yours," I whisper, wrapping my hand around her throat while continuing to stroke her throbbing clit. "I'm going to make sure you know exactly who they belong to."

"Oh God…" She groans as I kiss her neck, feeling my climax nearing.

"Say it, Abigail."

"No…" She whines.

"Go on, Foxy," I say, thrusting harder, squeezing her throat. "Give in. Say it for me."

"Fuckkkk," she gasps.

I pull out of her and her breath hitches.

"No…I mean…yes…what was the question?!"

Taking the opportunity I spin her around, grab her hips and set her back up on the bench, teasing her entrance with my swollen cock and crushing my lips to hers.

"Tell me who this pussy belongs to," I purr as I pull away, a wicked grin spreading across my face. "And I will give it what it needs."

Pressing my lips back to hers I gently push the tip just inside her slit before stopping.

"Oh God," she groans desperately, screwing her eyes shut. "It's…yours, Roman. It's fucking yours."

"Good girl," I growl, before ramming myself back inside her. "Now I'm going to make you cum."

I kiss her neck, thrusting harder and deeper, squeezing her hips and pulling her into me. When my lips make their way back to hers, she immediately moans into my mouth.

"I…I…" She whispers breathlessly. "I'm so close."

Fuck me this is incredible. She's so wet I actually *can* feel her dripping down my leg. But I know I'm barely holding on to my own climax.

"At the end of the day," I grunt, accelerating my rhythm. "I love you, Abigail Wayne. And I don't give a flying fuck if you love me back."

"Roman, I…" She starts to say, as her entire body begins to shake,

"This is mine. It's been mine the entire time…because you…were…made…for me," I grunt heavily.

With the last thrust I explode inside her, just as she throws her arms around my neck and seizes around me, lost in her own orgasm.

But as my climax slowly fades, and I'm left holding Abby's trembling body tightly against mine, I realize that what I said in the middle of our ecstasy was true.

I *do* love her.

I have loved her all along.

CHAPTER THIRTY-FOUR

Sex has never been like that before.

My entire body quivers as I come down from the high that only Roman can take me to.

But right now, my brain is only thinking about one thing:

Roman said *"I love you."*

How? How can he love me? After all I've done?

My thoughts are running a mile a minute trying to process everything that's just happened.

The truth is Roman scares me. Not because I think he will hurt me, but because of the way he makes me feel.

Free.

It's true, I felt free after I killed my husband. And then I felt free when I started my noble work as a vigilante killer of bad men. But even then, I had restraints. I had a code that kept my demons in check, and gave me limitations that kept me in control…but I was still a prisoner of my own morality.

The reason that Roman terrifies me, is because he is the hand that threatens to unlock them completely. He wouldn't fend off my demons. He would feed them, fuel them, fuck them mercilessly, and let them run wild.

Yes, he locked me in my house tonight. But not because he wanted to control me, rather because he wanted the opportunity to understand why I'd been killing his men.

He wanted to understand *me*.

One of the first things he ever said to me was "betray me and find out." And by all accounts, I've done that every time I've poisoned one of his men.

Technically I'd betrayed him before we'd even met. My motive for applying for the job as his secretary was solely in hope of finding more bad men to kill.

His bad men.

I should be dead.

He should have put me down and moved the fuck on with his life…but he hasn't.

Instead, Roman Antonov has embedded himself in my skin, inserting himself so far into my life it feels as if he's always been a part of it. I've told him things I've never told anyone, and when I look into his eyes, I see the same darkness, and need for control.

But perhaps what terrifies me the most is the way I *care* for him.

The last time I cared for someone and let them past the walls I'd built around my heart, it burned me. It destroyed me and obliterated any sense of existence. I lost so many years, submitting to another person's will for my life.

And while I've healed and forgiven myself for allowing Garrett's disrespect to continue and escalate the way it did, the one casualty I've never been able to forgive myself for is the loss of my unborn child.

On some level, I still hate myself for not fighting harder. For not leaving earlier…And for not killing the bastard sooner.

So, while part of my heart calls for Roman to set it ablaze, and the rest of it is terrified of the way I feel for him and how vulnerable those feelings could make me.

He might not be the kind of bad man that I put down, but he's no angel either.

He's a powerful man. And a *deadly* one.

But then again…I'm deadly too.

I am jarred out of my thoughts by a phone ringing.

Roman answers his phone pinning it into his shoulder as he tucks himself into his boxers and pulls his pants back up.

"What?" he demands.

The greenhouse is so quiet I could just make out a male voice rumbling on the other line. Roman stills, his eyes darting straight to mine.

"They confirmed?" He snaps, placing his hand on his hip. "When? Can't it wait?"

I hear him sigh.

"Fine," he barks, ending the call.

He throws his phone down next to me on the workbench, and I flinch in response, the loud noise echoing against the glass walls.

"Get dressed Abigail," he says, throwing his jacket at me.

"Excuse me?"

"Get fucking dressed," he repeats matter-of-factly. "We have to go."

He looks around, his jaw clenched and his hand running through his ruffled hair.

"Fuck! Where the hell is my shirt?"

"Roman, I'm not going anywhere," I state, sitting up on the workbench and closing my legs.

"Abby, I highly doubt you want to spend the rest of the day in a goodman greenhouse," he barks. "So, get dressed. Now."

Jesus, something has him on edge.

"Maybe I do, actually," I snap back.

"I have some shit I have to handle, and you're going to come with me."

"Why the hell would I want to go anywhere with you?"

"I don't give a shit about what you want to do," he snorts. "I can't leave you alone. Especially after catching you nearly killing Oleg."

"I never actually admitted to that," I shrug.

He walks toward me, forcing my legs apart, his fingers firmly grip my chin as he presses his lips to mine.

"You lie so prettily." He whispers against my lips, as my pulse races.

I would be lying if I didn't say I wanted to fuck him again already, something about this man was a drug.

"Something has come up, and I have to pull the men," he says as he pulls away, walking round the side of me.

"Good. Take them. I don't fucking need them, anyway," I snap. "As I've already told you, I'm not some helpless doll that needs protection, Mr. Antonov."

"I know that, Abby. That's not what this is about."

He picks up his shirt, and dusts it off before throwing it over his shoulders. However, when he looks down and sees that all the buttons have been ripped off, he sighs, and I have to fight the wicked grin pulling at my lips.

Despite the incredible sex we just had, he suddenly looks tired, and slightly…worried.

"Roman… what's going on?" I ask.

"Just get dressed," he sighs, picking up his phone again. "We're leaving in ten. And that's not a fucking request."

I flick my wrist, looking at the time.

5:58 a.m.

That gives me an idea…

If Mr. Bossy CEO thinks he can order me around, making all my decisions for me, then I'm going to teach him a lesson.

"Twenty minutes." I state.

"What?"

"I need a shower, and time to get ready. So, actually make it an hour," I say as I jump down from the workbench.

"Fine," he grunts.

I feel Roman's cum run down my thigh as I smooth my skirt down my legs.

"Go get ready to go."

"Okay, babe," I smirk, closing the door behind. "Have a nice shower."

I wave at him.

"What did you—" He looks at me, his head tilted to the side as all of a sudden, the greenhouse sprinkler system turns on, dousing him in water.

"What the fuck, Abigail!"

Laughing I race up the path to the back door, as he continues shouting and yelling my name. The men stationed at the front of the house come around the corner, concerned for their Boss. However, the moment they see him trapped in my backyard monsoon, they can barely contain their amusement.

"Shut the fuck up!" I hear Roman roar at them as he finally steps out into the frigid garden. "And someone get me a fresh set of clothes."

Wrapping the fluffy towel around my body, I walk into my bedroom, and see Roman lounging against the headboard of the bed, looking rather damp.

"You're ruining my sheets, you know," I smirk. "Did you have a good shower?"

"Abigail," he growls. "After that little stunt with the sprinklers, I suggest you don't push your luck right now."

"Maybe I like pushing," I sing, throwing my towel at his head and step into my closet.

"Oh, I'm well aware of that," he snaps.

I hear a knock at the door, and Roman storming across the room. There's a sound of crinkling plastic, and what sounds like Roman hanging something on the back of my bedroom door.

"Is this what you wanted, Boss?" I hear Oleg say.

"It will do. Tell Cal to make sure everything is ready to go," I hear Roman say. "And it's probably time to bring Ana up to speed."

"Yes, Boss."

The door closes just as I pull a shirt over my head. After grabbing a pair of panties, I step back out into the room, finding Roman ripping plastic off a freshly laundered set of clothes.

"That didn't take them very long," I say with a smirk. "And here I thought you were going to have to sit in your soggy clothes all afternoon."

"I pay them well," he says, pulling off his sopping wet boxers, and replacing them with a dry pair.

God his cock is huge. I had that inside me.

I snort to myself, shaking my head as I deliberately sit down on the bed opposite him, and begin to pull on my panties.

He's in the middle of throwing the fresh dress shirt over his shoulders when he looks up and stares at me. I try not to look at the bulge growing between his legs, but I can't help it.

The devilish look in his eye as I stand and pull the black lace over my hips nearly sets my entire bedroom on fire.

"I assume I'm not getting my other ones back?" I say sweetly, raising a brow at him.

He snorts.

"No, you're not."

"Why would you want a pair of ripped dirty panties?" I ask, scrunching up my nose as I walk past him toward my closet to pick out a skirt.

But the minute I pass him, he grabs my arm and pulls me in front of him, cupping my face in his hands and kissing me deeply. Shoving his tongue into my mouth. His hand slips down to my ass and he squeezes my left ass cheek, making me gasp.

I think we're about to go for round two when he pulls away, pressing his forehead to mine.

"Because, little fox," he growls against my lips. "As I told you the first time we fucked. I like your *scent*."

His words make me shiver, and I try to get away, but he holds me fast, gripping my throat tightly.

"In fact, if I had my way, I wouldn't have let you shower, and I'd have made you go out with me with my cum dripping down your legs. So, you could feel me trickling out of you all afternoon."

Even though he infuriates me, there's something about the cocky arrogance in his voice that makes my thighs clench.

He's such a prick….But I kind of love it.

But suddenly, a completely different fear takes root within my chest, making it tighten.

"You didn't use protection," I swallow, trying to hide the way my voice trembles.

"And I never will, Abigail," he says wickedly, whispering against my lips. "You are mine. There will be nothing between us. Ever."

While this might be incredibly romantic, or sexy to someone else, it actually breaks my heart.

Fuck. I don't exactly *want* to have this conversation.

But I can already feel myself getting attached to this man, and I'm suddenly unable to stop the words as they bubble to the surface.

"So…you know then?" I ask, turning away from him and pulling on my skirt in the mirror.

"Know?" He asks, fastening his belt. "Know what?"

I say nothing. Not because I don't want to say something, but because the words strangle me where I stand.

"Abby?"

His voice is soft as he steps behind me.

But I just stand there, staring at my reflection.

Gently his hand grips my shoulders, and he turns me to face him, but even then, I can't look him in the eye.

This is it. This is where he rejects me.

The one thing a woman is good for, and I can't even do that.

"Abigail…what are you talking about?" He says, softly gripping my chin and forcing my gaze to him.

"You've read my file," I say, feeling a tear streak down my cheek. "You said you know everything about me."

Instinctively my hands push against his chest, as if bracing myself for the impact.

His eyes scan mine, his chest rising and falling.

"I can't have kids, Roman," I say, the words choking in my throat. "After my husband pushed me down the stairs, the doctor told me that the damage was so extensive that I'd never be able to carry a child again."

"Abigail…" He starts to say but I step away from him, pacing slowly across the bedroom floor.

"So, I guess protection *isn't* really needed, is it?" I laugh, the sound bitter in the air. I inhale sharply, my heart hammering hard in my chest, which feels as if it's tightening around my lungs. "I mean…all this trouble you're going through to keep me? And I can't even give you a child!"

"Abby, I—"

"I've heard about the mafia," I continue, my steps quickening and my breathing becoming erratic. "You're all obsessed with heirs and continuing your family legacy. But I can't have kids. You'll never be able to have that with me."

He stays silent, his jaw ticking as he continues to stare at me as I pace the room, finally coming to a stop beside my bed.

"I'm damaged goods. Physically and mentally, so I'm going to save you all this trouble. Leave, Roman." I yell, my finger pointing at the door. "Just leave now and save us both the heartache."

I slam down on the bed, my hands covering my face as I pull at my hair.

Sweet Lily is scratching at my door to get in, her meow getting louder by the minute. She knows I'm upset.

I feel Roman move toward me, the fabric of his suit rustling as I feel his hands cup mine, gently pulling them away from my face.

My eyes remain closed, my lashes thick with tears as they run down my face.

"Look at me," he whispers, his thumbs running soothing circles against the back of my hands. I pull in a deep breath, trying to take back control of my emotions as my eyes blink open, my eyebrows shoot up as I see Roman's face directly in front of mine.

He's kneeling on the floor between my legs.

The Mafia king of New York city is on his knees…for *me*.

"I need you to take a deep breath for me," he says, a gentle calmness in his voice that I have never heard before.

But even in his softness, his words bid me to obey, so I do as he says. Taking a long deep breath, filling my lungs.

"There you go, now release it, and inhale again. Good girl. Do it again."

For the next few minutes, we repeat the process, with him breathing in and out, and me copying him. My spiral slows, and I begin to focus on his face, and the smell of his cologne, or the smooth tones in his voice.

"Abby," he says softly. "You should know, that wasn't in your medical file."

"What?"

All I can do is stare at him.

I know what the doctor said to me. I've replayed that moment a hundred thousand times. I can still remember how the pain, the crippling numbness, and how my brain froze and looped back his words over and over.

"You won't be able to conceive."

"It had to be," I whisper.

"It wasn't," he says firmly. "What *was* in your medical file, however, is that you received a shot every thirteen weeks."

"Yeah, it was a vitamin shot, to help with my mood swings." I say, shaking my head, "It wasn't a big deal."

Roman stares at me for a long moment before furrowing his brow and licking his bottom lip.

"You never questioned that?" He asks gently, his thumbs still rubbing circles on the back of my hands.

"No?" I ask, confused. "Why would I?"

"What did the doctor say to you?" He asks again, narrowing his eyes at me. "About the shot?"

"He said that it was crucial for me to keep up to date on it," I say, my brain spinning.

"And did you?"

"Yes, but when my husband died, I moved, I just never got another appointment," I shrug. "He was the one who said I needed it for my mood swings, and since he was gone, I didn't think I needed it anymore."

He sighs heavily, nodding slowly, his jaw flexing.

"Abby, that injection was *Depo Provera*, it was a contraceptive shot," Roman says slowly, swallowing hard. "It was meant to *stop* you from getting pregnant."

My head jerks back, as if I've been hit.

"What?" I ask, shaking my head. "That can't...I...I..."

But as I look into Roman's eyes, I can see the truth reflected within. And the longer I think about it, the more it sounds exactly like something my shithead husband would do.

My chest starts heaving and I grind my teeth so hard, I'm surprised I don't feel one crack.

"There was nothing in your medical file, in any of your medical files, that said you're unable to have children, Abigail." He says slowly. "In fact, the notes after your miscarriage said that you were expected to make a full recovery with zero chance of any reproductive issues."

"But... Dr. Downing said..."

"There's no Dr. Downing, Abby," he counters. "Not in the state of New

York anyway."

I sit here, just staring at him.

I'm sure my jaw is on the floor, but I can't seem to form rational thoughts right now.

That's when I feel the fire flooding my bones. The very same fire that spread through my blood stream to my brain and awoke my need to kill my husband.

Even from the grave that bastard is still fucking with me.

If he hadn't pushed me down the stairs I wouldn't be here right now, having my world turned upside down again.

I can have children. I've always been able to have children.

"Then who the fuck treated me?!" I yell, fighting the urge to get up and throw stuff against the wall. "Who the fuck told me all this shit?!"

"I don't know, Foxy, but I'll find him," he growls darkly. "I'll find him, and I'll deliver you whatever part of him you desire."

"No," I whisper venomously, my voice rumbling in my chest. "He's *mine*, Roman."

ANTONOV

CHAPTER THIRTY-FIVE

ROMAN

"Abby, stop this."

"No!"

"Let's go," I growl, twirling my finger around as I step into the hallway.

"I've already told you," she spits angrily. "If you need to go handle your business that's fine, but I'm not going."

Jesus Christ, what's the big deal?

"Yes, you are," I say firmly. "I have business to attend to, but I'm not leaving you alone. Either you can come willingly, or I will just take you. Your choice, Foxy."

She snorts, her jaw slack as she shakes her head in stunned surprise, before immediately trying to shut the door in my face, effectively trying to lock me out of the bedroom.

However, I anticipated this, and stop it with my hand, forcing it back open.

"I said I'm not leave—"

But I don't let her finish that sentence.

Instead, like I did at the gala, and that day at my office, I throw Abby's ranting ass over my shoulder and carry her out of the bedroom.

"I swear to God, Roman," she hisses at me angrily, smacking my back, as I thump down the stairs. "You're the most arrogant, controlling, possessive—"

"Yeah, I know. It's okay, sweetheart," I chuckle sarcastically. "I know you *love* me."

"Arrrrgh!" Abby hands slam harder onto my back as she pushes against me.

"Uh huh," I chuckle as Trevor opens the front door for me and I step outside.

"Boss," Oleg says, clearing his throat as he awkwardly looks up at me holding a squirming and cursing Abigail, and wisely decides to divert his gaze. "I…uh…brought your car around as requested."

"Go upstairs, and get my *girlfriend's* purse," I say, snatching the keys from his hand.

But if I thought Abby was going to be moved by my choice of words, I am sorely mistaken. Instead, she's completely unfazed and continues to smack and yell at me.

"Roman Antonov, you put me down or so help me I will—"

"What?" I chuckle, slapping her ass hard. "You'll do what exactly?"

I slip my hand between her thighs and smile when I hear her gasp, momentarily going limp in my arms as my fingers brush her panties.

"You know," I say darkly. "I think I love having you so close to my face that I can smell your pussy. Your scent is intoxicating."

"Ughhhh!" She grunts irritably as I ignore her pleas and carry her down the path toward the White Ferrari that sits rumbling at the curb. "You're such a pervert."

After hitting the button that opens the passenger door, I finally set Abby down on her feet in front of me. She immediately tries to smack me, but I grab her wrist, stopping her blow.

"Abby…Abigail!" I shout, as she tries to hit me again. "What on earth is going on here? I thought we were good? I don't understand this reaction to me asking you to just come along with me for the day?"

"That's not what you said!" She snaps at me. "You said you had some business to take care of, and wanted me to tag alon—"

"So *exactly* like I said," I snort, shaking my head incredulously. "Got it."

"…Yeah, but then you said we were going to go back to the *penthouse*."

I stare at her, my brow furrowed.

The penthouse is the problem?

"Um, Boss?" Oleg clears his throat beside me, and I look up to see him standing there, awkwardly holding Abby's purse out to her.

"Thank you, Oleg," Abby says, taking it from him without taking her eyes off of me. "I mean, I think that's what you're *supposed* to say. Unless you're Roman Antonov, it seems, and can just order people around without any kind of gratitude."

"Yeah, yeah, we can discuss my etiquette deficiencies later," I say, waving her off. "I'm still confused, what the hell is wrong with my penthouse?"

But before she can answer, we are interrupted.

"Hey man," I suddenly hear from behind me.

Instinctively I push Abby around my body with one hand while simultaneously yanking my gun from my holster with the other.

But I'm not the only one who does.

Because just as I turn to face the skinny dark haired white kid, in his Bob Marley beanie, drooping dark jeans and a brightly colored track jacket, I see *Abigail's* gun also pointing at the kid.

Holy shit.

I didn't even know she had a gun on her, and she must've pulled hers out at the same time I did. And while that is kind of sexy, I still have to deal with the now terrified wannabe gangster walking up on us.

"The fuck do you want?" I bark at him.

"Shit! Yo, man, sorry," he says, throwing his hands in the air at the sight of both Abby and I glaring at him, with weapons drawn. "I was just going to tell you that I liked the car and—"

"This is the part where you fuck off!" Abby snaps, her lip curling, and her chest heaving.

I find myself momentarily distracted by the breeze blowing her long dark brown hair as her eyes viciously stare down the kid with a smoldering intensity.

Yeah...very, very, sexy.

"S...sorry!" He says, turning on his heel and running the other way as fast as his legs can carry him.

That settles that.

Well, not exactly.

"Oleg!" I thunder whipping around to glare at him next. "What the fuck are you doing? We're on high alert and you just let some random cockface walk up on us like that?! What the hell do I even pay you for?!"

"Sorry, Boss," Oleg says, lowering his eyes to the ground.

He's lucky.

Because if I wasn't worried about Abby bolting back into the house and locking the door behind her, I'd be beating the fuck out of him right here on the sidewalk.

Instead, I turn back to her, finding that she hasn't moved.

In fact, she's still pointing the massive pistol at the kid who is more than a block away at this point.

"Foxy," I say, placing my hand on the top of the gun, and pressing downwards firmly. "It's okay, baby. He's gone."

With my other hand, I gently tuck a strand of her hair behind her ear. It takes Abby a few seconds to register what I'm saying to her, and I could be wrong, but it almost appears as if she doesn't *want* to put the gun down.

Eventually, however, she relents, throwing the safety on and putting it back in her purse. She turns, and just as I'm about to snatch her up into my arms again, she reaches for the car door handle and yanks it open, looking at me.

"What?" she says with a shrug, seeing my confusion. "It's not as if I can *stay* here right now. That kid knows my house and might send the police over. And honestly, orange really isn't my color."

And without another word, she hops into the passenger seat.

I stand there, trying to process everything that just took place, feeling as if I have a bit of whiplash.

One minute Abby is vehemently opposed to coming with me, and the next she is just climbing into my car?

Women.

Stepping into the driver's seat I throw on my seat belt and immediately speed off toward the city.

I'm just about to ask her about her issue with my penthouse, but once again I'm interrupted by my phone ringing.

Goddamnit!

I tell myself that I'm not going to answer, until of course, I see that it's Ana and change my mind.

"Good morning," I say.

"*Good morning?*" Ana scoffs loudly.

"What?"

"Seriously? Good morning? What the fuck, Roman? You never say good morning to anyone. Were you abducted by aliens last night?"

Abby giggles.

"Wait, is someone…with you?" Ana asks.

"Um…yes," I say, clearing my throat. "I'm with Miss Wayne at the moment."

There is a long silent pause.

"Alllllright then," she says, barely hiding her chuckle. "Well, I'm going to have Paulie pick him up in an hour. What does he know?"

"Nothing," I say firmly. "I thought it was better that way."

Ana laughs hard.

Why is she amused?

"Yeah, okay," she snorts. "Well, this should be fun then."

But before I have time to ask her what she means, she simply ends the call.

Damnit! I fucking hate when she does that.

My chest tightens, knowing what's about to happen. I've put so much thought and planning into this, but now I can't help but wonder…is this a mistake?

I'm so lost in my thoughts that I don't realize how long I've ridden in silence with Abby until we reach downtown. Glancing over at her, I find her sitting peacefully staring out the window, her arms crossed across her chest.

Right here, in the simplest moments, I realize how truly beautiful she is. She's pulled her dark brown hair softly to one shoulder and her perky tits heave against the low v-neck sweater she's wearing, poking out and teasing me.

God she's gorgeous. I can see the goosebumps on her skin—

"Roman! Watch out!" She suddenly shouts, slamming her hand on the roof of the car.

My attention is ripped from her bodice back to the road, and I swerve just in time to avoid hitting a car that is blasting its horn at me.

"Fuck!" I shout, sliding back into our lane.

I can feel the blood rushing to my face, realizing just how close I came to crashing this car, all because I was staring at Abby.

"So," I clear my throat. "I feel like we should, I don't know, talk about this?"

"Which part?" she says, crossing her arms again as I bring the car to a stop at the light, her tone suddenly quiet and cold. "The fact that you called me your girlfriend back there, or the fact that you have another girl's *panties* hanging from your rear-view mirror?"

"What?"

It's then that I look up and indeed see the pair of red lace lingerie dangling from around the mirror.

"Abby," I scoff. "I didn't even—"

"You know what," she says, throwing her hands in the air, "I don't even know why I agreed to this."

And before I can stop her, Abby unbuckles her seat belt, and yanks the door handle open. She's out of the car just as the light turns green.

"Abby!" I call after her, keeping the car in park.

But she ignores me, stepping into the crowded New York street crowd.

Godamnit! What the fuck is going on here?!

As the cars behind me start to honk, seeing the light has changed, and I haven't moved, I pull my phone from my pocket and dial Oleg.

"Boss, do you want us just to grab her?" Oleg says in my ear, as I slowly lurch the car forward.

"Absolutely not, I don't want a scene," I say quickly. "Just stay with her."

Without turning to look at me she continues storming down the sidewalk, I pull up beside her, rolling the window down.

"Abigail! Get in the damn car!" I snap.

"You know, Roman," she shouts back, but refuses to stop walking. "If you actually give any fucks about your current *girlfriend*, it's probably best not to have trophies of your old ones hanging about!"

Shit.

That's not at all what I'd intended.

"Are you seriously upset about fucking panties?" I laugh incredulously. "I forgot they were there, and I have no fucking idea who they belong to. I didn't know it was such a big deal. I'm sorry."

"You're not sorry and you don't fucking get it!" She snaps, suddenly turning on her heel. "Because they're still fucking hanging there!"

Fuck this. I'm not losing her over some damn panties.

My foot slams hard on the brakes, causing the car behind me with my men to slam on theirs. The sound of screeching tires and people honking echoes through the street as I rip the panties off the rearview mirror, tearing the delicate lace fabric.

Leaving the car running, I step out onto the street and chase after her on the sidewalk.

"Abigail!" I thunder, making her jump.

"Fuck you, Roman," she says, still walking wiping her eyes.

"Abby, will you just turn around and look at me for one—"

"Look at what?!" She shouts suddenly, whirling around to glare at me, the faint traces of tears streaking down her cheeks. "The trophy of some other nameless bitch who was marking their territory? No fucking thank you!"

She glares at me before suddenly storming back down the sidewalk toward me, pointing her finger.

"I'll have you know that I don't give a shit how rich or powerful you are, you ego-centric, maniacal, misogynistic asshole! I'm not a toy for you to play with! And I won't be just another one of your *conquests*! I have too much respect for myself to—"

But her voice fades the second she sees I've pulled my lighter from my pocket….and have lit the panties ablaze.

Right here on fucking Fifth Avenue.

The New Yorkers around us gasp and point, some stopping to stare, others choosing to move away, or ignore us entirely.

But I just stare at her, her brown eyes studying the old lace shriveling and crumbling to dust on the sidewalk.

Then without a word, I step toward her, grab her hand and yank her toward me, cupping her face and kissing her hard.

"You don't seem to get it, Foxy," I growl against her lips. "No one else matters but you. And no one ever will. The bitches that came before you, were a dime a dozen. They meant nothing."

I crush my lips to hers again, landing yet another bruising kiss on her soft lips.

"You have me, all of me, Abigail Wayne. And don't you ever fucking doubt that."

The last of the tears in her eyes fall down her cheeks and I wipe them away with my thumb.

Fuck. I hate knowing I made her cry.

"Now," I say, as softly as I can manage. "Will you please stop confusing the fuck out of me, and just get back in the car, so we can get on with our day?"

Silently her eyes scan mine, before she finally bites her lip. Slowly a wickedly playful grin spreads across her beautiful face.

"Fine," she purrs, batting her lashes at me. "But, if all of that is true, then you certainly won't have a problem with me driving your car then, will you, *darling*?"

"Well, I—"

But without another word she steps past me, storms over to the driver's side door, and gets inside.

Is she fucking serious?

However, Abby told me the night at my penthouse that she hasn't driven in years, and I'm willing to bet she has no idea *how* to drive a stick. So, taking a deep breath, I walk back to the car and open the door, as an angry driver whizzes past, honking and yelling at our little caravan of cars blocking traffic.

I have to stop myself from impulsively pulling my gun from my holster and shooting his back window out.

Probably not the best idea in the middle of downtown.

Foxy sits in the driver's seat, her arms crossed tightly across her body.

"Abby, if you want to drive the car it's fine, but I'll have to teach you *how* first. And even if I wasn't late for a meeting—"

"*We*," Abby says, raising a brow at me. "We are late for a meeting. You said back at my house that you wanted to share your life with me, remember?

If that's true, then *we* are running late for a meeting."

"Okay, but even if *we* weren't running late for a meeting, I don't think fifth avenue at rush hour is the best place for driving lessons in a $300,000 car."

She pauses for a minute, pursing her lips, before stepping back out of the car.

But before she can run off again, I take her hand, firmly, and walk around to the passenger side. Smiling, I politely open the door for her and motion for her to get inside. Without protest, she slips into the seat, crossing her arms again as I close the door.

That's when I notice Oleg and Trevor standing on the sidewalk. Looking utterly dumbfounded.

"What are you idiots waiting for?" I snap at them, waving my hand in the air. "Get back in the fucking cars we're leaving."

I yank open the door and step inside. However, as I do, I immediately notice that hanging from the mirror…is another pair of panties.

These are black lace, with the little blush pink bow at the back.

I look over at her, and she grins at me wickedly before leaning over the seat, pressing her breasts together.

She grabs my face and kisses me passionately.

"*Mine,*" she growls as she pulls away, biting her bottom lip with a wink.

My cock instantly throbs, and instinctively I grab her throat, making her gasp and kissing her again, shoving my tongue into her mouth.

"Yes, you crazy bitch," I whisper against her swollen lips. "I am yours."

I press my hand between her thighs grabbing her pussy aggressively, and slipping two fingers inside her, I make her moan like a slut.

"And when we get home, I'll teach you a few lessons, baby girl. Including how to drive a stick…the right way," I growl against her lips.

I reach up, this time gently removing the black lace panties from the mirror.

She opens her mouth, and I watch her tense and her eyes go wide.

Until I ball up her little thong, and press it against my nose, inhaling deeply.

"You smell so fucking good," I whisper.

I reach down slowly, twisting the soft fabric around the gear shift.

"But if I'm gonna have your panties in my car, I'd rather feel them under my fingers," I say, watching with satisfaction as her cheeks redden. "The *entire* time."

A half hour later, we pull up outside of my private jet's hangar.

"Let me guess," Abby sighs. "This is the part where you tell me you want me to wait in the car."

In truth, I was.

But only because I don't honestly know how any of this is going to go. And if it goes poorly then…well, let's just say, she won't get back *in* the car with the highest opinion of me.

…Or my family.

However, because Abby assumed I'd be asking her to wait in the car, I somehow want to do the opposite.

This is just part of the ongoing mental chess match we play, with each of us trying to out-maneuver, or out bluff the other. And like so many times before, the moment Abby underestimates me, and attempts to anticipate my movements, becomes the exact moment I decide to change them.

Just to keep my little fox on her toes.

Perhaps it's a bit sadistic. Or perhaps I get off every time surprise skates across her face, no matter the circumstances. Either way, the prospect of exceeding Abby expectations brings me the real first grin I've had since I was buried inside her.

"Actually, Miss Wayne," I smile broadly. "I was rather hoping that you'd join me. There's someone I'd like you to meet."

And I bet he is going to love this.

This time it's not just surprise I see written on her face, but genuine excitement.

After shutting off the engine, I walk around to Abby's side of the car and pull her up against my body, immediately pressing my lips to hers, and shoving my tongue inside her mouth.

"We're about to go meet some very important, powerful people, Miss Wayne," I growl, shoving her back against the car and burying my face in her neck. "So, if possible, try and not shoot anyone, alright?"

"No…promises," she groans breathlessly as I slip my hand between her thighs. And the moment I realize that her panties are *still* hooked around my gear shift and squeeze her now bare pussy between my fingers I feel my cock throb.

I have no idea how this woman does this to me, but I love it.

Kissing her once more, I finally tear myself from her and take her hand, trying to calm myself.

I can't walk in there with a hard-on, after all.

As we step past the giant steel doors, we find a little crowd of people standing between two massive Gulfstream jets.

"Oh, thank God," I hear Ana say, her voice tinged in anxiety and annoyance as she throws her hands in the air and shoots me a very reproachful look. "There you are!"

"Roman," a deep gravelly voice says loudly as we enter the now packed hangar. "How nice of you to join us, some of us were starting to get worried."

"Oh, you know me, *sweetheart*," I fire back sarcastically with a smirk as we approach. "I love to make an entrance."

"That you do," Jaxon Pace snorts, rubbing the smirk off his face before his hawk-like eyes immediately fall to the gorgeous brunette by my side. "And, you've brought company it seems."

"This is—"

"Abigail Wayne," she says, extending her hand to Jaxon without hesitation. "Nice to meet you, *Mr. Pace*."

My eyes turn to her, and she glances up at me with a shrug.

"What? Why are you looking at me like that? Roman, I manage your *calendar*, remember? I've known about this meeting as long as you have." She says, rolling her eyes. "Also, it's not like the man is keeping a low profile, he was on the cover of TIME magazine last year for fucks sake."

Jaxon chuckles, raising a brow, seemingly impressed.

"Oh, don't encourage him," a woman's sultry voice replies, stepping up behind Chicago's famous billionaire bachelor. "I've learned from experience that with mafia dons, it just goes straight to their heads."

And as the stunningly beautiful blonde threads her left hand, boasting a massive rock sitting atop her matching tattoo, around Jaxon's arm, I'm suddenly aware that *this* is the reason that the Don Supreme of Chicago has stopped burning the midnight oil at any of our old haunts.

…And also the reason he is no longer a *bachelor*.

"Noted," Abby grins, which is coincidentally something I've only seen her do around Lizzie, and Ana.

"Hi," Jaxon's wife says warmly, extending her hand to Abby. "I'm Natalie Pace, pleasure to meet you."

"Abigail Wayne," she replies.

"Enchanted," I say, politely taking Natalie's hand and kissing it respectfully.

"And congratulations on the wedding, I sincerely apologize that I was unable to make it."

"Roman," Ana says, huffing as she walks up to us, her stress evident on her face.

"Ana, have you met—"

"Yeah, yeah, yeah," she says, waving me off. "We had plenty of time to acquaint ourselves while we were waiting for you to arrive."

She turns to the group with a transparently polite smile.

"I'm sorry, would you excuse me for a moment? I need to have a word with my brother."

Yanking my arm, she pulls me forcibly away from Abigail and the Paces.

"Jesus," I say, shaking her off.

"Sorry to interrupt your little *circle jerk* here, Roman," she hisses. "But you knew we were on a strict timeline with this, and they are pulling up any minute. Do you have a plan?"

"Yeah," I sigh, rolling my eyes. "We're going to rip the Band Aid off and deal with it. No need in getting preemptively stressed out about it, dear sister."

She laughs sarcastically.

"I'm stressed about everything!" She snaps under her breath. "Our family is threatened, Polina has gone rogue, you're trying to buy billion-dollar skyscrapers, and now you want to do this—"

However, a loud buzzing interrupts Ana's panicked tirade as the gigantic hangar doors begin to slide open once more.

"Shit…" I hear her mutter defeatedly. "I sure as hell hope you know what you're doing, Roman."

And as two individuals appear in the doorway, I can't help the way my chest tightens around me.

I hope I do too.

Wesley, Jaxon Pace's weapon's expert, steps into the giant hangar bay… followed by Pasha, who has Caesar trotting along beside him.

"…I'd say it boils down to this," Wesley says animatedly. "If you're going for sheer distance, I would always trust the Barrett, it will never let you down. That or the AXSR for the sheer versatility."

"Yeah, but the sheer *fact* that it's British made, is the reason I wouldn't ever go with the AXSR," Pasha snorts, waving him off. "I'd have to go with my roots and trust the Dragunov above the AXSR."

"You can't be serious!" Wesley laughs loudly. "The Dragunov is practically a dinosaur! I mean…no offense or anything."

"Dinosaur or not, it's still wracking up body counts," Pasha counters.

"Your mom wracks up a bod—oh shiiit," Wesley gasps, as he and Pasha distractedly come skidding to a halt right in front of us.

"Jesus Christ," Pasha whispers loudly, clearly startled as he presses his hand to his chest.

"Not quite," I say quietly, watching as all the blood drains from *both* of their faces. "I trust you two gentlemen have had a successful morning of tracking down my missing *paintings*?"

"Um," Wesley says, gulping loudly and awkwardly running his hand through his hair. "Not yet, but we're still working on it, Mr. Antonov, Sir."

"Not anymore you're not," Jaxon Pace suddenly barks from behind Wesley, making him jump again.

"Fuck!" He yelps.

"Oh, I'd definitely say that's the right word for you right now, commander," Jaxon growls, his face instantly a clear mixture of frustration and rage. "*Fucked* is exactly what you are."

"Sir, I…I…" Wesley stammers, but Jaxon simply raises his hand in the air, silencing him.

"Believe me, I've heard more than enough of it already," he says darkly, glaring at Wesley. "And if Mrs. Pace wasn't so fond of you, no one would be hearing another word from you. *Ever.*"

Wesley immediately lowers his eyes to the floor and nods as Jaxon steps up close to him and whispers in his ear lethally.

"Get your damaged ass on the plane. And I suggest you be as silent as the grave that you are so *narrowly* avoiding, and not remind me that you exist for the next two hours."

"Yes, Sir," he whispers with his eyes still lowered.

"*Now*," Jaxon hisses venomously.

Without another word, Wesley walks off toward the plane where several other men stand waiting.

I'd bet that's Jaxon's famously chilly Alpha Squad.

He watches Wesley board before clearing his throat and turning back to face me.

"Once again," he says with a sigh. "I apologize for the unprofessionalism of my commander. Rest assured he will be doing every miserable assignment until I'm satisfied that he's learned his lesson."

"Mr. Pace," Pasha says quietly, swallowing hard. "It wasn't his fault. It was mine. It was entirely my fault."

Jaxon and I exchange a look before he crosses his hand in front of his body.

"Is that so?"

"The absinthe was my idea, well my friend's idea," Pasha nods. "I was the one who suggested we test out the weapons down by the dunes, and I was the one who shot *him*."

Of all the things I expected to hear this afternoon, my kid brother taking ownership of his failures in this ill-fated weapons transaction to the Don Supreme Chicago mafia was not one of them.

"Tell me, were you also the one who put a weapon in Mr. *Lee's* hands?" Jaxon asks, raising a brow. "And did you force him to shoot at you?"

Pasha opens his mouth to say something but then instantly closes it, and shakes his head.

"Then," Jaxon says quietly. "It *wasn't* entirely your fault. And what you just said was a lie. And a lie that accomplished nothing."

My brother shifts uncomfortably, but says nothing, evidently feeling the weight of Jaxon's words.

"I was just trying to protect him," he finally says, glancing up at Jaxon nervously. "And for the record, Mr. Pace, we all lie in this business."

Jaxon smiles, licking his bottom lip before looking over at me. Even though no words are exchanged between the two of us, I know that he's silently asking me for my approval to educate my little brother.

I consent with a nod.

"We do," Jaxon says quietly. "But as I'm sure you know, there has to be *some* honor, even between the damned. Otherwise, none of us would trust anyone, and the only thing we'd be accomplishing would be bloodshed. However, there's nothing admirable about stupidity, and nothing to be gained by protecting a fool from the consequences of his actions."

Pasha swallows silently.

"Think of it this way," Jaxon says, crossing his arms. "If I fail to punish him, then I subconsciously tell him that I condone his behavior. And as Mr. Lee is my wife's primary bodyguard, if his foolish, selfish, and grossly inappropriate behavior ever led him to slip in his duties, or miss his mark, causing harm to her, I'd be partially responsible. Which is something I will never allow."

I have to fight my smirk, because true to form, the smooth-talking Jaxon Pace, has eloquently made his point. And based on the way my kid brother can't even look him in the eyes, I know that it has hit its mark.

"In this business," Jaxon says, his voice low and lethal. "Leadership is a privilege. But it's also a responsibility. It's our duty to lead and protect the men that follow us…even from themselves."

Pasha, who always has a comeback, is silent.

"I've never thought about it like that," he finally says.

"I know," I reply quietly. "Which is why I've decided you're going back *with* him."

Pasha's head suddenly snaps up.

"What?" He asks, confused, looking between me and an equally perplexed looking Jaxon.

"Wait, you didn't tell him?" Jaxon asks, pointing at Pasha with his brow raised.

"No," I say, clearing my throat.

"What the fuck?" Pasha scoffs, the look of betrayal on his face conflicting with one of pain. "Roman?"

"I'll give you two a moment," Jaxon says, politely excusing himself while shooting me a look that seems to say, *"you're a fucking dumbass."*

"Oh my God," Pasha laughs sarcastically. "You're actually fucking serious."

"Pasha…"

"I knew you were pissed about the dunes and the painting, but I never thought you'd want to get *rid* of me," he says, shaking his head.

"That's not what this is."

"Of course, it is!" Pasha suddenly snaps at me angrily, his voice so loud it echoes in the hangar, making everyone turn to look. "You've got to be the big badass brother who orders everyone around and you just want me gone because I—"

Without thinking I grab him and wrap him in a tight hug.

"Pasha…Pasha," I say as he fights against me.

"Fuck you, Roman!" He chokes, the twinge in his voice nearly breaking my heart as he tries to elbow me in the ribs. "I'm not going!"

"I need you to—"

"No! I'm not! I've always done what you asked, but I'm not doing this!"

"Pasha, stop," I say, still holding him firmly. "Stop! Just listen to me!"

"No! I know I fuck up sometimes, but I always have your back, Roman and—"

"I know you do," I interrupt him, taking a hard blow to the ribs but still refusing to let go. "So now I have to have yours."

Suddenly he stops, and I finally release him.

"What?" he asks.

I sigh heavily.

I didn't want to show him this, but after realizing there's no other way to get him on Jaxon's plane today, I pull the envelope from my pocket and hand it to him.

"The fuck?" He asks, quickly looking through the photos.

"These were sent to me," I whisper to him, so that only he can hear me.

"By someone in the McCleary family who clearly knows that…"

My voice trails off and I swallow hard.

"Well, they know that I can't lose you, okay?"

Pasha stares down at the words scribbled on the back of the photo.

"I'm not sending you away forever," I say firmly, discreetly rubbing my side where Pasha's elbow had painfully connected. "Just until I can get shit under control here."

"But…" Pasha scoffs before his face turns red. "Roman, fuck these guys! If they want to come for me, then I got the answer for them right here!"

He goes to draw his gun from his holster, but I grab his hand, preventing him from doing so.

"*No*," I growl lethally. "Think about where you are right now. In a very flammable room, filled with heavily armed, trigger-happy individuals. And there are women present. One of whom is your sister."

Pasha glances over at Ana who is staring at us, her concern written plainly on her face. I watch as the realization of what could happen flashes across his eyes before I feel him release his hand, even if it does little to cull the anger radiating off him.

"Listen to me, I'm not sending you away because I think you can't handle yourself, or because I give a flying fuck about some stupid ugly painting some whores stole from me," I say quietly. "It's because Cillian knows that if I'm focused on *you*, I won't be focused on *him*. He knows that you are my soft spot. Just like father did. And you remember how that went down, don't you?"

Slowly, Pasha's face changes.

The reminder of our past, and the truth behind my words being enough to finally break through to him.

"But there's also another reason," I say softly.

"What other reason?" Pasha asks.

"Cillian has something I don't have," I breathe. "He has people who are good with money."

My brother snorts, and opens his mouth to say something but I continue.

"I'm talking about accountants or investment portfolios. I mean people who can read the market and oppositional weakness as a whole investment. Cillian has a lot of kin."

"Yeah, but I mean, so do we, Roman," Pasha says sarcastically.

"But they function as a *single* unit," I say, grabbing his shoulder and pointing at him. "We don't. And we need to, or we won't survive the next decade."

Pasha stares at me, his eyes scanning mine for potential misdirection, but finding none.

"So…what do you want me to do with Jaxon Pace?" He finally says.

"*Learn,*" I say, squeezing his shoulder. "Learn everything."

"Roman," Pasha rolls his eyes. "Come on. He's not *that* much older than you. What the fuck does he know that you—"

"Alot" I say, waiting until his eyes find mine. "When I was your age, I spent a little time with the Pace Family. I watched how they operate and how it gives them an advantage in more than just muscle. And muscle is all we have right now."

"I mean, muscle is good," Pasha shrugs. "It might've been all father could teach us, but it's not nothing."

"It's not everything either. And unlike us, Jaxon had a father who wasn't a total sociopath, one who taught him business and how to diversify his assets…as well as his *weaknesses.* Which is exactly what we need to do. Or we will die. All of us."

Pasha stares back at me, without saying anything, but at least he's not fighting me, or trying to run.

"Look, I've discussed it with Jaxon, and despite you shooting Wesley, he's willing to take you under his instruction and show you what he knows, which is a hell of a lot more than I ever got. Especially from dad. Which means at the very least, you'll be able to help me be…better than *he* was."

I watch as my brother's hesitance fades ever so slightly, replaced by the smallest flicker of *honor.*

Not wanting to waste any more time, I grab him and pull him into another tight hug.

"I know you don't want to do this. But I need you to do this for me, brother," I whisper. "Because I need to keep you safe, but I also need to keep everyone safe. And despite what I tell everyone, I'm not a God, and I can't be everywhere at once. I need someone watching my back…even from myself. So, please, do this for me. Go to Chicago, go learn what I didn't have the opportunity to learn all those years ago, and come back here and help me keep this family safe, okay?"

After what feels like an eternity, I feel my brother nod, and my chest finally releases.

However, twenty minutes later, after watching Pasha board the Pace jet, and watching Ana practically sob herself into a migraine, all I can do is hope that I just sent my brother to the safest corner of the world…and not to his death.

ANTONOV

CHAPTER THIRTY-SIX

Abby

Standing in silence we watch as the Pace plane, with Pasha aboard, slowly gets smaller and smaller in the distance.

"Where next then, *Boss*?" I say, forcing Roman back into the now.

"Let's go," he mutters.

He whistles loudly, and Caesar, who had been sitting with Ana, trying to comfort her, comes bounding over to us.

I take a step in the direction of the car we arrived in, only for Roman to grab my arm and pull me back.

Reading the look on my face, he smirks.

"We switch cars a lot."

"Fucking rich people," I mutter with a smile, shaking my head at him.

"It's not just for show. It's also for protection, it prevents our enemies from tracking us," he explains before pulling out a key fob and pressing it toward the wall.

Only it wasn't a wall, with a click it slides open, revealing a sleek yellow car.

"Got a thing for yellow?" I laugh, looking at Roman.

"No, but you do," he smirks, knowing damn well how much I dislike the color.

"What is it?" I ask, staring at what appears to be a mix between a sports car and an SUV.

"Lamborghini Urus. The best of both worlds."

"How so?"

"Well, it's a hybrid, with its streamlined body, it's fast, but is built like an SUV, allowing for modifications," he explains, opening the door for me. "And perfect for where our next meeting is."

"Wouldn't you want something… less *bold*?" I ask, staring at the carbon fiber hood. "If you're avoiding being tracked by your enemies and all?"

"You mean something boring," he states, reaching around and grabbing the seat belt. He buckles it, tugging on it lightly as he smirks at me.

"No," I say with a shrug. "It's just this yells *look* at me."

"They can look all they want," he grins, closing the door and rounding the car to the trunk.

He opens it and pulls out a harness.

"Caesar."

The dog obeys, sitting patiently while Roman attaches a harness around his chest and shoulders before snapping his fingers and instructing the pup into the backseat.

As he buckles Caesar in, my fingers trace over the raised custom *"Antonov"* embossing on the dash, leaning my head against the headrest I take in the rest of the car.

My nose scrunches at the new car smell. Most people would think that it's the crisp fresh leather, but it's not, it's mostly all chemical, and there's nothing "new" about it at all.

Roman slides into the car, and the engine roars to life in the confined space before pressing his finger against one of the screens.

Jesus Christ, it even has two screens.

Tires screech as he floors it straight out of the hanger.

"Jesus!" I squeak, slamming my hand down onto the dash. Roman turns sharply, forcing me to grab hold of the door handle.

Increasing in speed, we start to approach the airfield exit, which still has the barrier down.

"Uh, Roman?" I mutter, watching that barrier get closer and closer.

With a laugh, he slams on the brakes, as we skid to a stop just before the barrier.

"Open it," he barks out of the window at the poor security guard manning the exit.

"Yes, Mr. Antonov," the man replies curtly.

Slowly, the barrier opens, and before it's even fully lifted the car flies through it, turning sharply as we enter traffic.

Out of the corner of my eye I watch Roman.

Saying goodbye to his brother clearly wasn't easy for him, especially after seeing how badly Pasha didn't want to go.

"You okay?" I ask, setting my hand on his leg.

"Yeah," he replies, placing his hand on mine.

"Pasha thought I wanted to get rid of him," he says bitterly.

Turning my hand, I entwine our fingers, squeezing lightly.

"I need him safe. Out of all my siblings, I need *him* safe." He laughs, "Don't tell them I said that."

He doesn't wait for me to reply, before releasing my hand and placing both of his on the wheel. A comfortable silence descends between us as we zoom through the city.

But while the silence is comforting, it also gives me way too much time to think. Each and every possible thought I could have, I've had it, and then some.

Jaxon Pace was everything I thought he would be, but still he was *more*. From everything I'd seen online, it really hadn't done him justice.

I can't help but wonder how Natalie fits in so well in this new world she found herself in. In our brief conversation, while Roman tried talking Pasha out of shooting everyone, she'd mentioned how she hadn't been a part of the mafia life, but had somehow managed to navigate it.

Everything about her was feminine, and pure grace, yet even from a distance it is clear as day she would kill for that husband of hers, as well as for their men.

And they would die for her all the same.

"So, this mafia stuff," I say, biting my lip as I glance over at Roman. "Where do I fit in?"

"You're mine," Roman replies, completely dodging the question.

"And you are mine. But, Roman," I sigh, tilting my head at him, "that doesn't exactly answer my question."

"It's simple Abigail," he revs the engine, forcing the car to accelerate suddenly, before seamlessly switching gears. "I own this city. And for years I've done everything that this family has needed me to do. I've sacrificed a lot of things, for them and their protection. But you? You are everything to me. You're something I'm not willing to sacrifice."

"But I killed your men," I say curtly.

"No," he replies, "you killed *our* men."

Turning slightly in my seat, I watch as his hands tighten against the wheel, my hair whips wildly around my face as Caesar barks happily behind me.

"What about Igor?" I ask, holding my breath. "I imagine that's going to be a problem for you? You know, to keep me after I—"

"Fuck Igor," he growls.

"And Polina?"

"Fuck her too."

"But she's your sister and I killed her husband and—"

"Abigail," he says darkly. "I've already told you, I've wanted you for years. I've craved you from the moment I first saw you. No one takes you from me. Not even my sister."

I stare at him as realization slowly sinks in.

"I know what I do will have consequences, Roman," I grab my necklace, waving it. "*This* is my way out."

"What the fuck do you mean?" He growls.

"It's got my Widowmaker inside it. I always said that if I got caught, I'd have a…way out." I state.

It takes a second for Roman to register what I'm saying.

"Absolutely fucking not. I'll kill whoever comes after you. Do you hear me, Abigail Wayne?"

I shake my head, my stomach twisting as the car continues increasing in speed, down a long dirt road.

"If anyone even looks at you wrong, I will have their eyes. If they speak poorly about you, then I will take their fucking jaw. And I'll give them to you so you can wear them around your pretty little neck."

"You're not God, Roman,"

"Maybe not, but I am the fucking *king*," he says, turning his head to look directly into my eyes.

But as he does, mine glance over at the speedometer, before grabbing hold of the door.

"Eyes on the road!" I yell, adrenaline flooding my body.

"You are my fucking queen, Abby. Do you understand me?" He states, his voice calm and collected.

"Roman!" I scream, staring straight ahead as the car continues to speed down the dirt road, the building at the end getting closer and closer.

"Say it, Abigail!" He barks, his tone leaving no room for hesitation.

I stare at him, my eyes wide as he starts grinning widely, making him look completely and utterly deranged.

"I understand!"

"Say it!"

"I'm your fucking queen!" I scream at him, shaking my head back and forth as I laugh, watching him turn back to the road before slamming on the brakes.

We come to an abrupt stop, the tires kicking up loose gravel, the pebbles bouncing off the body of the car, and a cloud of dust engulfing us.

Silence descends inside the car, and all I can hear is the sound of my own breathing. Leaning forward, I crush my lips to his as adrenaline floods my veins.

"It was you," I whisper against his lips, as his breath hitches in his throat.

"What?"

"It was your eyes I could feel at every event I went to, wasn't it?" I run my thumb over his cheek. "You were watching me."

"If I had known, Abby… about your husband."

Quickly, I place my finger against his lips.

"Shhh, we don't need to talk of the dead," I say, swallowing around the lump in my throat, I know exactly what he wants to say. "I had to walk my road alone, so I could find my way *home.*"

Gently, he presses a kiss to my finger, before pushing it aside and lightly kissing my cheek, slowly trailing kisses along my jaw before recapturing my lips with his.

"I love you," he whispers reverently.

"I know."

He glares at me, grabbing both my hands in his.

"So, did you find your way home?"

I shrug, smiling at him, "meh."

He laughs, throwing open his door before walking round to mine. Looking around I see we're parked outside of a derelict building, and if I had to hazard a guess, it looks as if it used to be apartments before it was condemned.

I understand he has business to attend to, I do, but surely, they could find a building that doesn't look like it's about to collapse.

"Could we not do this somewhere else? This place doesn't look safe, Roman." I say, worrying my lip between my teeth, tasting metal in my mouth.

He doesn't even glance at me as he pulls out his phone.

"I know I said you can come to these meetings with me, but for this one, Foxy, I need you to stay in the car."

"Roman," I sigh, shaking my head at him. "I don't like the idea of you going alone."

"It'll only take a couple of minutes," he says, reasoning with me. "And I won't go alone. I'll have Caesar."

"A dog is not a human, Roman," I say firmly.

"Nah, he's better. And I mean it, Foxy. Stay. In. The. Car." His finger pointing at me with each word he says.

I roll my eyes as I cross my arms. "Fine. I'll stay in the car." I slouch down in the chair as I kick my legs into the footwell.

He crouches down in front of me, with a smirk.

"Good girl," he purrs, and instantly my core clenches.

Jerk.

He knows what that does to me, and I don't appreciate the manipulation tactic.

"Come boy," his eyes dart to Caesar in the back. "We have work to do."

Obediently he jumps into the driver's seat, but he pauses suddenly as if hesitating. He turns towards me, his tongue lolling out of the side of his mouth as he cocks his head to the side.

I can't be certain, but it's like he can sense my reluctance and anxiety. My gut is telling me that something bad is coming. I clutch my necklace between my fingers, rubbing it and feeling its grooves slowly calm me.

"Caesar!" Roman commands.

He jumps from the car, and Roman slams the door shut. I watch him walk into that hazardous building like he owns the place, with Caesar trotting behind him, his tail swinging wildly.

My ears twitch as they strain to listen for any noise, dread settling heavily in my stomach. Straightening my spine I lean forward, trying to clear the static ringing in my ears.

My eyes have been locked on the door he entered since he left, waiting anxiously for him to appear.

After a little while, I finally glance at the clock, he's been in there for ten minutes, but it feels like he's been in there for hours.

With numb fingers, I shakily reach forward for the radio, but before I turn it on, I suddenly hear muffled bangs coming from the building and my head whips around.

From the corner of my eye, I watch as Oleg and Cal run forward, with their guns raised.

I didn't even realize they were here with us.

But squinting through the dust I finally see what they are staring at and my heart stops.

My eyes widen as I throw open the door and jump out of the car.

"Roman!" I shout.

I freeze, staring at him. My eyes scan across his face to the raw pain I see all over it.

"Boss!" Cal yells. "What happened?!"

Everyone around us is yelling, Oleg runs forward grabbing Roman, only to be shrugged off.

"I'm not hit! Fucking go get *them*! Now!" He yells, storming forward. "Don't let them get away!"

"Go go go!" Cal shouts, leading three more men into the broken down building.

It's only then that I notice Roman's shirt is covered in blood and his jacket…is wrapped around *Caesar*.

…Who is limp in his arms.

"You need to drive Abigail!" Roman thunders as he races toward the car.

He throws open the back door, gently getting into the car, and cradling a whimpering Caesar.

Hearing this, my body instantly unfreezes, running round the hood of the car, I jump into the driver's seat, and freeze as I stare at the stick shift.

"Put your fucking foot down and drive, Foxy!"

"I—"

His hand slams into the back of the chair, jolting me forward.

"Foxy!"

"Okay okay!"

It's been years since I've driven a car. My hands tremble as the engine purrs to life, the wheel slick and smooth under my hands. I take a deep breath and throw the stick into drive. The car roars to life and jumps underneath my hands, bunny hopping down the road.

"Abigail?"

"It's been a few years and I…" I say, feeling my heart pounding and sinking at the same time. "You said you were going to teach me!"

My chest tightens as Caesar whimpers behind me, a sound that pierces straight through my heart and squeezes.

"Relax, Baby, you got this! Just ease your foot up… there we go, keep doing that. Just drive! And if a light turns red, fuck it, just go straight through it!" He commands, and I feel myself come alive with the order.

Somehow, he always knows how to settle me, even though I can feel his heart shattering from the front seat.

"Good boy, you're such a good boy," Roman mutters.

Glancing at him in the mirror I watch as he slowly strokes Caesar's face.

Caesar whimpers, forcing me to blink rapidly to stop the tears from escaping.

To the best of my ability, I race toward the animal hospital as Roman barks directions at me in the back seat.

"Turn right!"

"Turn left!"

"Go! Now! Floor it!"

Cars honk at me as I weave through the traffic, fighting to get the stick into the next gear, under Roman's instructions.

My stomach drops as I watch a light turn from green to red.

"Run that light!" He commands.

Slamming my foot down on the accelerator, I fight the desire to close my eyes as I fly through the light at nearly a hundred miles an hour.

As I skid to a stop outside the animal hospital, Roman is already out of the car and running before I can even throw it in park.

"Help! I need help!" Roman screams as he shoulders his way in through the door.

I take a deep breath, slumping down in the seat as I let my head thump against the headrest. My eyes catch movement in the rearview mirror of a black Range Rover.

A Range Rover that has wheel rims exactly like—

A knock sounds against the driver's side window, my body flinching with the intrusion.

"Miss! I'm sorry, you can't park here," A short balding man exclaims, as he gestures wildly at the *Lamborghini* currently diagonally parked across the emergency bays.

"Oh! I'll… move… I mean the car; I'll move the car!" I flap flustered, my brain completely shutting down. "I just need to erm… I—"

"Want me to move it for you, Miss? I saw your husband run in with the dog. I'd be happy to help," I glance back up at him, his eyes soft as he nods his head slightly.

"It's okay, sweetheart," he says gently. "Let me do it."

I hesitate for a moment, knowing that the longer I'm sitting out here, the longer Roman is in there alone.

It doesn't escape my notice that I didn't correct him when he called Roman my *"husband."*

I nod, my hand reaching for the handle.

"Please, I'm terrified of scratching the paint," I say, with a slight chuckle. He nods.

"Wait here. I'll park it up for you and bring you the keys."

He slides into the driver's seat and the engine revs as he smoothly shifts it into gear and pulls away.

As the guy walks the keys back over to me, I pull in a deep breath, and look over to the entrance, noticing that the car I saw is gone.

What the fuck happened in that 'meeting?' And how did it go so badly?

"It'll only take a couple of minutes."

That's how long it should have been.

My heart breaks as I close my eyes, remembering Roman stroking Caesar, whispering his encouragement and begging him to hold on.

I walk into the vet waiting room, my eyes scanning nervously for Roman, who I find leaning against the far wall, his leg bouncing up and down.

He suddenly pushes away and heads to the check-in desk and slams his hand down, making the frail receptionist jump.

"Update?!" He snaps darkly.

"Erm…no, Sir, it's been fifteen minutes…" She replies, looking toward me with a pained glance.

"Well, what the fuck is taking so long?!" Roman roars.

I walk forward quickly, placing my hand on his arm, squeezing gently as his tumultuous gaze finds mine.

"Thank you," I say, smiling at the receptionist gently. "Please let us know when you have an update."

"Of course, darling." she smiles, clicking her pen.

Roman huffs, stomping away. He slams himself down hard onto a waiting room chair, causing a woman who'd been sitting in a chair nearby with a cat carrier at her feet to get up and walk farther away from the scary brooding man.

I sit down across from him, giving him a moment as I scan the rest of the room. It's eerily quiet in here, and besides the little old lady with the cat carrier, it's empty.

After a few moments, I stand, and kneel in front of him, quickly pulling a pack of makeup wipes from my purse.

Avoiding his eyes, knowing exactly what I will find there, I slowly reach forward, grabbing Roman's blood covered hands in mine.

Without saying a word, I slowly start to wipe the blood from his hands, taking my time to make sure I can get as much of it off as I can. I shuffle forward, standing on my knees, as I grab a fresh wipe, and gently remove the drying blood from his face.

When I'm sure I got it all, or as much as I could get off, I silently walk the soiled wipes over to the trash can.

Suddenly, Roman stands, and paces continuously across the room, his fist clenching.

"Dogs are designed to go in first and take the bullet…it's just a dog, he did his job. He got between me and them. He took the bullet. He did his job," Roman rambles, his hands moving rapidly as his breathing increases. "It's just a dog."

Automatically, I walk forward and wrap my arms around him from behind, squeezing him tightly, I rock us slightly.

"He's going to be okay," I say, my voice cracking.

If this was reversed. If this was Lily... I couldn't.

"He's going to be fine," I repeat, trying to soothe him as his body tightens under my fingers.

I have no idea how long we've stood like this, before eventually Roman turns, wrapping me in his arms.

"He's not just a dog, Abby," he whispers.

"I know."

"He's family," his voice cracks.

"I know Ro, I know, he's going to be okay."

Roman breathes heavily before suddenly chuckling darkly, causing my body to stiffen. Suddenly, the room turns cold, as his darkness spills out of him.

"They are all fucking dead," he whispers his lips pressing against the top of my head. "I will hunt them. I will make each and every fucking one of those bastards pay for shooting my goddamn dog."

My heart thumps loudly in my chest and all I can do is nod in response.

"Every single fucking McCleary is *dead*."

ANTONOV

ANTONOV

CHAPTER THIRTY-SEVEN

ROMAN

"Are you sure this is the shooter?" I growl, staring from the edge of the enclosure, my breath turning to steam in the freezing fall air.

"No," Cal sighs, sounding disappointed.

"What do you mean, *no*?" I hiss angrily.

"Even on the security cameras we could hardly identify anyone as they scrambled from the building," Cal explains, crossing his arms. "And by the time we got there, the McCleary's had all cleared out of the place."

"Who the fuck is this then?" I snort, glaring at the man in the middle of the abandoned roller derby, his hands and feet shackled into the cuffs that are built into the metal chair he sits in. "Since you just said you couldn't identify anyone?"

Cal grins wickedly.

"I said *hardly* anyone. We did get one hit. On the license plate of one of the cars parked around the block."

My head snaps back to the man in the chair. It's then that I recognize the same green eyes, and facial features.

"He's a McCleary." I whisper under my breath. "Blood relative."

"Yes, Sir," Cal nods. "Sean McCleary. Second cousin."

The longer I stare at him, the more I recognize him. He was the man who tried to jump me at the warehouse. One of them.

After I got the pictures of Pasha, I'd gone there, alone, hoping to discuss a ceasefire or at least to cull their efforts to stalk Pasha.

I should've known they'd never honor their word.

Cillian and I had barely started our conversation before I heard movement in the darkness, and Caesar lunged, stopping a man from blindsiding me.

That's when the gun went off.

Three men were there that day, so to me, all of them are responsible for what happened to my fucking dog.

"I'm going to enjoy this."

Licking my bottom lip, I pull on my black leather gloves, watching the man in the chair.

"Wake him," I whisper darkly.

Cal holds his finger to a button on the small black controller in his hand and the power flickers, a loud electrical buzzing echoing in the building. The body of my unconscious prisoner suddenly goes rigid, shaking violently from the shock of electricity pumping through his metal chair.

Now he's awake.

"Hello, Sean," I say, salivating watching the instant panic flashing in his eyes as he realizes his inability to move. "How nice of you to join us."

"Mmmmpf!" He grunts, unable to talk from the gag in his mouth.

But tonight, isn't about talking.

"This is normally the part where I'd ask you if you know why I brought you here, and blah, blah, blah," I say, rubbing my hands together as I roll my eyes. "But you *do* know, Sean."

The man starts to mumble something, but I raise my finger in the air, and Cal presses the button once more, sending another wave of electricity though the man's body.

Lowering my hand, Cal releases the button, and the man can breathe again. His whole body shakes, and beads of sweat form on his skin as he blinks rapidly.

"Forgive me," I grin. "I just want to make sure that you are good and awake for what is going to come next."

"Mmmmpf!" He strains against the metal cuffs.

"What was that? Sorry, I can't hear you," I say, leaning in closer as the man continues to grunt and mumble against the gag. "Here, let me help you."

Reaching forward I pull the Antonov dagger from my pocket and press it to the man's face, slicing his cheek as I cut through the gag.

That's good…I need him to bleed.

"Arrrgh!" He grunts, as blood starts to pour down his face. "Fuck you man! I don't know anything anyway!"

"Oh, I know," I smile viciously.

"I won't tell you shit, motherfucker!" He says, straining against the chair.

"I know that too. But don't worry, I prefer it if you try not to talk anyway," I chuckle, turning away from him and nodding to Cal. "It definitely makes it more fun that way."

"Yeah? Well do your worst, you fucking monster!" He shouts at me. "I didn't do anything to you!"

Suddenly, I snap.

Turning on my heel I storm back over to him and land two hard punches across the man's face, breaking his nose, and sending blood spraying all over him…and me.

"No," I hiss, grabbing the man's throat and squeezing so hard I can feel his racing pulse as his face turns purple. "You did it to my fucking dog! You call me a monster? You and your kin shot a fucking dog!"

Releasing him, Sean gasps for breath.

"You think you're a big man for attacking a small animal?" I spit angrily, my chest heaving with rage. "Well, I'm about to balance the scales."

Smiling at the man on the chair, I turn and walk out of the ring, hopping over the guard rail. That's when I hear the commotion near the entrance, which happens to be behind Sean.

Walking through the rusty green metal gate, is my largest soldier.

Jeremy, a seven-foot monster of a man, wearing dirty jeans, suspenders, a white tank-top walks into the room…with a *bear*.

A 1400-pound behemoth, affectionately named *Baloo*, grunts and grumbles, walking alongside his beloved trainer and handler.

A smile returns to my face, especially when I look down and see Sean hearing the sounds of the bear snorting and dragging his six-inch razor sharp claws across the dirt.

"What…what is that?" Sean asks, terror blanketing his face as the gigantic bear nears.

"As I said, Mr. McCleary," I say, clicking my tongue. "This is balance."

I spread my arms wide, laughing darkly to myself.

"…And frankly, it's just plain *fun*."

I nod to Oleg, who with the help of Trevor, carries the hind leg of a dismembered deer into the ring. The two of them drop the bloody hunk of meat, and back away slowly before quickly climbing over the fence to safety.

Baloo raises his nose in the air, huffing deeply, smelling the scent of food nearby.

Perfect.

"What's up fuckers."

A male voice sounds behind me, and I jump, nearly pulling my gun as I whirl around, finding Lev standing there.

"The fuck are you doing here?" I ask.

"Jeremy phoned and said you asked for *my* bear," Lev shrugs, staring me down coldly. "I go where he goes."

"Technically he's *my* bear," I snort, rolling my eyes.

"You know as well as I do that Baloo is not your bear. He barely even recognizes you," Lev says, crossing his arms and glaring at me. "Father may have gifted him to you, but *I* was the one who took care of him."

"What, are you expecting a medal or something?" I snap irritably. "Because I'm a little busy here, Lev."

He stares at me saying nothing.

"Nope," he clicks his tongue inside his mouth. "As I said, I'm just here to make sure that nothing happens to him."

"Oh my God!" Sean suddenly yells as the giant bear slowly picks up the dead deer leg and drags it in front of him, gnawing on the meat. "That's… that's…that's a fucking *bear*."

"Yup," I reply to Sean, but deliberately look over at Lev. "He's a bear alright. Just a bear."

"Yeah, and Caesar was just a *dog*," he snaps back, now glaring at me. "And look where he ended up."

My fist clenches and my jaw tightens.

"Careful, brother," I growl, lethally as Sean begins to scream in terror. "Do not test me. Not tonight."

"Wouldn't dream of it," Lev says sarcastically, his quiet rage unusually loud behind his eyes tonight. "I understand you're the big Boss and all, but forgive me for wanting to make sure that *my* animal is safe. Otherwise, who knows, you might grow tired of him and just decide to send him off to Chicago…with Jaxon Pace."

Now I understand.

Lev is pissed about Pasha.

Which…to some extent I understand.

Besides Ana, I hadn't exactly told anyone about my plans to send my youngest brother home with Jaxon, but that's because I didn't trust any of them not to let it slip. However, I can't allow myself to think about that right now. I can't think about anything but making a man who is affiliated with the injury to my dog pay…in blood.

"Take the leg away," I snap at Jeremy, while still glaring at my brother. "He can have it later…if he's still hungry."

"Boss, I don't know if that's a good idea," Jeremy says cautiously. "Taking food away from a bear is—"

"I'll distract him," Lev says loudly, also not taking his eyes off of me. "Show my brother here that he's a pet, not a beast."

Part of me wants to scream at him, worried that he's going to derail my punishment of Sean by getting his stupid ass killed.

But my pride screws my mouth shut and before I know it, Lev is climbing the metal railing.

He puts his first two fingers to his lip and whistles loudly. The gigantic Kodiak bear looks up from tearing meat off of the dismembered animal carcass, and the moment he sees Lev standing there, he drops his dinner and comes galloping over to him, his thundering paws shaking the earth around him.

Baloo stops right in front of Sean, and as he stands on his two hind legs to nuzzle my brother. Even atop the railing, Lev is barely taller than the nine-foot bear.

"Holy fucking shit!" Sean screams, frantically pulling at his restraints.

"Hey Baloo," Lev chuckles, scratching the head of the grunting bear as Jeremy hops the railing back into the ring, and snatches the bloody deer's leg away. "Who's my big muddy buddy?"

Hearing Lev call this thousand-pound-wood-tank a pet name and watching him snuggle his head like he's a lap dog, is both ironic and terrifying.

"I changed my mind!" Sean shouts in the background. "I'll tell you whatever you want to know!"

Oh, right, he's still here.

"Lev," I snap. "You've proven your point. He's *your* bear. Now, get the fuck down so I can get on with my business."

I nod to Cal, who presses the button again, this time in a shorter burst, but still just as effective. When Sean stops seizing from the shock, he starts screaming…Which immediately attracts Baloo.

And as he slowly stalks his way across the dirt center of the roller derby rink, Sean's pitches nearly reach an operatic tone.

"Get him the fuck away from me! No! No! Don't come near me!"

But Sean's pleas do absolutely nothing to stop the advancing bear, who upon reaching the incapacitated man starts licking the blood from off his clothes, and face.

Exactly as I hoped.

It's true that on my eighteenth birthday, my father had given me Baloo as a symbol of my maturity and acceptance as the future don of this family. But my "lessons" were more than a fulltime job. Lev, being the animal lover of the group, found himself inadvertently delegated to the care and training of Baloo, and obviously that loving bond had lasted over two decades.

However, loving the bear wasn't the problem, keeping it was. As he grew, Baloo simply needed more space. And although Lev loved the Prius-sized teddy bear, he was ultimately a city boy at heart, who never wanted to be more than walking distance from his beloved fight club.

That's where Jeremy came into play.

Jeremy was a retired zoologist, who owned a large swath of land upstate, and with a few necessary renovations, and even a few paid relocations, Baloo's life got an upgrade. He had forests to roam, trees to climb, and all the sweet honey rolls his heart could handle.

The only rule that Jeremy enforced, whenever we'd visit, was that we were never ever to turn our back on Baloo, as it could trigger his natural instincts and cause him to see us as prey.

…But Sean McCleary doesn't know this.

"Get this fucker off me!" He screams, his pained voice echoing loudly in the room. "Let me out of here!"

"You know what?" I say facetiously. "I think I will."

Cal presses another button on the keypad, and all at once, the metal restraints unlock, freeing him.

And once again, Sean does exactly what I want him to do.

He *runs*.

Sean bolts from the chair, not realizing that directly behind him is a very curious Kodiak bear-chasing after him like a bakery vehicle. He doesn't even make it halfway across the ring before Baloo is on him, slapping at him with his giant paw.

I can tell that at first, the bear thinks that Sean is just playing with him. However, when the terrified bleeding man turns and starts kicking and hitting Baloo, I watch in real time as his attitude shifts entirely.

Pinned beneath him, the bear roars, nipping at Sean's ribs and slashing his face.

Sitting in the seats that are set up around the ring, I smile to myself but then I hear someone sigh beside me.

"Is this too much for you, darling?" I ask, turning to face Abby who leans back against the metal seat.

"No," she shrugs, looking down at her nails. "That's not it."

"Then what is it?"

"Oh no, I don't want to give you my opinions on how you conduct your business," She shakes her head.

I smirk.

Grabbing her by the hand I yank her into my lap and grab her chin as Sean continues screaming in the background.

"Since when have you ever hesitated to tell me your opinions on anything I do, eh?"

She laughs quietly to herself.

"Forgive me," she says looking up at me with a smirk tugging at the corners of her mouth. "But it just seems like such a…waste."

"A *waste*?" I snort.

"Yeah, I mean, I get it and all," she shrugs. "Having a bear tear him apart is poetic and ironic, but seems like such a waste of a good…kill. You don't get to see their life leave their eyes."

It's hard to describe the feelings that flood my veins as I digest her words.

I've never had someone tell me that they would prefer more of the agonizing screaming echoing in the room as Sean struggles to keep away from the angry bear.

And it's strangely…hot.

Abigail is unquestionably made for me.

I run my thumb along her smooth jaw, watching her pale cheeks flush with color.

She's beautiful. And she's mine. Finally fucking mine.

"Arrrgh! Please! Someone help me!" Sean wails.

But I don't care.

All I see is Abigail Wayne. My very own little psychopath.

Without taking my eyes off of her I yank my gun from my holster and fire one shot into the air, momentarily distracting every man, woman, and bear in the vicinity.

"Jeremy, take Baloo home, and feed him whatever he wants."

"Yes, Boss," I hear him say, but my eyes are still glued to Abby's.

He shouts a few stern commands in Russian and I hear Baloo grunting in response. Extending my hand, I pull the goddess before me into my arms and crush my lips to hers.

"Come."

Silently I lead her down the steps and back into the ring, its dirt floor now covered in Sean's blood and scraps of his mangled flesh.

He lays crumpled on his side, and after using my foot to turn him over, I realize that he is still breathing.

Good.

"P…ple…please just…kill…me," he groans.

"Oh, I'm not going to kill you," I smirk slowly, watching with satisfaction as a tear falls down Sean's face.

"…*She*'s going to kill you."

"What?" Abby breathes, turning to look at me.

However, as I pull the Antonov dagger from my suit coat, her eyes light up.

"And I think you should do it with this, it is an Antonov family heirloom after all. Since I know you like it."

"But I'm not family," she says quietly.

I suddenly grip her chin so quickly and forcefully, she gasps.

"You *are* my family now too," I whisper, slipping my hand between her thighs, rubbing the handle of the dagger against her soft slit. "And once you finish off this bastard, I'm going to fuck you and get to work on putting my *heir* inside you."

Abby gasps, but before she can say a word, I press my lips to hers and shove my tongue in her mouth. She throws her arms around my neck and kisses me back.

"So, you might as well just hold on to it," I growl, as I finally pull away from her. "Now, finish off this poor bastard."

Without warning I grab her soft pussy in my hands and rub her clit.

She takes the knife from me, carefully flipping the sharp obsidian blade around and twirling it in her fingers.

"You're sure?" she asks, raising a brow at me. "You want me to kill him. However, I want?"

I nod.

"Finish him off, my darling," I whisper against her neck, kissing her earlobe. "And then I'll return the favor. *Inside you.*"

As I pull back to look at her, Abby's wicked grin ignites every dark desire in my heart. I'm convinced I would burn the world to ash just to see her smile like this.

Turning back to Sean, she grips the dagger hard and then presses it to his throat.

"This is for the fucking dog," Abby sneers. "His name is Caeser."

One quick swipe of the blade opens the artery in his neck, and blood immediately starts to spray everywhere. I try to pull her backwards, but it's too late, the hot thick liquid coating her clothes, chest and face.

However, Abby doesn't react.

In fact, she stands rigid, as if she's in a trance, staring at Sean. Slowly she lifts her hand to her face, seeing that it too is covered in blood.

…And she *smiles*.

But perhaps the most disturbing of all, is the fact that looking at her now, in her most raw and vicious form, I realize that I have never been more attracted to her.

Jaxon Pace was right. I am fucked. And I want her. Now.

"Get out," I bark at my men. "All of you!"

Snatching Abigail's hand in mine, I follow after the men, and lock the doors behind them.

The moment we are alone, I immediately turn to Abby, wrapping my fingers through her curls and pulling her mouth to mine.

Immediately, her tongue is in my throat and my erection throbs. I need this woman like oxygen.

She fiddles with my belt buckle, but when I grab her wrist, stopping her from touching my cock, she looks up at me with confusion.

"Your hands," I growl breathlessly, pulling off my leather gloves. "Are covered in blood."

"Oh, do you want me to go wash—"

But once again, I grab the back of her head and press my lips to hers, kissing her while pulling my cock out of my pants.

"No, I just want you to hold on tight."

Abby grins, kissing me before wrapping her arms around the back of my neck. Pulling her skirt over her hips, I waste no time and shove my swollen cock inside of her.

"Fucking hell, Foxy," I grunt loudly, my voice trembling, holding her hips and slamming myself deeper. "You feel so fucking good."

"S…so…do you," she moans, throwing her head back.

She wraps her legs around me, and using my shoulders for leverage, she works herself up and down, bouncing on my cock.

"Ahhh!" She cries, as I thrust harder, slamming her back against the metal door, hearing it rattle on its hinges.

She groans, her whole body tensing and her pussy squeezing me hard.

"Roman…" She breathes, my name like a prayer on her lips. "I'm going to cum."

"So am I," I hiss. "Inside *my* pussy."

"Roman," she whispers.

"You're mine, Little Fox," I growl, biting her neck. "You've always been mine."

"Yes!"

Her last moan wracks her body, and I feel her climax hit right as I empty myself inside of her.

CHAPTER THIRTY-EIGHT

A moan bubbles out of me as he applies pressure to my sore muscles, his fingers circling and pushing, a devilish smirk gracing his face.

"You're missing the best part," I mutter, trying to draw his attention back to the TV.

"I don't really watch television to be honest," he mutters with a roll of his eyes. "And besides, I'd much rather be upstairs recreating the previous scene than watching it."

I chuckle, my head leaning back against the couch as I roll my shoulders, burrowing down into the soft cushions and turning my attention back to the movie we're currently watching. I haven't seen the film before, yet it's eerily predictable, like always.

If someone told me this would be my life a few weeks ago, I would have laughed in their face, yet here I am. Sitting here, watching a chick flick with a Mafia Boss, as he adoringly massages my swollen feet and ankles.

I do find it a bit ironic that he's attending to me, when he's the one who nearly lost his dog yesterday.

Caesar had thankfully survived the attack. The bullet that had been fired at him had grazed his shoulder, but according to the terrified vet who delivered the news, he was going to make a full recovery. However, they still recommended that they keep him there to monitor his progress for the next couple of days.

Roman wasn't exactly pleased with this decision, but I managed to get him to see reason, and reluctantly let his pup heal and recover at the animal hospital.

In the meantime, I knew my mafia boyfriend needed a distraction. Something to lighten his heavy load.

Which is why I invited him back to my place, for dinner and a movie.

And so, the mafia king of New York sits with me, his feet up on the couch, having a rare day of normalcy.

It's kind of amazing to think about how after my failed attempt at killing him, everything has just clicked into place for us.

Granted his men are still stationed outside of my house, guarding each door like they expect me to run.

But I have no intention of running.

Not only because I know he would chase me, but also because I no longer want to run.

I want to be here. With him.

The man is breaking all the rules to keep me in his life. From what he has told me about his family, he should've killed me for what I did to Igor. Technically, he should've handed me over to Polina and let *her* kill me.

Yet he didn't.

Nor would he ever.

"What the fuck!" Roman shouts, jolting me out of my thoughts. "Why would he do that?!"

He angrily gestures toward the screen.

"What?" I giggle.

Suddenly the door bursts open as Paulie, one of Roman's men, flies into the room, his gun drawn.

He anxiously glances between me, Roman and the television, nervously looking around the room.

"Boss?" Paulie asks, his spine straightening as he lowers the gun. "Is everything al—"

"What the fuck are you doing?!" Roman snaps, shaking his head as he taps his ring against my leg.

A laugh bursts out of me, and I cover my mouth, but I am unable to contain the giggles that pour out of me.

I gasp, struggling to pull in air as I point at Roman, and then at Paulie.

"Roman…he…thought that you… hahahahahah!"

Both men stare at me in shock, as I struggle to reign in my amusement.

Paulie quickly tucks the gun into the back of his trousers, before glancing at the screen.

"Oh! I've seen this one! My wife is obsessed with the actor… what's his name?" He clicks his fingers, as he thinks.

"It's—" I start to say but I'm immediately interrupted.

"What the fuck are you doing in here?" Roman hisses.

"I…well…you…um," Paulie stutters nervously. "You yelled, and we thought that—"

"You thought what?!"

My laughter dies in my throat as I feel Roman's demons slide silently into the room, ready to tear into his man to pieces for the interruption.

Paulie runs his hand through his hair, before rubbing the back of his neck, he glances at me causing Roman to stiffen.

"Don't look at her!" He growls. "Look at me."

"Sorry, Boss," he replies, glancing submissively at Roman. "I thought you were in danger."

"Why would I be in any danger with Abigail?"

Paulie clears his throat, his lips tightening into a thin line, before he takes a breath.

"I heard that she…might've," he gulps reluctantly. "*Killed* some of the men. So, I was worried that she was going to…"

His voice trails off as I shift in my seat, my face heating as I tug at the bottom of my sleeve.

Oh no. The men know now.

Roman had told me how important it was that we keep this as quiet as possible, until he could deal with Polina. But somehow, they'd found out.

I feel Roman's hand tighten around my ankle, and I flex my foot, as I clear my throat, hoping to draw Roman's attention to my discomfort.

He lifts my legs as he slides up off the couch, and stands to his full height, his frame towering over Paulie.

He steps toward him slowly.

"You heard that, huh?" He whispers darkly. "And who exactly did you hear that from?"

"I…I don't remember," Paulie stammers, his eyes wide. "It was just a rumor."

"And you think that your Don couldn't deal with a singular woman?"

"No! That's not it at all, Boss!" He states, his face reddening. "I was just worried and—"

"Roman," I interject. "Relax. He was just doing his job…"

"Quiet, Abigail," Roman snaps at me, without removing his murderous gaze from Paulie.

Excuse me?!

The vein in my temple throbs, and my skin heats as my own demons now flood the room.

"Don't you dare talk to me like that, Roman!" I snap, jumping up from the couch. "You do not get to dismiss me that way."

However, Roman still doesn't look at me, nor does he make any indication he's listening to me at all.

I can almost hear his thoughts out loud. I know his concern is about the rumor spreading that I have killed his men, and I can hear his resolve even before he pulls the gun from his holster.

The resounding click of the safety disengaging echoes through the room, louder than the movie playing on the television. He raises the gun slowly, aiming it straight at the sweating mess of the man standing in front of him.

A man who did absolutely nothing wrong.

No. This isn't right.

I slide past him, stepping between the barrel of the gun and Paulie.

"Abigial, what the fuck are you doing?"

"I'm not going to let you kill him," I say firmly. "He didn't do anything wrong."

"You can't just step in front of a fucking gun, Abigail!" Roman barks. "Especially not *my* fucking gun!"

"I will do whatever I please," I growl, narrowing my eyes at him. "But you will not shoot this man for doing his job."

"That is not your decision to make," he snaps. "Move out of the way."

"No. If you want to shoot him, then you will have to shoot me."

"Abigail—"

"I killed your men," I blurt out, my heart pounding in my chest. "I disrespected your family, your name. I deserve to die. But he doesn't."

"Stop this!" Roman snaps angrily. "I'm not going to shoot you! But I cannot have these rumors spreading amongst my men, I need to make sure that doesn't happen. Now move!"

"I'm not fucking moving!" I shout at him. "So, if you insist on shooting him, then you need to shoot me first."

"Move, Abigail."

"No."

"Move!" He bellows again, his jaw ticking.

"No!" I scream at him, crossing my arms as I hold my ground.

He stares at me in silence, the fury shaking through him as he fights with himself.

"Paulie," I say, my eyes locked firmly on Roman's.

"Y…yes, Miss?" He whispers shakily.

"You can go."

I can feel the reluctance from behind me, but I know the moment Paulie starts to move from the sound of his shoes scuffing across the floor, and from the way Roman's eyes darken.

"Where. The. Fuck," Roman snaps out. "Do you think you're going?"

"He's leaving." I reply firmly.

"He doesn't take orders from you."

"He does now," I smirk, as I hear the front door softly click closed.

I stare down the barrel of Roman's gun, still raised at me.

Slowly I take a step forward, feeling the cool metal of the barrel pressing straight into my forehead. I raise my chin, my eyes locking onto Roman's.

He stares at me in shock, before clicking the safety back on, and throws the gun to the side.

"Jesus Christ!" He gasps, running a hand through his hair. before gripping my shoulders to pull me against him. "What the fuck are you thinking, Abigail!"

I shrug out of his hold, "You dismissed me."

"It was business."

"Business," I snort. "Roman, you ignored me! You pretended I wasn't in the room with you."

"That man disrespected me!" He roars.

"So that means you can disrespect me?" I mutter.

"Abigail—"

"He didn't disrespect you, Roman," I snap. "In fact, he did the opposite, he was looking out for you. Which is his job. He did absolutely nothing wrong."

"He was questioning my leadership. My strength."

"Like hell he was!"

"Abby, there are rules in place. And I have to maintain the respect of my men."

"Well, shoot me then," I shrug, crossing my arms. "If you want to follow your precious rules."

"No."

"Then, don't talk to me like that. If you want to keep me, then treat me like you fucking want to keep me, Roman!"

I hold my ground, staring him down.

"You know what, you're right. Your men do need to respect you. But they also need to see you, respecting me," I growl at him. "If you want to quell the rumors, then they need to see you unafraid of me. And if you claim that I'm your queen, then treat me as such."

My body is shaking but I know I need to say this.

I refuse to be about to be treated how I was by my ex-husband.

I will be treated how I deserve to be treated and won't *accept* anything less.

He sighs, cocking his head to the side as he inspects me, his eyes roaming down my body before returning to my face.

"Okay, Abigail, okay." He concedes, as he pulls me in for a hug, his arm wrapping round me. "I'm sorry."

Holy shit.

"I shouldn't have yelled at you," he continues, pulling my body from his, his fingers tipping my chin up. "But, I think you need to remember, this is *my* city."

I jerk myself from his hold, and walk backwards away from him, my head shaking.

"Then go back to your city then," I state, turning to face him.

"Abigail. These are my men, they are loyal to *me*."

"I get it."

"No, you don't, if you did you wouldn't have intervened like that."

"You keep saying you want to *keep* me," I snap at him. "But I don't think you understand what that actually means. Because if you did, you would ensure that I'm treated with respect by your men. And to do that, they need to see you doing it!"

Roman opens his mouth to say something but I don't give him the opportunity.

"Let me make one thing clear, Roman. If you want to have me in your life, then you will give me the equality I need. Because if you think you're going to treat me like a possession to flaunt, or some object wrapped in bubble wrap, then you may as well go over there and pick up that fucking gun," I gesture toward it. "...And shoot me right here, right now."

His eyes appraise me, taking in my words.

"Because, if you treat me like *he* did, that would be a fate worse than death." I growl, raising my chin. "And maybe that would be my death, or maybe it would be yours, but either way, death will come for us."

"Are you," he says cautiously, narrowing his eyes at me. "*Threatening* me, Foxy?"

I shrug, smiling at him brightly.

"You might have demons, Roman Antonov, but so do I. And mine have claws."

A
ANTONOV

ANTONOV

CHAPTER THIRTY-NINE

ROMAN

3:01am

The Witching Hour.

At least that's what my mother used to call it.

I glance over at Abby, who lays sleeping on the bed next me, after I fucked her brains out. The pale moonlight filters through the window, illuminating her naked body wrapped up in the dark gray sheets, her hand resting on my chest.

Softly, I raise mine and place it gently on top of hers.

I still can't believe she's here.

Well, I guess it's more like I can't believe *I'm* here.

This clusterfuck of a romance has been insane to say the least. And it's even more insane to think about the fact that a few months ago this woman was the very ghost who only haunted my dreams…and my regrets. But now I'm here, in her house, in her bed, with *her*.

And she is *mine*.

But even that sentence feels so surreal to say out loud, because I never wanted this.

To me, choosing to be with just one person, forever, sounded like the equivalent of stuffing your dick into a blender: self-imposed misery.

It's actually a big part of why Jaxon Pace and I had gotten on so well for nearly a decade. We'd had countless discussions, albeit *inebriated* discussions, on the emotional prison that was monogamy. In fact, in one of those drunken philosophical word-vomit sessions, the two of us had made a pact that we'd never allow the other to walk off the matrimonial plank.

But then, a few years later, he *did*.

In truth, I'd lied to him the other night at dinner.

I *could've* attended his wedding to Natalie, but I chose not to. And it wasn't because I was disappointed in him, or trying to uphold some stupid promise made between two drunk guys in a bar.

It was because I was jealous.

Jaxon might be older than me, and have more money, power, and influence, but none of those things had ever intimidated me, or made me feel inferior.

Yet somehow *this* did.

We'd only had one conversation about Natalie, but even I knew from just that one conversation that my oldest friend, confidant, and even occasional brother-in-arms, was utterly enamored by this woman. And yeah, after seeing her, I could understand the appeal.

But it wasn't just the fact that she was pretty.

Because we'd been so close, I'd seen him with plenty of pretty women, models, influencers, socialites. And I'd even seen him with Rachel, his first real girlfriend, and the mother of his child. But their relationship had been chaotic and toxic, often leaving him pissed off and spiraling, needing to trip out on some drugs and bury his dick in a stripper.

In a way, women had always been just another drug to Jaxon. Another vice to occupy his time.

Until *her*.

Natalie had changed Jaxon in a way that I'd never thought was possible. She had bravely accepted his life, and his darkness, while also giving him hope of a future. She'd taken on her role more than just his paramour, but as his wife, supporting him, bolstering him, while also being able to settle him when he threatened to go off the rails.

And listening to him tell me about how things were "different," and "real," had made me happy for him, but it had also made me envious that he had found someone who was capable of doing and being all of those things for him.

Because I *hadn't* found it.

I wasn't settling down with anyone. Hell, I was the "Russian Rooster," and the "One Night Stand Man." I was the prick who would bring a bitch home, fuck her, and then kick her out of my penthouse in the morning without feeling a drop of remorse.

However, deep down, in the darkest corner, of the most reclusive and clandestine parts of my soul, the truth sat defiantly staring back at me. No matter how I denied it, or fought against it, I knew that I craved the very thing I disparaged: A *family*.

And not just any family. No, a happy family. A wife, and kids, and a life with my siblings that brought me joy.

The truth was, that I didn't *want* to do this all alone, and I *wanted* a worthy partner by my side.

My muse. My Aphrodite. My *home*.

But this was nothing more than a fantasy.

After all, I'd never *seen* that kind of love before.

On their best days, my parents had just avoided each other.

On their worst days, they'd plotted to kill each other.

No one knew where the breakdown had happened, but there'd been rumors. Some whispered tales about how before meeting my mother, my father had actually been in love with the Irish mafia lord's daughter, Sinead McCleary. But how her father had denied their love, and forbade them from seeing each other.

Some of those rumors said that her father had killed her.

Others said that she died of a broken heart.

But either way, my father had been denied the only woman he had truly loved and wanted, and over time it had turned his heart to stone.

At first, he was kind and gentle to my mother, but it wasn't long before he was cold and distant. And then after Pasha was born, looking so different with his blue eyes and blonde hair, my father had checked out entirely.

He used his "suspicions" about Pasha's parentage as a way to justify having a mistress, even though my mother had rarely ever left our house.

And the way he treated Pasha was absolutely despicable.

…Especially when he had used him as a weapon against me.

Pasha and I had always been close, and my father hated it.

And so, every time I would fuck up, or fail or even disappoint him slightly in my training, he would use Pasha as a way to punish me.

One time, I was less than perfect on my target practice sheets, and my father, in his rage and delusion, had decided I needed to be punished. His punishment? Locking my claustrophobic brother in a crypt in Calvary Cemetery in the freezing cold…and telling me to find him…all on my own.

I'd scrambled around that cemetery for hours, screaming for my brother, certain that I was going to be the cause of his death. And if Cal hadn't shown up to help me find him in secret, I might've.

Pasha had survived that day, and my father had taught me a valuable lesson: That love, in all its forms, was dangerous.

Perhaps that's why I keep everyone at a distance, and why love has always been such a hard concept for me to wrap my head around.

And then, out of nowhere, *she* wandered into my life.

I'd loved her from the moment I saw her. Every curve of her body felt familiar, as if somehow, I had designed her, and manifested her out of thin air.

The only problem was, she belonged to someone else. And even as selfish as I was, after watching the horrific dissolution of my parents' relationship, I could never wish that misery on anyone. But it felt as if the universe was playing a cruel trick on me, taunting me with the very thing I desired, while keeping her just out of reach.

In a way this only further hardened my already jaded heart, and confirmed what my father had tried to drill into me: I was meant to be alone.

Yet as I lay here in the darkness, feeling Abigail curl her body around mine, I realize that nothing could be further from the truth. Sure, my life is dangerous, and yes, being with me comes with risks that the average, sane, rational woman would never willingly sign up for.

But Abigail Wayne isn't average.

Nor is she sane or even rational.

She's a killer.

And yet, somehow, she's been the only woman I've ever wanted. And the one I know was made specifically for *me*.

Somehow, I know that I would sacrifice my soul to the devil if it meant I got to have her.

I meant what I said to her that day in the greenhouse.

I do love her.

I want to marry her.

I want to have a family with her.

Fuck, I want it all.

And I am going to have it, even if it kills me.

…Or even if *she* does.

CHAPTER FORTY

Abby

My eyes open slowly, the room dark and quiet.

Behind me, Roman's body heats mine, and I snuggle further into him. I lay there for a moment, just basking in the heat of him before slowly turning to face him. The morning sun slowly casts a light glow from behind the curtains, highlighting his features.

My breath hitches in my throat as my eyes devour the sight in front of me.

Watching Roman sleep is something I could get used to. He's so attractive that it should be illegal. But, looking at him right now, I realize he isn't just attractive.

He's beautiful.

His features, which are usually chiseled hard lines and jagged edges, are smooth, his face the picture of peace that rarely encompasses him. They are softer, and more pronounced like this. His long lashes flutter against his cheek as his eyes flick under his lids. A light dusting of stubble coats his cheeks. With each soft, even breath, his chest rises and falls ever so slightly.

It occurs to me that seeing Roman like this is something most people will never see. Not because he doesn't sleep, but because he would never allow anyone to *see* him sleeping.

Yet here he is, next to me, my vulnerable king.

Leaning up on my elbow, I gently run my fingers over his skin, admiring the intricate tattoos that paint his chest, each line leading into another, canvassing his body.

I pause as he moves, his arm lifting to cover his eyes. Biting my lip, I trail my fingers lightly over the veins in his arms.

His demons demand to be worshiped, and seeing him like this, I fully understand why women throw themselves at his feet, ready to be used and completely destroyed. A man like this could never be a soft, slow lover, everything about him screams violence and bloodshed.

He goes to war on your body, and you welcome it.

He goes to war on your soul, and you let him.

I unintentionally went to war on his family, and he embraced it, completely rewriting our outcome.

For all I know, the end game could still be death. And that shouldn't turn me on.

But it does.

Slowly, I peel away the thin blanket that he's wrapped himself in, exposing more of his chest and stomach.

He tenses in response, my eyes flick to his face. I watching his fist clench slightly before he relaxes once more, I continue, exposing his body to me as he sleeps.

His legs widen, leaving a gap in the middle of the bed. As carefully as I can, I rise up on my knees, lifting one leg, then the other to kneel between his thighs.

His cock rests against his stomach, lengthening as my eyes take it in. Gently, I run my fingers up his leg, before grasping it in my hand.

He twitches, a low moan escaping him. Staying still, I stare up at him, waiting for him to wake.

When he doesn't, I pump my fist, feeling him harden in response.

Lightly, I press soft kisses to his hips, before pressing my lips gently to his head, and watch as precum beads on the tip, his need lighting me on fire. My heart thunders in my chest, I really should stop, but the thrill of having this man keeps me going.

Parting my lips, I take the head of his cock in my mouth, pausing when his body tenses and then twitches as he moves his hips slightly, pushing himself further inside.

I moan, the sound vibrating against his cock as he groans back. Relaxing my jaw, I take in more of his impressive length, before pulling back and sucking lightly on the tip.

The taste of this man is a drug, and my downfall, yet I crave it. He could ruin me, and I would let him.

Glancing up at him, his arm still covering his eyes, I catch him biting his lip.

He's awake.

Sucking more of him into my mouth, I press my tongue to the underside of his cock, before swirling it around as I come back up. His hips rock automatically, chasing my mouth as I move up and down, with each dip of my head my speed and pressure increase, until his cock is touching the back of my throat each time.

Swallowing around him, I fight the urge to gag.

"Fucccck, Foxy," he groans, his arm falling away from his eyes, which still haven't opened.

Moaning around his cock, I suck harder, watching his neck tense.

His hands move, gripping my hair tightly in his fist, with an audible pop he pulls me off his cock. His blue eyes meet mine with a lazy smirk, before forcing my head back down.

"If you wanted me to fuck your mouth, you could have asked," He growls, causing my legs to clench, and feeling myself dripping with need.

His tattooed hand reaches down, gripping his hard cock in his hand, he pumps it once, then twice, before slapping it against my lips.

"Open your mouth and take my fucking cock like a good girl."

I moan against him as he rams his cock into my mouth.

With each thrust he hits the back of my throat.

"Fuck," he groans, his hooded gaze locked on mine.

Reaching down, I grip his balls in my hand, squeezing tightly as my mouth sucks him.

"You were fucking made for me," he says, his head dropping back down the pillows.

Suddenly he tenses and holds me down, his cock filling my mouth, as his cum pours down the back of my throat. I nearly choke swallowing it all.

Before he's even finished, he's dragging me up his body and slams his lips to mine, tasting his release on my tongue. My pussy clenches as he moans against my mouth.

"I love the taste of me on your lips," he growls. "It drives me fucking crazy."

He lifts me, and the tip of his still hard cock teases my entrance.

"You're so fucking wet for me baby. You're dripping."

With a growl, I push against his chest. I shove him back against the bed before mounting him and impaling myself on his cock as my muscles tighten around him.

"Shut up, and give me what I need." I bark at him, rolling my hips and clawing at his chest.

His hands grip my ass painfully, spreading me further open as he lifts and slams me back down onto him.

"That's it baby. Fucking take it."

With each thrust our breathing becomes rapid, his groans driving me wild. He reaches down and gently presses a finger to my entrance, feeling his cock thrust in and out of me. Tensing, I feel his finger push against his cock, gently sliding into me as well.

Without warning his other hand grips my throat tightly,

"You," he whispers, his lip curling. "Take my cock so fucking perfectly."

He pulls his other hand out of me and suddenly rubs my asshole at the same time.

I stiffen on top of him, my eyes darting to his as he gently runs his finger over my tight little hole.

"And one day Foxy, you'll fucking take me here too."

Holy. Shit.

Flipping me over suddenly, he pounds into me, every thrust punishing my traitorous pussy.

"Fuck Roman," I moan, drowning in the feel of him.

Heat pools low in my stomach forcing me to arch up against him.

Gripping my hair tightly, he yanks my head back, exposing my neck to him, biting down his teeth digging into my skin.

"Fucking cum," he grunts, forcing me closer to the edge.

"No," I snap back, knowing that he's riding that edge with me.

Biting harder, his hand reaches down to my clit, rubbing fast as the pressure peaks.

"Now."

A scream tears through my throat as I climax, my muscles clamping down around him, my vision blurs as everything goes dark.

He doesn't stop, forcing my orgasm to continue, before he tenses, his hips shuddering as a long low groan comes from him and empties himself inside of me.

Flipping us back over, I collapse across his chest. He's still buried inside me, the aftershocks fluttering through me with each twitch of his cock.

We lay here, frozen in our ecstasy, our ragged breathing echoing in the room.

This man is everything I've ever wanted in a lover.

Pressing a light kiss to his chest, I finally push off of him.

"Breakfast?" I smile.

And when Roman Antonov looks up at me with that mesmerizingly playful smirk of his, there is only one thought that fills my brain:

I could get used to this.

As I round the corner to the kitchen, I freeze.

My entire kitchen is full of Roman's men.

Oleg smirks at me, tipping up a steaming cup of coffee before his eyes cast back down as I feel Roman against my back.

"Everyone out," he says, his voice hoarse. "Trevor, you stay behind."

Without a second of hesitation everyone evacuates, a few of them casting sympathetic looks toward Trevor on their way out. After they close the door behind them, my house falls silent.

"Yes, Boss?" Trevor asks nervously.

"Go to the penthouse," he starts, pausing when he feels me stiffen. His arm wraps round my stomach, giving me a light squeeze before he continues.

"I want it prepared for our arrival."

"Consider it done," Trevor says with a nod, taking a final sip of his coffee, before placing it in the sink.

Untangling myself from Roman's hold, I walk into the kitchen and open the cupboard to get Lily her food.

"Ugh," I sigh, slamming the door closed.

Shit. I don't have any food for her.

I turn, seeing Trevor fighting with his impulse to clean his dirty cup, indecision coating his features.

"Out." Roman states, making the decision for him.

"I'll wash it, Trevor."

He nods, and scurries to the door, clicking it closed behind him.

"So," Roman claps. "Breakfast?"

Roman doesn't wait for a response, before rifling through the cupboards and pulling out sausage, bacon, and eggs from the fridge.

Food that I have no recollection of purchasing myself.

"I had the men stock your fridge," he turns, glaring at me. "You know, since it was *empty.*"

"Haven't had the time—"

"Not acceptable."

"Well, if my boss didn't keep me so busy, and naked," I say, glaring at him. "I'd have time to shop."

"Oh, I'd say you've had plenty of time to *shop*, Abigail," he says, condescendingly. "And make donations."

"Well, it would've been more helpful if they'd gotten Lily some food too." I say with a sigh, ignoring his remark regarding my abuse on his card.

"Abby, you were my priority, not the damn—"

"If you're about to say what I think you're about to say," I spit, pointing toward the foyer. "Then there's the door, Sir."

He snorts to himself, shaking his head.

"I'm going to have to run to the store to get food for her."

"I'll send one of the men."

"No, I'll get it myself."

With a sigh, he turns back to the stove.

"Only if one of them goes with you."

"Seriously?" I huff. "I can take care of myself."

"I'm in the middle of a war, woman."

"It's not our enemies that defeat us, Roman. It's our fear. Find a way to make them fear you." I state, "Because I'm telling you now, they don't get to lock me down or get me thrown on a plane."

"Abigail…" he laughs.

Roman places a plate in front of me, before sitting down next to me at the island.

The smell makes my stomach roll.

"Talking of the men, what are we doing about the… you know…" I trail off, trying to distract myself.

"I'll deal with it."

"How, Roman?"

"It's handled."

"You keep saying they are *our* men," I say slowly. "Well, I'm telling you that *our* men see me as the villain who kills them."

"I kill them too," he snorts, shrugging slightly before throwing a piece of bacon in his mouth.

"Roman," I sigh.

"You're not a villain, Foxy," he shakes his head. "You have your reasons."

"Don't romanticize murder."

"I'm not," he shrugs, "you kill men who hurt women. I don't see anything wrong with that." He smiles, cutting open the egg. "And my opinion is the only one that matters."

The arrogance in his words makes me bite my lip.

"Why do you hate the penthouse?" He asks, not missing a beat.

"My husband."

"No," Roman snaps, dropping his fork down with a bang. "Let me make one thing abundantly clear, you *had* a husband, that's not something I can erase. But, that fuck is no longer your husband, And the only person that is going to have that title is *me*."

All I can do is stare at him.

The idea of Roman being my husband sends shivers down my spine. I thought that after Garrett, I would never marry again, I would never give anyone that amount of power over me.

But marrying Roman? Surrendering to *him*?

…Doesn't sound so bad.

We are the same, him and I.

Kinda funny to me that a few months ago, "home" was a cat, and now it's this man, who is my equal in all ways.

"Home feels pretty good," I whisper under my breath.

"Would be better if you lived at the penthouse," he grumbles.

"Okay, seeing as we are stating our terms, I nearly died in that building, Roman." I take a breath, trying to calm myself. "And my child *did* die in that building. The only time I'll happily return to that building, is to set it on fucking fire."

After breakfast, Roman went upstairs to shower before he had to head out for a few meetings. The moment the shower switched on, I threw on some clothes and snuck out the back door toward the greenhouse and slipped between the fences.

A sigh of relief escapes me as I glance over my shoulder and see that none of Roman's men saw me leave and are following me.

While I genuinely enjoy spending time with Roman, and I may have mildly swooned at the idea of waking up next to him every morning, having constant company is vastly different from how I've lived for the last few years.

I'll have to adjust, but I don't need armed guards to go and get some cat food.

As I reach the sidewalk, I see a familiar black car, one that was outside my house the other night, creeping toward me slowly. Quickly, I cross the road, and take a quick right before picking up speed.

Only to run directly into a wall of muscle.

"Hello, Abby baby."

A
ANTONOV

ANTONOV

CHAPTER FORTY-ONE

ROMAN

"What the fuck do you mean she was *taken*?!"

"Boss!" Cal says firmly, his voice panicked. "He can't answer you because you're choking him. If you don't let go, you're going to kill him!"

"I *am* going to fucking kill him!" I roar, feeling Oleg's windpipe closing beneath my fingertips.

As Oleg's eyes roll back into his head, I finally release him, slamming him through the drywall in Abby's living room, leaving a giant hole.

"You had one job you fucking idiot!" I snap at him as he crumples to the floor, moaning. "You were never supposed to let her out of your sight!"

But as I violently yank my pistol from my holster, resolved to shoot Oleg in the face, I accidentally manage to knock over a lamp in the living room and send it shattering to the floor.

"Yerrow!" A loud hiss echoes in the room, and before I can yell at Cal to close the front door, Abby's cat darts between his legs and out the front door.

Shit! I can't lose the cat too!

Leaving the debilitated Oleg on the floor, I immediately shove past Cal and out into the garden.

My head is spinning.

The Irish took Abby.

One minute everything was fine, next my girlfriend was kidnapped, and her cat got out.

"Hey cat! Come back!" I call out. "Fuck!"

"Did you see where she went?" Cal asks, as the two of us comb the garden.

"Are you referring to my girlfriend?" I snap angrily. "Because, no, I didn't. That's what I pay you people for!"

"We will find her, Boss," Cal says reassuringly before gently whistling for the cat.

"Yo! Cat! Get the fuck over here!" I shout.

"Sir," Cal clears his throat. "You're going to have to be a little…"

"What?!"

"Softer," Cal finishes. "And the cat is named Lily, by the way."

"Lily!" I call out again, but I already know my tone is still far too aggressive to convince this poor terrified cat to trust me.

Suddenly, I snap.

"Fuuuuck!" I shout loudly, my hands balled into fists as I grab the small flimsy lawn chair near the small fire pit and smash it violently against the brick pavers. "How the fuck did this fucking happen?! How?!"

"Boss, I—" Cal starts to say but I toss the chair to the side and storm over to him, pointing at him.

"Did you fucking do this?!"

He tries to respond, but I grab him by his jacket and shake him violently.

"You did this!" I roar, trying to punch him in my blind rage. "You deliberately got rid of Abby, didn't you? Didn't you?!"

But just like always, Cal doesn't fight back, remaining the strong silent force that he is when there's a crisis. For every blind jab I throw his way, he blocks it, using up all his energy just to stay calm and upright as the two of us grapple in the small garden.

"No, Boss," he finally whispers quietly. "I would never touch Abby. And I promise, no one on our team would dare touch Abby."

I can't explain why, but I know that I can trust the authenticity in his voice when he says this.

Slowly I feel my hands lift off of him.

"We're pulling all the security camera footage in the area," Cal says, checking under the other lawn chairs around Abby's fire pit. "We will get a hit on a plate, or a face, and we will get her back. But she will murder you herself if she finds out that you lost her cat."

"I know," I growl.

Behind us the men flood into the garden.

"Look everywhere!" Cal bellows, waving his hand.

We have to find Abby.

"Lily!" I feel my chest tightening. "Come here, girl."

We will find Abby.

And that's when we hear it.

The faintest of meows, coming from the greenhouse.

I look down the path to see Lily the cat, pacing back and forth at the door to Abby's glass plant warehouse.

"Oh, thank God," I mutter softly.

But what I see when I pick her up immediately makes my blood run cold.

Because right there, at the door to the greenhouse, is a soft pink...Juliet rose.

"This wasn't the Irish," I whisper only so Cal can hear me. "It was *Polina.*"

CHAPTER FORTY-TWO

Clang… clang… clang…

The noise is loud, but it isn't clear. It's distorted, almost as if I'm underwater. I feel the air ripple around me in the darkness as the clanging gets louder and louder. I flinch when it bangs right next to my head and instinctively my arms tense to cover my ears…but they don't move.

They can't move. My chest starts to tighten with the realization.

Oh fuck.

I can't move. I can't see.

Fuck I can't see!

My skin feels clammy, a droplet of sweat running down my back as I inhale as much air as I can. But my lungs tighten, as if a boa constrictor is squeezing, preparing to make a meal out of me.

Squeezing my eyes shut, I focus on slowing my breathing, trying to picture Roman walking me through my breaths like he did back in my bedroom.

But the panic and shock of my predicament is making that difficult.

Still, I try to count softly, feeling my lips crack as I mutter the numbers.

With the last of my sanity, I try to focus on what's around me.

Think Abby! What can you touch, hear and smell?

It feels and smells damp and musky.

I can hear birds outside, and the sound of men chatting as they kick up gravel.

I'm sitting in a metal chair.

The blindfold is covering my eyes and nose, making my face feel hot.

"Awww look! Our guest is awake," comes a shrill feminine voice to my right.

…A voice with a *Russian* accent.

"She's a pretty one, ma'am, do we get to play with her?" Another voice, this one male, comes from my left, his tone instantly making me cringe, my stomach twisting.

I know *that* voice.

Heels click against the concrete floor, echoing off the walls.

I straighten as much as I can in my chair, but my arms are pinned behind my back, tied tightly with something that is painfully digging into my skin.

"Not yet," she chuckles viciously. "First, I need to have a little chat with my brother's new *toy*."

Wait a minute…brother's new toy?

My thoughts are interrupted as the blindfold is pulled from my head. I groan as it catches in my hair, yanking it painfully and snapping my head back.

The light is blinding, and it takes me a few seconds to adjust.

But that's when I see him.

No. It can't be.

My chest tightens, and I bite down on the inside of my cheek, my mind instantly recalling every past interaction, looking for signs I must've missed.

Trying to find any reason that *he* would do this.

"Why?" I choke, my voice rough, strangled by the suffocating feeling of betrayal.

He shrugs, smirking at me.

Only, it's not *sweet* Teddy that answers.

"You silly little girl. You killed my husband," she laughs, the edge in it sharp enough to slice the air. Polina glares at me, her gun held loosely in her hand.

"He…" I clear my throat, "he was cheating on you. He had a mistress!" I state, keeping my eyes focused on hers.

Taking a deep breath, I stare at her.

"He disrespected you," I continue. "He even did it in your house! She was in the cupboard when you came home!"

"Oh, Abigail, I know."

"He probably fuck—wait…*what?*" I blink at her, my head cocked to one side.

"I already know that bitch was in the cupboard," she snorts, narrowing her eyes at me and licking her lip. "Because I put the little bitch there. She knew what she signed up for when I picked her."

"You… picked his mistress?"

"I picked *our* mistress," she grins wickedly. "I always prefer the young and desperate ones. And, of course, her fantastic fertility results helped too."

My heart freezes in my chest.

"What? I don't understand…"

"Why would you, Abigail Wayne? Who's twenty-eight, currently resides in Forest Hill's, with a cat. Lily is her name, right?" Polina taunts, a disgustingly sweet softness in her voice. "Hmm…and you had a husband who was very wealthy, didn't you? I chatted to him once. He was a lovely man, wasn't he a lovely man, darling."

She looks pointedly across the room at Teddy, who leans against the wall with his arms crossed licking his lips.

"Oh yes, Mr. Adams was a blast. He had a thing for small blonde things, if I recall correctly," he grins, his teeth on full show.

Small blonde things.

"We were so sad to hear he had died. So suddenly too. And we were shocked to learn he died of a heart attack in the middle of his own home! At such a young age!"

My eyes stay locked on Polina's, my necklace burning a hole in my chest.

"I'll admit, it took us a while to piece it all together," she laughs. "But you have an awfully nice greenhouse…*Abby.*"

My thundering heart comes to a stop.

"What I couldn't figure out, however, is why my brother would take notice of a nobody like you. A plain Jane."

Polina leans down in front of me, reaching for my face. I strain, trying to avoid her, but it's no use as I cannot move.

"And then I saw it," she purrs, gently stroking my cheek with the back of her icy cold fingers. "He sees his darkness lurking beneath your skin. How poetic. My ruthless, vicious, cold-hearted brother finally found the perfect woman."

Suddenly she snaps, grabbing my chin hard between her fingers, the gun in her hand gleaming in the light.

"…But she fucked around and killed someone she shouldn't have," she grips my jaw painfully before violently ripping her fingers away, scratching my cheek. "I'm owed a life for a life. And I'm here to fucking collect it."

A
ANTONOV

CHAPTER FORTY-THREE

ROMAN

"Roman, I'm tracking Polina's phone but it's showing that it's at her house. Same as her car," Ana says into my ear as two of my men carry a mumbling Oleg out of Abby's house and into the nearest car.

"...And I know they aren't there because the cameras at her house have no activity. No one is there."

She knew. She knew we'd track her.

"What about the city cameras outside of Abby's house?"

"I'm still trying to get into those, but I've already told you that's harder because of the—"

The phone suddenly beeps in my ear.

Unknown Caller.

That shouldn't happen. No one has this number.

"Hold on," I say, switching over to the other line.

"Who is this?" I bark.

"Well, good morning to you too," a gravelly voice replies.

Cillian McCleary.

"You have some balls," I growl venomously.

"As do you," he scoffs. "I received your little package this morning. Don't think the man who watched the tape made it halfway through without vomiting."

I figured I'd get this phone call.

And I'd planned to enjoy his disgust when he received the video tape of what Baloo did to his cousin. But right now, neither he, nor the ongoing war with the Irish, are my primary concern.

My only focus right now is getting Abigail back.

"As much as I'd love to have this little chat right now about our little shituationship," I hiss acidly, my jaw clenching. "I do have a few more pressing issues at the moment."

"Oh, I assume you do," Cillian purrs. "Probably not a good look for the girlfriend of a mob boss to get kidnapped. I assume it's counterproductive in instilling confidence in your leadership."

My heart stops beating, and my blood runs cold.

How the fuck does he know?

"Now, right about now, I bet you're asking yourself how on earth I would know that," Cillian chuckles darkly. "And as much as I'd love to string you along, and watch you fumble around for the answer, I know that if I don't dispel the rumors, then you'll likely assume I did it."

"I sincerely doubt you're worried about my opinion of you Cillian," I whisper lethally. "Not after you had your men kill my cousin, and threaten my entire family."

"...Which was in retaliation for your men killing my cousin, and threatening my entire family," Cillian says softly. "That's how these things unfortunately tend to go. Wars, as you know, are messy."

"You shot my fucking dog!" I roar angrily, holding the phone away from my mouth.

"No, I did not—"

"And you were the ones who broke the truce first," I continue. "You drew first blood!"

"No, we did not!" Cillian snaps back angrily. "The fucking truce was broken the minute *you* had *your* men come into our part of town, and take two of our women. One of whom was my sister!"

"Are you kidding me?" I laugh sarcastically. "That's fucking bull—"

"It's not bullshit!" Cillian shouts at me down the phone. "I have the proof! I have the video footage!"

"What proof?" I snort. "And what video footage!"

"He was your fucking brother-in-law, Roman!"

"Cillian," I growl, my jaw clenching. "I haven't the foggiest fucking idea of what you're talking about, and right now I have other shit to deal with that's more important than any of this bullshit!"

The call goes quiet, with the only sound being the heavy breathing on the other end of the line.

"You really don't know," he whispers. "Do you?"

I'm about to hang-up when suddenly I get a text chime.

I open it, and see that it's a surveillance video from a street camera.

It's grainy, and the rain makes the beginning of the video hard to see.

But then I recognize a man in the video…Igor.

In stunned silence I watch as he basically drags a clearly drunk woman towards his black Range Rover SUV, while another male, who I don't recognize at all, puts another unconscious woman in the backseat.

"What…the fuck…is this?" I say, my breath hitching in my throat.

"This," Cillian growls into the receiver. "Is my fucking sister. She's been missing for two months. And the last time I saw her was with *your* goddamn brother-in-law."

I clench my eyes closed.

Igor was a whore. Everyone knew that, even my sister. And I of all people certainly enjoyed the thrill of the hunt along with the next rich, egotistical, fuckboy.

But I never did this shit.

This is *predatory*.

And with everything I'm learning about Polina, and whatever her association with these "Jewel Rose" girls, my stomach clenches thinking at the possibility of where those two drunk girls may have ended up.

"Cillian, I can assure you I knew nothing about this—"

"I don't want your fucking assurances!" He roars. "I want my sister back! And since you clearly had no idea, this was even going on in your organization, I knew that your incompetent ass would try to pin this shit on me. And I refuse to have my name associated with your sins."

I open my mouth to say something, but no words come to my lips. In truth, there's nothing I can say.

"I never wanted war with you Russian pricks, but war is what you got when *your* men came across the line, into our territory and took *my* sister Aoife, and her roommate Erin," he says darkly. "So, as they act for you, this atrocity is on your fucking hands! And war is what you will get!"

"…And what if I can get her back?"

Cillian laughs.

"You wouldn't even know where to start," he snorts sarcastically. "Hell, you don't even know where your own girlfriend is."

My fist clenches.

"But," he continues with a sigh. "I might."

I freeze, hearing my heartbeat in my ears.

"What do you mean?"

"I haven't just been watching you and your little band of heathens," Cillian says darkly. "I've been keeping a close eye on your brother-in-law, and your sister."

"Where are they?" I snarl, glancing at my watch.

Fuck we're wasting time.

"...Although, I did find it a bit suspicious when he wound up dead," Cillian continues, ignoring me. "I heard the papers said it was a heart attack, though to be honest, I always thought it was his spoiled cunt of a wife who offed him."

"Cillian…" I growl. "Where are they?"

"But after studying them for quite some time, I discovered something… interesting. There was one place they both used to go, when they thought the other wasn't paying attention."

My fist clenches and I inhale deeply, frustrated as fuck that this bastard is wasting so much time telling this long-winded story.

"I'll tell you where I think they are holding her," Cillian says, evidently sensing my irritation. "But in return I want my sister back."

"I'll find her for you," I growl. "I promise."

Cillian snorts.

"The promise of a liar is never worth very much to me, Mr. Antonov. No, I want your *commitment* to finding her. And you will find her, or you will find every single person you love dead by spring…Including your little brother in Chicago."

My heart stops beating.

"Chelsea Pier, three buildings west of the one I had you meet me at," Cillian says softly. "And if I were you, I'd come loaded, because from what I've seen, they already are."

Then the line goes dead.

"Cillian must've known I didn't know about Polina and Igor's little warehouse the night we found Stetson. He was watching us that night, and would've seen how unfamiliar we were with this side of the marina," I say as I load my weapon from the backseat of the Cadillac. "But what he couldn't tell us, about how to get into the place, I know you can...*Heather.*"

My shaking and disheveled ex-accounting manager sits beside me in the car, outside the warehouse where we had originally come to meet Cillian.

"Fuck you," she says, her voice trembling. "I'm not telling you shit, Roman. And I don't give a shit about what happens to your little bitch of a girlfriend either."

I smile.

"You know, I thought you'd say that," I say, licking my bottom lip.

Cal hands me a tablet from the front seat.

"But I suggest you rethink that statement, one more time."

Pressing play, a video pops on to the screen, of a man, woman, and an elderly woman, all blindfolded and tied to their kitchen chairs.

...With one of my men standing behind them with a gun.

"Oh my God," Heather gasps, snatching it from me. "That's...that's my parents house!"

"Bravo. And yes, if you're wondering," I sneer. "That is a live feed. See that man there? That's Giorgi, he doesn't say much. Say hi, Giorgi!"

The man with the gun waves briefly at the camera before resuming his rigid stance.

"Mama! Papa!" Heather gasps, tears welling in her eyes. "Nona!"

"Oh, sorry, I should've specified," I smile darkly. "They can't hear you. Only Giorgi can hear you. Which, admittedly, has made *Nona's* participation in this entire thing a bit of a gamble. You know, given that she was dragged out of her bed and tied to the chair at one in the afternoon. Probably not very good for that heart condition of hers."

"You fucking monster!" She wails, trying to hit me.

However, I'm too quick for her, and given my restraint has teetered on the edge of my rage all fucking morning, I finally snap.

Blocking her with one hand, I grab her throat with my other, and smash her head against the glass window of my Cadillac so hard that the entire car shakes.

"Let's get one thing straight," I growl lethally. "I *am* a fucking monster, Heather. And if anything happens to Abigail, while I'm sitting in this motherfucking car wasting time with your trashy ass, I will make you watch as I slowly and mercilessly dismember your parents limb from fucking limb. And then, if she survives watching it happen, I will skin your sweet grandma alive. Do you understand?!"

Heather frantically scratches at my hand, crushing her windpipe.

"I'm giving you one opportunity, just *one*, to rethink your answer. And if it's the wrong one, I promise I will make you listen to their screams until your ears bleed."

When her face starts turning a dark shade of crimson, I finally release her, hearing her sharp intake of breath as she slumps against the window.

She coughs loudly, before breaking into a soft sob.

"So, tell me, Miss Jenson," I ask, folding my hands politely across my lap. "What's it going to be?"

ANTONOV

CHAPTER FORTY-FOUR

I always thought that I was immortal.

I'd convinced myself that the steps I took to cover my tracks would make it too hard for anyone to piece together who I've killed.

But Polina did.

"Tell me, Abigail," she says, brushing my hair from my face. "How much has Roman told you about our family business?"

"Not much," I hiss, pulling back from her.

"Liar," she chuckles darkly, stepping away from me, her heels clicking loudly against the concrete. "Each member of our family has a role. A purpose. But *I* was never given a role."

"How sad," I mutter sarcastically.

"I was set adrift in an empty void. And I accepted that life, for many years, until I saw an opportunity and decided to fill it," she says, shrugging arrogantly. "Do you want to know what I do?"

"Not as much as you apparently want to tell me," I whisper through gritted teeth.

She walks forward, stopping directly in front of me as her wild, unhinged laughter echoes off the walls. She brushes a strand of hair from my face, following the line of my jaw until her fingertip is under my chin and pushes upwards, leaving my neck completely exposed.

I glare down my nose at her.

"I find the *women*," she whispers seductively. "The lonely ones, with no friends, no family. The girls that no one will miss. Like Clarissa here."

She releases me, and walks over to a beautiful blonde woman standing like a statue by the door. Her hair and makeup are perfect, her only clothing being a lace bra and panties. Her arms are crossed behind her back, red lips pressed together, and her blue eyes staring listlessly at nothing.

Polina runs her fingers through the unmoving woman's hair, before trailing them down her breasts and stomach, touching her as if she is her personal property.

"It's a process. It takes time. But after I've broken them, and trained them, I sell them to men who want them."

"Want them for what?" I hiss, my heart racing as she turns and walks back toward me.

"For whatever. Maybe they just want a good fuck. Or maybe want a wife who doesn't talk back," she leans in and snickers darkly. "That's what all the girls hope for."

She steps back, placing her hand on the metal table behind her.

"But you know men," she shrugs with a disaffected sigh. "Most of them just want a hole to fuck, whenever they want, *however* they want. Or something they can take their frustrations out on. But *you* know all about that don't you, Abigail?"

"I have no idea what you're talking about," I say defiantly.

"Sure you do!" She says excitedly. "After all, your husband spent all those years training *you* to be the perfect woman. Silent and submissive."

She glares at me, narrowing her eyes with a wicked smile.

"Where do you think he learned it from?"

My jaw drops, my stomach sinking through the floor.

What the fuck?!

I say nothing, refusing to look at her.

"Did you know he *sold* you to me?" Polina coos viciously. "For a decent penny too. Of course, you were younger back then."

"No," I mutter, shaking my head, my stomach twisting.

"I'd already given him a downpayment for you. But then he died, and you disappeared, and I thought I'd just lost my investment." She says with a shrug. "Happens sometimes. Not all the girls make it, I'm afraid."

Garrett sold me? To her?!

The thought makes me nauseous. The idea that all of his abuse and brainwashing hadn't just been a result of his narcissistic sadism…it had been *intentional*.

"…But then out of the blue, you just happen to show back up as my brother's secretary!" Polina laughs. "Took me a minute to recognize you, after all, your appearance had changed so much from that frumpy girl Garrett Adams had shown me. But what a lucky coincidence. I guess life is just funny sometimes."

Jesus fucking Christ. This bitch is a monster.

"You're sick," I say, biting my lip hard, wanting nothing more than to break these restraints and put my thumbs through Polina's eye sockets.

"You know, Abigail," she teases. "You've gone quite pale. Are you feeling alright?"

"I'd feel a lot better if you'd untie me," I snap sarcastically. "Or at least kill me so I don't have to listen to your mouth talking anymore."

Polina laughs again, the painful sound echoing off the walls.

"Do you think I was just going to kill you like you killed my husband?" She sneers viciously. "Oh Abby, death is too good for you. No, you're going to *live*. And you have my dearest brother to thank for that."

My heart leaps into my throat.

"Because if Roman had just handed you over, like our laws dictate, then it would have been quick for you. Well, *quicker* than this anyway. I do have a bit of a temper I'm afraid," She snickers in a whisper. "But he didn't. He tried to claim you for himself, thinking that would keep you *safe*."

Her mouth is pinched into a thin line, her expression sour. She reaches down and grabs my jaw, pushing my cheeks together.

"But now you'll fetch me a large amount of money," she presses a quick kiss to my lips before she straightens, gesturing to Teddy. "Darling, take the King of New York's *whore* down to holding cell three."

Teddy slams his fists against the hard metal door, the noise echoing through the room as my heart drops.

"Got one for admission, boys!"

The door flies open, and a group of men rush in, quickly encircling me, licking their lips and salivating in front of me like rabid dogs.

However, my eyes lock onto a beautiful dark-haired woman who steps in behind them. Her face is soft, her expression cold. She doesn't acknowledge any of the men around her, leaning against the doorframe, keeping her chin raised.

But when her eyes find mine, my heart drops at what I see.

They are *empty*.

Almost as if her soul is dying inside the prison of her body.

"Look, Leigh! I have a new one for you," Roman's sister exclaims, clapping her hands together.

"I can see that, Polina," Leigh replies, shooting her a quick smile, before her eyes find mine again.

A blade suddenly nicks my skin as someone slices through the restraints. My eyes dart between each man who encircles me, leering down at me as they do. Sweaty hands grab at my legs, my arms, my breasts causing my stomach to roll and twinge.

They laugh as they pinch my skin. One of them nuzzles into the crook of my neck, his teeth grazing against it.

"I'm going to fuck you so fucking hard," he groans, making me recoil.

He fists my hair tightly, pulling me against him as he thrusts his erection into my hip. A shudder runs down my spine as I press my knees together, anchoring them closed as their hands travel down my legs.

"You want that, don't you, whore?" Another asks, his breath disgustingly thick with the smell of cigarettes and alcohol.

My legs wobble as they force me to my feet.

Pulling away I drop my eyes to the concrete floor, staring into the cracks as I feel the walls in my mind slowly rise, trying to protect me from what I know is coming.

The static noise has returned, as they continue to grope and fondle my breasts and ass.

I screw my eyes shut, struggling to swallow.

But then Leigh releases a breath, drawing my eyes to hers as she clears her throat, her head tilted slightly to the side.

"Polina, is this really necessary?" She sighs. "I mean, she's not going anywhere."

"You always were too nice, Leigh." Polina spits, rolling her eyes.

"I'm just thinking about her worth at the auction," she says suggestively, raising her brows. "Because as she is right now…"

Polina laughs, her eyes widening as I watch her suddenly understand whatever Leigh is insinuating.

"You're brilliant."

Leigh smirks, nodding her head stiffly.

"Stop!" Polina snaps, causing the hoard of men groping my body to freeze. "No one touches her. I want her *exactly* as she is for the auction."

No one will touch me?

"Babe," Teddy protests, echoing the disappointed sighs of the men standing around me. "Come on, I mean she's—"

"No!" Polina hisses, glaring at him. "No one breaks her in. That's an order."

She walks toward us, smiling at me.

"After all, she's worth more with my brother's cum still inside her."

The door opens and a short man walks into the room, stopping briefly to stare at the sight in front of him, before silently passing Polina a manila folder.

The men around me start shuffling me to the door, But Polina holds up a hand, stopping them.

"Excellent," Polina smiles, opening the folder. "Thank you...*Dr. Downing.*"

My heart stops, and my eyes immediately flash to his man at her side. It's then that I recognize the curves and lines of his face, the same as the man who delivered the worst news of my life.

Holy shit...it's him.

"You fucking bastard!" I hiss, lunging at Dr. Downing.

But I'm stopped by Teddy, who grips me hard by the arm, pulling me backwards and shoving me back into the group of men standing at the door, their hands groping me once again.

Suddenly, Polina's face hardens as she stares down at the file in her hands.

"Well, *that's* something we need to take care of."

She extends the folder to Leigh, whose eyes widen as well, before glancing up at me in shock.

Polina steps forward.

"Question, Abigail," she whispers venomously, her voice sickly sweet. "Have you been with anyone else besides Roman?"

I look away from her, refusing to answer.

"No, of course you haven't," she exclaims in delight. "Well, isn't this excellent!"

She claps, snatching the folder from Leigh once more and grinning wildly at me as she flips it back open.

"While you were unconscious, we performed some tests. Standard procedure you know, just to ensure that you're not carrying any diseases," she shrugs arrogantly. "Can't be selling faulty goods you know, it's bad for business."

Looking down, she reads directly from the file.

Why would she ask if I'd fucked anyone else?

"STD tests were negative, however, sample A's hCG count is elevated at 138,094 mlU/ML," she looks up, glancing at Leigh before turning her vicious smile to me. "Congratulations Abigail! You're *pregnant!*"

My heart drops to my stomach, as my brain struggles to make sense of her words.

"No," I whisper, my chest tightening. "I can't be."

Polina shakes the file in her hands.

"Blood work doesn't lie," she smiles. "But, unfortunately, that isn't *something* our clients would appreciate."

This isn't happening. It can't be.

"So, I guess we're going to have to take care of that, before you go to auction." She laughs to herself.

"No," I hiss, finding my voice as I suddenly understand her intention.

Polina says nothing, biting her bottom lip as the evilest of grins spreads across her face.

"I won't let you kill my baby!" I scream at her.

"You think I'm going to *abort* it?" She sneers, throwing her head back. "Sweetie, an Antonov *heir* is far too valuable to just throw in the garbage."

A single tear rolls down my cheek. I try to breathe, but the air strangles in my lungs.

I'm pregnant. With Roman's child. *Our* child.

"No, I'm going to keep you, until you pop. And then I'm going to take the child from you."

"No, you won't," I spit, pulling away from the hands that hold me, only to be yanked back again. "That's *my* baby! I will never let you have my fucking baby!"

"I will have it. And there's nothing you can do about it. The moment that little brat enters this world it's mine. I'll have the *heir* to the Antonov bloodline." A sinister smile fills her face. "The best bargaining chip to secure power."

"My child is not your fucking bargaining chip!" I shout at her, fighting against the strong arms that restrain me.

"Don't worry, I'll take good care of it, at least until Roman is dead and I'm in charge," she smirks. "And then? Well, you know… *accidents* sometimes happen."

A sweaty hand reaches across my stomach, rubbing it roughly before whispering in my ear.

"I've always wanted to fuck a pregnant lady."

"Get the fuck off me!" I snap, flinching away from him.

My body is shaking, my mind flooding with pain as I realize that I can't save my baby from a fate worse than death.

"Take her away."

The world around me becomes hazy.

Screaming, kicking, and shouting, I try my best to fight against the men hauling me out of the room, and down some musty corridor. But they are all too strong for me.

Step by step they drag me down the hall.

Frantically I try to remember the route, my brain still clinging to some hope of escaping this nightmare. But I cannot.

And even as my world crumbles around me, one thought rings out inside my head, screaming louder than the rest:

I won't let them win. I will go out fighting.

My knees slam into the floor as I'm pushed inside the cell, tearing the skin on my palms against the rough concrete as I catch myself.

"Enjoy your stay," a man grunts at me as he grips himself over his dirty jeans. "Little *whore*."

Leigh walks toward me, and I scramble backwards on my hands and knees until I press against the wall.

"Leave," she barks at the men still salivating and gesticulating around me, her finger pointing to the door.

It slams shut, the locking mechanism snapping into place.

My eyes scan the room. There's a dirty mattress in one corner and a bucket in the other, with mold growing up the wall next to it. Other than that, it's just a concrete box.

"Trust me, do not fight this, Abigail," Leigh says quietly as she scratches at her neck.

"Trust you?" I laugh. "Fuck off!"

"I know how this works," she says softly. "I've seen it hundreds of times, with hundreds of girls. The more you resist, the worst things will be for you."

"I'm sorry, do you expect me to just *accept* this?!" I spit, "to just lie back and let some psychopathic bitch rip my baby from my womb, and sell me off to the highest bidder?!"

My anger reaches a boiling point, and I clench my shaking fists.

"She wants to take my child!" I hiss, a mirthless laugh escaping me as I glare at her. "My *child*!"

Leigh's mouth opens and closes before her lips press together in a slight grimace.

"I'm a fucking human being! You cannot keep me here like a breeding mare and try to take my baby!"

"Keep your voice down," Leigh suddenly whispers loudly, glancing around. "I cannot help you if they hear you!"

Her words stun me.

"*Help* me?" I ask, that small flicker of hope reigniting in my chest. "Great! Then how do we get out of here?"

She sighs, shaking her head.

"There is no getting out of here," she says quietly. "Once Polina has made up her mind, there's no changing it. I did the best I could do with making sure *they* didn't touch you."

"Do you want me to thank you?!" I snap sarcastically.

"Abigail," she sighs, crossing her arms tightly across her chest. "I know it's hard. But things *will* be easier for you if you just accept this fate."

"Never!"

"Look, no one will touch you until the child is born. And if you're lucky, you might even be sold to a nice man who just wants a wife."

"A nice man who wants a wife?!" I shout at her throwing my hands in the air. "Are you fucking kidding me? How is that lucky?!"

"You have a fire in you," Leigh shrugs. "I get it. But I've been around a long time, and I'm telling you, things will go easier for you if you just…don't fight back. Because if you do, that fire will get you killed."

"I can't believe this…" I whisper to myself, scoffing quietly.

She sighs.

"Do you want anything?"

"Yes, actually," I snap. "To leave, with *my child*!"

"Anything I can actually do, Abigail?"

I snort, clicking my tongue inside my mouth and shaking my head.

This is a nightmare. I am living in a fucking nightmare.

Suddenly I remember what hangs around my neck, and an idea comes to me. It's a horrible idea, but it appears to be my only way out of this living hell I have so quickly found myself in.

Leigh turns and steps for the door.

"Wait," I call after her. "I *do* need something."

"Which is?"

"A glass of water."

"Water? I can do that," she says, shooting me a small smile.

She turns for the door, but then spins back around to look at me.

"I know you're thinking of running," she says, almost sympathetically. "But I'm warning you, don't. If you try, you won't get out of this room before they take you down."

I roll my eyes.

"Couldn't be worse than this," I gesture around me.

"Yes, it could," she says, her face paling in the fluorescent lights above us. "Because before they kill you, they'll use you however they want."

"Polina just said they can't touch me."

"The moment you run," she sighs, rubbing her arm. "Polina's word won't mean shit."

I stare at her, my mind trying to figure this woman out.

Leigh seems to be one of them, and yet, she acts like she's afraid of them. She claims to want to help me, but yet she's trying to convince me to just lie back and accept my fate.

And why does she want to "help" me at all?

Who is she and how did she get here?

I'm still asking myself this as she walks over to the door. A door that I happen to notice lacks a handle on the inside. She bangs her hand against the metal twice in quick succession, and I hear the lock disengage before it swings open.

A small muscular man steps into view, his hand gracing the gun on his hip as she steps into the hallway.

Perhaps Leigh was right.

Running *isn't* an option.

The rusty metal door quickly slams shut behind her with a resounding bang, vibrating my bones.

As I look up at the cracked ceiling, my eyes begin to burn.

There is no other option.

Resting my hand on my stomach, I slowly slide down the wall, feeling the panic and defeat bubbling in my chest.

There's nothing I can do.

There's no way I can save us both.

If Polina gets her way, I'm going to be kept locked in here, in this miserable cell, until my baby is born. Then she will take my child from me, for use in her nefarious plans. She'll use this baby as a weapon against Roman, one that will likely cost him his life.

And then, when she has everything that she wants, what will happen to my baby?

No. I will not allow that.

There's only one way I can see us both getting out of here without suffering Polina's fate, but it's something I wish I didn't have to do.

I wish that my child could live a safe and happy life with me...and *Roman*.

And even if I knew that there was a way for my child to go on, and live, safely, I would happily sacrifice myself to make that happen.

But there isn't.

We're both now helpless pawns in Polina's game.

We mean nothing to her, and she'd have no remorse for either of us ending up in a body bag.

My fingers pull against my necklace, feeling the cool chain run against my skin.

I thought I'd never have to use this.

But I guess I'm *not* immortal.

It's my own fault. I got careless and sloppy, and now because of me, my child will pay the price.

Tears streak down my cheeks as I realize a heartbreaking irony. I always wanted to be a mother more than anything in the world. And now, my one and only act of motherhood will be to save my child from a monster…before I even get to hold my baby.

And then there's Roman.

The only man who ever really loved me.

He will scour the earth for me. I know it.

My chest tightens, thinking about him searching every darkened corner for me, never to find me. The hopelessness he will feel. The uncertainty, and doubt, wondering if maybe I just left him once again.

It breaks my heart knowing my disappearance will break his.

He was the only man who ever made me feel alive. The only man who made me happier than I've ever felt, even happier than when I took out monsters.

I pull my legs into my chest, resting my head on my knees, the heartbreak consuming me, as I sob softly to myself.

I'm playing with my necklace as Leigh returns with a large glass of water, which she places on the floor in front of me.

"For what it's worth, I am sorry that I can't help you more," she whispers, her eyes misting with tears as she looks at me.

When I say nothing, she sighs heavily, and turns on her heel to leave.

"Could you pass someone a message for me?" I ask, my voice quietly echoing off the walls.

"Um, I can try."

"Could you tell Roman…" I trail off, my voice cracking.

No. I have to try.

Mustering my courage, I take a deep breath and continue.

"Tell him I don't hate him… tell him I…" I pause, biting my lip and lowering my gaze from hers. "Fuck. He knows, he's always known."

Leigh stares at me, her eyes soft and sad before nodding slowly.

"Yes," she whispers. "I'll find a way to tell him. You have my word. You're going to be okay, you know?"

I hum quietly to myself.

And without another word, she bangs on the door, and walks out of the room, leaving me alone in the silence.

Rubbing my hand on my stomach, over the bump that hasn't even formed, my heart shatters.

"I'm sorry," I whisper, tears streaking down my cheeks once more. "You have no idea how much I want to meet you. To see you smile. And your father…well, he would've loved you. So much."

Reaching my hands around my neck I unclasp my necklace, the chain running across my palm as I untangle it from my hair. I twist it gently between my fingers, feeling the capsule unscrew.

As I stare down at the Widowmaker, my heart beats steadily in my chest, thinking of all the things I will miss.

My child.

Roman.

Lily.

My greenhouse.

I hope that Roman will take care of Lily. He might not be a cat person, but he's a good man, he will find a good home for her.

A bittersweet giggle escapes me, realizing he'll likely burn the greenhouse down though.

I could never see him watering a plant, let alone an entire greenhouse. I thought I'd be sad at the idea of my flowers burning, but they could burn for Roman if that made him feel better.

I pour the powder into the glass, watching it sink down to the bottom, and knowing that when it's completely dissolved, this glass of water will become a glass of death.

…And my only way out.

It's strange, a few months ago no one would have missed me if I died.

Then there was Roman.

God, I feel bad for anyone who gets in his way when he learns the truth. I'd have loved to watch his rage unleashed on all of these fuckers.

But I won't get that opportunity.

My lips quirk as I reach for the glass, the condensation cold against my skin as I lift it to my lips.

ANTONOV

ANTONOV

CHAPTER FORTY-FIVE

ROMAN

"Make sure we keep an eye on her. I don't want her getting any…ideas."

"Yes Ma'am. However, I do think that I should mention that round the clock medical supervision, especially for them both, is going to cost you extra."

"Of course, it fucking does. Everything costs extra with you. You tiny, money-hungry little man."

"Well, obviously, if my work isn't valued here, Mrs. Ivanova—"

"What did you just say? Do not ever fucking call me that!"

"Do you want me to kick his ass, babe?"

"No! Please! I…I meant no disrespect, I assure you!"

"Get the fuck out of here you swine! Before I have one of my men crush your fucking head against the wall!"

"Yes! Of course! I…I will leave!"

"You heard her! Get the fuck out out! Now!"

"Arrrgh!"

The door to the room slams open and my sister storms inside, followed closely by Teddy.

But as the lights flick on, the safety on my gun flicks off.

"Hello Pol…" I growl, looking up at her.

She screams, and her new little fuck toy Teddy goes to pull his gun from his pants but from the shadows behind the door my brother Lev emerges, cracking Teddy in the face with his rifle. The blow is so hard that Teddy's head whips around violently before crashing to the floor. Foolishly he again reaches for his gun, but Lev is faster, pulling his and aiming it directly at Teddy's head.

"I've already proven I'm faster than you twice, fuckface," Lev smirks darkly. "I wouldn't try a third time. Or do. I don't really care either way."

Teddy throws his hands above his head, breathing heavily as his broken nose drips blood on the floor.

Silently, Polina appraises the sight in front of her.

I sit at the table, steadily holding my gun on her, Lev has incapacitated her shithead boyfriend, and Nikolai stands in the corner, in front of the half-naked, terrified girl we found here, who is now wrapped in his jacket.

"Roman," my sister says cautiously, finding her words and smiling at me as she tries to take a step toward me. "What are you—"

I fire, hitting her hand.

Even with my silencer, the reverberations of the gunshot echo around the cold room. But the bullet hits its mark, shattering the bones within her hand, and sending blood spraying all over the floor.

"Oh my God!" She screams. "Fuck!"

Kicking the chair backwards, I storm toward her, and grab her by the throat.

"Where is Abigail, Polina," I ask viciously. "And believe me, I don't need you *alive* to figure it out."

"Boss, we've got company!"

Cal's voice in my ear combined with the gunfire erupting in the hallway momentarily distracts me. Polina takes the opportunity to knee me in the crotch, sending me stumbling backwards.

"You took away my justice!" She croaks at me. "That bitch killed my husband!"

"You never gave a shit about your whore of a husband!"

"I gave a shit about the business we were starting, and that slut nearly ruined it!"

"A business that was never sanctioned by *me*!" I roar. "I've already told you, we don't fuck with the sex trade Pol! You already know the reasons."

"I don't give a fuck about the reasons!" She snaps back, cradling her bleeding hand. "It was ours! And we were making money!"

"On the backs of slaves!" I snap, pointing to the cowering woman in the corner.

"That's rich coming from you, Roman!" She spits, tears streaming down her face. "Everyone is a slave to you! And I wanted to be free of all of you!"

"Then you wanted the impossible," I snarl darkly. "You never get to be free of me, and we don't fuck with the sex trade! It could jeopardize our relations with other contacts in this business!"

She laughs, collapsing into the chair on the opposite side of the table.

"If you're referring to Jaxon Pace, then fuck you, and fuck him too."

"It's not my fault he didn't want to marry you," I hiss venomously. "But none of this matters. This little business venture of yours is done. You're going to release all of these captives, and you're going to tell me where the fuck my goddamn girlfriend is."

"They aren't captives," she snarls. "They are my property. I bought them. Fair and square. Just like I bought your little girlfriend from her husband."

The fuck did she just say?!

All I see is *red*.

Grabbing her long blonde hair, I yank her out of the chair and throw her hard into the concrete wall. Her head slams back hard, and she screws her eyes shut, the impact causing her knees to buckle.

I catch her by the shoulders, lifting her and slamming her down hard on the table, denting it down the middle. I grab her throat as she scratches and claws at me, her long acrylic nails slicing into my skin, and smearing blood all over my arm.

But I do not fucking care.

"If I find out," I hiss, as she squirms and thrashes, trying to get away. "That you've harmed a single hair on my girlfriend's head, I will remove yours, Polina. So, where the fuck is she?!"

My sister says nothing, unable to speak or breathe as my fingers dig into her neck.

With my free hand I snatch my knife from my pocket and hold it close to her eye.

"Where…the…fuck…is…she."

She frantically plunges her hand into her pocket and pulls out a small remote, clicking the bottom button with her thumb just as her eyes start to roll back into her head.

I release my grip, allowing her to breathe, but placing the blade against her neck as the TV screen above us illuminates.

The moment I see Abby, holding her knees and staring blankly I step backwards, breathing a small sigh of relief.

My sister coughs, gasping for air.

"See," she hacks, her voice now hoarse and raspy as she starts to sit up. "The bitch is fine."

I backhand her hard across the face, sending her falling back to the table.

That's when I see movement on the television out of the corner of my eye and I watch as a dark-haired woman walks in the room carrying a glass.

As the feed has no sound, I can't hear any words exchanged between the obviously nervous woman, and Abby who sits fidgeting with her necklace.

That's when I remember what she told me about that *particular* necklace, and a horrifying realization suddenly hits me like a freight train.

Abby's necklace contains her Widowmaker, and she always said that if she was ever caught, that it was her way out.

And now, having been kidnapped by sister, she's asked for something to drink, and plans to add the poison…and kill herself. Right here. Right now. In front of me.

No.

"Abigail…" I whisper.

Pouncing on my sister, I immediately smash her hard against the table.

"Where is she?!" I roar in her face. "Where the fuck is she being held?! Tell me now!"

"Just…down the—" Polina stammers.

"Where?!" I thunder, shaking her again.

"Go down the hall and turn left!" Polina wails, twisting away from me.

I'm around the table in seconds and bolting from the room, nearly tripping on the pile of dead men just outside, taken out by Cal.

"Keep an eye on them!" I shout as I sprint down the hall. "Abigail! Abigail!"

I have to make it to her in time.

As I round the corner, I catch sight of a brunette peeking nervously from an open doorway. The minute she sees me, her terrified eyes go wide, and she tries to retreat, but I aim my gun directly at her.

"You! Get out here now!" I bark at her angrily. "Where the fuck is Abigail Wayne?!"

"Abigail? She…she's down the hall!" The girl whimpers, dropping to her knees and throwing her hands above her head. "To the right! It's the door with the yellow graffiti!"

"Show me!" Grabbing her by the arm I yank her upright and shove her forwards with my gun.

"Go! Now!" I snap. "And know if you lie to me, I will shoot you in the fucking head!"

The two of us take off in a sprint, with my heart pounding inside my chest. What if I don't make it? What if it's too late?

"*Abigail!*" I shout as we round the corner, seeing a singular guard standing in the hallway.

I fire three shots before he even has a chance to pull his from his belt.

…And then all the lights go out.

EPILOGUE

Forcefully I throw Roman against the old oak door, which rattles and groans against his weight.

He smirks at me.

"Abigail," he says, drawing out my name in that husky tone he knows I like.

"Roman."

"If you wanted—"

But the words die in his throat, and his entire body freezes.

"Nothing to say, *Sweetie?*" I say, smiling up at him, holding my arm steady.

He swallows sharply, the obsidian Antonov dagger digging into his skin as a small stream of blood runs down his neck.

I have to fight the urge to lick it.

My hormones and cravings have been absolutely wild, and I'm pretty sure I'm carrying a vampire at this point.

But I've grown tired of our games these past few weeks, and so I've been carefully planning this moment as he slept.

The moment when my precious King let his guard down.

His business trip to Vegas was the perfect cover.

"While this certainly has been fun," I whisper, watching the blood seeping into his crisp white shirt collar. "I'm tired of waiting."

With each word I watch as his face pales, his lust melting slowly into fury as he fights to hold his body in place.

We both know if he moves too fast, this blade will shred his skin like paper, and he'd be dead faster than he could draw that gun of his.

"Why?" He asks, his voice pained.

"Why not? You certainly made it easy," I smile, stepping forward and pressing my body into his, "So very easy. I just had to play the long game."

With my left hand, I slowly stroke his face, before running the other down his body and reaching behind him to grab the handle. With a quick twist he falls backwards through the doorway unable to catch himself.

"Abigail…why?" He questions, crawling away from me before hitting the back of the pew chairs.

"Because you took too fucking long," I snap at him, fighting the smile that's begging to unleash itself.

"But…I emptied the penthouses!" He blurts out suddenly.

My jaw drops as I stare at him.

"What?"

"I did it for you! So, you can burn it down," he states, using his arms to lift himself from the floor without dropping his eyes from mine. "The whole building."

"You did that for me?" I whisper, fighting the burn behind my eyes.

"For *us*," he says, gesturing between us, trying to reason with me. "And I bought all your neighbors' townhouses."

"What?" I ask breathlessly. "But…*why*?"

"Because I know you love it there," he says, still inching his way backwards. "We can turn that whole neighborhood in Forest Hills into its own gated Mafia community. Someplace safe for all of us. A *home*. You know, for our family."

I shake my head slowly.

Sometimes I can't believe how far we've come.

From the moment I met Roman Antonov, I was certain that one of us was supposed to die.

And four weeks ago, I nearly *did*.

But he got to me before the poison touched my tongue.

We rewrote our narrative. And even though we began with death, somewhere along the line, we created *life*.

A little heart that beats inside my womb, fathered by the man who even now is building our future one brick or emptied penthouse at a time.

But also the man who has coincidentally neglected to ask me the most important question.

"A home?" I ask softly.

He opens his mouth to continue, but freezes, hearing hushed whispers behind him. He whips around, coming face to face with his family, well... *our* family.

All of his siblings.

All of our most trusted men.

Jaxon Pace and his Alpha Squad.

All of them standing in front of a conveniently placed priest.

...Exactly as planned.

"What the..." He mumbles, looking back at me.

I throw him a dazzling smile, slowly lowering the dagger before sliding it into my thigh sheath.

"You took too long to ask me, Roman, so now you don't get to ask. You just get to *do*."

"You two are fucked in the head." Ana says humorlessly, shaking her head. "Can we get this over and done with? There's a gig tonight I wanna rock the fuck out at."

"Ana!" Pasha shouts, his finger pointing at the priest. "Don't curse in front of God!"

"What fucking God?" Lev laughs back.

"All of you shut up," Cal mutters, slapping Lev on the back of the head.

Roman turns back to me slowly, his eyes darkening. He takes one step, then another, before he prowls lethally toward me.

"How?" He asks.

I grin.

"How did I manage to get your family, men and best friend together in Vegas, without you hearing about it?" I ask smugly.

"Well, despite you thinking that you're God, or some one-man-army who needs to take on the world alone, it turns out you have an army of people who love you and want to see you happy. And who are pretty good at keeping secrets when they have to."

I wink at him, amused by the shock blanketing his face.

"...And you sleep like the dead."

"No, Abigail, I really don't," he chuckles softly, running his hand through his hair. "But I still don't understand. Why did you do all this?"

"You didn't ask me, Roman," I state, shaking my head at him slowly. "So now you don't get to ask."

"You think you can escape me fucking asking?"

"Can't escape something you never did, you idiot," I sneer, narrowing my eyes at him. "But yeah, for the guy who empties penthouses, and constantly claims to want to marry me, I'll admit it *is* a bit surprising that you never did just come out and ask me to marry you."

Stopping before me, he threads his fingers in my hair and yanks my face toward his. His soft lips are so close to mine I can almost taste the whiskey he had before we got here, reminding me exactly how much I miss drinking.

And my greenhouse. Which is off limits to pregnant ladies.

Roman grins deeply, his blue eyes locking on mine.

"Foxy, you've carried your ring with you," he says softly, pressing his lips to mine. "...Everywhere you've been."

He steps away from me, extending his hand to me.

"Give me the dagger."

Numbly, I unsheathed the dagger, flipping it in the air before placing the hilt in his outstretched palm.

Without breaking eye contact, he grips the blade, and smashes the handle against the back of the nearest chair. The brittle whalebone handle splinters into pieces, as my hands cover my face.

And before I can utter a word, he reaches down, and holds up a ring in his blooded fingers.

…The ruby ring that had sat on the hilt.

"You said "*yes*" the moment you took the dagger," he grins, biting his lip. "You've had your ring for months."

I can't explain the feeling that erupts inside my chest as he says this to me, holding the ring out to me.

But then a thought sneaks into my brain and I inhale sharply before starting to giggle. That giggle quickly grows, however, bordering almost maniacal after just a few seconds.

Roman raises a brow. "Are you alright?"

"I carved slut into that bitch's chest with that dagger!" I cackle, my sides beginning to ache. "So, in a way, I carved her up…with my fucking *wedding ring*!"

"Fuck me," Ana gasps, her jaw dropping. "That was *you*?!"

"Fuck yes it was me," I snort. "That *slut* touched my fucking man."

"Jesus," Jaxon mutters, tugging at his tie, only to get smacked immediately on the arm by Natalie who stares pointedly at the traumatized priest.

"You and I need to discuss who you can and cannot carve up in the office!"

"Not now, Ana!" Roman barks.

My attention snaps back to Roman, staring at the ring before staring at him.

"Why didn't you ask?" I whisper, feeling a tear roll down my face.

"I wanted it to be your decision," he says, locking eyes with me. "And, you know *why*."

It's then that I understand that Roman is giving me a choice. He knows how important control is to me, especially after everything Garrett Adams did. Not only did he control me, but he also abused me, and sold me into the sex trade, like I was worthless.

Roman would *never*.

My mafia man has always made me feel desired and worthy.

He gives me strength, without wanting anything in return.

Smiling at him softly, I step forward grabbing his hand in mine. But instead of taking the ring, I open his palm, causing him to drop it. Thankfully he quickly catches with his other hand before it hits the floor.

"You're bleeding," I say tearfully, yanking his tie aggressively from his neck.

Gently I wrap his fingers, pressing a kiss to each fingertip as I do.

"So, what do you say?"

"You broke the dagger."

"Just the handle," he shrugs, "I'll get it fixed."

There's no stopping the tears that stream down my face uncontrollably, and I inhale sharply.

"You've been mine, Little Fox, since the moment I saw you," he says, his blue eyes holding mine with ferocious intent, as he leans in to whisper against my earlobe. "...in that horrible pale yellow dress."

A gasp escapes me, realizing that dress was the first dress I burnt after Garrett died.

Silently I stand, appraising this man, the same man who wanted me for years, but selflessly gave me up because he thought I was happy.

My happiness has always meant more to Roman than his own.

"I'm pregnant," I blurt out, my chest heaving.

"Awww!" Natalie sighs.

Slowly as I watch as the secret I've kept quiet for these past four weeks, slowly registers in Roman's eyes. The most beautiful smile fills his face, and I watch his eyes glisten.

 Slowly he reaches for my stomach, pressing gently.

"Mine," he growls, possessively.

"It's so romantic!" Natalie gushes.

"Are you *crying*, woman?!" Jaxon exclaims.

"Shut up!" She sniffles, smacking him again.

"So, Abigail," Roman asks, taking my hands in his and biting his lip. "What do you say?"

But looking into his eyes, I know he already knows my answer, and he knows that he never really needed to ask at all.

"I do."

He barks out a laugh, one that our family behind him echoes.

"Forever, I do," he states back.

Without hesitation he slides the ring onto my finger, kissing me like a man on fire, consumed by every emotion that rages beneath his skin.

However, as he pulls away his head whips to the priest.

"We said I do!" He snaps over his shoulder,

"Oh! Right!" The nervous priest stammers, before quickly clearing his throat, "By the power vested in me, by the State of Nevada, I now pronounce you husband and wife."

Roman pulls me against his body, before dipping me back and kissing me hard.

"I love you, Abigail," he whispers against my lips.

"And I love you, Roman," I whisper back, cupping his beautiful face. "I hate how much I love you."

He grins wickedly, pulling me back up on my feet and kissing my earlobe.

"How about I take you back to the hotel," he whispers darkly against my ear. "And you can fuck me like you mean it?"

"Or," I smile, biting my lip. "*You* can."

ANTONOV

BONUS CONTENT

ANTONOV

BONUS EPILOGUE

ROMAN

SIX WEEKS LATER

"Holy Shit…" Jaxon Pace says quietly. "No wonder you didn't want to tell me all of this over the phone."

"Yeah."

The two of us stand in the bustling lobby of his hotel, The Jefferson, in downtown Chicago, people coming and going around us.

"Morning, Mr. Pace," A man says politely, dipping his head respectfully as Jaxon politely returns his salutations with a silent nod.

"And, uh," he says, clearing his throat as he turns his attention back to me. "What about Polina?"

I shift uncomfortably, feeling my body stiffen at the mere mention of her name.

"We haven't spoken since."

"Wait… she's still *alive*?" He asks, shock blanketing his face. "After what she did? How?"

"Her and her little twatstain of a boyfriend managed to shoot Lev, disable the warehouse breaker, and sneak away in the darkness.”

“Jesus,” Jaxon says, with a nod, raising his brows as he looks away from me. “And what about Lev?”

“The bullet just grazed his ribs,” I say, waving him off. “The asshole was a bit insufferable when the doctor told him he couldn’t go back to his precious fight club for a few months, but he’s making a full recovery.”

Jaxon nods.

“Anyway, Lev isn’t my biggest concern right now.”

“What do you mean?” He asks.

“It’s Nikolai,” I sigh. “The night we rescued Abby, we also rescued a few girls my sister had been holding there. Apparently, he’s gotten attached to one of them. And well, you know how it goes…”

I shift, rolling my eyes.

“He thinks it’s love or some shit. I keep trying to talk him out of it. Hell, we’re all trying to talk him out of it. But he’s being a stubborn little fuck about it. Convinced she’s the one and refusing to listen to reason.”

Jaxon chuckles softly to himself, crossing his arms and wiping his thumb across his chin.

“What?”

“Nothing,” he shrugs with a smirk. “Seems a bit ironic is all. Considering *you’re* the one who married a serial kil—”

“What about *me*?”

From behind me, the most beautiful brunette emerges from the hotel tour she took with Natalie, interrupting our conversation.

She slides her arm in mine, and smiles up at me, biting her bottom lip.

“Foxy,” I say, placing my hand over hers. “You remember, Jaxon Pace?”

“How could I forget?” she says with a smile. “He stood up in our wedding.”

“Yes, he—”

“And you said he was the only man with more patience than you.”

“I’m sorry…what?” Natalie scoffs, looking at me while pointing to her husband with her thumb. “You can’t possibly be referring to this Jaxon, right here?”

“Hey, I *am* patient,” Jaxon says defensively, only for Natalie to fold her arms across her chest and raise her brow.

“The crazy saint,” Abby says, snapping her fingers. “That’s what you called him! Right?”

“Abby…” I say with a nervous laugh.

“The crazy saint?” Natalie chuckles.

“Well,” Abby says, looking up at me. “Roman said that he thought Jaxon

Pace must be either a madman or a saint…Actually, wait a minute…maybe it was that Jaxon had the patience of a saint? You know, for taking in Pasha and—"

Shit.

I clear my throat, squeezing her hand.

"I'm sure that's not *exactly* what I said," I say, tugging at my tie, and shooting Abby a look.

But Jaxon just laughs.

"Oh no, he was definitely right," he chuckles, pulling Natalie close to him. "Well, about the *madman* part anyway."

A calm silence settles over the four of us. I can't help but find it a bit amusing that somehow, Jaxon and I ended up married after all.

Married and happy, so different from how our younger selves thought we'd be.

"Well," Jaxon says, finally breaking the silence. "I think it's about time. Everyone should be close to being assembled in the ballroom. Shall we join them and get this party started?"

"I suppose," I say, taking Abby's hand in mine. "But Roman never did tell me who was all meeting us here?"

Jaxon grins.

"*Everyone.*"

COMING SOON IN THE ANTONOV LEGACY:

BOOK 2

NIKOLAI'S STORY.
COMING 2024.

THANK YOU FOR READING!

Thank you for taking a chance on a new to you author. There are no words that we can write here other than to say:

We love you.

We appreciate you.

And thank **you**.

If you enjoyed this book, please consider leaving an honest review!

ACKNOWLEDGEMENTS

First and foremost, we would both like to say how blessed we are to have the support of our families, both blood and chosen. Thank you for lending us your strength when we had none. Neither of us would be standing here today without you, and your love and encouragement.

To our significant others, who have been patient, and selflessly sacrificed personal time to watch us create and publish our first debut novel, we are so grateful for your support, your resilience, and calm reassurance no matter how stressed, grumpy, or occasionally unbearable we've been. We love you.

To Mikayla: Thank you for reading our scribbles, for devouring our words, and for dedicating your time and energy into helping us make this book baby everything it could be. Thank you for just being you. We don't know what we did to deserve a friend like you, but we couldn't imagine walking this author journey without you.

To all our friends, and fellow author community, who believed in us from the very beginning, thank you for allowing us to ramble about our fictional characters without judgement. You are the REAL ones, and we are honored to have you in our lives.

To all the fans who took a chance on a debut indie author duo-we are so grateful to you, and will consistently strive to deliver dark, delicious, debauchery in every new book.

To all the exes in the world, who have ever done anyone we love dirty, thank you for providing limitless villain material. We aim to off you in interesting ways. ;)

To all our pets, who have dutifully napped while we hustled, thank you for cuddling our imposter syndrome away, and loving us no matter what.

And finally, to all the haters, and the people that treated us less than we deserved, thank you for the motherfucking motivation.

STAY IN TOUCH

If you'd like to stay in touch with us, then you can follow us here!

Tiktok:
@AuthorCharlyNicole

Instagram:
@AuthorCharlyNicole

Author reading group:
Charly Nicole's Chaos Corner.

You can also subscribe to their newsletter at:
Authorcharlynicole.net/

ABOUT THE AUTHORS

Charly Nicole is a writing duo, made up of Charly Jade and Nicole Fanning. Who are separated by an entire ocean, but even that isn't enough to stop them. They are dedicated to writing darkly twisted villains that you just can't get enough of.

Charly Jade lives in the rainy UK, with her two cats. She spends her days either writing delicious villains or messing around with photoshop. When she isn't doing that, she's working in retail, daydreaming about her latest book boyfriend. Charly always roots for the villain, no wonder she decided to write about them getting the girl.

Award winning author Nicole Fanning lives on the east coast with her husband, two dogs and her cats. She has a background in marketing, and Human Resources. She has often found that the human element is by far the most colorful, complex, and most interesting in the world. You will often find Nicole cuddled up in her writing cave, when she isn't writing you'll find her spending time with her friends and family.

The duo connected online, and the rest is history.